Dear Ell...

THE
TRADE
OFF

The Life of a New York
Personal Shopper

Inspired by True Stories

Enjoy! Louise

Louise Maniscalco
& Susan Rudin

Happy Shopping!
xxx
Susan Rudin

DIVERSIONBOOKS

To all those inspired by the fashion industry.

Diversion Books
A Division of Diversion Publishing Corp.
443 Park Avenue South, Suite 1008
New York, New York 10016
www.DiversionBooks.com

For more information, email info@diversionbooks.com

First Diversion Books edition November 2014.
Hardcover ISBN: 978-1-62681-546-9
Paperback ISBN: 978-1-62681-523-0
eBook ISBN: 978-1-62681-521-6

PART ONE

September:
The Surprise Party

Chapter One

Late was always bad, but the first Monday after summer vacation was the worst. As she ran for the subway, Bonnie Salerno Madden pictured her boss peering over his glasses at her, reminding her, "You're not indispensable. Everyone can be replaced."

The train pulled into the 103rd Street Station in Corona, Queens just as Bonnie hit the platform. The ride from Queens to Manhattan was only forty minutes, but the two boroughs were light-years apart. Queens was made up of working-class, multigenerational families flying American flags outside tract houses with two cars in every driveway. Stick your nose in the air anywhere in Queens, and you'd pick up the scent of garlic, cumin, gas fumes, cut grass, or garbage. Bonnie was the youngest of five kids from a proud Italian family, the first (and only) of her siblings to go to college and get a job in the city.

Bonnie's Manhattan, the few square blocks she worked in, was for the upper strata of the upper class, where the top 1 percent lived in luxury high-rise buildings along Central Park, dressed glamorously to walk the dog (if they even did that themselves), and kept Mercedes and BMWs in underground garages that cost more per month than Bonnie's mortgage. When Bonnie thought of the difference between Corona and the Upper East Side real estate, her mental shorthand was "closet-size bedrooms versus bedroom-size closets." That also spoke directly to the priorities that defined Queens versus Manhattan dwellers. In her borough of birth, the prime directive was to keep families close, fitting as many people in one house as possible *by choice*. Her father's brag was, "I was born in this house, and I'm going to die here, right in this lounger." In rich Manhattan, a sign of success was a family's ability to spread out. The brag was, "My daughter's studying in Paris, my son's on safari in Kenya, my husband's in China on business, and I'm going for a spa week at Canyon Ranch." Kids were sent away to schools, given cars and houses of their own for "healthy" distance. Bonnie loved her large family and lived only a few blocks from the house she grew up in. But Bonnie had to get away, at least during work hours, to a fantasy version of reality among the Manhattanites. It was like working undercover. No matter how well she'd infiltrated the scene, she knew all too well where she'd come from. You could take the girl out of Queens, but Queens stuck to Bonnie like hot tar. Although she was a part of her clients' world, she was not of it.

On the ride to Manhattan, to ease the transition, she played her makeover game, imagining the work-a-day commuters around her transformed in designer dresses and suits from Frankel's, a.k.a. "the most luxurious store in the world." She'd spend the next ten hours on site at Frankel's, styling clients. Politicians, socialites, celebrities, and royalty relied on her taste and knowledge of the market to make them look flawless and powerful. Some needed a fabulous look for their work. But most of Bonnie's society ladies had other reasons to appear perfect.

Since the dawn of civilization, women had sought men who would be good providers. In this particular sector of New York culture, the men were like providers on steroids. Not just millionaires or multimillionaires—they were billionaires. The things women did to attract and keep them were put on steroids, too, including extreme styling, pampering, dieting, surgical adjustments, exotic sex practices. The dream of marrying well drew hundreds, if not thousands, of young women to Manhattan each year, each hoping to land her very own billionaire. Some succeeded as wives, girlfriends, mistresses, "special friends," and so on down the ladder of male-female interaction. Some relationships lasted twenty years, some two weeks, others one night or one hour. From what Bonnie had seen in her years of dressing women up and down this ladder of success, once they'd had a moment's exposure to that first-class world, they were determined to do whatever they could to stay there. There was always some kind of trade-off, of course. The women wound up paying a high price for a foothold on their rung—more precious than anything available at Frankel's. No matter how levelheaded a woman might be, how grounded, how jaded, the dream of partnering with a rich man was always in the back of her mind. It could happen. It *did* happen. Bonnie had seen it, many times. But not, of course, to her.

Bonnie's first appointment, at ten, was a red-carpet gown hunt with a reality TV show starlet. At noon, a wardrobe update with a middle-aged political candidate. At two, a consultation with a nineteen-year-old hip-hop singer, who usually wore jeans, a hoodie, and basketball sneakers. Bonnie had special orders arriving, inventory to inspect, and a trunk show for an up-and-coming designer. In other words, a slow day.

She transferred at Grand Central. The train inched along, moving much too slowly. The starlet might be waiting for her already. More likely, though, she'd show up two hours late. Regardless, Bonnie would greet her like she was right on time. Half of Bonnie's job was styling. The other half was ego stroking.

The reason her clients came to the Salon at Frankel's was only, in part, because of Bonnie's talent and instinct for knowing the perfect clothes for the person and the occasion. If they knew about her modest background, they might not trust her taste as implicitly. If one of their children showed an aptitude for style, she'd get signed up for classes at Parsons or do an internship at Ralph Lauren. Bonnie had to pursue her interest by browsing Macy's, reading magazines in salons, and watching fashion TV shows. She was the only thirteen-year-old in her neighborhood who had gone to the library every afternoon to read *Women's Wear Daily*. Her mother, Sylvia, clued into Bonnie's passion and helped her nurture it by buying her magazines and taking her on occasional browsing missions in Saks and Bergdorf Goodman. Sylvia noticed in her youngest daughter a chance to break free of a predictable life. When her siblings laughed at Bonnie's often strange outfits, Sylvia whispered to her, "Don't listen to them. You have an eye. You're special. You can do anything."

Bonnie would never forget the stricken look of horror on her father Vinny's face when she announced she'd applied to the

Fashion Institute of Technology, had been accepted, and was going to take on loans to pay for it herself. She and Sylvia had done it all behind his back, waiting until she got in to tell him. Vinny, a sanitation worker, acted personally insulted that any of his children would aim higher than the down-to-earth life they had been raised in. What was worse was that one had chosen a field as phony and stupid as fashion. It's hard for people who didn't grow up with her background to understand, but going to college was seen as a rejection of her father's values. Vinny was so angry with Bonnie for going to college, he stopped speaking to her for a month.

College and fashion were how Bonnie rebelled against her father's authority. Her mom's encouragement turned out to be how Sylvia rebelled against the confines of her small life. A year after Bonnie enrolled at FIT, Sylvia made her escape, too. She announced her plans to divorce Vinny and moved into a rental a few blocks away. Shocking the family, she got a job at a restaurant and started keeping company with the owner. Vinny blamed Bonnie for inspiring Sylvia to leave him. It was years before he could talk to his youngest daughter without starting a fight. Only Sylvia and Bonnie's boyfriend, Mike (who would later be her husband and then *ex*-husband) came to her graduation ceremony. She didn't care that her sisters and father blew it off. Although she was in debt, she was also in love and employed. Right out of college, she got a job as a stylist at Bloomingdale's. Then she worked at a handful of other jobs, learning more in a few months in-store than she had in four years of school. Her client list grew along with her expertise. Fifteen years in the trenches eventually led her to her current position as the head stylist at the best store in the greatest city for fashion in America.

Along with her elegant taste, her discretion, and her dedication, her availability was what Bonnie's clients valued most. She was *there*. She was always there, or at least accessible via BlackBerry 24/7. Some of her clients might think she lived at Frankel's. It certainly felt like she did.

Bonnie switched her Prada tote to the other arm and noticed a man staring at her. He held on to the overhead subway bar and wore a well-tailored, navy cashmere coat. Handsome face. When he saw her looking at him, he smiled.

She smiled back, but he wasn't her type. At thirty, he was too young. Her fantasy man was slightly older, had a seen-it-all look in his eye without being jaded. Unfortunately for her, she hardly ever met drop-dead gorgeous older men who weren't gay, married, or morally bankrupt.

She peeked at her admirer's body. Not bad. She felt flattered. It was a vote of confidence. She made an effort to put herself together well. Bonnie's role model was Jackie O. She'd been told more than once she resembled the former First Lady. She could see it, sort of, and had decided in her twenties to go with that crisp, classic style. Today, like every fall and winter day, she wore wool trousers, modest-heeled leather boots, a black sweater, and a cashmere coat of her own. Her hair, chestnut and thick, was pulled into a neat ponytail that highlighted broad cheekbones. Her heart-shaped face and wide-set eyes gave her face a feline impression. The smooth olive skin was a genetic gift from her mom's side of the family, as was her height, thick eyelashes, and good posture. She looked thirty and claimed to be thirty-two. Her real age? She'd rather not think about it. She hoped to appear timeless, neat, maybe a bit buttoned-up. Her clients and colleagues had no idea that underneath the elegant separates, Bonnie lived in very naughty underwear. The silken garments were her secret, a constant reminder that she had a beating heart and wasn't only a workaholic.

This man across the subway car grinned at her like he was in on the secret. Even if he did have X-ray eyes and could see her frilly unmentionables, a thirty-second conversation with her would crush his interest.

He: "Tell me about yourself."

She: "I'm an almost-broke, divorced, single mother of an autistic six-year-old. And you?"

He'd claw at the subway doors to get away.

She laughed out loud, picturing it. When the train pulled into Fifty-Ninth Street, Bonnie ran up the steps and out onto the street. As she walked, she replayed the scene of dropping off her son, Peter, at school this morning. She'd taken him to Mason (a private school in Queens for special needs kids) each day since first grade began one week ago and carefully handed him off to his new teacher, Ms. Whitman. Peter liked the teacher from their first meeting. "You smell like Mommy," he said matter-of-factly. He was right. Ms. Whitman and Bonnie both wore the perfume White Linen. Bonnie had never before been so grateful for her signature scent on another woman. It pulled hard on her heartstrings to leave him in the classroom. In fact, she wasn't able to do it and hovered just outside the door for an hour every morning, just to make sure he was okay.

Ms. Whitman assured her she was highly trained and was prepared to care for Peter. That had to be true. The school only hired qualified teachers. But Ms. Whitman was so young, only twenty-five or so, and she didn't know Peter, at least not yet. He could fool people into thinking he was all right by being quiet. When he was around two, he'd sit in a corner and stare at the wall in stony silence, swaying slightly, unblinking, unreachable. He rarely made eye contact. He'd build a tower of three blocks in the same way, same order, and then deconstruct it, repeatedly, for an hour, then two. He'd fly into a tantrum if he heard a loud sound, like a motorcycle on the street, or if she turned on the lights or touched him unexpectedly. His emotional whiplash was unnerving, and it was the earliest sign he wasn't like other toddlers. Since then, there'd been testing, a diagnosis, treatment, and education about autism for Peter as well as for Bonnie and her ex-husband Mike. They had intervened early with meds and behavior modification. He was fairly high on the autism spectrum. Peter would, however, never live a completely "normal" life, but he was doing well. That said, as skilled as Ms. Whitman was, she didn't know Peter like Bonnie did. His demeanor could change at any minute, whether Bonnie was hovering outside the classroom door or not. Every day, she had to make a leap of faith to go to work. Some days it was harder than others.

Bonnie checked her watch. The store doors would be opening any moment. She forced herself to shift her attention away from

Peter to Frankel's, away from Queens and to Manhattan. As she hustled toward Madison Avenue and Fifty-Seventh Street, she had a sudden realization that she'd been hustling for fifteen years. Style changed every season in the fashion business. But the business of fashion was enduringly hectic.

Irma was outside the store, as usual. Old, black, blind, and homeless, Irma sat on a milk crate by the main entrance to Frankel's on Madison Avenue from nine in the morning until closing at eight. Every day, Bonnie gave her a dollar on the way to the employee entrance. Bonnie was superstitious that way. It came from her Italian-American upbringing, her mom spitting on the kitchen floor to ward off the evil eye at every opportunity.

Irma sniffed the air. "White Linen. I missed you last week."

She missed the money. "Here's a five," said Bonnie, putting a bill in her cup. *How does Irma know it's really a five? It could be a single.* But Bonnie would never do that. Lying to a blind, homeless woman would land her on the express train to hell.

"Have a nice vacation?"

"Yes, thanks," said Bonnie. Most of it had been spent sitting by the phone, waiting for Ms. Whitman to call her. "I caught up on my worrying."

"Good for you. Mr. Charles got here a half hour ago."

The boss. Bonnie tried, and usually failed, to be at her desk before he entered the building. She rushed in. Store hours began only minutes ago, and Frankel's was already bustling with customers. The first floor housed the Fragrance and Makeup Departments. After five years as Salon director, Bonnie's eyes still had to grow three sizes to take it all in. Vivid colors, sparkling objects, crystal chandeliers, shining display cases. Every mirror was engineered to slim. The lighting, a soft pinky yellow, erased wrinkles. Walking into Frankel's was like losing ten pounds and ten years.

Bonnie walked in time to the music toward the escalators. Like the lighting, mirrors, and temperature, the music had been tested by researchers for optimal shopping. Bonnie almost felt sorry for the customers. They didn't stand a chance. Everything they saw, heard, smelled, and touched had been carefully chosen to lower their spending resistance.

She turned right toward the escalators when she caught a glimpse of her boss, Mr. Chase W. Charles, cutting through Men's Accessories—wallets, money clips, hats, and gloves. He'd pause to examine a display case and nod lordly at a salesperson before barking a terse order at another.

Despite her being the Salon director with years of seniority backing her up, Bonnie might as well have been a teenage assistant to Mr. Charles. He treated all his employees with equal condescension. Considering where she'd come from, Bonnie might've taken the condescension a little more to heart than other employees. She always felt a bit like she was passing at Frankel's, just managing to hide her outer-borough roots.

Ordinarily Bonnie would have hidden behind a column to avoid her boss during his morning walk-through, or else risk being commanded to re-dress a mannequin. But she was too distracted today by his companion to duck out of sight. She was sure she'd never seen the man in the gray suit before, but he might as well have walked straight out of Bonnie's fantasies. As if she'd summoned him, she marveled at the slightly older man with his worldly air, full head of salt-and-pepper hair, manicured good looks, and beautiful fluid strides. The main draw was the bemused expression on his face, like he had a secret. Maybe the same secret Bonnie had? Was this man wearing black silk panties?

Bonnie blushed and managed to board the escalator before Mr. Charles saw her. The mystery man did, though. There were dozens of sophisticated women milling around the floor, but he zeroed in on Bonnie just as the escalator lifted her out of his line of sight. He caught her staring at him, just as she caught the man on the subway staring at her. In that second and a half, they held eye contact and Bonnie waved. It was an impulse. Her hand lifted on its own. As soon as their connection was lost, she felt like an idiot, standing on the escalator with her arm in the air.

That summed up Bonnie's romantic interaction for the last four years. A lot of furtive glances, but no contact. If her worst fears were realized, she'd turn forty with nothing touching her intimately but her expensive and ridiculously pornographic underwear.

Escalator up.

Second floor: Jewelry.

Third floor: Menswear.

Fourth floor: Home Decor.

Fifth floor: Shoes. A football field of shoes. Shoes of every color, style, and strap. The Shoe Department was so gigantic, it should have had its own zip code.

Sixth floor: Lingerie. Her 30 percent employee discount was exercised here.

Seventh Floor: Designer Ready-to-Wear. Another frequent stop for Bonnie—in particular, the Donna Karan and Armani boutiques.

Eighth floor: Valhalla, a.k.a. Designer Couture. One practically required a special passport up here. The floor was divided into twenty-five mini-stores, each displaying one-of-a-kind garments. The Salon at Frankel's suite, where Bonnie worked, was tucked in the back of this floor. The offices were a respite for the elite from the whirlwind of shopping. For the people who worked there, it was the eye of the hurricane.

As she walked through the mini-stores, Bonnie took a second to touch the beading on a bodice, a yummy sweater, and a whisper-soft chiffon dress. Her fashion passion felt red-hot today. After a week off spent tending to her son and fretting about the start of his school year, returning to work felt like a relief.

"Welcome back," said Fran Giagoni, forty-five, at the Salon reception desk, with her thick Brooklyn accent. "You look... the same."

So did Fran, her beehive at its usual Marge Simpson height. "Did you notice the man with Mr. Charles today?" Bonnie asked.

"He hasn't come up yet."

"Is Lilah here?" The starlet in need of a gown.

"She's running late."

Bonnie walked down a short corridor crammed with cases of accessories, jewelry, and fully dressed mannequins displaying the merchandise. It opened into a large circular room they called

Grand Central, which was also crammed with racks of clothing, piles of cashmere sweaters on the floor, stacks of shoe and boot boxes, and tables dripping with baubles, scarves, bags, hats, and gloves.. Two plush couches in the middle of the room faced windows with city views. Between them was a glass table bearing platters of catered snacks.

On the other side of Grand Central, opposite the windows, were three fitting rooms. Each had a dress platform, a couple of chairs, a three-way mirror, and racks for clothes. Down a corridor to the left was Bonnie's closet-size office. Opposite that, the bathroom. Down a corridor to the right were overflowing closets and the largest fitting room, known as the Private Studio, or PS. Use of the PS was exclusive to A-list Salon clients, celebrities, and the fantastically wealthy who paid extra for the privilege of privacy.

At present, a half dozen people flitted around the Salon. Their movements seemed chaotic, but Bonnie knew exactly what each person was doing and why. It was the bustle of a busy ballet, the principles spinning in sync with one another.

Bonnie's assistant, Megan, a freckle-faced brunette, balanced a raft of Starbucks coffee cups.

Junior shopper Roman pushed yet *another* groaning rack of clothes into an already bursting fitting room.

A middle-aged redhead, Mrs. Gloria Rodkin, a B-list client, sat on one of the plush couches. An exhibitionist, she wore only her bra and a skirt slip and chatted on her iPhone while nibbling a brioche.

A busty blond, Mrs. Vicki Freed, thirty-four, A-list, stepped off a dress platform in a fitting room to tear through the rack of clothing Roman just wheeled in.

Bella, fiftyish, a no-nonsense Russian native with gray hair, steel eyes, and a gift for fitting, knelt on the carpet, pins in her mouth, in front of Mrs. Freed, attempting to hem her dress.

Bonnie shouted "Morning!" to everyone and went straight to her office. She went behind her desk, sat down, and booted up her computer. No sooner had her bottom hit the chair, her BlackBerry vibrated. A text from Mr. Charles read, "Friend in town needs new tux. When are you available today?" He must mean the man downstairs. Bonnie felt her skin heating at the idea of shopping with him, whoever he was. It'd been a long time since she'd felt a visceral reaction, a gut crush, at the sight of a man. The butterflies were awful. It was almost like being sixteen.

Emotional regression. That was the result of being alone for a week with a six-year-old. She started to compose a reply when another call came in—probably security alerting her to Lilah's arrival.

"Salon at Frankel's. How can I help?" answered Bonnie.

"It's Cody," said the caller. "I'll be there at noon. Order me a tuna sandwich, hold the bread, and a water, hold the ice. I'm bringing my hair guy, makeup guy...Chester, hurry up!...Also my party planner and personal assistant...Make a *right*, Chester, you idiot!...We have a tasting at one in Soho. That gives you thirty minutes. Make sure Bella is ready...I'm hosting a last-minute surprise party for Dan at the St. Regis. What? The planner is saying no to the St. Regis...I don't care if they're booked. Make it happen. Just...okay then. So Dan is turning forty, and he's been grouchy about the economy. So I thought *party*. Fun. Friends. Champagne. Get his mind off business for a few hours. I'm such a good wife, you don't even know. I need two dresses, one short, one long. The theme is Hot Night in Vegas. Think sexy, but not sleazy. Maybe a little sleazy, but *chic*. Don't forget the tuna." Click.

Bonnie stared at the silent BlackBerry, amazed that she continued to be surprised by Cody Deerlinger's egomania, as well as insulted by it. More money than manners. Obsessed with her own appearance but blind to how she came off, Cody was a top-down person. Anyone beneath her perceived status might as well be a trained chimp, there to amuse and serve her and to appreciate the occasional pat on the head and tossed cookie. If it weren't for Cody and others like her, however, Bonnie wouldn't have a job.

She replied to Mr. Charles's text: "Cody D. on her way in. Have to work exclusively with her for a while."

He replied, "Okay."

So. Two dresses for a surprise party. The challenge, if not the client, inspired Bonnie. For obscenely rich Cody Deerlinger, the sky was the limit. Bonnie could show her *anything*—a $25,000 Chanel ball gown—and it would be a viable option. This unscheduled emergency was, in a way, a blessing. Bonnie needed a big sale. It was September of a bad year. Bonnie's numbers were off by 35 percent from last year. Her annual bonus depended on a strong finish.

Bonnie summoned a subtle attitude shift. Frankel's needed the Cody Deerlingers of the world. The store depended on them. Cody's husband's hedge fund had to be hurting in the recession, though. Could she really afford this party and two new dresses? Not for Bonnie to say, nor to worry about. Her business was to sell taste, style, and clothes at a premium. She was an enabler to her clients' clothing addiction. Encouraging restraint was the opposite of her job. If a client spent more than she intended, *so be it*. Occasionally Bonnie felt guilty. Should a client really buy a new dress when her family's net worth had dropped from a billion to a mere $500 million? How were they managing? Honestly, Bonnie was afraid for them.

The truth? Bonnie loved the clothes. She loved her family. She even loved working with famous people—although once you've seen the twentieth hot young thing in her underwear, you really have seen them all, since they all went to the same plastic surgeons. Professional athletes, however, continued to amaze, if only because they got bigger each year. She adored the sights and smells of Frankel's. Although she wasn't a designer, she did have influence in the larger world of style. She styled the trendsetters. In all of New York City, there were ten jobs like Bonnie's.

The rumors were true. It *was* lonely at the top of her profession, as well as precarious. Despite her experience, Bonnie had no more job security than a salesgirl at the Gap. That was the nature of working in a world where the next big thing was the most desirable. That included designers, stores, muses, and stylists.

Text message from the doorman out front. Lilah was on her way up with her mother/manager and PR woman.

"Megan, are you out there?" Bonnie beckoned. On cue, her assistant appeared in the office doorway, bearing coffee.

Megan Houlihan, twenty-five, had been at Frankel's for a few months now. She'd landed the job via her family connections. Megan's father was a former governor of Iowa—how he had pull in New York City fashion retail was a mystery to Bonnie. Megan had entitled-girl syndrome. Bonnie had seen her type come and go through these doors. Megan had been waited on by nannies, and now her job was to fetch coffee. She did it with enthusiasm. It couldn't possibly last. The girl would either quit or start whining for a promotion in—Bonnie checked her watch—approximately three months, give or take a week. Six months as an assistant wasn't paying your dues, not by Bonnie's calculations. If Megan stuck around for a couple of years, maybe …but that was highly unlikely.

"Mrs. Deerlinger will be here at noon," said Bonnie. "We have to pull ten dresses—five short, five long. Evening, sexy, color, embellishment, size four. Start walking the floor— I'll catch up after I deal with Lilah—but first call Mr. Bianco in Footwear and tell him Mrs. Deerlinger wants glamour on heels, size eight."

"You mean now?" asked Megan.

She finally gets something interesting to do and she's stalling? "Right now. And ask Roman to come in," said Bonnie.

Roman Jones, twenty-seven, multiethnic, and a dedicated flirt, appeared in Bonnie's office. He'd been working at Frankel's since he was a teenager, starting in the stock room and later moving up to the eighth floor. Bonnie respected Roman's work ethic as well as his having a life outside of fashion—he was getting a college degree from the City University of New York, taking law classes at night. Too many people in her business lived and breathed clothes. Roman was an outside-the-closet thinker.

"What's up, Chief?" he said.

Bonnie quickly explained the Cody Deerlinger situation. "She has a reserve on the Private Studio. We have to get Mrs. Freed out of there."

Roman said, "Bella is working as fast as she can."

Mrs. Deerlinger refused to use any fitting room other than the Private Studio, the same space Gwyneth Paltrow and Robert DeNiro used. The acts of debauchery that went on in there over the years pickled the mind. It was the inevitable result of giving insanely wealthy people—who often traveled with an entourage, including some very *personal* assistants—a private room in a store that inflamed desire and encouraged indulgence. If the Private Studio walls could talk, they'd be on *Access Hollywood*. Bonnie had found some shocking items.

The glamorous world of high fashion has its darker side.

Mrs. Vicki Vendercamp Freed, thirty-six, the client currently using the PS, had recently returned to Manhattan from a Swiss spa with the hips of an adolescent boy and the breasts of Dolly Parton. In her previous figure, she'd purchased a fall wardrobe—$300,000 worth of dresses, skirts, tops, and pants—that no longer fit. Each item had to be altered by hand. Bonnie wondered if she'd had her new parts installed because her husband asked her to. Or it could be prescriptive on Vicki's part. Her marriage was past the ten-year mark, a watershed year. Bonnie could almost set her watch to the every-ten-year divorce/affair timetable.

Bella Orloff, the fitter slaving over Vicki's new cleavage, had been an OB/GYN in Soviet Russia who'd delivered "thousands of babies into poverty," as she told Bonnie once. She thought she'd be a doctor in the United States when she arrived in the early 1990s, but her degree wasn't recognized in New York. Bella's skillful suturing translated into sublime sewing. Her understanding of the female form helped her become the most sought-after fitter at Frankel's and, therefore, all of Manhattan.

Bonnie frowned on Bella's behalf. She was in for a crazy amount of pinning and chalking today.

"Cody wants to see ten dresses in thirty minutes."

He whistled. "Three minutes per dress? No one's that fast."

"First things first. Get Vicki Freed out of there."

"Me?"

"Vicki loves you," said Bonnie. The busty socialite did enjoy flirting with Roman, the only apparently straight man at the Salon. Roman tolerated the attention well enough.

Roman smiled. "What's not to love?"

"Is Mrs. Rodkin still out there? We need room on the couches for Cody's entourage."

He took a peek. The fifty-eight-year-old, cherry redhead exhibitionist was still there, lounging around in her bra and slip. "She's on the phone with her daughter. It's a very intense conversation."

"It always is. I'll take care of her." She scooped up her BlackBerry and exited her office with Roman on her heels.

"How are you today, Mrs. Rodkin?" asked Bonnie solicitously of the over-groomed Park Avenue matron.

"Hold on one second," said Gloria into her iPhone. She muted it. "I'm *terrible*. My daughter Shelley is very upset. Her husband, Elliot, has been to three doctors without getting a diagnosis. He's had every test in the world. And they can't find what's wrong with him. *They* say he's healthy. Elliot says he feels fine. But I know he's sick. I've buried two husbands. I know what sick looks like. He's only thirty years old! He's going to drop dead any second, and won't those doctors feel terrible then? Meanwhile, all this has been so hard for Shelley. She's having a *total* nervous breakdown." Replacing the iPhone to her ear, Gloria said, "Shelley, are you there? Put *down* the cheesecake."

"I'm very sorry to hear about it. I'm sure he'll be all right," said Bonnie. If anyone could harangue a healthy man into an early grave, it'd be Gloria Bernstein Lawrence Rodkin neé Schwartz. "Mrs. Rodkin, I'm afraid I've made a mistake. I don't have you on my schedule."

"No appointment. I just popped in to see what was new. Hortense is sending up some things for me."

Hortense Clout, fifty-two bitchy years old, was a salesperson on seven, Designer Ready-to-Wear. She would love a promotion to Salon stylist. As long as Bonnie was the director, that would never happen. Hortense regularly parked customers on Bonnie's couch, where they'd be lulled into purchase mode, then swooped in and made the sale.

Roman gave Bonnie the eyebrow. He knew that the very

name "Hortense" made Bonnie see red all day long. Naturally intuitive to mood, Roman would make an excellent therapist if law school didn't work out.

Megan was just heading out to the floor on the Cody Deerlinger mission. Bonnie stopped her and said, "Scratch gowns. I want you to pull suits, size six—Yves, Valentino, Prada—for Mrs. Rodkin here."

"Like, now?" asked Megan, confused.

"From this point on, if I ask you to do something, assume *now*."

Megan smiled and left. Bonnie could tell that corn-fed smile was starting to crack.

Roman said, "You're scaring her."

If Megan couldn't take a direct request, she shouldn't be here. Stopping at Fran's desk, Bonnie said to her, "Don't let Hortense Clout into the Salon. If she tries to get in, tell her Jennifer Aniston was seen in the Shoe Department."

Next, Bonnie and Roman went to the PS to check on Vicki Freed's fitting with Bella. The blond third wife of manufacturing giant Lee Freed stood on the dress platform in a thong, demi-bra, six-inch heels, and a super white smile. She looked like Trophy Wife Barbie.

Vicki leaned forward, as if tilting by the weight of her boobs, to poke through the jewelry on the fitting room display table. It was for sale, of course, but primarily used as placeholders for the client's precious pieces locked in a vault somewhere. Vicki fingered a string of pearls, stared at Roman, and said, "I just love pearl necklaces."

Bella said, "Step in, please." The fitter held a black, sequined Zac Posen open at Vicki's feet. For balance, Vicki put her hand on Bella's head and stepped into the low-cut strapless gown. It had fit perfectly before. Now it hung loosely around the hips, and her breasts exploded over the top like Poppin' Fresh dough out of the tube. Bonnie felt for the fitter, whom she respected. A professional enthusiast, she said, "Just a few tiny adjustments." In fact, a major restructuring job would have to be done. Vicki really had destroyed Bella's work with those cartoon boobs.

"Tiny adjustment? It's a disaster. Chernobyl," said Bella, a professional hyperbolist.

"My man loves them, and that's what matters," said Vicki. "Do *you* like them, Roman?"

"Is that a trick question?" He grinned, and Bonnie resolved to get him a raise this year, no matter the salary freeze.

Vicki smiled. "Which necklaces with this dress?"

Roman poked around the display and selected two choices: a ribbon necklace with a cluster of diamond-encrusted daisies and a choker of oversized gold baubles, big and round as cherries. "You'd look great in both."

"That one," said Vicki.

Roman stepped up on the platform to fasten the baubles around her white neck. She caressed the golden spheres and gazed at Roman's reflection in the mirror. "I just love balls," she said.

Roman fell off the platform.

Bella said, "Enough. Get out of here. Mrs. Freed, stand straight. Stop tilting hips."

Bonnie's hip pocket vibrated—phone. "Salon at Frankel's," she answered.

"Ms. Madden?" asked the caller. "It's Bethany Whitman from the Mason School. I'm sorry to bother you at work, but we have a problem."

Bonnie's stomach crashed to her feet. She hurried back to her office for semiprivacy. "Is Peter okay?"

"He's fine. Physically, he's fine," she said. "But he won't come out of the coat closet. He's been in there for an hour."

Instant flashback. When Peter was in preschool—at a different school—he locked himself in the bathroom. When the teacher banged on the door, he crawled behind the toilet and got stuck. The custodian had to take the door off the hinges and dismantle the toilet. The noise and crowd were so terrifying to Peter, he went into a fugue state—limp body, no talking, dead eyes—for three days. This wasn't supposed to happen at Mason. That's what they were paying in tuition to prevent. Bonnie felt panicked. Her heart tightened in her chest. It'd take her at least an hour to get to her son.

"Have you called Mike? Detective Madden?" Bonnie asked. Mike was a detective in the NYPD, and his precinct in Queens was only a ten-minute drive away.

"Mr. Madden said to call you."

Bastard. With her hand on her forehead, Bonnie said, "I'll call you right back."

She hung up and dialed Mike, who answered on the first ring. Before he could even say "hello," Bonnie said, "You need to go get Peter at Mason, or at least calm him down."

"He'll be fine," said Mike. "A little stress is good for him."

"*Are you out of your mind?*" she yelled.

"They know what they're doing at Mason."

She almost exploded at Mike. But screaming at one's ex was not how things were done at Frankel's. Catching herself, she whispered, "You're only ten minutes away. Drive over, *now*, or I swear to God, I'll make your life a living hell."

Then she hung up. Although it was beside the point, Mike was right. Mason was the best private facility in the five boroughs for kids on the autism spectrum, with a backbreaking tuition to go with it. But Bonnie had been right about Ms. Whitman. She was clearly out of her depth. Bonnie would try to get Peter back in the classroom with his teacher from last year, whom he was comfortable with and adored.

She called Ms. Whitman back. "Peter's dad is on the way," she said. "Call me if things get worse."

Closing the phone, she did a little prayer. But that was the most she could do about her unique work/life challenge. None of the other Salon employees had small kids, let alone one with special needs. Bonnie learned years ago that the mere mention of her son made Mr. Charles cringe and change the subject. It wasn't only that her boss didn't like children. He hated his staff to talk about *anything* but work. Bonnie did her best to comply. When she walked into Frankel's, she left one world and entered another. Compartmentalizing wasn't easy. It wasn't always possible, but she'd trained herself to focus. She had to maintain the façade in order to do her job, which paid for the

Mason School, her afterschool babysitter, Peter's therapy and medication, and provided their health insurance. She was cool and calm. She wouldn't crack under pressure. The turmoil might be rising inside, but her surface was as smooth as glass.

Her BlackBerry vibrated again. Text from Fran at reception. "Lilah's here."

She let loose a single sob, sent Peter a telepathic message to hang in there, and gathered her wits to do the same. Then she left her office to do what she did best.

Bonnie went shopping.

Chapter Two

"The Walmart Special," as Fran referred to the conservative political candidate, "canceled."

That helped. Bonnie smiled at Lilah Sheridan, her mother/manager, and her PR woman. "Good to see you all," she said. "Shall we hit the floor?"

Lilah flipped her blond tendrils. "Show me the tightest, brightest, shiniest, sparkliest, shortest dress you've got," she said in her pip-squeaky voice. "I want to kill on the white carpet."

"White?" asked Bonnie.

"At the MTV Video Music Awards! White carpet, not red. This is serious, yo. I need to kill, leave a body trail behind me."

Mrs. Sheridan added, "We want Lilah to look like she's completely naked, but not naked."

The PR woman nodded mutely. They conspired to exploit a child. If Bonnie had a daughter, she wouldn't treat her like a meal ticket. Mrs. Sheridan's Mama Rose act had landed Lilah on the red carpet—pardon, the *white* carpet. It was Bonnie's job to style Lilah, not judge her mother. It was possible Mrs. Sheridan had selfless motives. She pushed Lilah into the spotlight to make her feel beautiful and talented. Her mother's love and pride drove the bus. What mother didn't think her child was worthy of acclaim?

"If you want sexy, we should start with Versace," said Bonnie. She'd try to steer her toward tasteful options, which might be a hard sell. Bonnie would draw the line, though, at anything too revealing. It'd be like participating in child pornography. Her boss, Mr. Charles, would be furious if he knew she held back in any way. As Roman had said, "Mr. Charles would sell cigarettes to a cancer patient."

They browsed through the Versace, Rodarte, and Hervé Leger boutiques. "This is it!" said Lilah of a gold bandage dress with a crew neck in front and a deep scoop to the butt crack in back. The hem was what Bonnie called "Vee Length."

"You'll look incredible in that," agreed Bonnie. "I have to tell you, Lilah, that someone else already ordered that dress. I think she plans to wear it to the VMAs, too."

Mrs. Sheridan's eyes narrowed. "Who?"

"Does it matter? You don't want to show up in the same dress."

The PR woman pushed it. "You can't throw that out there without telling us. Come on, Bonnie! Just a hint."

In her years as a stylist—she used to be called a "personal shopper," or a "salesgirl"; semantics changed with hemlines, much to Bonnie's amusement—Bonnie had learned that honesty was the best policy. If she obfuscated or lied and was found out, Lilah would shop elsewhere. If she told the truth, Bonnie became a source of gossip and an instant confidante. It never occurred to clients that Bonnie might have an ulterior motive for divulging certain bits of information.

"Okay," Bonnie pretended to give in. "It was Anna Maytag."

The trio of women gasped. Anna was Lilah's rival on her reality TV show. If Anna bought the dress, Lilah wouldn't dare. As it just so happened, Bonnie had another choice at arm's length, one with twice the impact—and price tag. And it showed a bit less skin.

The three women huddled. Lilah twirled her tendrils and, as Bonnie watched in amazement, scratched the inside of her nostril.

The three reached a decision. "We'll take it," said Mama Sheridan.

"You will?" Bonnie was shocked. "Are you sure? Should we take ten more minutes and look at Azzedine Alaia?"

"I know what I'm doing."

Bonnie wasn't going to argue with success. Lilah et al. had been on the premises for twenty minutes and would spend $6,000. Bonnie would send some shoes to her fitting next week which would increase the total. Now *that* was some good hunting. Bonnie didn't celebrate in her mind too hard. For every easy client, there were five troublemakers.

Which reminded her: Cody Deerlinger was expected shortly. Bonnie's time flew as she rushed from boutique to boutique for her number one client. A true shopaholic, Cody spent half a million dollars last year at Frankel's buying clothes, gifts, and decor for her many children, friends, and homes—and for herself, of course.

At noon on the dot, the main doors of the Salon burst open. Five people—three women and two men—entered the space. They were talking on phones, Bluetooth headsets, or into a tote bag with a furry creature inside.

"Hey, Mrs. Deerlinger," said Fran, putting down her eyelash curler, which was a true sign of respect. "Right on time. I got your tuna right there."

If Fran had said the same sentence on the streets of Bensonhurst, a dozen horny Italians would have surrounded her, cupping their groins. Mrs. Cody Deerlinger acted as if Fran hadn't spoken. The thirty-two-year-old princess of Manhattan society—by way of Fort Worth, Texas—glided right by the reception desk and into the Salon proper. The "personal assistant"—ten years ago, she'd have been a "secretary"—who carried Cake, Cody's Brussels Griffon, took the sandwich from Fran with an aloof smirk.

Bonnie watched the exchange from Grand Central, a smile plastered on her face. Fran Giagoni, a woman who'd put three kids through college by working two jobs, apparently didn't deserve respect from a snotty twenty-five-year-old who bagged dog shit for a living. The gulf between wealth and character only got bigger as the years went by. When Bonnie started out, the wealthiest clients were overly polite, almost chagrined by their fortune. Nowadays? Money didn't sleep or apologize.

"Cody Deerlinger just walked in," said Gloria Rodkin on the iPhone to Shelley. She was still there on the couch, half-dressed, munching her third brioche. "She's in a red Chanel suit, carrying an Hermés Kelly bag in black croc…I'm not sure.

Around $20,000."

Roman stood to Bonnie's right, Megan to her left. They were as prepared as they could be on such short notice. Bonnie took a deep breath and shifted into sell mode. Before an important presentation, Bonnie always made the sign of the cross, a superstitious hangover from her Catholic childhood. She did it tiny, so no one would see. It looked like she was adjusting her blouse.

Cody sat on the plushest couch. The party planner stood at attention behind her, iPad out, ready for instruction. The hair and makeup stylists were rummaging through the jewelry and accessories on display. The assistant sat next to Cody and took the dog out of the tote to massage his shoulders.

"Not so rough," barked Cody.

The assistant said, "I'm sorry."

"Don't apologize to *me*."

The girl nodded, tilted Cake's furry face toward her, and said, "I'm *so* sorry, Cake. I didn't mean to hurt you." Bonnie sympathized with the girl. She knew what it felt like to trade dignity for salary.

"Mrs. Deerlinger, excuse me. I just got a text. We have the St. Regis ballroom," said the party planner.

"*Of course* we do," said Cody.

"She's sitting right next to me!" gushed Gloria. "Yes! I can see her pores."

"Lunch," said Cody, her hand open in the air.

The assistant placed the sandwich in her boss's hand. Cody unwrapped it. "Bonnie, what the hell is this?"

Fran said, "What's the problem?"

Cody spoke only to Bonnie. "This is a *sandwich*. I said 'tuna, hold the bread.' And where's my room temperature water?"

Fran rushed forward, put a crystal stem on the table within Cody's easy reach, and poured Fiji into it. Fran retreated, knowing she might as well wait for pigs to fly for a thank-you.

Gloria relayed, "Apparently Cody asked for tuna, no bread. But she's eating the sandwich anyway…yes, even the bread. I don't know. Multigrain? Wheat?"

With her mouth full, Cody said, "Begin."

Bonnie and Megan wheeled a rack forward. Roman alerted Mr. Bianco in Fitting Room B to be ready with the shoes. Mr. Bianco was a Frankel's lifer. He'd worked in Footwear for thirty years and planned to stay until "they carry me out in a box—feet first," as he loved to say, perhaps nine times a day.

"Not to get too high-concept," said Bonnie, who knew that Cody Deerlinger loved high-concept, but would never admit it, "the two dresses represent the first and second half of a hot Las Vegas night. When you step out in Vegas, you start slowly at an elegant dinner in a full-length gown. Then things loosen up. You have a glass or two of champagne. You win at roulette. For the second half of the night, inhibitions go down and the hem goes up. From soigné to soiree."

"Soigné to soiree!" repeated Raj, Cody's makeup pro. "Love it! I'm so stealing that."

Bonnie shot him a grateful glance. Any support was appreciated. She quickly ran through her picks. Just as quickly, Cody rejected four of the ten dresses right off the rack. Of an Oscar de la Renta, she said, "Is that...*taffeta*? Have you lost your *mind*? I'm not going to the fucking *prom*!" Cody agreed to try on the remaining six and pick two. Bonnie had suggested specific pairings of long and short, but the client would make the final decision.

Cody said, "Where is Bella? I've got...six minutes per dress." She marched down the corridor to the PS and yanked the door open.

Oh, Christ. Bonnie knew she forgot something.

Inside the fitting room, Bella was helping Vicki Freed peel off a sheath dress. With the door wide open, everyone in the Salon was treated to the sight of Vicki's scientifically engineered curves.

Raj said, "I think I just went straight."

Gloria did the blow-by-blow for her daughter: "Cody Deerlinger and Vicki Freed are air-kissing! And Vicki is practically nude!"

Cody pulled back from the air-kiss and said, "Wonderful to

see you. And so much of you!" She gave Vicki the once-over, in slow motion, twice.

Mrs. Freed could smile just as phonily as Cody. "You look fantastic! You've lost so much weight. Good for you."

"And you've gained," said Cody.

"In all the right places," said Vicki, slipping on a robe. "Although it does get tiring, having to fend off so many of my friends' husbands."

Vicki's blue eyes stayed fixed on Cody's. Something had to break the tension soon, or Cody might storm off in a snit without choosing a dress.

Dog to the rescue. Cake sniffed Gloria's brioche and then snatched it out of her hand. "Oh my God! Cody Deerlinger's dog is eating off my plate. I don't know. Terrier? It looks like a gremlin."

"I hate to do this to you in the middle of your fitting," said Cody to Vicki. They both knew Cody had a reserve on the room, even if someone else was currently using it.

Vicki said, "Don't give it another thought. I'm ready for a lunch break anyway." Bella helped her into a robe, and she left the room, asking the fitter if she wanted a water or a sandwich.

Bonnie exhaled gratefully. Beneath the *vavavoom* body, Vicki was a lady. She'd gracefully sidestepped what could have been a difficult moment. As she took a seat on the couch next to Gloria, Vicki winked at Bonnie. The message was clear: Bonnie now owed her a favor.

Roman wheeled Vicki's rack out of the PS. He wheeled Cody's rack in. "That's one minute of my life—*wasted*," said Cody, following the rack and closing the fitting room door.

Meanwhile, back on the couch, Vicki acknowledged Cody's party planner with a nod and said, "Congrats, Simone, working with Mrs. Deerlinger."

Simone seemed anxious. "Thank you, Mrs. Freed."

"What kind of event are you planning?" Vicki was trolling for information. Although her influence in society wasn't at the Deerlinger level, as chairwoman for the Peace on Earth Foundation, a major celebrity-affiliated charity, Vicki carried weight.

Simone smiled enigmatically. "It's a small, intimate party."

"Sounds divine. How intimate?"

"Close friends and family."

"I thought the St. Regis ballroom had a minimum of three hundred."

Busted. Simone said, "It's a business thing."

"With a Las Vegas theme?"

Gloria whispered into the phone, "Drama!"

"My husband and I adore the St. Regis," said Vicki. "I was thinking of hosting the next Peace on Earth fundraiser there."

The subtext came in loud and clear. Vicki was dangling a possible fundraiser gig to Simone in exchange for wrangling her an invite to Cody's party. It was pure extortion. Everyone in New York, including the Freeds, would want to party with the tippy-top of Manhattan's elite. The event would be a spare-no-expense spectacle, covered by every newspaper and society blog. If her picture found its way onto the right style pages, Vicki's stock would skyrocket.

Cody emerged from the PS wearing a strapless, blush pink evening gown of draped silk jersey by Halston. She paraded down the corridor to Grand Central to get a verdict from her paid people.

Bonnie's first impression: wrong. The pink was too pale for Cody's coloring. Her B-cup breasts were crushed flat, negating any curves. Even social X-rays wanted to show a bit of a figure. Cody was an attractive woman, and anything looked good. But this wasn't making the most of what she had.

Raj grabbed his heart as if stricken. "Love ittttt!"

Perry, Cody's hairstylist, said, "I'm seeing straight, high gloss, middle part, a la Demi. Or a *Mad Men* chignon."

Vicki said, "It's *very* flattering." A lie. Society ladies could be pathologically competitive.

"Halston," Gloria said into her phone. "At least $5,000."

Mr. Bianco, a balding, short man in a rumpled brown suit, came out of his makeshift mini shoe department in Fitting Room B with a pair of six-inch, gold, peep-toe heels. He helped

Cody into them. She looked at herself in the three-way mirror. "I'm a rail."

Exactly. That was Bonnie's objection to the dress. No curves. But Cody didn't want to look feminine. She wanted to look skinny. Bonnie turned to Megan and Roman. "It's a maybe."

While they waited for Cody to change, Megan asked Bonnie, "Is everything okay? You seem distracted."

Bonnie turned toward her assistant and found what appeared to be genuine concern in her freckled face. A rare sight at Frankel's. Bonnie was thrown by it and let down her guard. "My son is having a rough day at school," she said.

"Is he okay?" asked Megan with what seemed like real sympathy.

Bonnie had forced that question out of her mind for two hours. But the expression on Megan's face…it was sincere. Whenever someone showed the slightest hint of authentic emotion at work, Bonnie felt the weight of the pressure she was constantly under.

Damn it! She *hated* feeling vulnerable. Bonnie would have preferred it if Megan punched her in the jaw. Her BlackBerry hummed. A text from Mike. "All is well. Peter is fine," it read. Bonnie had to bite her lip to keep in her sigh of relief.

Cody emerged from the PS in another dress. Gloria said into her phone, "Black organza Stella McCartney. Short. Too young for her."

"Gor…GEOUS!" gushed Raj.

"Catwoman back-comb. Think Julie Newmar," concurred Perry.

Vicki must have thought Cody looked sexy. She crinkled her nose and said, "You look like a precious doll. Very cute." *Cute* was the kiss of death.

Mr. Bianco brought out a pair of black zip-up boots that came over Cody's knee. Roman whispered into her ear, "The boots go for $4,000."

Bonnie thought, *I love them*. She'd love them even if they were $5,000.

"Next!" Cody proclaimed loudly and returned to the

fitting room.

In and out in record time, she now wore a black halter dress that clung to her body like a jealous lover. Bonnie's jaw nearly dropped. It was a knockout.

"Narciso Rodriguez, supertight cocktail dress," said Gloria, who knew her designers. "Cody looks fifteen years lighter."

Raj and Perry adored it. Bonnie wondered if Cody paid them to be stylists or cheerleaders. This time, they were right. If Cody didn't buy this dress, she was a fool, blind, or nuts.

Vicki said, "Please don't take it the wrong way, Cody. You look chunky. A real friend would tell you the truth."

Chunky was a bigger kiss of death than *cute*. Cody didn't wait for shoes and returned to the fitting room. She emerged in a long dress.

Gloria called it correctly. "Valentino. Pale yellow, silk chiffon, embellished bow neckline."

Cody asked doubtfully, "Yellow, Bonnie? Really?"

"Not the hottest color this season," nodded Bonnie. "But it's flattering to your skin tone. The line of the dress— so slimming."

Cody examined her reflection carefully. Bonnie sensed she had a winner—a $6,000 one, at that. Bonnie said, "Mr. Bianco! The McQueens, please."

The shoe man shuffled forward. Wordlessly he put a box on the floor and ceremoniously removed the top. Eh, voila! Sparkling rhinestone-studded Alexander McQueen stilettos.

Cody, Gloria, the assistant, Simone, Raj, Perry—even Cake—couldn't help themselves. They chorused, "Oohhhhh!"

"Plus a white mink capelet," said Bonnie. "Bella, the Lanvin?"

Bella ducked into the PS to find the mink. "Not here," she announced.

"It's not?" Bonnie was sure she'd seen it on the rack herself not fifteen minutes ago. She mouthed to Megan and Roman, "Find it."

Roman walked briskly back to the Lanvin boutique to grab another stole, if they had it. Megan rushed into the PS to recheck the rack. Cody peered into the fitting room, appalled by Megan's frantic searching. "Why is that fat person touching my clothes?" she asked Bonnie.

Fat? Megan was a perfectly proportioned size eight. A lean six, Bonnie was probably plus-sized in Cody's eyes.

Cody took a hard look at Bonnie. "What in God's name is the matter with you today?" she asked. "I hated most of your picks. The PS was occupied. You're misplacing important pieces. And," she added, extra disgust in her voice, "for Christ's sake, you look like you're about to *cry*."

Every head in the room swiveled toward Bonnie. She blinked away her humiliation and said to herself, "Bitch, you gave me one hour to pull ten dresses when I was already booked. My kid was sitting in a closet at school, which is an hour away on the train. My ex-husband is a lazy prick. I haven't had a decent meal in a month or felt a man's hands on my body in years. I'm paying 30 percent interest on a mountain of credit card debt. Your stupid *dog* is eating his weight in catered food, including the mozzarella sandwich that I was going to have for lunch. You're a mean, selfish person, and I hate you."

Of course, Bonnie couldn't *really* say that out loud. She screamed it in her head, so loud she thought her skull might explode.

"Cody! My favorite customer! Dear Lord, you are a vision!" The boisterous entrance of Mr. Chase W. Charles broke the silence. He was dressed in his usual charcoal suit, high-collared white shirt, brown wing-tip shoes, and wireless glasses. He was alone. His "old friend" didn't want to wait for his tux shopping. Bonnie felt disappointed. She'd powered through the morning imagining Mr. Charles bringing up his friend this afternoon, the man's warm and rough hand shaking hers, maybe a smoldering glance or two. An indulgent fantasy to power through the day. No crime in it. In a way, she was relieved not to have to put on her game face for a new client. Being positive and up all the time was grinding her down.

Cody said, "Chase! Darling!" Manhattan ladies adored dapper Mr. Charles. When he embraced Cody, she visibly softened. When they separated, he held her at arm's length and looked over his glasses at her, emanating joy in her presence. He loved all his big-money clients to death.

Bonnie found it ironic that Mr. Charles, the president at Frankel's, didn't really know much about fashion. He was a salesman. Clothes, widgets, or turnips—it didn't matter to him what the store was selling. He hadn't picked a pocket square for himself in years. Bonnie styled his outfits for him and organized his home closet, too. When the press applauded Mr. Charles's taste and the Frankel's aesthetic, the brand "look," he took full credit. His great talent was hiring talented people. His staff watched hemlines. Mr. Charles watched the bottom line.

Very closely lately. This was the last year of his ten-year contract. He lived in constant fear that the store's owners would ditch him for young, fresh talent, this year's Harvard MBA. The recession wasn't his fault. Nor was the drop in annual sales. But Mr. Charles might take the fall for it anyway—unless he could find someone else to blame.

So the sight of a Cody Deerlinger in a Valentino dress set Mr. Charles's heart aflutter. He heaped on the praise, kept his chatter at top speed and volume. Bonnie rubbed her forehead. Headache coming.

Mr. Charles himself helped Mrs. Deerlinger into the McQueen sparklers.

Cody said, "Now, Chase, I want your honest opinion."

Mr. Charles said, "You're stunning. Absolutely stunning."

"I'm not sure…" she said.

"You can't not buy those shoes, darling."

"I'll take them," said Cody, "but only for a 20 percent discount."

"It'd be a crime to deny the world the sight of you in those shoes," replied Mr. Charles, grinning and looking over his glasses. Bonnie didn't fault Mr. Charles. He'd do whatever it took to close the deal. Eighty percent was better than nothing.

Simone, on the couch, started grumbling about being late for the meeting with the caterer.

Roman ran into the Salon, mink stoles piled in his arms—

but not, as Bonnie would later learn, the white Lanvin.

Raj and Perry fluttered at him to stroke the minks. Roman placed one on Cody's shoulders.

Bella pinned the Valentino dress even tighter across Cody's hips and tried to shoo away the stylists.

Vicki watched jealously from the couch, her smile fake and frozen.

Cake lifted his furry face from the people food and snarled. He started barking at something. Cody's assistant struggled to keep him on her lap.

Out of the corner of Bonnie's eye, she caught a flash of movement on the floor. Cody's assistant yelled, "Mouse!"

It might as well have been a lion, by the way the ladies reacted. Vicki and Gloria jumped up on the couch, screaming. Raj and Perry shrieked and clutched each other. Mr. Charles leapt up on the dress platform with Cody.

Bonnie was not a lover of rodents, but she pitied this one. Its rear foot was stuck in a glue trap that he dragged across the carpet behind him. He looked at the frightened humans, whiskers twitching, probably wondering how the hell he wound up here, stuck in a bad situation with no visible way to escape. Bonnie thought: *Of all the creatures in this room, I have the most in common with the mouse.*

Thwap. Fran dropped an open shoebox over the critter and slid a top underneath to capture him. She held the box aloft. "Got him. Crisis over. The mouse can't hurt you now." Fran lifted the lid for a peek. "Eh. Kind of puny. I've seen bigger cockroaches."

Chapter Three

"You should remember to lock this," said Mike Madden, forty, as he walked through the back door at Bonnie's bungalow-style house in Corona, formerly *their* house. It was a two-story building with graying white paint on a small plot of land that looked almost identical (except for paint and landscaping) to the homes on either side and up and down the block. The interior left a lot to be desired. Although Bonnie hated the 1980s earth-toned cabinetry and wallpaper left over from the previous owners and the flea-market-find furniture that dated back to the earliest days of her marriage, she hadn't redecorated. No time. No money. And no motivation. Fashion changed every season. The famous storefront windows at Frankel's changed every couple of weeks. But Bonnie's Queens home and life were fixed. Same people. Same furniture. She took comfort in the familiar.

In off-duty jeans and a too-tight navy T-shirt, Mike still looked like a cop with the hard-set mouth, cut cheekbones, and intense dark blue eyes. He glared at everyone like they were up to something. Bonnie used to love Mike's intensity, until his unblinking eyes made her feel like a guilty perp in her own marriage.

She gestured for him to sit at the beige Formica kitchen table and got him a Coke. Bonnie watched him drink, his Adam's apple moving up and down on his muscular neck. His dark hair, wavy and thick, needed a cut. When they were married, Bonnie loved this stage, when he was two weeks past needing a trim, the curls both rugged and soft.

He was a gorgeous man. There was simply no getting around that fact. When Bonnie looked at him—when *any* woman looked at him—she had to take a giant step back or else be drawn into his orbit. That he had a gun tucked into the back of his jeans used to make Bonnie sweat whenever she thought about it. They met in high school, long before Bonnie knew what she wanted to do or become. If she met him now, she'd be attracted to him. She'd think he was a good person. But he wouldn't clear a first date hurdle. A cop? What woman with kids would want to date a cop? It was like asking for heartbreak and stress. If Mike just met Bonnie, he'd probably give her a pass as well, like the half dozen men she dated after the divorce did before she said goodbye to all that. He'd say, "I'm sorry, Bonnie. You're a very attractive woman, but you've got too much baggage."

She couldn't really blame them. Men didn't waltz into a relationship with a woman knowing they'd never be her top priority. Men wanted to be number one. With Bonnie, no matter how perfectly a man fit her checklist, he would be second to Peter or maybe third, after her career. Four years post-breakup, Bonnie had accepted her dismal romantic fate. Dreaming of the perfect man would have to, and did, suffice.

"I'm still pissed off at you," she said.

"It was fine. I already told you. By the time I got there, Peter was back in the group. Enough about that. What're you doing tonight?" Mike asked. "Hot date?"

Bonnie nodded. "Yes, with the president of France. Are you going to Vivian's?" Vivian was Mike's mother. She lived a few blocks from where he lived now, which was a few blocks from Bonnie's. Which was a few blocks from Bonnie's dad's house and her sisters' houses. The entire family lived within two square miles, and most of them were in and out of each other's houses all day long, transporting food and gossip. Bonnie's house wasn't a high-traffic stop, though. Too much commotion affected Peter.

"Vivian's first," said her ex. "Then we might make the rounds."

On the weekends Mike had custody, he always took Peter to his mother's house. *Couldn't he spend time with Peter alone?* she wondered. Why did he rely on his mother so much? Vivian worshipped her grandson, and she was excellent at handling him. But still.

"You could get help from your mom, too, you know," he said once, and they both burst out laughing. Bonnie's mom wasn't exactly the nurturing type. Sylvia Salerno had raised five kids and then, when the youngest left home, she announced, "I'm *done*." Within six months, she'd divorced Bonnie's father, taken half of their savings, and moved to her own house—one mile away from her old one. Sylvia vowed never to change a diaper or fix a grilled cheese sandwich ever (ever, ever, ever) again. She'd been true to her word. When Sylvia saw her grandkids, including Peter, she was affectionate and loving. But she didn't babysit. And she never cooked.

Bonnie had packed Peter's weekend bag of clothes, meds, books, DVDs, and music. All his essentials. At the moment, Peter could not live without the penguin cartoon *Happy Feet*. He slept with the DVD box and carried it in his backpack to school. If anyone tried to take it away, Peter might have an episode. His 100-times-normal reaction to stress was due to the unique construction of his brain. It wasn't his fault. He was born that way.

Mike had custody every other weekend and Wednesday nights. Bonnie looked forward to the break. But then five minutes after Peter left with Mike, Bonnie felt the ache. She missed her son, his sweet face, the way his benevolent spirit filled the room, the concentration of caring for him. When Bonnie was by herself, she had no choice but to look at her life. She didn't like what she saw. Especially the rear view.

Mike said, "You look good. Tired."

"Good and tired?" she asked. "Or good, but tired?"

Mike laughed. "You always look good, Bonnie."

He smiled, long and slow like a river, and Bonnie felt the flutter. It was embarrassing, how attracted she was to her ex-husband. It'd been four years since they split up. Maybe if she had sex with someone else, her body wouldn't reflexively overheat near him.

She said, "We need to talk."

He groaned. "I'm tapped out, Bonnie."

"Work is horrible," she said. "I'm afraid for my bonus." Her bonus was calculated by her annual sales total, which was off by 35 percent from last year. Without a fat check, Bonnie wouldn't be able to make the January tuition payment to the Mason School. Mike had never missed a child support payment. But his monthly check was a fixed amount. The cost of Peter's needs went up constantly.

"I'm giving you all I can. Citywide wage freezes on public employees, including cops. A lot of guys have been forced into early retirement. I'm lucky I still have a job."

Bonnie sighed. "I know." He was protecting the peace, putting his life at risk. But she still resented having to carry the heavier financial burden. In her part of Queens, she might be the only woman who outearned her husband, or ex-husband.

"We could take Peter out of Mason," suggested Mike again.

"No," she said firmly. She Skyped with the school administrators for an hour Monday night, and they were able to move Peter back into a classroom with his beloved teacher from last year. Bonnie had probably made an enemy for life in Ms. Whitman. But she was willing to add her, or anyone, to that list for the sake of Peter's well-being.

Buzz. Bonnie's BlackBerry started scooting across the kitchen table.

"Oh no," she said, her heart speeding up. Caller ID showed Cody Deerlinger's number. It was seven o'clock. She should be preparing to greet her guests at the St. Regis.

This can't be good. Bonnie answered, "Mrs. Deerlinger?"

"Get over here *now*!" said Cody. "These shoes are ridiculous! I can't walk ten feet in them."

She had to be referring to the Alexander McQueens. They were on the weird side, and difficult to walk in. But Cody *knew* that. Bonnie had warned her—repeatedly—that she might prefer a lower heel.

Stupid, thought Bonnie of herself. She should have anticipated this and sent other choices to the St. Regis. The Deerlinger primary residence was in Greenwich, Connecticut. Cody had reserved the suite at the hotel for the party night.

Dan Deerlinger had found out about the "surprise." Apparently, when the St. Regis tried to charge $40,000 on Cody's Visa Black card, Dan was the first to hear about it. He would agree to the party only if Cody uninvited sixty of her "friends" to make room for some of his new Japanese business contacts.

Bonnie could imagine Cody's face when she was told to change her hat from the crown of social royalty to the hood of dutiful business hostess. She felt a little spiteful glee, picturing Cody cowed by her husband.

"Bonnie!" screeched Cody into the phone. "*Are you listening to me!?*"

"Sorry, Mrs. Deerlinger. I was thinking about the logistics of getting to you as quickly as…"

"I don't give a crap about your logistical problems. Just be here in thirty minutes with new shoes."

She hung up. Bonnie's blood ran cold. She didn't want to lose Cody as a client. Cody would tell her friends she'd changed stylists. The friends would follow like lemmings. An open appointment book was death to Bonnie and would mean the end of her Frankel's career. No job, no tuition money. No Mason School. Peter wouldn't get specialized help that could make all the difference in his life. Bonnie choked on the panic that came a few times a day when she had time to think about her son's iffy future.

Mike read the situation. "Shopping alert?"

"Code red," she said. Bonnie had to get from Corona to midtown Manhattan in thirty minutes on a Friday night. It was impossible.

"Just tell me what you need," he said, standing up, shoulders back, ready to be a hero. This was Mike's happy place. Along with the family tradition—his father and grandfather had been NYPD—riding the rescue was why Mike became a cop. His problem-solving compulsion was also one of the reasons they split up. They had philosophically different ideas about how to raise their son.

She quickly explained the situation. Mike knew all about Cody Deerlinger. When they were married, Bonnie filled him in about all her clients. They laughed about their entitlement, excess, and brattiness. Venting to Mike had been a huge stress reliever. Besides the sex, if she had to say the one thing she missed most about her marriage, it was swapping stories at night with Mike, under the covers. His down-to-earth perspective adjustments helped her deal with situations like this.

Peter ran into the kitchen. Father and son—big and small versions of the same mold—kissed hello, a sight that, even in a jam, warmed Bonnie's heart. Peter held up his *Happy Feet* DVD and said, "Good ending."

The boy had seen the ending approximately eighty-seven times, and he would probably find it just as reassuring and satisfying after another fifty viewings.

Mike said, "Ready to go?"

Peter said, "Grandma's house."

"Yup," said Mike, "with a quick stop on the way."

Mike was already hustling his son and ex out of the house. Bonnie grabbed Peter's bag and her purse.

Peter liked plan changes as much as a frying pan to the skull. He asked, "Where are we going? How long will it take to get there? How many miles? How fast are we going?"

All good questions that Bonnie was curious about herself. She and Mike put on an excellent show of acting calm, despite moving as fast as they dared. More than so-called normal kids, Peter sensed mood. He could sniff out the slightest trace of tension, and that set off his own anxieties.

Bonnie buckled her son into the backseat of Mike's Crown Victoria. The cop car was Peter's favorite vehicle, apart from U-boats. One of the many contradictions of Peter's autism was that although he was terrified of bright lights and loud noises, Peter loved it when Mike turned on the Crown Vic's sirens and LED flashers. If Peter knew when the siren was coming, he could prepare for it and delight in it.

Bonnie asked Mike, "Are you allowed to do this?"

"Who's going to stop me?" he replied.

Flashing cherry red on the roof, a warning to Peter, then a siren blast, and they were off. Mike sped toward the Queensboro

Bridge. Traffic opened up in front of them like the parting of the Red Sea. While Mike drove, Bonnie called Mr. Bianco on her BlackBerry. Thank God the shoe man was still on site at Frankel's, checking returns before he went home to his wife. Bonnie explained the situation. Mr. Bianco agreed to pull five new pairs and personally walk them the few blocks from Frankel's to the St. Regis. Since Cody would only work with Bonnie, he'd meet her by the correct elevator banks to hand off the shopping bags on her way up to Cody's suite.

Bonnie hung up and looked at Peter in the backseat. He was grinning, covering his ears, and saying, "Do it again, Dad!"

Mike switched on the siren. Peter laughed.

"We're coming to the tunnel," said Mike.

"Thank you so much for this," said Bonnie, daring to relax.

"Cody hasn't changed," he said. "You'd think she'd know how to do her own shopping by now."

Why *didn't* Cody Deerlinger—or any of the Salon's clients— pick out her own clothes? Most women enjoyed shopping. It was entertainment. They had time and money. Why did they rely on Bonnie to choose their wardrobe for them?

The truth was, society types and celebs didn't have as much time to shop as one might think. Cody had four kids in two schools, three houses, and a staff of ten. She sat on the board of three major charities, spent two hours a day with her trainer, and had daily lunch dates and grooming appointments. Granted, Cody was not holed up in a science lab finding a cure for cancer. But she was a very busy woman. She'd traded off the simple life for the complications of having it all. It was her job to stay current, for her homes, children, husband, and self to look and present a certain way. No question, she was a spoiled, selfish, privileged person. But she was constantly under pressure. Granted, Cody wasn't worried about food on the table or a roof over her head. But pressure was pressure. If you felt it, it was real. Bonnie could certainly relate and sympathize with Cody about that.

Plus, Cody had bad taste. Left to her own devices, the woman would dress like Linda Evans on *Dallas*. That was not

Cody's vision of the glamorous life in New York. Cody grew up on *Sex and the City*. Lloyd Proctor, Cody's daddy, would have preferred if Cody married a billionaire oilman like himself, but Lone Star society wasn't nearly big enough for Cody. She wanted a national arena, to be at the center of the universe. Doing a big-haired impression of Veruca Salt, Cody stomped her feet on the marble floor of her Fort Worth mansion and screamed, "But I want to be the queen of New York City *now*, Daddy!"

"Whatever you want, sweetheart," had been Lloyd's response. He couldn't deny her anything, including a suitable New York husband. He probably saw the upside for himself as well. Having a moneyman on Wall Street couldn't hurt, especially in these uncertain times. Father and daughter moved to Manhattan to begin the husband search. Lloyd wouldn't leave town until he'd found someone he could trust to stay under his thumb. Financier Dan Deerlinger seemed like a good bet in his ruthless ambition and lack of integrity. Dan agreed to all of Lloyd's requests, including that he change his surname from Dershewitz to Deerlinger, and to marry in a Unitarian church. It was one thing for Lloyd Proctor's daughter to marry a Yankee, but quite another for her to marry a Jew.

Dan used Cody's dowry of $50 million to form a hedge fund. Cody used her platinum credit cards at Frankel's. With Bonnie's help, Cody had turned herself into a style maven, trendsetter, and icon of the New Society. Her photo was regularly found in the *New York Times* Styles section. Cody's existence was about maintaining her place at the top—and she could not do it alone.

Bonnie said, "Should I call you later? Tell you how it went?" The emergency shoe delivery was exactly the kind of thing they used to laugh about in bed. She used to save up funny stories and little moments and bring them home to Mike like gifts.

"I'll check in with you tomorrow." A brush-off. Her stories weren't fun for him anymore. *Were they ever?* she wondered.

"We hardly talk anymore. We're still friends. Friends talk."

Mike's jaw tensed. Bonnie noticed he spent less time at her place lately. He was pulling away. Bonnie knew he had a girlfriend. Peter had been mentioning the name "Emily" a lot after his weekends with Mike. Bonnie hoped it was just a fling. The thought of Mike replacing her knotted her stomach. She was afraid for Peter, too. Would this Emily be patient and kind? Would she watch *Happy Feet* a hundred times?

The conversation was cut short when Mike stopped short in front of the St. Regis Hotel, a 1904 Beaux Arts masterpiece on East Fifty-Fifth Street. It'd been only twenty-five minutes since Cody's hysterical phone call.

She kissed Mike on the cheek and said, "You are my hero." Bonnie leaned into the backseat to kiss Peter. Her son was distracted by the crowds on the Manhattan street, but he said goodbye. She'd have preferred a kiss, but a wave would have to do.

She got out of the car and ran into the hotel. Mr. Bianco was waiting exactly where he said he'd be. "You're my hero, too," she told him and kissed his shiny head.

He gave her an avuncular cheek pinch and said, "For you, I'd walk *five* blocks on a moment's notice."

They shared a conspiratorial smile. Bonnie relieved him of two heavy shopping bags, pushed the up button, and zipped up to the tenth floor to Cody's suite.

Sweet, indeed. The Imperial Suite looked like a movie set for *Marie Antoinette.* Walnut, satin-upholstered furniture, damask drapery, wallpaper made of patterned silk. Two bedrooms. The living room was bigger than Bonnie's whole downstairs. She'd been sufficiently awed by the suite earlier that day, organizing Cody's racks for her two outfits. Each held the dress, accessories, footwear, and appropriate undergarments. Cody was bringing her own jewelry from the Greenwich mansion vault.

She knocked and Raj let her in. Unlike this morning, every surface was now covered with boxes, luggage, room service debris, and gift baskets, dozens of them. A lot of the boxes were oblong and orange.

Raj whispered in her ear, "I know. It's like an Hermés bomb went off in here. What do you give the man who has everything? Apparently he needs ties."

Cody, in an ivory silk robe, her hair done up in a high

chignon, rushed out of one of the bedrooms. Perry ran after her, an aerosol bottle in his hands, saying, "One more squirt…"

"Show me," said Cody to Bonnie. No greeting. No "sorry for ruining your night." Not a hint of "thank you."

Bonnie's placid façade was up and uncracked. Putting on a servile performance was part of her job. She smiled and unpacked Mr. Bianco's selections. He wisely stuck to conservative-yet-sexy metallics. Raj and Perry, in sync with each other like bats, swooped down on a pair of Manolo Blahnik three-toned sandals with an ankle strap. Simple, elegant, worked with either dress.

Cody nodded at their choice. "Let's try them," she said and put on the $900 shoes.

She scrutinized the sandals in the bedroom's full-length mirror as if they contained the secrets of the universe. "Is there a God?" and "Why are we here?" were trumped by Cody's question, "Do these sandals make my toes look fat?"

"No!" said Raj.

"Your feet look totally skinny," said Perry.

Bonnie remained absolutely quiet, did her mini sign of the cross. Superstitious? *Yes.* If she breathed too loud, Cody might take off the shoes and throw them at her.

Cody stopped pacing in front of the mirror and said, "Okay."

Bonnie exhaled so hard, she felt dizzy. When in doubt, Manolo. She should have bumper stickers made.

Raj and Perry ushered Cody back to the vanity for more hair and makeup primping. The mood was bright again. Cody actually smiled as Perry sprayed her last strand into place. She puckered playfully for Raj to blot her lipstick. Bonnie sank into a chair. Her back muscles unclenched.

And then, a dark energy filtered into the room. Bonnie felt the presence like an icy finger on her neck. Raj and Perry sensed it, too. They froze mid-polish and turned toward the doorway of the bedroom.

There stood Dan Deerlinger. A tall, brooding Heathcliff, he had dark hair, eyes, and aura. Paradoxically, his body language spoke of ease and comfort in his skin.

"Three hundred people are waiting for you downstairs," said Mr. Deerlinger softly—but chillingly.

Cody flinched. "Almost ready!" she sang. Bonnie had never heard her sound sunny. Cody had a placid façade to master as well.

Mr. Deerlinger pointed at Bonnie, Raj, and Perry one by one with a finger gun. "Am I paying these people?"

Bonnie had met Dan several times before, but she'd learned to re-re-reintroduce herself to the husbands. They paid the bills after all. "Bonnie Madden, sir. I work with your wife on her beautiful wardrobe."

Mr. Deerlinger inspected Bonnie's outfit of jeans and a black turtleneck. "Let's see how beautiful," he said. To his wife: "Waiting."

Cody stood up and went to the first rack. With Bonnie's help, she got into the Halston pink empire-waist, boob-crushing gown that Bonnie had voted against. Once she was zipped, with her diamond earrings and necklace in place, Cody faced her husband with a forced smile.

Bonnie was the first to admit when she was wrong. The complete picture—gown, hair, diamonds, Manolos—was lovely. Cody looked like a twenty-first century Audrey Hepburn. It read Park Avenue, not Las Vegas. But who cared? It was Cody's party. She could dress any way she wanted.

Mr. Deerlinger slowly appraised his wife. He walked a small circle around her, his fingers stroking his clean-shaven chin.

"You sold my wife this gown?" he asked Bonnie.

"Yes, sir."

"How much did this cost me?"

Bonnie cleared her throat. "Around five thousand dollars."

He laughed. "That's five thousand dollars of my money—*wasted*," he declared. An echo of Cody's comment at the Salon earlier in the week: "a minute of my life—*wasted*." To his wife, he said, "There are sixty Japanese investors downstairs who expect American wives to have big American tits. You're flat as a fifth-grader in this dress. Can't you..." he reached into Cody's bodice, groping at her modest breasts and trying to yank them upward,

"...make them *bigger?*"

Cody's skin turned white as ash. But she just stood there, letting her husband manhandle her roughly in front of other people. The sight made Bonnie queasy. She could only imagine how Cody felt.

"It's hopeless," sneered Mr. Deerlinger, jerkily extracting his hands from inside the gown. Cody seemed relieved. To Bonnie, he ordered, "Shove some socks in there."

"The dress has been fit to Mrs. Deerlinger's body," said Bonnie.

"If I can get my whole hand in there, you can cram in a sock," he said, holding up his hairy knuckles. To Cody, he said, "I want you downstairs in five minutes. And don't think about wasting time crying to your daddy about what a bastard I am."

And then he left, taking his black aura with him. A man who brokered deals all over the world for billions of dollars, at the end of the day, was insecure about how big his wife's breasts looked in a dress.

As soon as the door closed, Cody cracked. She sobbed gustily and sank onto the bed, resting her head softly on her arm.

Raj and Perry rushed forward to stroke Cody on the back and shoulders.

"What a meanie," said Raj. "He doesn't deserve you."

"And you look *amazing,*" said Perry. "He's an idiot."

Bonnie wished she had two cheerleaders on call to make her feel better.

Cody sat upright. "That's enough. How's my hair and makeup?"

"You're divine," said Raj.

"Perfection," agreed Perry.

To Bonnie, Cody said, "What are our options?"

"You mean...stuffing the gown?" Was she seriously going to do it? From the look on Cody's face, she was dead serious. Where Bonnie came from, literally and metaphorically, a man couldn't expect to shove his grubby fingers inside her dress and expect to keep the hand. But Cody, a take-no-prisoners type of woman, would allow her vulgar husband to grope her and humiliate her semipublicly? There wasn't enough money in the world, as far as Bonnie was concerned. If Dan would talk to her like this in public, imagine their private life. Horrible. Bonnie actually felt sorry for her. But this was the life Cody wanted, and Dan was what she got.

Bonnie turned her mind to practical matters. What could they do on a moment's notice? She asked Raj, "Any cutlets?" Sometimes makeup artists carried the silicone bra inserts as part of their kit.

He shook his head. "I can run to a drugstore on Lex and buy some."

"No time," said Bonnie, dejected. And then, a flash. "The shoe boxes!" she said, rushing back into the living room of the suite. Inside the sandals were tight balls of tissue used to keep the shoe's shape. "You have a bra for the second dress. You can wear it without the straps."

Cody voice changed, her anxiety growing. "But it won't stay up. This won't work!"

Raj said, "It will. I've got tape."

Perry helped Cody out of the gown while Bonnie and Raj taped the tissue into the bra cups. Then they reconstructed the bra itself, taping the straps down, putting it on Cody while taping it across her chest. They zipped her back up.

It wasn't much. Cody was not in Vicki Freed's DD-cup league. But she looked bustier.

"No tight hugs," said Raj. "You'll crinkle."

"And don't overdo it on the dance floor," said Bonnie.

Cody snorted. She inspected herself for one more minute. "I'm such a good wife," she said to her own reflection. Catching Bonnie's eye, she added, "You don't even know."

The flatness of Cody's voice was disturbing. Bonnie could guess the hundreds of compromises Cody made to be a good wife. Mike always used to say, "The richer they were, the lonelier." As hard-edged as he was, Mike had his empathetic moments. Bonnie flashed to leaving him tonight, her rushed kiss and his warm cheek.

Cody said to the men, "I'll be back at ten-thirty to change.

Be ready. You can order room service."

To Bonnie, she said, "I'd like to treat you to dinner as well."

"Really?" Bonnie was pleasantly surprised. Was Cody inviting her to stay in the suite for room service? It'd been a long, long time since she'd eaten a gourmet meal.

Cody headed for the door. She stopped to inspect a few of the gift baskets on a side table. She lifted the smallest one with tacky blue cellophane wrapping and handed it to Bonnie. The basket was full of dry crackers, cheap cheese wheels, and spotty fruit.

"Bon appétit!" Cody said, and left the room.

Bonnie took the insult for what it was. She was being punished for having seen with her own eyes the sham of Cody's marriage. The gift basket was how Cody made sure that Bonnie knew her place, and it wasn't at the table with the grown-ups, or even in the kitchen with the kids.

Bonnie felt deflated. She'd been on an adrenaline rush since she got Cody's phone call an hour ago, and now she was crashing. She leaned against the wall and stared blankly at the door Cody had just closed.

Perry put his hand on her shoulder. "Stay for dinner, Bonnie. Cody won't know."

But Bonnie didn't dare. On the off-off-off chance Cody came back up to the suite, Bonnie didn't want to be there. She shook her head. "Thanks. I've got to be somewhere. Congrats, guys. She looked exquisite."

"What about the shoes?" asked Raj.

Damn. She couldn't leave $5,000 worth of footwear behind. A pair might go missing, and then Bonnie would be held accountable. "I'll take them back to the store on my way. It's no problem."

While repacking the boxes, Bonnie wondered why she was hiding her feelings from Raj and Perry. They'd be sympathetic and could help her feel better. It was ingrained in Bonnie, from childhood, as Peter's mom, and from dealing with clients, to spare everyone else her feelings. Her role as a parent and stylist was to clue into the emotional needs of others and ignore or squash her own needs. In a way, it was easier.

Ten minutes later, Bonnie walked through the St. Regis lobby with two shopping bags full of shoes and a gift basket. As she headed for the hotel front doors, she passed a dozen or so beautifully dressed couples. They were most likely headed for the Deerlinger party. Most were younger women with older men. The women smiled radiantly, knowing their pictures would be taken. Bonnie detected a certain smugness, too. Those women, like Cody, like Vicki Freed, had achieved their goals. They'd come to New York and found their billionaires. Bonnie would be lying to herself if she didn't admit that, yes, she fantasized about a rich man swooping in and relieving her of the pressure of fending for herself.

At the revolving door, Bonnie and her packages were a tight fit. She had some trouble getting into the glass wedge and then fumbled when she tried to push. A man entered the opposite wedge from the street. He noticed the problem of Bonnie's too-full compartment. Instead of frowning with irritation, though, the man smiled, nodded to let her know he was aware, and slowly inched the door forward so she could walk without also having to push. It was a small civility. Or a small chivalry.

When she got on the street, she put down her bags to right her coat and turned around to wave a thank-you to the man who'd helped her. Her view unobstructed, she could see him clearly.

It was him. Mr. Charles's friend, the mystery man who'd caught her eye earlier at Frankel's. He wore a tux that was out of style with its too-wide lapels and three buttons. But the fit was impeccable, as was his lean body. He waved back, smiled, and went on his way. There was no indication he recognized her. He appeared to be alone. When he held up his left hand, Bonnie admired his long fingers, none of which bore a ring.

After the drama of dressing Cody, Peter's mini-episode at drop-off that Monday morning was cake. He was happy about being back with his old teacher, but he didn't like the configuration of the classroom. Bonnie had to remind herself, for the millionth time, Peter didn't retreat or protest to be difficult. He simply couldn't help it.

Once, when Bonnie was doing the dishes at the sink, Peter put his hand on her arm and said, "I wish I was what you wanted me to be," which nearly crushed Bonnie's heart. He shocked her with statements and comments that seemed to come out of the mouth of a sixty-year-old. She lowered to her knees to hold him and told him he was wrong, that he was exactly what she wanted and would ever want. She cried a little. He patted her shoulder, mechanically, until she released him.

By the time Peter was calm enough for Bonnie to leave school, she was already late for the Monday morning meeting at work. Mr. Charles, her staff, and two store buyers—June and Tiffany—were already seated on the couches waiting for her when she rushed into the Salon.

Mr. Charles held up yesterday's *New York Times* Styles section's full-page coverage of Cody Deerlinger's party at the St. Regis, under the headline "September Surprise."

"Explain this," he said to her.

"I saw it already," said Bonnie. "What's the problem?"

The short write-up described the party as a huge success. Despite the recession, the generous and glamorous Mrs. Deerlinger was determined to celebrate her husband's fortieth birthday in style. Mr. Deerlinger had been genuinely touched by the party, and how proud and honored he was to have such a wonderful wife.

In other words, complete bullshit. It was to be expected.

Mr. Charles pointed to a photo of Cody in her first dress selection. The caption: "Mrs. Deerlinger in Halston. 'I had a sneak peek at this dress at the designer's showroom last month,' said the hostess.'"

"So she lied," said Bonnie.

"I'm talking about the *other* photo," said Mr. Charles testily.

Bonnie made a quick survey of her staff to see if they knew what was up. Megan, on the other couch, looked nervous. Roman wore his blank "I'm out of here as soon as I get my law degree" expression. Fran, vigorously chewing her gum, seemed entertained.

June and Tiffany, store buyers, glared pointedly at Bonnie. Tiffany Redstone, thirty, single, and bitter, openly pursued the male clients, seeing each Wall Streeter in a suit as her future husband, or a vehicle to ride out of her current life and into a better one. June Purcell, thirtyish and also single, was a dedicated follower of trends, switching favorite designers every month. It made Bonnie wonder if she had any loyalty at all.

The relationship between the store buyer and the stylist was inherently adversarial. A stylist, like Bonnie, told the buyers, like Tiffany and June, what she needed for the client—a dress in a certain size, for example. It was the buyer's job to go get it from the designer. The client told the stylist: jump. The stylist told the buyer: fetch. The buyer put in the request to the narcissistic, unreliable designers. Stylists and buyers were caught between two colossal egos—the client's and the designer's. One would think they'd join forces. But instead, the stylists and buyers saw each other as natural enemies.

Bonnie looked at the photo that so offended them. It was a wide shot of the party. She'd styled many of the women there and sold six dresses in that one picture alone. And then she saw what had upset Mr. Charles and the buyers.

How could she have missed it? Mrs. Vicki Freed had wrangled an invite to the party after all and was shown in the photo, her new boobs packed in the Narciso Rodriguez dress Cody had tried on right in front of her.

"And now, Bonnie, please explain to us why Mrs. Freed went to another store to buy the dress that you showed her last week in the Salon?" asked Mr. Charles. "You'll also notice, she's wearing a Lanvin mink stole, which we also happen to sell here."

Bonnie gulped. "You're sure she didn't buy it here?"

Mr. Charles laughed ruefully. He studied the sales orders with a magnifying glass every night. He could tell you how many Chanel lipsticks were purchased on a Tuesday in January two years ago.

Tiffany said, "Narciso told me *himself* that Mrs. Freed bought the dress at Bergdorf. He personally fit the dress for her."

Why would Vicki go to Bergdorf? Bonnie absorbed the blow. It felt like a personal betrayal. Mrs. Freed spent $300,000 at the Salon at Frankel's last year. Had the in-house stylists at Bergdorf offered her a deep discount? Losing her to them would cut to the marrow.

"I'm sorry," said Bonnie. "I don't know how this could happen. We do everything for her. Right, Bella?"

The Russian, who'd been pretending to ignore the conversation, shrugged. "Vicki bought one dress at Bergdorf," she said. "You make big thing out of nothing. No one has been sent to Siberia."

Megan raised her hand to speak. Mr. Charles barked, "What?"

"It's not Bonnie's fault that there were so many people in the Salon that day," said the assistant. "Things were so hectic. Mistakes happen. In the grand scheme, does it matter that Mrs. Deerlinger's lunch order was wrong? Or that Bonnie double-booked the Private Studio and misplaced the stole? It's *somewhere* around here. It'll turn up! Bonnie can't possibly show every dress in the store to every customer. She's got a lot on her mind, including some personal problems."

Megan made it sound like Bonnie had been unorganized, disrespectful, and incompetent. Mr. Charles listened to her passionate defense with increasing fury. Turning to Bonnie, he erupted, "You double-booked the Studio?"

"Okay, stop helping me," said Bonnie to Megan. She'd underestimated the girl's ambition. Her rebellion had come a few months ahead of schedule. Unfortunately, Bonnie's arms weren't flexible enough to pull the knife out of her back.

Roman said, "I mislaid the stole."

Bella said, "Maybe it was me."

Their *mea culpas* were sweet, but they made Roman and Bella sound like loyal soldiers stepping in to take the bullet for their leader.

June Purcell said, "I don't know how long you've been here, Megan, but it's Bonnie's job to show every client every dress in the store. Because every dress has to sell!" She aimed her brow lift at Mr. Charles. "Business is off the cliff," she reminded him, as if he'd forgotten. "We can't afford this kind of damage. When Bonnie messes up, everyone in this room suffers a *personal* loss."

"A personal loss?" said Bella. "Someone died?" Bonnie had to hold back a smile at the comment. Bella could always be counted on to supply perspective. No one died. No one was hurt. But her boss and colleagues were acting like their worlds had been turned upside down. How had this become her life?

"Bonnie, you *are* responsible for everything that happens in the Salon," scolded Mr. Charles. "Mrs. Freed's defection is your fault. If your personal problems affect your job, they're professional problems."

"You're talking about the day that Cody Deerlinger's one-day purchase came to…what was it?"

"Twenty-two thousand, one hundred and fourteen dollars and twenty seven cents," said Mr. Charles.

"Which pushed the Salon total sales for September well over last year's number," said Bonnie. She wasn't exactly sure about that.

Mr. Charles nodded. "By 2 percent." Of course, if Mrs. Freed had bought the Rodriguez dress and Lanvin stole here, the number would have been much higher. The boss either decided to overlook that or had another appointment. "Back to work," he announced abruptly. The staff dispersed. "In your office," he said to Bonnie.

A private dressing-down was the last thing she needed. She went down the hallway into her office, her boss following. She sat behind her desk. He remained standing. "I'm still angry. But moving on. Steve Kline, that friend of mine I texted about last week? His schedule is erratic. I'd like you to be available at a moment's notice when he calls."

Drop everything, in other words. If Mr. Kline was who Bonnie thought he was, it would be a pleasure. But she still didn't like being ordered around. She asked, "Do you have any idea when Mr. Kline is coming in?"

"Does it matter?" snapped Mr. Charles. "I asked you to

be ready."

And then he left. Bonnie exhaled. Her cheeks burned from being yelled at, first in the staff meeting and then in private. The spark of excitement about working with a sexy man went out. She checked her messages and saw a text from Lori Fortuna, a colleague and friend from her Bloomingdale's days that read, "Just fired an idiot. I need you. Call me."

Knock. Megan hovered sheepishly outside Bonnie's office. The girl was contrite. "I didn't realize how it sounded," she said.

"Next time, leave the excuses and groveling to me." Was she really that clueless? Bonnie found that hard to believe.

"I'm so sorry! I didn't think. I just blurted. I'm sure you'll never forgive me for being so stupid. To be *completely* honest, I'm distracted myself lately. It's horrible, like a sickness. I can't shake it."

Just then, Roman walked in. "You need anything, Chief? Some coffee maybe?"

Megan blushed under her freckles and shifted her weight from side to side. Bonnie caught Megan stealing a peek at Roman and then hiding behind her thick eyelashes.

"Oh," said Bonnie. The girl had a crush. Bonnie's crushes for the last four years had been theoretical, a man on the train or in the store, a stranger who was safe fodder for fantasy. Maybe Bonnie's anxiety about actually meeting Mr. Kline at some point in the near future made her sympathetic to Megan's plight. But Bonnie was still annoyed.

Roman said, "Ohhh…kay? You want coffee."

"Yes, please," she replied.

Off they went. Then an email from Mrs. Sheridan, Lilah's mom, came in. It read: "Ka-ching!" with a link to a popular celebrity gossip website.

Bonnie clicked the link and came to a photograph of Lilah Sheridan standing next to Anna Maytag on the white carpet at the VMAs. They were wearing the same gold bandage dress. Lilah was all smiles, but Anna looked like she'd swallowed a pincushion. The item head was "Seeing Double." The caption underneath read, "Lilah and Anna: Matchy-matchy. Did they call each other the night before? Or was this a naturally occurring fashion disaster? According to my side-by-side comparison survey, 67 percent of my readers think Lilah is hotter. Sorry, Anna! Better luck next year."

Bonnie said, "Shit!" and slammed her laptop. Bonnie should have seen this coming. She'd inadvertently created a bad situation for a client. Lilah's mom was thrilled, but Anna would never speak to her again.

Win one, lose one. At least Bonnie was breaking even.

Her BlackBerry hummed. A new email. It read, "Ms. Madden: I got your contact info from Chase Charles. He tells me you're the best. I hope that's true for my sake."

The email was sent from an unknown address. The new client/friend of Mr. Charles. She couldn't help smiling at the idea that anyone called her "the best." After the meeting, the kind words were deeply appreciated.

She replied: "I'm flattered. I don't dare contradict my boss. I'm booked solid today, though. The 'best' is busy." She hit send and then wished she hadn't. Her reply was too cheeky for the average Frankel's shopper who was above bantering with the staff. Oh well. What was done was done.

A reply came right away. "Too busy? You don't drop everything at a moment's notice for a complete stranger?"

She laughed, relieved. This man was clearly from out of town and on the older side (emails were the giveaway; the under-50 crowd texted). She emailed back, "I can see you tomorrow."

Send. "Tomorrow's no good. I'll be in touch."

She hung up, her heart trotting surprisingly. Jumpy? Over a few emails? That was new. She felt dangerously excited, yet wary.

PART TWO

December:
Christmas Shopping

Chapter Four

In the bowels of Frankel's, almost as deep as the subway tunnels that ran under Madison Avenue to Columbus Circle, Bonnie pulled her black cashmere cardigan closer and walked quickly through the dark corridor. She passed the boiler room, a knot of banging pipes overhead, rounded one last turn, and saw the glow of her destination.

Out of the black, a flashlight beam hit her face. "Who's there?" asked a menacing voice.

"Now I'm blind," she said. "My retinas were wide open."

"Bonnie, I've told you twenty times to call before you come down here," said Jesus Cruz, turning off the beam and taking her by the elbow. "Especially during December. We shoot unidentifieds on sight."

Jesus, twenty-eight, was the head wrapper/shipper at Frankel's. He'd worked in the subbasement since he was twenty. In those years, he'd proven himself invaluable to Mr. Charles and the store's operation. Jesus and his Vitamin-D-deprived staff wrapped and tracked every item that left the building, from a tiny key chain to a huge sectional couch. Jesus knew what Frankel's customers purchased—and to where they shipped. A cheating husband bought lingerie and sent it to his downtown mistress? Jesus had folded the tissue paper. A lobbyist sent an inappropriately expensive gift to a dirty politician? Jesus had printed the address label.

And yet this young man, this keeper of intimate information who could single-handedly bring down careers, marriages, and businesses, was invisible to the wealthy women and men shopping on the floors above. Only a select few clients were even aware of the power that lurked below.

Despite spending so much time underground, Jesus had sun-kissed, hot Latino looks. It was a crime against masculine beauty to keep him tucked away down here. But it'd be a terrible blow to Frankel's if he left shipping. He was a natural organizer and leader.

Jesus walked Bonnie farther down the corridor. When her vision returned, she rattled the Cage door and said, "Let me in."

The wrapping/shipping/handling space was surrounded by chain-link walls and ceiling, a secure area that most Frankel's employees were forbidden to enter. No one was allowed inside "the Cage" without written permission from Chase W. Charles. If too many people were coming and going, purchased items could be misplaced or stolen. Restricted access minimized the risk.

"What's the magic word?" Jesus asked.

"It's freezing down here!"

"Close enough." He unlocked the Cage door.

Only a week to go until Christmas. Bonnie had been working twelve hours a day, seven days a week since Black Friday, the day after Thanksgiving. As each day passed, clients' last-minute demands and impossible requests increased exponentially. It'd be like this until December 20, when the entire Upper East Side left town. Meanwhile, Bonnie was running on coffee fumes, adrenaline, and an occasional Ritalin pinched from Peter. She'd been so busy this week she hadn't had time for her daily ritual of staring at the wall of her office and imagining Mr. Kline entering the small space for the appointment that never happened. Bonnie had been fantasizing for weeks about their first meeting-to-be. The awkward conversation quickly giving way to a comfortable banter, like they'd known each other forever, the frisson of sexual chemistry between them. As more days went by without hearing from Mr. Kline, Bonnie settled nicely into her daydreams about him. Should he, the real person, ever actually appear in her office, she'd be so shocked and intimidated, she'd probably swallow her gum.

"What's the crisis today?" asked Jesus, bringing her back to reality.

"I have to check a label from the Deerlinger mailing."

Cody was sending holiday gifts to 500 of her intimate friends, each one near and dear to her heart, even if she couldn't remember their names. "Make sure you send something to that woman who was at that thing that time—you know, the event I did at the park or the library two or three years ago," she'd told Bonnie. The sad part was Bonnie knew exactly the woman Cody was referring to: a Mrs. Henry Ridgewood, who would soon be in possession of a titanium Christmas tree ornament.

"Nice haul this year from Mrs. D.," said Jesus. "Skimping on her B-list, I noticed. A pair of wine glasses? Two years ago, they got gold candleholders."

"Right, in the shape of the letters C and D." An example of Cody's singular hubris. Who on earth wanted candleholders in someone else's initials?

"If the economy recovers next year, she can send a silver framed photo of herself."

They indulged in some merry seasonal snickering, but only for a minute. "Did the Freed mailing go out?" Bonnie asked.

He nodded and asked, "Did Vicki get her boobs done? If not, Mr. Freed sent the wrong size bra to his wife."

Bonnie cupped her own boobs and mimed them growing, and growing. "Out to here," she estimated.

"Right this way," he said, escorting Bonnie to a mini-forklift built for two and helping her into the passenger seat. Jesus drove fifty yards into the depths of shipping, past cages within the Cage—the bridal cage, the rug cage, the vault-like jewelry cage that had its own security guard. The Cage tour might be a waste of time, but to be off her feet, even for three minutes, was heaven.

Pulling to a slow stop about ten feet away from the car-size shipping elevator, Jesus pointed at a pile of beautifully wrapped boxes and said, "The Deerlinger mailing. Scheduled fifth for departure."

"*Fifth?*"

"It'll be gone in the next three hours."

"I'm sorry," she said. "It's the crunch. I hate myself

for bitching."

"I forgive you. Now get out of my truck."

Climbing down, Bonnie reminded herself to hurry. She had three VIP appointments this afternoon, including a couple from Chicago that Mr. Charles asked her to see today and a Venezuelan oil heiress flying in on her Gulfstream V for the afternoon to buy cheese and caviar. Was there no cheese and caviar in Venezuela? Why did Mrs. Valdez need to travel thousands of miles just to shop at Frankel's gourmet shop during the busiest shopping week of the year?

Easy. Because she could. Because she had the urge. As entitled as she was, Mrs. Valdez was a lovely woman. Unlike most New York heiresses, Mrs. V. said, "Muchas gracias," and apologized when she was hours late. (Punctuality, in Bonnie's experience, was optional for South American aristocrats.)

She started hunting through the stack of boxes in the Deerlinger mailing. Cody had emailed earlier, asking for a triple confirmation that the wife of a prospective client of Dan's had been sent the one-of-a-kind, pearl gray Hermés shirt. It'd been custom designed at a cost of $15,000. She wondered if rare worms had been nurtured in tiny cradles from birth, fattened on the finest dirt, and then, after spinning just enough silk for one shirt, been slaughtered in a salt bath?

She chided herself for this momentary slip into cynicism. That was a downward spiral she couldn't easily crawl out of.

If she told Cody she'd triple-checked the label and then something went wrong, Bonnie would have to go through the rest of her life without a head. After a few minutes of searching, she found the shirt box wrapped in gold paper with a ribbon bow on top. Name, correct. Address, clearly typed. The safest thing to do would be to taxi the package to Trump Plaza and place the box into the hands of Mrs. Yoshi Takati's doorman herself. Any other day, Bonnie would do it. But today, she didn't have five minutes to spare.

"Anyone home?" shouted a shrill voice, followed by the sound of the Cage door rattling. "Knock, knock!"

Bonnie recognized the high-pitched tones of Hortense

Clout, the bony brunette salesperson of Designer Ready-to-Wear. Super aggressive Hortense worked on commission, whereas Bonnie had a salary and bonus, so Hortense scratched and clawed for every sale. She surely made a very good living, but money wasn't enough for Hortense. She wanted status, too. Ambitious and anorexic, Hortense wouldn't stop until she'd reached the top—which, for all intents and purposes, was Bonnie's director job at the Salon.

If Hortense saw her, she'd tell Mr. Charles about Jesus's letting Bonnie in the Cage during the holidays. That was a fireable offense. She ducked behind the Deerlinger mailing pile and, from her hiding place, watched Jesus pull up to the Cage door… slowly…in his forklift. He took his time climbing down, too, just to annoy Hortense. Voices bounced off the Cage's cement floor like a rubber ball. Bonnie could hear their conversation.

Hortense said, "Jesus, you look very handsome today." For two weeks each year, she kissed his ass. Otherwise, he didn't exist.

"Mailings go out in the order they're received," he said matter-of-factly. "Including yours."

She held something up, a couple of pieces of paper. "Two Giants tickets—last home game of the season," she said.

Bonnie bit her lip. Even she'd be tempted by the bribe. Mike lived and died by the New York Giants. That last home game was always a raucous event, and Mike wanted to go desperately. When he picked up Peter last Wednesday, he said, "I'd give my left nut for just one ticket to that game."

"Why the left?" Peter asked. "Is your right nut ugly? Is *my* right nut ugly? Why do we have nuts anyway?" Bonnie sat back in her chair, grinning, and watched Mike explain his way out of that comment.

Hortense rolled up the tickets and fit them through the diamond of chain link. Jesus took the tickets and examined them closely. Smelled them, pressed them against his heart, kissed them a few times. He glanced over his shoulder toward where Bonnie was.

He said, "You know I can't speed up your mailings. The system doesn't work that way."

"I'm not asking you to deliver my mailings first. I want you to deliver Bonnie Madden's last. Or not at all."

That bitch! thought Bonnie.

"Okay," said Jesus, slipping the tickets into the pocket of his jeans.

WHAT?!? Bonnie could not have heard right.

"You promise?"

"Cross my heart."

"Our little secret?"

"Unless you want me to broadcast your bribe," he said. "Don't come down here again. Or the deal's off."

"Of course," she said. "I'll skulk away now."

As soon as the coast was clear, Bonnie ran to Jesus. He held up his hand. "Before you speak, remember who you're talking to."

"I've got some very tasty Tic Tacs in the bottom of my purse," she said. "They don't compare to Giants tickets, but it's the best I can do."

"Keep your candy. You're the only salesperson who doesn't treat me like a gift-wrapping monkey. Now go away. I've got work to do." Yelling at his foreman over the metal-on-metal crash of the elevator doors, he said, "Moving up the Deerlinger mailing. It goes out next."

She left the Cage and headed for the back elevators. When the car opened, Roman was inside.

"Chief!" he said. "I've been looking all over for you."

Bonnie stepped inside and pushed the button for the Salon. "Donning the gay apparel?" she asked, appraising his green jacket and red tie.

He didn't take the bait. "Lobby security called," he said. "Stacy Watson's team just arrived for a sweep. She'll be here in five minutes with her son."

Ms. Watson was a movie star. More importantly, she was married to Tim Watson, an Academy Award-winning actor. Tim and Stacy wed five years ago, and it was widely rumored he'd used his Scientology hoodoo to brainwash her into the role of a lifetime: subservient wife. They had a son together. The gossip mill claimed Archer had been conceived in vitro, since the only time Tim Watson could bring himself to touch an icky girl was for his love scenes. Stacy Watson was a Salon semiregular and an unpredictable spender. Some days, she dropped a bundle. Others, not a single dime.

Roman said, "I tried to call you down here."

"No signal," she said. Bonnie's mind spun. She'd have to fit Stacy into her already packed day. How on earth would she do it?

"Your three o'clock canceled. That's the good news," said Roman.

The couple from Chicago. Good. "I don't want to hear any bad news. I don't want to know if the building is on fire."

"Yesterday, I'd put aside a red Valentino for Mrs. Rodkin. I looked for it today, and it's gone."

She knew the gown in question. The gown was a one-of-a-kind vintage piece, priced at $30,000. "Is it back on the floor?" she asked.

He shook his head. "I turned the place upside down."

Valentino gowns didn't disappear into thin air. It had at least two sensors on it. No one could get it out of the building. "It'll turn up," said Bonnie. She had to shelf this emergency, with others taking precedent.

The elevator doors shushed open on eight. Bonnie and Roman walked quickly toward the entrance of the Salon. Along the way, Bonnie noticed four large men in black suits stalking the floor with Bluetooth headsets. One of them guarded the Salon door.

Fran at the reception desk whispered, "Stacy got here five seconds ago. The kid is adorable! I just want to *pinch* him."

"Please don't," said Bonnie. With Fran's fingernails, a pinch could draw blood.

Bonnie looked around the space for her famous client. The Salon was crammed to the rafters with boxes, bows, bags, ribbons, and festive decorations. Typical Christmas chaos. Stacy stood next to the pair of couches, also covered with clothes and boxes. Archer, three, angelic, with his father's thick, dark hair and his mother's creamy skin, was jumping on and off the dress platform.

"Welcome, Ms. Watson! What an unexpected pleasure to see you!" said Bonnie. Bubbly! Cheerful!

"Where *were* you?" asked Stacy, tremulous, as if waiting for five seconds had been emotionally trying. A six-footer in black with a platinum buzz cut, Stacy looked like a glamazon warrior, but she acted like a confused little girl. "I walked in and *no one* was here. I was alone."

Alone, save for Fran at the desk, Megan cataloguing racks in the PS, two members of Jesus's staff loading packages on a dolly, and Bella in Fitting Room A with a client, any one of whom would have gladly helped her. Regardless, if the actress felt neglected, Bonnie had a problem.

Fortunately, she also had the solution. "Let's go shopping! Are we looking for gifts today?"

"I've got a little list." From her Prada tote, Stacy removed a scroll of paper that unfurled to the floor.

A joke. Bonnie thought, *Laugh.* "Ha! A little list on a long piece of paper. You're so funny, Ms. Watson. You should do more comedy."

The sparkle faded from Stacy's eyes. "I don't want to talk about my career."

Shit! "Where shall we begin? Jewelry? Accessories? Are we shopping for your friends, family?"

"I don't want to talk about my family," warbled Stacy.

Bonnie remembered reading once that Stacy's conversion to Scientology required her to cut all ties to nonbelievers, including her parents and siblings. Was being the wife of a Hollywood legend worth her family? Another "bad trade," in Bonnie's eyes. Her own family drove her crazy, but she wouldn't give them up for any man. Maybe the ache for family connection was why Stacy famously took Archer everywhere she went. He was all the family she had, except for her workaholic husband. Bonnie could relate to maternal clinginess. She was guilty of it, too.

Meanwhile, Archer was lashing a mannequin with a belt. It wobbled and then crashed into a pile of blue boxes. The sound of glass shattering filled the room. A just-arrived shipment of

Swarovski crystal was destroyed.

The kid started crying. "Don't worry about that," said Bonnie. "Totally my fault."

Fran got on the phone. "This is the Salon. Can you send a team of custodians up here? And the insurance underwriter?"

Her BlackBerry hummed. A text from a blocked number. Her heart sped up. She and her anonymous new client had been texting once or twice a week. Sometimes forwarding funny little things. He'd send, "What am I wearing?" or "How important is it, from a design standpoint, if the carpet matches the drapes?" At some point, Bonnie stopped worrying about tone and just went with it, almost as if it wasn't really happening. It was amazing how much she enjoyed the communiqués. In her mind, she'd given him the face and body of that handsome man who'd helped her through the revolving doors at the St. Regis the night of Cody's surprise party. What a disappointment it'd be when he turned out to be some older, fat, bald troll.

The text read, "We must meet. This week."

Bonnie gasped. A pang of fear hit her. Her secret relationship was going to enter the real world. And then the fun would be over.

"What's the matter?" asked Stacy.

"Nothing at all. Shall we?" Bonnie gestured for Stacy to follow her. She told herself to focus on her client. In classic compartmentalizing mode, Bonnie shelved thoughts about Mr. Kline and put her mind to the task. Shopping with Stacy would be easier without Archer in tow. But how?

"I've got an idea," she said. "Megan!"

The freckle-faced young assistant peeked out of the PS when she heard her name. Bonnie asked her, "Do you mind entertaining Archer for a little while?" Stacy would spend twice as much without the distraction of her son. If only Frankel's had an on-site playroom for busy moms. It was a good idea. Mr. Charles would never go for it, though. He loathed children. He'd sooner allow a doggy daycare than babysitting.

Megan said, "I was doing an inventory for Mr. Charles…"

Bonnie glared at her. The girl was refusing? Megan had

forgotten who her boss was. She couldn't say as much in front of Stacy. That would look bad. Instead, Bonnie pretended Megan hadn't said anything. "Good. So that's settled. We'll be back soon," she said.

"Er, okay," said Megan.

The boy sized up his new guardian. He seemed unsure. Archer walked over to Megan and kicked her in the shin, like testing the tires on a new car.

"He likes you!" said Stacy. Leaving a bodyguard with Archer, she signaled the others to follow her out of the Salon. Bonnie kept up.

On the Accessories floor, Stacy tried on fifteen pairs of gloves before deciding, "Too predictable." On the Jewelry floor, Stacy examined twenty different bangles before deciding, "Too ethnic." On the Lingerie floor, Stacy tore through thirty pairs of lace panties and then vetoed them as "Too personal."

"Perhaps if I knew who you were shopping for," said Bonnie.

"I don't like it when people pry in my business. I'm a very private person," declared one of the most famous women in the world.

On the Home Decor floor, Stacy touched and rejected every gift item in sight. Bonnie was running out of places to browse. As a last resort, they went down to Fragrance and Makeup, the most visible floor, where dozens of shoppers gawked at Stacy and took her picture.

"Hey, it's my scent," she said, picking up a sample bottle of Clear, her own brand of perfume, named after Scientology's highest level of enlightenment. Clear—the perfume, not the mindset—was not, as one might think, clear-*colored*. It was a pale yellow and smelled like cat pee on an orange blossom. Everything smelled offensive to her. Olfactory overload. Bonnie thought, *The seasonal stress is even getting to my nose.*

"Have a spritz," said the starlet.

"I'd love one," said Bonnie, nearly gagging when Stacy squirted her wrist, neck, and hair.

"I just got a brilliant idea!" announced Stacy. "I don't know why I didn't think of this *before*. I'm going to call the marketing department and have them send bottles of Clear to everyone on my list. It's great publicity —and won't cost me anything!"

"Yes, that is brilliant," grumbled Bonnie, realizing she'd just wasted an hour and a half on one of her busiest days of the year. Plus, she smelled like a brothel.

Bonnie's BlackBerry vibrated in her pocket. "Salon at Frankel's," she answered.

"I lost Archer," said Megan. "We were playing hide-and-seek at Tory Burch, and he disappeared."

Bonnie's throat closed. Could Megan be that stupid to play hide-and-seek with a three-year-old in a store, among hundreds, if not thousands, of people? Kids got lost at Frankel's every Christmas season. The store had cameras and a system in place to find them. But Archer was no ordinary kid. If he got hurt or was kidnapped... *Do not go there*, thought Bonnie.

"What about his bodyguard?" said Bonnie, moving a step away from Stacy.

"He was in the bathroom," cried Megan into the phone. "Bonnie! I'm freaking out!"

"I'm on it." Struggling to stay cool, she hung up and called security, where twenty people were, at that moment, staring at a wall of monitors. One of them must have seen Archer. She explained the situation and got off the phone. Bonnie wished she could just let the system take over and keep Stacy occupied until Archer was found. But that would be wrong. If Peter went missing in the store, Bonnie would want to know immediately.

The fragrance counter was not the place to deliver bad news. Bonnie said, "Ms. Watson, we need to go back to the Salon now."

Stacy saw the seriousness in Bonnie's eyes and knew something was wrong. She dropped the bottle of Clear. It shattered on the floor.

The bodyguards closed ranks, surrounding Stacy and Bonnie in a tight circle. "Is Archer okay?" asked Stacy, her long fingers closing on Bonnie's shoulder.

Bonnie explained what had happened. Stacy let out a wail

of concern, which drew a crowd of onlookers. The security team moved Stacy and Bonnie, a bit roughly, toward the VIP elevators. Stacy started to swoon. The guards practically dragged her. Once inside the elevator, she slumped against the wall. By the time they reached the eighth floor, Stacy was in full hysterics.

The team moved her into the relative privacy of the Salon. Bonnie readied herself to call Mr. Charles. Before she could push the button for speed dial, she heard Stacy cry, "Archer!"

"Mommy!" he said, running toward her.

Looking up, Bonnie watched Stacy scoop the kid into her arms. "Where were you?" she asked.

The kid struggled to get free. He looked fine, no sign of tears. Megan stood, ashen-cheeked, next to Hortense Clout. "I found this little cutie on the seventh floor," she said, oozing smugness. "I recognized him, of course, and figured he was supposed to be up here."

Stacy said, "Thank you," to Hortense, took Archer's hand, and left the Salon, her team following.

When they were gone, Megan started crying. Bonnie felt like crying, too, with guilt and relief. As bad as that experience had been for Stacy and Archer, it could have been worse. Bonnie made a big mistake by putting her assistant in charge of a three-year-old. Megan wasn't a professional babysitter. For all Bonnie knew, the girl didn't know kids at all.

Bonnie swallowed her pride and said, "Thank you, Hortense."

"Think nothing of it," she said. The implication was clear, though. She might as well have said, "I've got you under my thumb now."

Buzz. BlackBerry. Heart still beating rapidly, Bonnie answered.

"Mrs. Valdez and I are on the way up," said Mr. Charles, apparently giving a personal escort to the Venezuelan heiress. Bonnie had completely forgotten about her. She checked the time. It was after five. Mrs. Valdez made Stacy Watson look like a speed shopper. Her workday, at hour nine, had only just begun.

"I'm ready," she said to her boss. She tried to calm herself, but struggled to relax. Next, Bonnie called Lucee, her trustworthy babysitter, to say she'd be home late.

Although she felt bad every time she worked late since Peter was born, Bonnie's guilt was particularly acute around the holidays. She pictured Lucee and Peter at the kitchen table: his excited chatter, how he'd dip his chicken nugget into the ketchup exactly three times. He loved Lucee and talked to her as comfortably as he did with Bonnie. Even their wonderful relationship gave Bonnie pangs. She should be home with her son, not spooning caviar onto toast for Mrs. Valdez or anyone.

The face of the St. Regis man flashed through her mind. He'd smiled at her and waved. She'd cast him as Mr. Kline. Bonnie felt another pang of guilt. She shouldn't bother thinking about a fantasy man or letting a dream bubble up from her subconscious. There was only one male in her life, and his needs were bigger and more important than hers.

Chapter Five

"Be at Home at ten for new client meet," boomed Mr. Charles on the phone the next morning. He meant the Home Decor floor of Frankel's. New client? Man? Woman? Mr. Charles didn't bother supplying necessary details just to make her life easier. Hedging her bets, Bonnie would bring backup. She'd once arrived at an impromptu client meet to find a family of five. They splintered off, and Mr. Charles had been furious she couldn't keep up with all of them.

"Megan, are you free?" Bonnie asked when she found her assistant going through a rack in Grand Central. "I need you downstairs with me for an hour or two."

The girl cringed when she heard her name and asked, "Is it about Archer Watson?"

Bonnie closed her eyes. She'd rather pretend the lost celebritot nightmare never happened.

But Megan would not let it drop. On the elevator down to the fourth floor, she said, "I blame myself, even though it really was your fault."

"Can we please stop talking about it?"

"It's also my parents' fault for not letting me babysit. They wouldn't let me have any job when I was a teenager. People worked for me. A nanny. A cook. A tutor. Daddy gave me a big allowance. This is the first job I've ever had."

No kidding. The only person not to blame for losing Archer was the person who'd actually lost him. Megan's sob story about being a child of privilege was supposed to make Bonnie feel sorry for her? If Bonnie could, she'd fire Megan just for being annoying. But there was a long process of warnings and suspensions, and Megan had mysterious pull with Mr. Charles.

"For the eight hundredth time, forget about Archer. Things happen. Mistakes are made, and then you move on. We have a new client coming up, a friend of Mr. Charles. So put on a happy face," said Bonnie, quickly crossing the department to the elevator banks, where the client would be arriving.

"Just tell me if you hate me," said Megan. "This job is my chance to prove myself. I have to prove myself, or it's back to Iowa to marry some boring lawyer. Tell me you like me. Please, Bonnie!"

"Enough," said Bonnie. "He's here."

Chase W. Charles's head appeared first as the glass elevator rose. He was facing out toward Bonnie. A man stood next to him. Bonnie almost had a heart attack at the sight of him. It'd been weeks since she'd seen him at the St. Regis. Watching him follow Mr. Charles out of the elevator, Bonnie realized the dream man she'd fantasized about was even sexier in real life. He was a *man*, for starters. Tall, over six feet, lean and muscular inside his navy pin-striped suit, wearing brown shoes, and holding a black cashmere coat draped over his arm. His hair was graying naturally, unapologetically. His eyebrows were masculine, too—bushy, but well-shaped, darker than his hair, which gave his face and his eyes a certain intensity. His walk was pure animal elegance. Each step seemed both languid and purposeful. His head moved casually to the left and right as he approached, studying the environment. He was wide awake and taking it all in. Totally alert.

Bonnie struggled to maintain her neutral "Here to serve!" expression for meeting clients. Any woman meeting this man for the first time would have a hard time keeping her jaw from dropping to the floor. Bonnie felt nervously exposed. Surely he'd sense that she was pumping out pheromones by the bucketful. She realized, to her amazement, that he'd zeroed in on her and smiled. His hazel eyes found hers, and she couldn't look away. He didn't either.

And then he was standing right in front of her. She confirmed: no wedding ring. Mr. Charles, who'd been prattling all this time, said, "Our Salon director, Ms. Bonnie Madden.

Bonnie, my old, old friend, Stephen Kline. I told you about him."

"A pleasure to meet you," she said, shaking his dry, warm hand.

Mr. Kline smiled broadly, holding on for a beat too long. "We finally meet."

From the playful look in his eyes, Bonnie realized that Mr. Kline was her text friend. She'd been correct to put his face into her fantasies. How often did that work out? She was amazed—and then terrified. If Mr. Charles knew about those too-friendly texts, he'd be livid. Clients and stylists should not be cheeky.

"Steve and I met at Exeter," said Mr. Charles proudly. From the way he was acting, it was obvious he didn't know that she and Steve had been texting. That helped. She calmed herself down by calculating Steve's age. Mr. Charles was forty-nine. So Steve was around that age. Apparently he was wealthy. From his emails and texts, she knew he was funny and wise. In other words, he was Bonnie's romantic ideal.

"What brings you to Frankel's today, Mr. Kline?" asked Bonnie, locking into his hazel eyes.

"I've recently relocated to New York from Chicago. I'm thinking about expanding my business back East and…"

Mr. Charles laughed. "Since you already own every strip mall in Chicago, you have to go somewhere."

A real estate mogul? Bonnie felt her stomach flutter again. He really was perfect. How on earth was this man unmarried?

Mr. Charles laughed, continuing to suck up to his dear old friend. At her side, Megan fidgeted, waiting to be introduced. The girl was just as excited to be near this dynamic man as Bonnie was. If she could, Bonnie would get rid of her assistant and work alone with Steve Kline. She lifted her phone, to act like she just got a message that required Megan's immediate attention…

"There you are!" said a woman's voice behind her.

Mr. Charles said, "Oh, good. We're all here. Bonnie, this is Mrs. Joanne Kline."

A serviceably attractive, well-groomed, rich lady with a decent honey-blond dye job and one face-lift down walked over to Mr. Charles and Mr. Kline. "I got here early and had a look around, Chase, you look wonderful." She lowered her intelligent blue eyes and kissed Mr. Charles. Then she kissed Mr. Kline on the cheek, the sight of which made Bonnie feel irrationally jealous.

Style-wise, she was exquisite, but she had no personal flair. When a woman was dressed head to toe in one designer—in Joanne Kline's case, Chanel—she was playing it safe. She didn't trust her own sense of style to experiment and mix it up. Although her navy cardigan jacket with big buttons and pencil skirt, ivory blouse, and pearls were classic, the overall impression was uninspired.

"A pleasure to meet you, Mrs. Kline. That's a handsome suit," said Bonnie.

The woman took the compliment well. "Thank you."

So he was married after all, despite his naked finger. Well, that explained the flirty messages. It was classic married-man style. Covering up for her major disappointment, she said, "This is my assistant, Megan Houlihan. She'll be helping us today."

Megan smiled and lifted the handheld bar code scanner, as if to say, "Ready, set, shop!"

"We're in the process of decorating the Manhattan apartment, and we need everything. Furniture, bedding, kitchenware. I hate the sight of empty rooms," said Mrs. Kline.

"I hope this is a permanent move," Mr. Charles said. "Are you keeping the Evanston house?"

Mr. Kline said, "Headquarters are in Chicago. But I need a base of operations for the new venture—the one I told you about."

"The boys still live in Evanston, too," said Mrs. Kline. "We'll have to bulldoze the mansion to get them out."

He had kids, too. Bonnie's fantasy man just turned into a pickle.

"I've got to hand it to you, Steve," said Mr. Charles. "Back in prep school, I was the Romeo and you were shy. Now you've got beautiful, brilliant Joanne—and I'm a lonely bachelor."

"We've been friends for decades, Chase," said Mr. Kline. "You don't have to kiss my ass."

"I'm not kissing your ass. I'm kissing *Joanne's* ass."

The wife laughed. Bonnie did, too. Mr. Charles, not kissing *everyone's* ass? That was funny. Also, the "lonely bachelor" had his pick of young, aspiring fashion world women, up-and-coming designers, stylists, and clients. He was hardly pining for the shackles of domesticity. Bonnie was surprised he did his shtick for old friends. But then again, if you removed Mr. Charles's shtick, you'd be left with an empty suit. His patter was all a polite, phony way for him to flatter the client and pass them off to Bonnie in a good mood.

Mr. Charles left with a bow. Bonnie said, "Right this way," and ushered the Klines into the exotic splendor of Home Decor. For the next hour, they wandered through the floor. Mrs. Kline was a woman who knew what she wanted. She'd point at something that caught her eye, and Bonnie or the department salesperson would describe the item in detail—for example, a set of 800-thread-count sheets made of 100 percent hand-picked and washed Egyptian-grown gypsum cotton. If Joanne liked them, she'd order them. "Three queen sets in cream for my bedroom. Three in white for your bedroom, Steve. Two more in beige for the guest room. We'll need three queen-size Tempur-Pedic mattresses as well."

Frankel's didn't carry mattresses, but if Mrs. Kline wanted them, Bonnie would arrange for the delivery with an outside vendor, even if the Salon didn't make a penny out of the deal. That was her job, to say yes to her client.

Meanwhile, the Klines had separate bedrooms? That was interesting. A flare of hope went up in Bonnie's chest. But she squashed it. If she were to compromise romantically, which she had yet to do, it'd never be about dating a married man, no matter how sexy and rich. Half of her clients met their husbands when they were other women's husbands. That was fine for them. Bonnie didn't judge them. But if she cheated with a married man, she'd go to hell. A holdover from her Catholic upbringing.

Mrs. Joanne Kline ordered plush sets of microfiber towels for her bathroom, Mr. Kline's, and the three other baths. This couple didn't share a bed or a sink? They didn't sleep or wash in the same vicinity. Did they need separate pots and pans for separate kitchens as well? More interesting information. Perhaps they'd divorce soon. Tomorrow would be good.

Megan and Bonnie scrambled to scan all the bar codes as the purchases were made. It was a challenge. Mrs. Kline had a fast finger. Her taste was predictable and conservative from a design standpoint. Bonnie appreciated her decisiveness. She'd walked through the floor with clients who spent twenty minutes agonizing over a soap dish.

While looking at formal dinner services, Mrs. Kline admired an oblong, oval-shaped well and tree designed by Philippe Starck. It was a serving platter for a roast with a shallow well and long indentations running vertically down the middle (the "trunk") and horizontal indentations alongside (the "branches") to catch juices. Bonnie loved this piece. It was simple and elegant. Although she rarely prepared roasts—she'd read that animal fats were high in acid, and autistics did better with an alkaline pH— Bonnie would display the platter on her dining room wall. The silver bottom with its divots cast a fractured reflection. She saw Mr. Kline's face inside it. Two beats later, she realized that, while she was staring at his reflection, he was looking at hers.

Mr. Kline asked, "You like this?"

Bonnie flushed—couldn't be helped—and said, "I do. For service or display."

The well and tree was solid silver and cost a fortune. The price didn't seem to ruffle Mr. Kline when he asked. Mrs. Kline said, "It'll just collect dust," and moved along.

Mrs. Kline made all the decisions, but Bonnie kept an eye on Mr. Kline, just to make sure he concurred with his wife's choices. Mr. Kline seemed amused and entertained by the fawning salespeople, the five-paragraph description of a washcloth, Mrs. Kline's occasionally asking, "What do you think, Steve?" and then ordering a $10,000 armchair before he responded.

While she considered an antique Iranian rug in the unusual size of fifteen-by-fifteen feet, she said, "This rug would really tie the dining room together."

"It's very impressive," he replied.

"I'm sure it's a fortune," said Mrs. Kline, stroking the wool and silk weave.

The rug salesperson, Mr. Amin, who was born in Iran and moved here with his family ten years ago, considered each of the Persians a work of art. "It's priceless," he declared. "A unique master work."

Mrs. Kline sighed impatiently. Bonnie typed a figure on the notepad of her BlackBerry. She showed the screen to Mrs. Kline, who said, "Oh."

Mr. Kline leaned in to see. He said, "There's your buy-in to the Peace on Earth committee."

Peace on Earth was a major New York City charitable organization. Their proceeds went to feeding starving children around the world. If *People* magazine ran a photo of a movie star surrounded by rag-clad African or Indian children, Peace on Earth probably paid for the trip. Many of Bonnie's clients were committee members. Vicki Freed was the outgoing chairwoman. Gloria Rodkin was involved to a lesser degree. Anyone could volunteer for the organization, but to join the committee, you had to be invited by three active members. In lean years, like this one, you could buy your way in with a donation. Mrs. Kline had obviously done her homework and calculated how much a straight shot to the top of New York society would cost.

Was it an either/or situation? The committee "in" or the rug? The sale would push the Salon's volume over the top in a relatively anemic holiday season. Bonnie had been working harder than ever, but her clients weren't spending like they used to. Fewer gifts were going out, at lower prices. But the rug would make it all better, guaranteeing a decent annual bonus. Half of Peter's annual tuition was due in January.

Her brain went into overdrive. How to make this sale happen? Bonnie could introduce Mrs. Kline to three Peace on Earth committee members, women who might bestow invitations. Then she wouldn't need to buy her way in and could purchase the rug. But Bonnie couldn't state that explicitly. That would be presumptuous.

"Peace on Earth is a wonderful charity," she said. "I hear

such incredible things about it from my clients. So many of them are committed to the cause." Like dropping a baited sinker.

Mrs. Kline did not bite. "Good to know," she said flatly.

Damn, thought Bonnie. She'd played that wrong. Mrs. Kline would not be bargained with or lured by vague promises. And she didn't like Bonnie nosing into their conversation. Had she offended the woman? She glanced at Mr. Kline to check his reaction.

He mouthed at her, "Nice try."

Flustered, she quickly looked away.

Mr. Amin said, "I'd be happy to show you other Persians."

"We'll take it," said Mr. Kline.

"We will?" asked his wife.

"Why not? We can always resell in ten years and double the investment."

His wife lifted an eyebrow. "Have you ever bought anything without planning to unload it later?"

He rolled his eyes. A sore point? Was Mr. Kline unsentimental to a fault? The whole exchange reeked of a secret marriage context, coded words and phrases that had meaning only to the spouses.

"Fine, then we won't buy it," he said, irritated.

"No. We will. It's perfect for the dining room. Our guests will be duly impressed. And our decorator will love it."

He wanted to make an investment, and she wanted to make an impression. Where was the love of beauty, the passion of wanting something special? Did this couple blow cold from too many Chicago winters? Bonnie glanced again at Mr. Kline, and he smiled at her.

She was so surprised, she almost gasped. Was he just friendly, or was he flirting with her? The idea was astonishing. Her heart started pounding wildly. Bonnie felt flattered, flustered, thrown off guard. Her façade cracked.

Megan whispered, "You're sweating."

Bonnie drabbed at her brow and tried to get control of her emotions. She hadn't felt a direct hit like that in years. Men flirted with her, lots of them. She laughed off the looks and comments or ignored them. But every cell in Bonnie's body yearned to flirt with Steve Kline. He was married and a client. Two major "stop" signs.

Joanne said, "We'll need papers of authentication as well as certified documents about the piece's origin and history. Once our lawyer has reviewed the material, we'll do a price comparison before we negotiate with Mr. Charles on the final figure."

Shaking herself back to reality, Bonnie said, "We can arrange all the paperwork today. If it's convenient, we can do it right now in my office upstairs."

"Shelley! Calm down! It's not the end of the world!" Gloria Rodkin was on her iPhone, stationed on the couch at the Salon. Pressing mute, she said to Bonnie, "I was right! My daughter's husband *is* sick. Elliot has a bleeding ulcer. She's hosting twelve this New Year's—tremendous job even with all the caterers and housekeepers. Shelley? Put down the fudge!"

Bonnie said, "Mrs. Rodkin, I'd like to introduce you to Mrs. Joanne Kline. She's just moved to New York from Chicago. Mrs. Kline, this is Mrs. Gloria Rodkin, a committee member at Peace on Earth."

"Her name is Kline; Jewish, I'm guessing. From Chicago. Yes, I know," Gloria reported to Shelley. Then she shook Mrs. Kline's hand. "Everyone who is everyone is interested in Peace on Earth. As the newly elected chairwoman, I'm making that my priority. Save the children from Islamic extremists."

Mrs. Rodkin was the new chairwoman? That was huge. Bonnie didn't think she had the cash or clout.

Mrs. Kline smiled. "I couldn't agree more," she said. "May I join you on the couch?"

Gloria recognized a potential new ally in tidy Mrs. Kline. "Shelley? I've got to go." She hung up. "Where in Chicago? Driving distance to Neiman Marcus, I hope."

Megan whispered, "Bonnie, should I start downloading their itemized list?"

"Yes, go," said Bonnie. Turning to Mr. Kline, Bonnie said,

"My office is right this way."

Mr. Kline said, "Lead the way."

Bonnie detected an eagerness, but about what? Spending a huge amount of money, or being in an office alone with her? Ha! Wishful thinking. Bonnie wasn't the type to attract the Stephen Klines of the world, the moguls and billionaires. Unless a woman was famous, twenty-two, a sylph, or ridiculously wealthy in her own right, she was relatively invisible to the masters of the universe.

"I'm afraid we won't have much privacy," she said. She ushered him into her office. "As you see, no door," she said, going behind her desk. She navigated to the store's program for creating a line of credit for a new customer.

Mr. Kline took the chair opposite. He looked just as good sitting down as he did standing up. Bonnie had to concentrate. She wasn't 100 percent confident with the new software, installed only last year when the Frankel's board of directors stopped offering quick credit to customers. A dozen old accounts had been "Madoffed," as Mr. Charles loved to say, and the store took a substantial loss. Since then, Bonnie had to verify four ways that a client could afford to buy a paper clip.

"Name and address, please," she started. "Might as well give me the New York one."

"Stephen Jerome Kline," he said. "740 Park Avenue."

"Date of birth?"

"February fourteenth."

"Year?" she asked.

"You're just trying to figure out how old I am," he said. His hazel eyes had some gold in them.

"It's just for the file," she said.

He nodded. "How old is George Clooney?"

Bonnie said, "Fifty?"

"Let's go with that," he said.

He sure didn't look older than Clooney, thought Bonnie. He was just as sexy. In an Armani tux, he'd be devastating. Yes, Bonnie could see it now. She could almost feel the fabric.

"Ms. Madden?" he asked, calling her back to reality.

Shaking her head, she forced her eyes back to the computer screen. "Married: yes. Spouse's name?" she asked, her tone back to business.

"Joanne Warren Kline," he replied.

"How long have you been married?" she asked. The question was not actually in the program.

"Twenty-five years. We've got two sons. Brian and Jack. Brian's twenty-three, finishing up at Northwestern. Jack is twenty-five. He works for me."

A twenty-three-year-old undergrad? "Brian is in graduate school?" she asked.

His face tightened. "He's on the six-year college plan."

Touchy subject. "Moving along. What is your profession?"

"I'm a bookie," he said. "I can give you a ten-point spread for the Giants game on Sunday."

"I could be wrong, but I doubt our vetting department will open up a credit line for a bookie."

"Just give them my name," he said. "I'm a pretty well-established bookie."

He was enjoying himself, and Bonnie found herself drawn in. They smiled at each other. She felt a zing in a sensitive place.

"I have some questions for you," he said.

Huh? "All right."

"Are *you* married?" he asked, glancing at her bare left index finger.

"Divorced," she replied. No shame in it.

"Children?"

"My son, Peter, is six."

"How long have you worked at Frankel's?"

"Five years," she said. Remembering her boss was his "old, old friend," she added, "Five glorious, no-complaint years."

He laughed. "What are your professional goals?"

She was stumped by that. It'd been a while since Bonnie aspired to anything but paying the bills each month. "I love the job I have."

"Let me rephrase. When you were twenty, and you dreamed of your future, was this how you pictured it?"

"I was in design school at twenty," she said. "I wanted to be a designer."

"Why aren't you?"

This was starting to feel like an inquisition or a job interview. "My real talent is appreciating and understanding the designs of others."

Steve nodded. "Are you happy?"

"That's a very personal question," she replied.

"I didn't ask to see your tattoos," he said.

Bonnie bit her lower lip, trying not to imagine what or where his tattoo might be. How had this conversation turned around, anyway? She looked back at her computer screen. A million questions about banking info, income, collateral, debt. The pixels were swimming on the screen. He'd asked if she was happy. What a question! What did that even *mean*?

"Look, Mr. Kline, we've got a lot of ground to cover here," she said, gesturing at the computer.

He registered her discomfort. "Sorry, sorry. I'm just curious. When I hear someone referred to as 'the best,' I want to know how they got that way and how it feels."

Bonnie sensed a presence in her doorway. Looking up, she was surprised to see Jesus. He had to be insanely busy today in the Cage. What could possibly bring him above ground?

"Sorry to interrupt," said Jesus. "Can we talk for a sec?"

His pained expression meant this had to be bad. Bonnie said, "Excuse me," and edged around her desk in the small space.

Once she was in the main Salon, Bonnie smiled blandly at Gloria Rodkin and Joanne Kline, who were hotly engaged in a three-way conversation with Shelley on speakerphone about the big Peace on Earth spring fundraiser.

Fran was serving the women coffee in china cups. She asked, "How do you like it, Mrs. R.?" in her thick Brooklyn accent.

Gloria snagged Jesus by his belt loop. "You tell her how I like it, Jesus."

"Hot and black," he said, by rote.

"Like my men!" Gloria said.

"Mother, that's disgusting," groaned Shelley on Gloria's

speakerphone.

Bonnie had heard ten times worse in these walls. When women were out of their husband's earshot, in the safety of the Salon, they turned into foul-mouthed truckers. Jesus and Roman were the usual targets. Even Mr. Charles had had his butt tweaked.

Jesus took Bonnie into Fitting Room A for privacy.

Bonnie leaned against a rack of garment bags. "What's up?"

"One of our drivers was hijacked at gunpoint yesterday."

"Is he okay?" asked Bonnie. Last Christmas season, a UPS driver had been shot and thrown into traffic on Forty-Second Street.

"He's fine. Two scumbags pulled guns, but they didn't use them. They did drive off with the truck, which turned up abandoned on the West Side Highway."

Bonnie froze. "The Deerlinger mailing."

Jesus said, "I'm sorry, Bonnie. Insurance will replace and resend the gifts. We've been in touch with the warehouse in New Jersey. As soon as the items arrive, we'll wrap and ship immediately. Mr. Charles is so freaked out, he wants to hire a private fleet for all Manhattan deliveries."

"Tell me the package addressed to Mrs. Yoshi Takati at Trump Plaza was delivered before the hijack." Her heated blood suddenly ran cold.

"They hit the driver almost as soon as he pulled out of the loading zone. The store computer said one item on Mrs. D.'s list was irreplaceable. That's what you're talking about?"

"A shirt. Hermés. Pearl gray," said Bonnie. "Will you tell Mrs. Deerlinger what happened? Please? Starbucks for a year!"

"Get the old man to call her." He meant Mr. Charles.

They both scoffed at that ridiculous suggestion. Mr. Charles was not a bad-news bearer. He left the dirty work to his staff.

"Cover me," said Bonnie, taking out her BlackBerry. "I'm going in." She pushed Cody's number and held the phone so both of them could listen.

Cody answered, first ring. "Bonnie. I was just going to call you...Chester! The light can't get any greener!...That Japanese bastard screwed Dan over on a big deal. Dan is *very* upset… Chester, go left. LEFT!!!…Do not, I repeat, DO NOT send that bitch Mrs. Takati the Hermés shirt. If you've already sent it, go to her place and tear it off her back. I should send her a box of Cake's fresh shit for what her husband did to Dan. I'll take store credit for the shirt. I never want to see it again."

Cody hung up. Bonnie lowered her arm, in shock.

"It's a Christmas miracle."

"Praise Jesus," she said.

"You're welcome."

They started laughing hard with relief. From the Salon couch, Gloria shouted, "What's going on in there?"

When Bonnie opened the door, Gloria sang out, "Keep your hands off him. He's mine."

Jesus bowed to the ladies and jogged out the Salon door.

Gloria said, "Bonnie, tell Joanne about the time the Saudi princess shows up with twenty assistants. Remember, Shelley? You were here—well, on the phone. The princess came to Frankel's to shop with twenty muttering women, covered head to toe in black. They each had their own job to assist her, even in the ladies room."

Bonnie was already back in her office on a cloud of cosmic gratitude. Stephen Jerome Kline watched her float in, his grin matching her own. He said, "Whoa. *Now* you're happy."

He meant it nicely. But his comment made the roller coaster of Bonnie's emotions take another turn. She looked happy. She *felt* happier than she had in weeks, but why? Because by sheer dumb luck, Cody Deerlinger wouldn't be chewing off her head today. She needed and deserved a better reason to be happy. She sat down behind her tiny desk in her small office and looked at her new client. His texts had made her feel good, too, like a small secret bite of candy. In the cosmic scheme, Bonnie wondered why he'd suddenly appeared in her life, riding in with a killer smile on a magic carpet, much like the one that he just purchased. Could this man, this stranger, be important to her?

The thought flashed brightly and then faded. She exhaled, not too loudly, smiled blandly at him, and asked, "Where were we?"

Chapter Six

On Christmas morning, Bonnie watched Mike and Peter on the plush-but-worn brown carpet of their living room unwrapping gifts from under the brightly lit tree. She sipped coffee on her tawny, cracked-leather couch and let herself remember the last holiday when they were still a family. That year had been rough. Peter was not yet two but was showing early signs of his autism. He had been an early talker—at ten months, he knew the alphabet and could speak in sentences. But then, the quirks and questions about his behavior started to crop up. The fall from "Peter is a genius!" to "something's wrong" had taken only six months, but it felt like a sudden splat. Now Bonnie knew that "genius" and "different" weren't mutually exclusive. She and Mike separated soon after Peter was diagnosed. And here they were now, sharing custody but little else.

Mike glanced at her thick, white porcelain mug, stolen years ago from a local diner. "Is that still hot?"

"Do you want some?" she asked.

"I'll get it." He took her cup to reheat it. She watched him walk into the kitchen. His jeans fit perfectly. She sighed, enjoying the view.

How had she let him get away? Mike left her, but she'd shown him the door, metaphorically. The separation had been a blur of legal papers and adjustments. Hiring a lawyer, a babysitter, a therapist. She'd moved from Bloomingdale's to Frankel's around the same time. Her life was upside down, absolute chaos. It was years before the dust settled—it was still settling, actually. When she started at Frankel's, the new job distracted Bonnie from her crumbling home life. Nothing like personal problems to turn you into a workaholic.

They'd been happy, and then, splat. According to Peter's shrink, Bonnie and Mike had typical gender-specific reactions to their son's diagnosis. Mike wanted to pursue; Bonnie wanted to protect. Instead of compromising, they dug in their heels. It wasn't long before they disagreed about everything. What brand of toilet paper to buy. Where to go for a long weekend. How often they had sex.

The night Mike left, he asked, "If Peter were normal, would this be happening?"

Bonnie couldn't accept that the son they both loved was to blame for the split. The parents-of-autistic-kids books confirmed her belief. If the marriage had been rock solid, they would have grown closer in a crisis. Peter's diagnosis widened already existing cracks. In a way, they were lucky to figure out they were better as friends relatively early in life. They weren't too old for second chances. But Bonnie couldn't imagine any man taking a chance on her. She hadn't compromised her position for Mike. She certainly wouldn't for another man.

Peter held up her gift, an Xbox game. "Sea Explorer Five," he said. "Thanks, Mom!"

A guaranteed winner. He'd loved Sea Explorer One through Four. "I'm glad you like it."

"Dad gave me a mitt," he said, showing her. "And a baseball."

"That's a nice gift," she said, even though she knew Peter was afraid of hard objects hurtling through space toward him.

"Except I'm not good at sports."

"Don't say that."

"It's true." He chucked the mitt at her.

"Man, you do stink at sports," she said. "You're supposed to throw the ball. You *catch* with the mitt."

He smelled himself. "I don't stink. And how am I supposed to throw the ball and catch the ball at the same time?"

Peter looked uncomfortable and confused. Bonnie said, "Come here." He jumped on the couch next to her. She hugged him tightly, and he rocked, which seemed to calm him down. Bonnie reminded herself for the millionth time that Peter took everything literally. Figures of speech only confused him and got him upset.

After a few minutes he asked, "Can I play Sea Explorer now?"

"Yes, and you can play at Grandma Viv's later, too," she said. "You have to socialize for an hour first, though, okay?" It was Mike's year to get Peter for Christmas dinner. They alternated.

"Thirty minutes," he said.

"Forty-five."

They bargained down to thirty-seven minutes and twenty seconds of human interaction, which Peter would time exactly on his watch. That was long enough. He wore out quickly, especially at the high testosterone Madden gathering. Bonnie would go to Christmas dinner at her dad's house with her siblings, nieces, and nephews. The Salerno clan's women had the men outnumbered two to one.

When Mike returned from the kitchen with a cup of coffee, he had another wrapped gift.

Bonnie's heart flipped. Had he bought something for *her*? They hadn't exchanged gifts since the split. She felt touched and almost started crying. Apart from Peter's Popsicle-stick picture frame, Bonnie had received only impersonal and inexpensive candy boxes from clients. She didn't have time for friends.

Mike moved toward her and then put the box in Peter's hands.

"Here you go, buddy," said Mike. "It's sort of a gift. Sort of a new therapy thing."

Bonnie's skin prickled. They'd had too many fights about Mike's kooky alternative therapies that set them up for high expectations and crushing disappointments.

Peter opened the box and removed a pair of what appeared to be blue sunglasses. Mike showed him how to push a button on the inside lens, which started a pulse of red light blinking on the left side every ten seconds. "Try them on," said Mike. Peter was reluctant, but he put on the weird glasses.

To Bonnie, Mike said, "It's a light therapy device. The flashing lights on the left side stimulate right brain development. I spoke to a psychologist who said that a lot of autistic kids have a brain imbalance —their left hemispheres are more developed than their right. So if Peter can stimulate his right hemisphere to grow, his brain will be in balance. He might show improvement."

It sounded like he was reading from a brochure. Bonnie looked at her son in the blue shades with the red light flashing. "How long is he supposed to wear them?"

"Three times a day, building up to twenty minutes each time. Three months from now, Peter could be on the mend."

Bonnie glared at Mike and shook her head. How many doctors had told both of them that there was no cure for autism? How dare he promise Peter a passive, easy fix?

"Honey, go get dressed," she said. "Almost time to go to Grandma's."

Once Peter was out of the living room, Bonnie glared at Mike and said, "What the hell are you doing?"

"Why not just try it? There's a book in the box that explains the science. If it doesn't work, then we'll be exactly where we are now."

"Our son is not an experiment. He's a fantastic kid, and he's perfect the way he is. Every time you drag out your latest magic cure, it's like you think he's defective."

"He knows I love him," said Mike, his voice colder. "I'm trying to help."

Right, Mike. It helps to give Peter a mitt that makes him feel inadequate. "You can hurt by helping."

"What about you? Sea World Five? Another book about submarines? A goldfish tank?" He pointed at her gifts as he listed them.

"I'm encouraging his interests." Exactly what the shrink advised her to do. Dr. Rubenstein also said there was a hair-thin line between encouragement and nurturing an obsession, especially for kids on the autism spectrum.

"You're complacent, Bonnie. I'm not giving up on finding ways to help him, even if you think they're a waste of time. Even if they *are* a waste of time."

Was this what had finally driven Mike out? Her alleged complacency? Bonnie searched for a grain of truth in his accusation. She hadn't given up. She was being realistic. Before she could get a grip on her thoughts, Peter came out of his room, the shades blinking.

"These glasses are cool," he said. "It's like having the police car light in my eye."

"See? He likes it," said Mike. "Just try something different for a change, Bonnie. You've got nothing to lose."

By five o'clock, Bonnie's father had planted himself in his pilling recliner to watch football. Bonnie's brother and brothers-in-law parked themselves in matching chairs on either side of Vinny or on the ancient, orange sectional couch that Bonnie had jumped on as a kid. The big plasma TV blared. (It was the only newish item in the living room, and the most expensive.) The cousins—ten kids in all, eleven when Peter came—had been tearing around the house all day, stampeding up and down the stairs, through the kitchen, out into the yard, with Vinny 's dog barking and running alongside them. Now they'd finally hit a wall and were zoning out in front of the TV, too.

The day had been typical Salerno family holiday madness. Bonnie, her three sisters, and one sister-in-law spent the entire afternoon plating and serving and clearing tray after tray of food to the men and kids. As usual, Ragussa's, a neighborhood restaurant, supplied the Christmas feast. The table groaned under platters of tortellini, spaghetti alla puttanesca, chicken florentine, garlic bread and focaccia, and tricolore salad in creamy dressing. Her share of the leftovers would feed Bonnie and Peter for a week. Bonnie's mom, Sylvia, was in charge of acquiring and bringing the meal. After all these years, Mom still considered it her duty to feed her family on Christmas. In the past, Sylvia cooked the feast, including the Christmas Eve traditional seven fishes meal. She'd more or less lived in the kitchen from December 20 to New Year's Day. Sylvia was a talented cook—like all Italian mamas—but she'd always resented having to do all that work and then having to clean up after dozens of people. Bonnie couldn't blame her for blowing off that huge undertaking. Her family, however, ate the delicious Ragussa's food while making subtle jabs. "It's good, but not as good as you used to make, Mom," etc.

The men and children had fallen into their food comas right on schedule, and now it was time for the women to clean up. They carried the trays and plates from the dining room through the hinge door into the kitchen, washing and putting things back in cabinets. They'd been using the same dishes and cabinets since Bonnie was a child. The wood paneling was worn, and the cabinet liner was rolling up. But being at her dad's house was like stepping back in time. Only the people got older.

They loaded leftovers into containers and taped scraps of paper on top of each, designating who got to take them home. When the kitchen was clean and all the food stored in the fridge, the sisters and sisters-in-law decided to go to the corner bar for some girl time. The last two women in the kitchen were Bonnie and her older sister, Anita, a classic, natural Italian beauty with long, dark hair, a tan, and heavy black eyeliner. She was dressed in a black outfit of jeans, a pullover sweatshirt, and sneakers. Bonnie had offered to put some flare into Anita's wardrobe, but her sister refused. "It's stupid," she said. "I'm too busy to worry about the cut of my jeans or the color of my shirt." Their relationship was crackly, to say the least.

Anita asked, "So. How's Mike?"

"He's good." All her sisters wanted Bonnie and Mike to get back together.

"I saw him at the deli," said Anita. "He looks good."

Eager to change the subject, Bonnie asked, "How's the shop?"

Anita shrugged. She and her husband owned a car repair business on Queens Boulevard. "We're staying alive. Got some new ideas for expansion. We'll see." After a pause, Anita asked somewhat reluctantly, "And how's business?"

Bonnie was reminded that Anita rarely asked about Peter. It wasn't that she didn't like her nephew or ignored his very existence. But the subject of his condition and treatment made her uncomfortable. Anything different chafed Anita. That included

Peter as well as Bonnie's career. She was the only member of her family to go to work in Manhattan. She was the only one who'd gone to college, too. Her sisters said they were proud of her, but they also thought she lorded her career over them. Not true. Bonnie just wanted to share her life, and they interpreted her stories about the glamour at Frankel's as bragging. "I got a new client last week," said Bonnie about Steve Kline. (The man had been on her mind, and now, in a safe setting, she could talk about him.) "He's insanely rich, handsome, and owns every strip mall in Chicago. He's been working with me to buy furniture and decorate his new place on the Upper East Side. Super high-end, crazy expensive stuff. He bought a Persian rug for...I can't say the price out loud; it might shatter the windows." Bonnie whispered the price in Anita's ear.

Instead of a low whistle, Anita said, "Whatever."

"Oh, come on. You're not impressed?"

"Why should I care that some rich idiot wastes his money? What's he to you?"

"He's a client," said Bonnie defensively. "I'm just saying how cool it is to get to spend time with people who..."

"...who have more money than sense? You see this man as some kind of hero. How does he see you, Bonnie?"

"He values my taste," she said.

"You're a shopgirl," said Anita. "Whether you're selling Persian rugs or packs of gum. That's who you are and how he sees you. He knows it. I know it. But you can't see the truth, even though it's right in your face."

When Anita said that last part, she was right up in Bonnie's face. Bonnie struggled to keep her expression frozen and not let Anita see how hurt she was. Her sister had no idea what Bonnie did or why it constituted more skill than selling gum. None of her family understood or appreciated beauty and style the way Bonnie always had, from birth.

"Look, I'm sorry," said Anita, pulling back. "I'm halfway drunk. You coming to the bar?"

"No, thanks. I'll finish cleaning up in here." The kitchen sparkled. It was obvious to both that Bonnie was blowing off Anita.

"I just want you to get your priorities straight," said Anita. "Peter and Mike are your family. Work is just something you do to keep your family going."

Then Anita left. Sylvia, Bonnie's mom, came into the kitchen a few seconds later. "Where is everyone?"

"They went to Louie's."

"Oh. Did you get the Old Navy card for Peter?" asked Sylvia.

A $50 card to each of her grandkids was Sylvia's gift each year. "Got it," said Bonnie.

"What's wrong with you?"

"Anita just slammed me pretty hard." Bonnie told her mom about their conversation.

"She's just jealous," said Sylvia. Like Bonnie, her mom was dressed casually to serve and clean, in jeans and a black turtleneck. They both wore their hair in a ponytail. Sylvia used to have dark chestnut hair like Bonnie's, but had been bleaching it blond since she left home. "Anita doesn't like people to think too highly of themselves. When you were little, she took it upon herself to keep all of you kids humble. Don't let her get you down. Your career is exciting, and Anita can't stand to hear it. I love your Frankel's stories, Bonnie. What movie stars came in lately?"

Bonnie rattled off some A-list names, Oscar and Emmy winners, chart-toppers. Sylvia exclaimed and cooed appropriately, soaking up the stories, making Bonnie feel important and special. Bonnie couldn't remember the last time they'd been alone together like this.

Sylvia cracked the swinging door between the kitchen and living room. "They're all asleep," she said of her ex-husband, son, and sons-in-law. "The food is packed up. I'm going to change my clothes, kiss you, and say goodbye."

"It's only seven o'clock." Bonnie felt abandoned suddenly, a replay from when Sylvia moved out and declared her independence.

"I've got a party to get to." Grabbing her shopping bag, she went into the hallway powder room. She emerged ten minutes later in a pair of trousers, boots, a black sequin jacket that was too thin for the weather, and pink lipstick. Her hair was teased up in a pouf.

"You're gorgeous," said Bonnie.

"Carmine should be here in the limo any second." Carmine Ragussa, 70, owner of his namesake restaurant, was Sylvia's boss and boyfriend. She'd been hostess at Ragussa's forever. Carmine's wife died of cancer not too long ago, and Sylvia stepped right in.

Ragussa's was, as everyone in Corona knew, a mob joint. The downstairs dining room was for tourists and regulars. The secret upstairs lair—known as "The Marilyn Room" with dozens of Monroe objects d'art—was an exclusive parlor for wise guys.

Bonnie said, "Where's the party?"

"At the restaurant. It's just a little something for the regulars," said Sylvia. "Want to come?"

"No, thanks." She was childfree until tomorrow evening and planned to go home, soak in the tub, and then sleep. After the frenzy at work for the last three weeks, Bonnie desperately needed a night off. Or she might be hiding from the world. Either way, a party at Ragussa's didn't tempt her in the least.

Sylvia asked, "What's Mike doing tonight?"

Here we go. "He's at his mom's."

"Did he bring a date?"

"Mom, please. It's none of our business." Peter had mentioned Mike's new girlfriend, a detective named Emily. They'd been together for a few months at least.

"Are you seeing anyone?" asked Sylvia.

Bonnie groaned. "I don't have time to date. Between Frankel's and Peter, my life is booked solid."

"You're wasting what's left of your youth, Bonnie. How can you stand it, year after year, alone?"

By not thinking about it. By latching onto fantasy crushes that had no risk of actually turning into real relationships. Honestly, Bonnie would be overjoyed to find a man to love, who loved her back, would take care of her, and relieve the constant pressure she was under. But who would take her on? The idea that she could find lasting true love was a setup for disappointment. It was like one of Mike's miracle cures.

"Here's what I want for Christmas," said Bonnie. "A break from nagging."

"How does it make you feel to see Peter suffer?" Sylvia was speaking of her own suffering, of course, from watching Bonnie.

She groaned. "I'm not suffering!" *Change the subject*, she thought. "Nice jacket."

"Carmine gave it to me. And take a look at this shirt," said Sylvia, peeling off her jacket to reveal a pearl gray, silk shirt that was as smooth and glossy as melted butter with real pearl buttons and stitching detail on the collar. Funny, how much it looked like…uncanny, actually, like… Not believing her eyes, Bonnie spun her mom around to check the label.

Sylvia said, "It's Hermés."

Voice like ice, Bonnie asked, "Where did you get that shirt?"

"I told you. Carmine gave it to me."

"Where did he get it?"

Sylvia drew herself up and said, "At Frankel's."

"At Frankel's. Bull*shit*."

"You don't recognize it?"

Only too well, thought Bonnie. "It's small on you, Mom. Why don't you return it and get a bigger size?" Not that the one-of-a-kind shirt came in a bigger size.

"Carmine likes my shirts to be snug. Besides, he's such a scatterbrain. Lost the receipt."

"We'd have the purchase on record," said Bonnie.

Sylvia put her jacket back on, irritated now. "So it's small. And maybe he got it through a friend. What's the big deal?"

"This shirt was stolen by two men with guns who hijacked a delivery truck yesterday."

"Even if that's true, Carmine had nothing to do with it," said Sylvia, waving away Bonnie's concern. "He's a gentleman and a very sweet person. He treats me like a queen. Do you think your father ever gave me anything? Vinny barely paid attention except to yell at me to cook or clean. Look at him. Go ahead. Take a peek."

"I don't have to."

"Because you know exactly what he's doing right now. Asleep with a beer on his belly after being waited on by me. Did he say, 'Thank you'? No. He didn't for twenty years of marriage. Now I have a man who gives me gifts and takes me to parties. He's coming to pick me up in a limo."

"A stolen limo?"

"I'm sixty years old, Bonnie. I worked hard and raised five kids. Now I want to live a little. I deserve this."

Her mom had made a justifiable trade. She'd exchanged her integrity for luxury. Bonnie flashed to Dan Deerlinger's rough handling of Cody the night of her party and Vicki Freed's XXL breast implants. Now that she thought about it, most of her clients had traded something for something. Dignity for social status. A natural-born body for a husband's devotion. Sylvia's trade seemed delusional. She was risking her personal safety for a few nice things.

Bonnie wouldn't have taken any of those trades. But would she trade her morality to have an affair with a married man? A week ago, she wouldn't have considered it. Not that Steve Kline made a clear offer, but Bonnie knew when the door was open, even slightly. Could she walk through it? What would she stand to gain? Affection, relief, fun, adventure, a break from the drudgery her life had become. She'd have a delicious secret and a boyfriend to nullify the sting of Mike's having a girlfriend. And what did she stand to lose if she somehow managed to connect with Steve Kline?

People cheated all over the world and didn't hate themselves for it. She wouldn't be the one cheating anyway. Steve would have that honor. But Bonnie would have guilt, no matter how much she rationalized it. That would be her trade-off. Perhaps the guilt wouldn't be as bad as she imagined. Look at Sylvia. Her own mother, the person who'd instilled the Catholic guilt in Bonnie, had managed to sidestep ethical issues to be with Carmine. If there was any possibility that Bonnie and Steve could one day fall in love, that he'd leave Joanne for her, that he'd accept Peter and love him like a father, didn't she owe it to herself to pursue it? The chances of that actually happening were zero. Steve Kline should and would stay where he belonged—in her fantasies.

As a salesperson, Bonnie walked on a fine moral edge. It was wrong to use a woman's insecurity or vanity to make a sale, but Bonnie did that every day. This moral dilemma came up a lot in her business. Would she sell a suit to Osama bin Laden? Many of her clients would see that as a great opportunity to raise their social profile. They routinely stole each other's husbands and betrayed each other for a higher rung on the society ladder. They thought only of their appearance, status, and short-term desires. Bonnie might be their social inferior, but she believed she was their moral superior. She *wouldn't* sell a suit to Osama bin Laden. She wouldn't steal or stab a friend in the back—or cheat. She had to live by her own code or risk behaving like the spoiled women she made fun of.

Bonnie shook her head at her mom. "You're playing with fire."

Sylvia shrugged. "And you're playing it safe."

An uncomfortable echo from Mike's "complacent" comment earlier.

"You ended your marriage without the slightest bit of guilt and never felt inclined to get back together with Dad. You never remarried. So I don't see how you can find fault with my being single."

"Well, I waited until you kids were grown to leave your father," she said. "I did my time. And now, I deserve my freedom."

"So you'd rather I do 'time' in a bad marriage than be single? Really?" said Bonnie, shooting her a look only a daughter could give her mom when things don't make sense.

"You've got a lot on your plate," said Sylvia. "I'm just saying, it'd be nice to have someone who could take care of you."

A pair of headlights shone through the kitchen window. Sylvia pulled back the curtain. "The limo just pulled up. Carmine's here. Kiss everyone goodbye for me. A special big kiss for Peter."

"Okay, Mom," said Bonnie.

Sylvia gave Bonnie a quick squeeze and said, "I love you." Then she was gone, out the door in a flash of sequin. Bonnie watched her run down the path toward a big black limo with blackout windows. The rear door opened as Sylvia approached, and then she disappeared inside.

Bonnie made it on time for the Monday meeting after the long Christmas weekend. She wasn't able to check the Sunday style sections yesterday or the gossip columns this morning, unfortunately. If any of her clients were featured, she hoped the reviews were positive. Mr. Charles used the fashion pages as a weekly report card.

She walked into the Salon only moments before Mr. Charles. The room was crowded already with no place for Bonnie to sit. She leaned against the wall by her office and gave her attention to the boss.

One look at Mr. Charles's face gave her an accurate measure of his mood. Bleak. This had to be about money. The first Monday meeting after New Year's was traditionally when Mr. Charles presented the staff with their annual bonus checks. Bonnie noticed immediately that he carried a copy of the *New York Post*, but no stack of white envelopes.

"First order of business," he said. "Our annual revenue was flat compared to last year's, which was down considerably from the year before. The board members voted not to give annual bonuses this year. I'm sorry. This isn't my decision. If you feel compelled, send your complaints to the Frankel family."

Groans around the room. Bonnie knew they'd all worked twice as hard for half the sales. She felt the sting keenly. She needed her bonus to pay for the Mason School.

Before she could wrap her mind around that and figure out how on earth she'd cover the tuition, Mr. Charles opened the *Post* and turned to "Page Six," the most popular gossip column in New York. He held up the page and pointed to the item circled with an angry red marker. Judging by their expressions, a lot of people in the room had seen it already.

Mr. Charles cleared his throat and peered over his glasses to read. "'Are You My Mother? Archer Watson Found Wandering

Alone at Frankel's,'" he recited.

Whoosh. The air rushed out of Bonnie's lungs like she'd been punched in the solar plexus.

Lowering the paper, Mr. Charles said, "We got a call from Tim Watson's lawyer today. They plan on suing the store for negligence." He looked right at Bonnie. "Explain."

She flubbed, "I haven't read the article."

"Well, read it now!" he shouted. Mr. Charles never shouted.

The paper was passed back to her. The item was short, but deadly:

> Shoppers beware. At Frankel's, you might lose your shirt as well as your child. Sources tell Page Six that on the Wednesday before Christmas, Stacy Watson left her son, Archer, in the care of Frankel's on-site babysitting service before heading off to shop. Within minutes, the boy escaped his incompetent tenders. "It's probably the first time in his entire life that no one knew where Archer Watson was," said an anonymous source at Frankel's. "A salesperson found him curled in a corner, crying for his mommy. He was extremely upset. This might have scarred him for life." When Stacy Watson was told her son had been missing for an hour, she swore never to shop at Frankel's again. Repeated calls to Frankel's for comment were not returned.

Little white dots exploded behind Bonnie's eyes. When she could speak, she said, "It's lies from top to bottom."

"Was Archer Watson lost in this store?" asked Mr. Charles.

"Yes, but not for an hour," said Bonnie. "Five minutes, max. And he wasn't upset. No crying. Stacy Watson didn't swear off Frankel's."

"How did this happen?"

Megan raised her hand. "Bonnie told me to watch him, even though the store doesn't have certification from the city to provide babysitting services, and childcare isn't in my job description, and I have no experience with kids, not that Bonnie asked. She passed Archer off like he was a bag of potatoes. She seemed…desperate…for Stacy Watson's undivided attention. Archer was in the way. I felt weird about it, but Bonnie's my boss. I thought she'd fire me if I refused. I feel terrible about what happened, but that kid was slippery."

Mr. Charles was livid. "And who, might I ask, was the savior salesperson?"

As if she'd been waiting for her cue, Hortense Clout walked into the Salon. "Sorry I'm late," she said, thick and sweet as syrup. "What's going on? You all look so *tense*."

Megan said, "Hortense found Archer."

"Are we talking about 'Page Six'? It was exaggerated. Little Archer wasn't upset. He was a trooper. Stacy blamed herself for leaving him behind in the first place," said Hortense. "At least, that's what she wrote in the thank-you note she sent me."

Mr. Charles pounced on that. "She wrote you a note and said she blamed herself?"

"Would you like to see it?"

"We have to get that note to our lawyer immediately." Leveling his eyes at Bonnie, he said, "I should fire you for not calling me the minute this happened. You're on probation. One more mistake and you're out. Hortense, come."

They left. Everyone was so embarrassed for Bonnie, they scattered like roaches when the lights come on. Roman had the courage to say something to her. "It'll blow over, Chief."

Megan edged toward her. "I had to defend myself, Bonnie."

Cylinders clicked into place in Bonnie's mind. "That was a setup from the moment you took charge of Archer," she said. "I bet you handed him off to Hortense and then conspired to make me look bad."

"What kind of person do you think I am?" asked Megan, hand at her heart. "I'd never do something as devious as that!"

But Bonnie saw the spark in her eye. She'd underestimated Megan, having sized her up as just another entitled brat who'd burn out after six months of hard work. The politician's daughter was an expert schemer and manipulator. Her target was clearly marked.

"No way, Chief," said Roman. "Megan feels terrible about what happened. The Archer thing was an honest mistake. No one's to blame."

Roman put his arm around Megan protectively. She smiled up at him, her eyes glistening. He gazed at her with tenderness, affection, and—God help him—dumb love. Roman was smitten. Megan had seduced him to her side. Bonnie felt sorry for him.

She's going to eat him alive, thought Bonnie. "I'm not to be disturbed, for anyone or anything." She retreated to her office. If she had a door, she'd have slammed it. She sat behind her desk and buried her face in her hands.

In five minutes flat, Bonnie sank from revered Salon director to friendless outcast. Talk about whiplash trending cycles.

The public shaming was one thing. The personal betrayal was another. Being put on warning was yet another. She'd obsess about all of that later and wallow in the sad realization that fifteen years of hustling in this business might've been undone by one misjudgment of character.

But none of the above compared to the practical catastrophe of not receiving an annual bonus. She was stuck for the tuition money. She'd have to take out a third mortgage or beg her family for a loan. Oh, her sister Anita would love to see Bonnie humbled with her handout.

"Stop," Bonnie extolled herself. If she went down that road, there really was no coming back. "Bitter" was the ultimate kiss of death.

Lifting her face up from her hands, Bonnie noticed a box on the floor by her desk, with a note from Jesus. "In-house delivery addressed to Ms. Bonnie Madden at the Salon. Secret admirer? XO, Jesus."

Probably more chocolate from a client, she thought. Bonnie opened the box. She peeled back several layers of tissue paper and stared down at a fractured reflection of her face at the bottom of the Philippe Starck silver well-and-tree platter.

Someone had sent her a real gift after all this season. Bonnie found a card. "Looking forward to our next encounter," it read. Unsigned.

Bonnie's heart, deflated only moments ago, was now engorged and pumping wildly. Her mom was right about this. It was a great feeling to receive an extravagant gift. Bonnie could definitely get used to it.

Taking out her BlackBerry, she texted, "Thanks for the beautiful gift."

Steve Kline texted right back. "You're most welcome."

PART THREE

February:
The Bar Mitzvah

Chapter Seven

"In Moscow, I make house calls," said Bella Orloff. "Women giving birth on dirty floor of crumbling building, too poor to go to hospital. House calls were life and death. Now I do house calls for hem adjustment."

"I can't tell you how much I appreciate this," said Bonnie as she lumbered under the weight of heavy garment bags.

The two women trudged into the marble lobby of Vicki Freed's building on Fifth Avenue at Eighty-Sixth Street. Bella carried only her sewing box. Bonnie wouldn't have dared to ask her to lug one of the garment bags, too. It'd taken a full day of begging—as well as a tense monetary negotiation—to get Bella here for the emergency Friday night fitting.

Vicki's son Zachary, thirteen going on three, would become a man in the morning. His bar mitzvah would be at B'nai Jeshurun in Short Hills, New Jersey, followed by a swank affair at his paternal grandparents' nearby mansion. Bella had already done several fittings with Vicki's three outfits. For the religious service and Kiddush afterward (ten types of nova; the Manischewitz would flow like water), Vicki would wear a silver Akris jacket, silk skirt, and shell. For the Saturday evening pre-dinner cocktail party, Vicki had chosen a Versace purple organza dress with teardrop cutouts. She'd change again for the formal reception into a gunmetal gray Hervé Leger sheath with thigh-high side slits.

Not long ago, Vicki was a perfect size four and looked gorgeous in everything. But since her husband, Lee Freed, gave her a breast enlargement and ass liposuction for her birthday, nothing fit. Bonnie wondered how he presented the gift. Silicone implants in a box? Now Vicki was a size two on the bottom and a size eight or ten across the chest. Hence, the four rounds of fittings for Vicki's bar mitzvah wardrobe. Bella had deconstructed and rebuilt all of her outfits. The crisis tonight? Vicki had lost a pound.

Bonnie nodded at the doorman in Captain Crunch epaulettes and a gold-buttoned, double-breasted jacket. Bonnie didn't know if she should tip him or salute. He waved them through, but didn't offer to carry the garment bags for women who were clearly "the help." That was the Upper East Side for you. Even the doormen were snobs.

Good thing Mike had Peter tonight, or Bonnie would have had to pay Lucee time and a half to work late. Once she asked Mr. Charles to reimburse her extra costs for after-hours situations like this. At least pay for a car service home. He said, "It's not Frankel's fault you live in Queens and have a dependent."

If she asked about tonight, he might say, "You're lucky you still have a job at all," even though the "Page Six" debacle faded quickly. Stacy Watson didn't sue the store. No lasting harm done. But Mr. Charles stubbornly held on to his anger. Maybe she didn't deserve to be back in his good graces. In hindsight, asking Megan—or anyone—to babysit Archer had been a foolish idea. Bonnie felt terrible guilt and shame each time she flashed back to Stacy's face when she told her Archer was missing. If it'd been Peter, Bonnie would have lost it.

"What floor?" asked Bella when they stepped into the elevator.

"Penthouse."

They ascended. The elevator doors opened directly into the Freed household. The living room was two stories high. Looking up, Bonnie marveled at the dangling crystal chandelier that hung low off the ceiling. And what a ceiling! Painted gold leaf, it shimmered Versailles-like in the light, bathing the vast room in a pinkish glow. The furnishings were from the 1980s Mario Buatta school of decorating, with overstuffed velvet settees, lion's paw chair legs, chintz wallpaper, and paisley patterns. The room had probably been decorated by the first Mrs. Lee Freed. That woman, formerly a high-ranking New York socialite, was now chintzing it up in Palm Beach off her multimillion-dollar divorce settlement.

Bonnie wondered if wife number two or Vicki (number three) had tried to update the decor but been denied, or whether they genuinely liked all those chaotic patterns.

"You made it!" trilled a voice, which echoed in the vast room.

Bonnie's eyes traveled up a spiral staircase to a second floor balcony. Vicki stood at the railing in an ivory demi-slip and bra, waving. "Come on up!"

Bonnie and Bella trudged up the stairs, through an outer chamber, into the master bedroom with a California king-size bed, through the master bathroom with his and her sinks, his and her toilets, his and her Jacuzzis, and finally, into Vicki's closet.

Calling it a "closet" was like calling Versailles a "cottage." Two hundred pairs of shoes were displayed on one wall. The overburdened racks of dresses, coats, minks, sables from J. Mendel, skirts, sweaters, shirts, and slacks reminded Bonnie of Bloomingdale's. Three mannequins stood in position on one side of the closet, dressed and fully accessorized. Apparently Vicki played with them like life-size dolls.

In the center of the room, there was a dress platform, just like at the Salon. Vicki climbed on top of it now and turned in a slow circle. "You see what happens when I have to talk to my monster-in-law five times a day?" asked Vicki.

"I should force a dozen cheese blintzes down your throat," said Bella.

Most people would be happy if they lost a few pounds, not that anyone else would notice. But on Vicki, every pound showed. The meticulously re-fitted dresses wouldn't hang properly now.

Of course, it would be far worse if Vicki had *gained* a few pounds, which was usually the case with code-red, night-before, emergency alterations. So Bonnie should be grateful. That was what Mr. Charles kept telling her, so it must be true.

Bonnie lay down the four garment bags on a well-stuffed chair. Her back and shoulders wept with relief. She unzipped.

Inside the first bag, Vicki's Akris skirt suit for the ceremony. In the second bag was the Versace and Leger.

The third bag contained a pair of men's suits for Mr. Freed and Zachary. Both of the suits had been made by Frankel's esteemed men's department tailor, seventy-one-year-old Herm Weiss, a native German. His family escaped the Holocaust when he was an infant and came to America. He worked in the *schmatte* trade on the Lower East Side before moving to a sweatshop on Delancey Street, where he sewed one dollar aprons. Sixty years later, his suits sold for $5,000 to $15,000 at Frankel's. This garment bag contained $30,000 worth of cashmere, life experience, and talent.

The last bag held Vicki's mother-in-law's gown, a gold-and-black sequined Oscar de la Renta. The elder Mrs. Freed—Bunny, Lee's mother and Zachary's grandmother—had ordered her dress by phone, telling Bonnie, "I tried it on at Neiman Marcus at the Mall. It's fine. Just put it on Lee's bill." When Bonnie suggested that the elder Mrs. Freed come in for a fitting, she replied, "I don't want it to fit! For God's sake, I'm eighty!" Bonnie knew many eighty-year-old Manhattan matrons who would schedule fittings for a pair of pajamas. But if Bunny Freed thought her Oscar was fine off the rack, she'd get no argument from Bonnie.

Vicki and Bunny had been at war since Lee and Vicki got engaged. The bar mitzvah battle had been waging for years already, starting with the argument about having it in Short Hills vs. Manhattan.

"Lee just rolled over and played mamma's boy," Vicki said from atop the dress platform. "He justified it by saying, 'It'll probably be the last bar mitzvah Bunny goes to.' Ha! I should be so lucky."

Bella took the Akris off the hanger. Vicki lifted her arms up for Bella to slip the tank over her head. Vicki's ribs stuck out sharply.

"If we had famine tomorrow," said Bella, "you would not last the weekend."

"I'll swim in chocolate as soon as the bar mitzvah's over,"

said Vicki.

Once Vicki was dressed, the three women assessed. Vicki examined herself in the three-way mirror. Bella and Bonnie stood next to her, also staring into the glass. The skirt sagged a bit at the waist, but it still looked magnificent—sexy and chic, but conservative for temple.

Bonnie said, "Button the jacket."

Vicki tried that and turned left, right. "It does look more respectful of the Torah this way." She pronounced it toe-*rah*. "I know we decided to leave the jacket open. But is it *Jewisher* like this?"

Jewisher? Was that a noun or an adjective? Was it someone who wished she were Jewish, or at least wanted to marry a rich man who was?

Bella examined the look. "Jacket open" meant the Friday night for both Bella and Bonnie was shot. "Jacket closed" would make life easier for all of them.

"Jacket closed," she declared.

Bonnie and Vicki exhaled their relief.

The phone on the dresser rang. Vicki was in the process of removing the shell. "Bonnie? Can you put it on speaker?" She did as she was asked, and a voice came through.

"It's Bunny," said the meddler-in-law. "We have to talk about the carpeting."

Vicki balled up a scrawny fist and shook it at the phone. "We already talked about that, Bunny. Lee doesn't think it's a good idea."

"He thought it was a good idea when we carpeted the cul-de-sac for Lester and Rodney's bar mitzvahs." She was referring to Lee's sons from his first marriage. "If we don't carpet the street, the guests will have to walk *on the road* from their cars to the house. As I've told you *ad nauseam*, Laurel Lane doesn't have sidewalks. I will not have the guests walking on the street where they could stumble on loose gravel. There *will* be carpeting, and that is my final decision."

Vicki said, "People don't care about walking on the road. In New York, people walk on the street every day!"

"I'm sure they do all kinds of things in New York. In Short Hills, we *drive* on the street. We walk on sidewalks. Since there are no sidewalks, we carpet the pavement. I've already arranged it," crackled the voice on speaker. "I'll have them send Lee the bill."

"I've really got to go," said Vicki, struggling to stay civil. "I have friends over."

"Some girls from the pool?" Bunny asked, then hung up.

The pool? Was Vicki a swimmer?

"Goddamn her!" shrieked Vicki. "I haven't been a secretary for fifteen years!" Then she flung one of her pumps at the phone with deadly accuracy, sending pieces of plastic all over the dresser.

Bonnie and Bella gasped. Rushing forward, Bonnie picked up the Louboutin. Cradling it gently, like a kitten, Bonnie said, "It's okay. Not a scratch. Just a little shaken up, that's all."

Vicki pouted. "This has been a five-phone bar mitzvah."

"In times like this, we need *wadkeh*," said Bella.

"What the hell is *wadkeh*?" asked Vicki. And then, "Ohhhh. We have some in the freezer. The kitchen's downstairs. Go through the hidden door, walk down the secret hallway, and make a left where the portrait of Zachary used to be."

Bonnie pointed at her chest. "Me?" She didn't want to roam through Vicki's house by herself.

Bella was on her knees with pins in her mouth. Vicki was half-dressed with a Versace at her feet. "Yes, you," said Vicki. "Come on! I'm thirsty."

Should. Be. Grateful. "Of course. I'd be happy to serve. Is there anything else I can get for you?" asked Bonnie slightly sarcastically.

"Fresca," said Vicki. "For mixing."

Amazingly, Bonnie was able to find the hidden door—painted with wainscoting and paper that matched the living room wall— as well as the secret hallway, which was down a short flight of stairs. The Freed's apartment was actually three floors: the upstairs bedrooms, the main floor with the gilded living room and dining room, and a third floor below for the kitchen and probably a home movie theater and whatever else they had room for.

At the end of the hallway, Bonnie noticed a blank space on the wall. Zachary's portrait was now hanging in his grandmother's house over the front door in a weatherproof glass box that had been custom-made for the occasion, at Bunny's insistence, and charged to Lee's credit card.

Bonnie went left into a brightly lit Tuscan kitchen, which included a wood-burning oven and floor-to-ceiling, climate-controlled wine storage shelving. She found the freezer, although it was also designed to match the cabinetry. A frosty bottle of Grey Goose vodka was the only thing in there. Did the Freeds eat out every meal? Did Vicki eat at all?

Vodka was easy. Fresca, however, was hard. Not a can in the fridge. Maybe in a pantry? Bonnie started opening cabinets and doors. Lots of glassware, crystal, stoneware, and china. No Fresca.

She pushed a swinging door into another room. Red carpeting, a wall-size projection screen, three rows of seating. The Freed home theater looked like an actual theater, right down to the popcorn machine. Her eyes following a trail of kernels on the carpet, Bonnie came to a sneaker. With a leg attached.

Catching her heart, Bonnie said, "Oh my goodness, Zachary. You scared me."

The boy sat on a red velvet chair, playing with his Nintendo DS. Peter had one, too, and played for hours without looking up. Zachary seemed equally transfixed. He pushed buttons, concentrating, but he didn't say a word.

"Are you nervous for your big day tomorrow?" asked Bonnie, trying to be polite. She'd spent three hours with Zachary at Frankel's, choosing fabrics with Herm Weiss. Granted, that had been a few months ago. Had Zachary forgotten her? Didn't seem possible.

But the kid kept playing his game, wheezing slightly. He probably had earbuds in and couldn't hear her. Maybe with those long bangs swept over his eyes, he hadn't seen her. Bonnie stepped forward. "I brought your suit. It's upstairs if you want to try it on."

Nothing. She was close enough now to see his unobstructed ears. "Do you know where your mom keeps the Fresca?" she asked.

If he did, he wasn't telling. Zachary *had* spoken to her—grunted "whatever"—at Frankel's. His mom was poking him in the ribs, saying, "Well? Whaddaya think?" But here? In his own home? Zachary Freed wouldn't talk to anyone if he didn't want to.

Bonnie said, "Good luck tomorrow," and left. *That kid is going to have a rude awakening one day,* she thought. *If only I could be there to watch it, with a bag of popcorn.*

Back in the kitchen, Bonnie spotted yet another faux cabinet door. Afraid of what might be behind it, Bonnie pushed it open gently, just a crack, and peered inside.

Not a pantry. She could see only a mirrored wall, reflecting a treadmill, elliptical machine, free weight stand, and a trio of yoga balls. The thud of techno music made Bonnie's bladder vibrate. A female voice said, "Up, come on. Five more."

Bonnie opened the door a smidge wider. In the mirror, she could see them now, in profile. On a mat, Lee Freed lay on his back, bent knees, hands behind his head. A woman in black bike shorts and a sports bra straddled his groin.

She slapped him across the cheek and barked, "Get UP!"

Mr. Freed jackknifed at the waist to do a marine style sit-up until his nose, dripping sweat, touched the trainer's ample cleavage. He then lowered himself and repeated. Each time he dug his snout into the woman's chest, she counted. "One, two, faster, three…"

Bonnie closed the door. For a nanosecond, she hesitated, wondering if she could ask Mr. Freed where to find Fresca. *I think not,* she thought with a smile.

The first Mrs. Lee Freed had been her husband's peer, a Manhattan society lady. The second Mrs. Freed was the nanny hired to help his wife. The third Mrs. Freed, Vicki, was the secretary he'd hired to organize the new nanny and his two previous wives.

The fourth Mrs. Freed? A personal trainer? A woman he'd hired to help him to "get up," as it were? Did Vicki know? She'd been distracted by the bar mitzvah, but surely she'd been paying attention to her husband's leisure activities. Vicki could spot a loose thread on a dress from twenty yards. It hardly seemed possible she'd fail to notice how pretty her husband's trainer was. With huge knockers! What did a trainer need with those implants? Maybe the trainer's boobs were why Vicki got her own matched set. She was just keeping up with the help. Was it possible Vicki Freed was that threatened by Workout Barbie?

Bonnie took another peek.

Mr. Freed was now doing push-ups.

On top of the trainer.

Whose legs were spread-eagle beneath him.

Horrified, Bonnie grabbed the *wadkeh* bottle on the counter, ran down the secret hallway, through the hidden door, up the spiral staircase, through the master bed and master bath, and into the drive-thru closet. Breathless, she said, "Couldn't... find...Fresca."

"Not to worry!" said Vicki. "I forgot I had some up here already."

The client pointed at a mini fridge—faux cabinet veneer—which was stocked with cold cans.

"On ice, with a splash of the vodka," said Vicki.

"Sounds good," said Bella. "I'll have same."

Bonnie, the cocktail waitress, found chilled tumblers in the fridge as well as a dish of ice. She fixed the drinks and passed them around.

Then she sat back in the chair to catch her breath. She was just about even with it when a figure appeared in the closet doorway.

Mr. Freed, sweating in *way* too tight black bike shorts and a soaked T-shirt, stood there, face flushed and breathing labored. He looked two push-ups away from a heart attack.

"My mother just called my cell," he said to Vicki, completely ignoring Bonnie and Bella. *Like father, like son.* "She was crying.

She said you insulted her."

Vicki hopped off the platform and rushed at her husband, almost stepping on Bella's hand at her hem.

"Don't hug him!" warned Bonnie and Bella.

Vicki placed her hands on his shoulders, keeping his sweaty body at arm's length. "Bunny ordered the carpeting. Did she tell you that?"

"Shit," he said. "It's a fortune! Has she lost her freaking mind?"

Since when did Mr. Freed worry about what things cost? Sure, he had ex-wives and children to support and a bar mitzvah to pay for. But he hadn't batted an eye thus far, not when Vicki spent hundreds of thousands on clothes. Mr. Freed was a manufacturer, a "garmento." His family's factories produced all the licensed merchandise for top designers. Calvin socks, Ralph scarves, Gucci sunglasses. If Mr. Freed's business was suffering, that meant retail stores weren't ordering his product, which meant customers weren't buying it, which meant retail cutbacks. Bonnie had even more reason for serious anxiety.

Vicki asked, "Can't you tell her no?"

Mr. Freed looked at his wife as if she'd lost *her* mind. Just then, the sexy trainer came up behind him. Bonnie got a better look at her now. Blond, of course. Young, perfect body. Tanned, smooth legs and arms.

Vicki said, "Chris! I didn't know you were here."

"Last chance to work out before the big day," said Chris. "I want to make sure Lee looks great in his suit tomorrow. Not that he wouldn't. He's a rock!"

Then she slapped Mr. Freed on the belly, which rippled slightly on contact. He flinched a bit and said, "That's enough, Chris," with an unmistakable warning.

Bella blinked at Bonnie, who lowered her lids with embarrassment. How could Vicki not read the situation? Maybe she chose not to.

Mr. Freed said, "I'm going to shower."

"What about the street carpeting?" asked Vicki, climbing back onto the platform.

"Just humor her," he said. "She won't last much longer. And then we'll have enough money to carpet all of Short Hills."

"Fingers crossed!" said Vicki, as if she were praying for good weather and not the death of a relative.

Bonnie could easily imagine a similar scene taking place thirty years from now. Zachary would play the role of his father, speaking to his future wife on the eve of their child's bar or bat mitzvah, chatting casually about his own father's death, which wouldn't come soon enough. A lump formed in Bonnie's throat that Fresca couldn't wash away. God rue the day Peter talked to his future wife about Bonnie's death. Not that he'd stand to inherit much. One blessing about being relatively poor: no one was coming after her money.

Zachary appeared next in the closet doorway, his face just as red and agitated as his father's. "Look, Mom," said the kid, with full use of his vocal cords. "I need TiVo in my room."

Vicki said, "When I was a girl in Spokane, we had one TV in the whole house. We voted on what shows to watch."

"Spare me the walk down poverty lane," groaned Zachary. "All of my friends have TiVo and HD in their rooms. I've had the same cheap plasma for, like, three years."

"You should be watching less TV," said Vicki.

"Exactly! TiVo means no commercials. I'd have more time to do homework."

"That *is* a good argument. Why don't we wait until tomorrow to talk about it? You might really like one of your bar mitzvah gifts."

The kid got the not-so-subtle hint and skulked away.

Vicki sighed warmly. "My two men. They're why I do what I do. The aggravation, suffering, and stress are worth it."

Personal sacrifice in the name of love. That was how Vicki rationalized the compromises and trade-offs she'd made to stay in this marriage and family. The self-delusion was bone-deep. It had to be. Vicki was a pampered society wife, but she was a decent person. If she didn't love her husband and son, there was no way she'd stay.

"You're an amazing wife and mother," said Bonnie, hoping

she sounded sincere. If only Vicki's husband and son were half as attentive and kind, she thought.

Bella, who'd witnessed more than her share of true human suffering and had made devastating personal sacrifices for her son and husband (both deceased), held up her tumbler and said, "More."

"Oh, yes. Me too!" said Vicki.

Bonnie freshened their drinks. Only as an afterthought, she refilled her own.

Chapter Eight

A man in a tux. Was there anything sexier?

No, thought Bonnie. Nothing was hotter than a tall, slender man with good hair wearing a black Armani dinner jacket.

Bonnie mentally flipped through the pages of her fantasy catalog, trying to summon a more mouthwatering image. Mr. Depp, Mr. Wahlberg, and Mr. Bridges didn't hold a candle to Mr. Steve Kline in a tux.

In his studio in Menswear, Herm Weiss slipped an Armani jacket over Mr. Kline's broad shoulders. Bonnie nearly swooned. The sight was like a first bite of chocolate. Sinking into a Jacuzzi. Fresh peonies. Bonnie recalled her former compulsion of replaying the short scene from *Casino Royale* of Daniel Craig putting on a dinner jacket and checking himself out in a bathroom mirror. She must have gawked at that scene a hundred times.

Steve Kline made Daniel Craig look like the dog's dinner.

"What in the world are you thinking?" he asked, jerking Bonnie out of her reverie.

She stammered, "I…you need shoes. What size are you?" Even that sounded forward.

Steve said, "Eleven."

Bonnie gulped. The heat rose a few more degrees.

Herm Weiss stopped chalking, midline, and peered at Bonnie through his bifocals. "Mr. Kline, please face forward," he said.

"What do you think of this jacket?" he asked. Unlike 99 percent of her clients, Mr. Kline didn't stare at himself in the mirror while being tended to. Mr. Kline kept his eyes on Bonnie, which was unnerving.

"It's beautiful."

"Thanks for coming in on a Saturday," he said.

"Happy to."

When Bonnie woke up this morning, she lay in her rumpled bed thinking about her to-do list. Clean out the fridge. Go shopping for food and toilet paper. Pay a visit to her dad's to check on him and bring some food. Go to Anita's husband's repair shop about those weird rattling sounds her Camry was making (and have to endure the weird rattling sounds Anita would make about Bonnie's life). Peter was with Mike. Bonnie would fill the hours until Sunday with errands and chores, staying busy but always worrying about her son. It was the usual childfree weekend paradox of counting down the hours until she got some time to herself, and then missing Peter and wanting him to come home.

Weekends used to be full of friends and partying at Louie's or another local bar. What happened to all her pals? Life happened. People moved away. Their kids and careers took priority over friendship. Bonnie back-burnered her friends when she had Peter. How tight could the ties have been if they unraveled so easily? Friendships required work. Marriage required work. Parenthood was tremendous work. And, of course, it went without saying: work was work.

Bonnie's life had turned into nothing but responsibility and duty. As she lay in bed, she wondered, *What happened to fun? Pleasure? Bliss of the romantic variety? Would she ever feel that again?*

Her BlackBerry hummed on the crowded nightstand. She nearly toppled a box of tissues and stack of books when she reached for it. "Bonnie Madden," she answered.

"Steve Kline," he said.

"Good morning," she replied, sitting up in bed, her heart pounding. She thought about fun, and he called. At Christmas, when she was feeling miserable, he sent a gift. A man she barely knew had rescued her twice already.

"I'd like to buy a few suits to keep in my New York apartment," he said. "I've been packing a full suitcase whenever I fly in from Chicago. It's been a pain in the ass, frankly."

"Have you considered a second wardrobe? You'd never

have to carry luggage again," she suggested. The thought of styling an entire wardrobe for Steve Kline was like giving a kid the candy store.

"I can be there in ten minutes."

There? In Queens? God, no. What would he think of her if he saw her neat, but decidedly not-chic house? His opinion on her would plummet. *He didn't mean Queens,* she thought. He meant he could be at Frankel's in ten minutes. This was typical of clients who believed stylists didn't have a life outside of Frankel's.

It was a Saturday. Did she want to go to her job on her day off? *Let's see,* she thought. Spend the day watching the star of her sexual fantasies try on designer suits or drag herself up and down Queens Boulevard running errands? It was the definition of a no-brainer.

"Can we make it an hour?" she asked.

"Sure," he said.

"Okay. See you at the Salon."

Bonnie threw back her covers and jumped out of bed. She dressed in her standard work ensemble: gray wool slacks, a black cashmere sweater, and black leather booties. Classic and sexy.

Two hours later, she was staring at Mr. Kline in an Armani tux as Herm drew chalk alteration marks on the shoulders. Mr. Kline fingered the sleeve. "What's the fabric?" he asked.

"Wool," said Bonnie.

"It's heavy. Here, feel it."

"It's lightweight year-round wool," she said. She stood up and stepped close enough to touch the lapel. From within the circle of Mr. Kline's personal space, Bonnie could smell his clean hair and the chalk.

"Do you honestly like it better than my old tux?"

Bonnie flashed to seeing him in the revolving door at the St. Regis in his wide-lapel, three-button dinner jacket. "I don't…"

"You saw it," he said. "We went through the revolving door at the St. Regis together back in September. I was wearing my old tux. You think this is better, right?"

I think I might melt. She couldn't believe he remembered that random small encounter. She could barely speak, but got out,

"This is much better."

Herm said, "Should I leave you two alone?"

Bonnie must have blushed fire engine red. Mr. Kline cleared his throat.

Herm bent to his knees to pin the trouser hem. For suit pants, Bonnie liked two breaks in the fabric before the shoe. On a tux, though, she preferred one break, as did Herm, who was, at the moment, having some trouble getting the hem to fall evenly. "Oy," he said. And then, "Bonnie. Come outside with me for one minute. Mr. Kline, stay right there."

Taking Bonnie's elbow, Herm brought her into the Menswear Department.

"Problem?" she asked Herm.

"I can't tailor Mr. Kline's trousers with the *schwanz* like that."

"I'm sorry, the…" Was he saying what she thought he was saying?

"The *schwanz*! He's dressing to the *right*, to the *left*. It's all over the place. The hem keeps rising."

Bonnie almost died of embarrassment right there by the sweater display. "I had no idea he was…uncomfortable," she claimed.

"*Nisht keshtoygen, nisht kefloygen,*" said Herm.

"My Yiddish is a bit rusty," said Bonnie.

"It means *bullshit*. You know *he's* uncomfortable. He knows *you're* uncomfortable. And I'm too old to be part of a threesome. You're banned until I finish hemming. I'll tell Mr. Kline you went for the shoes." And then he went back into the studio.

Is Steve Kline really that attracted to me? Couldn't be. Bonnie was attractive. In New York, everyone was attractive. She wasn't a movie star, a legendary wit, a social peer, or young. But she was available. She was *there*. Sheer availability and servitude had a geisha-like appeal to a certain type of man. But Steve Kline didn't seem like a power-crazed jerk.

He had sought her out. He'd been pursuing her nonaggressively for over a month. God knows, Bonnie was flattered by the attention. She took it as friendly, not daring to imagine he was seriously after her. If he did come right out and ask her to dinner, she had no idea how she'd react. Logically, she shouldn't. He was a client, and he was married. Her feelings on the moral matter had been swinging back and forth since she'd met him. No matter how she rationalized it, cheating was wrong. She just didn't know yet if being wrong was such a terrible sin. If so, Manhattan would have sunk into the Atlantic Ocean by now.

Her BlackBerry interrupted her thoughts. Bonnie checked caller ID. "Mrs. Freed?" she answered. "How's the bar mitzvah going?" The temple portion had been over since noon. The cocktail party would begin at five.

"The service was great," said Vicki. "I looked sensational in the Akris. Everyone stared at me."

Narcissist, thought Bonnie. "That's wonderful. And the Versace? The party is ready to go?"

"Pretty much," said Vicki. "A few minor hiccups with the caterer and heating the outdoor tents. I hate to tell you this, Bonnie, but we've got a problem with my mother-in-law's dress."

Darn. Bonnie knew she should have insisted the woman come to Frankel's for a fitting with Bella. "The hem?"

"It's got a plastic security tag on the underslip," said Vicki. "I called Neiman Marcus and Bloomingdale's at the Short Hills Mall, but they said they couldn't remove it. I almost took a wire cutter to it, but I'm afraid to damage the fabric. No one will see it, but Bunny is furious. She's blaming me."

Frankel's had a unique zonker—the two-part plastic tag that set off alarms if passed through security scanners. Every major store had a custom design. The only way to get a Frankel's zonker off was to use a Frankel's zonker remover. Department checkouts had one built into the counter. Handheld remover keys were kept in the shipping department in the Cage. Jesus, the Key Master, would sign out a handheld, but only in exchange for a pint of blood. And it was *never* to leave the premises. Maybe, if she begged, Jesus would let Bonnie take a key to Short Hills, but she doubted he was working on a Saturday.

She'd left a zonker on Bunny Freed's dress. This was a major blunder. Bonnie felt dizzy. Bunny would surely lodge a complaint with Mr. Charles. This carelessness on her part—she was *sure* she scanned for zonkers and removed two from the Oscar before she put it in the garment bag—would be the last straw. Why did the dress have a *third* zonker? One was standard. Two for pricier items. But three? Unheard of.

"I am beyond sorry, Mrs. Freed. I'll take care of it. If you text me the address in Short Hills, I'll come to you."

"The party starts in an hour and a half," said Vicki. "The traffic on the turnpike on a Saturday—it'll be an hour just getting through the tunnel. You'll never make it."

"I'll make it."

Her next call was to Jesus, who picked up from his home in Jamaica, Queens. Bonnie told him the story. "How'd you get it out of the building with the zonker attached?"

"No clue."

"The zonker could be defective. That's why it didn't beep when you scanned for the other two." He paused. "So you need a key to take to Jersey. We'll both get fired if Mr. Charles finds out."

"I swear on my ex-husband's life," said Bonnie.

Jesus guffawed. "For what that's worth, right?"

"Starbucks for a year, still on the table."

"Don't worry about it. Go to the Cage. I'll call Roger and tell him you need to sign out a handheld for the Salon. Bring it back to him *before the store closes* tonight."

Bonnie hung up and loudly cursed her life. At that moment, Mr. Kline walked out of the fitting room with Herm.

"That bad?" he asked.

"It's not the tux. It's magnificent. I have an emergency in New Jersey," she said. "I'm so sorry, but I have to go. Can we reschedule?"

Mr. Kline frowned. "Jersey, huh? How are you getting there?"

She hadn't thought that far. "Car service, I guess. Or taxi." Bonnie would wind up eating the cost, probably $200 roundtrip, maybe more.

"I'll take you. I've been meaning to pick your brain about a project of mine. This way, we can do each other a favor," said

Mr. Kline.

She hesitated. Pick her brain? Was that why he was being so nice to her? The well-and-tree platter. This New York wardrobe. The ride. What on earth could she tell him that he didn't already know? How to style a socialite? Why would he care? She couldn't help feeling disappointed, too, and a little insulted about the "brain" remark. He wasn't after her body?

She said, "That's very nice of you to offer, but…"

"You're only wasting time by refusing."

Oh, why *not*? She had to get there fast, and he had a car. Spending more time with him was like a fantasy come true. "Okay, yes. Let's go. I have to grab something first," she said.

"I'll wait on Madison."

"How will I know which is your car?"

"It's a black limo parked right out front. My driver, Serge, is a 300-pound Serbian with a scar across his cheek. Literally, you can't miss him."

"Thank you, Mr. Kline."

He smiled and said, "You really have to stop calling me Mr. Kline."

Ten minutes later, Bonnie ran out the Madison Avenue entrance with the zonker key in her purse and coat on her arm. Her eyes went to a man mountain with a red bolt across his cheek and a chauffeur cap standing beside a sleek black limousine.

He said, "Ms. Madden?"

"Serge?"

"Allow me." He opened the rear door, took her hand, and helped her into the limo's cavernous interior.

Steve Kline was already seated inside, dapper in his gray suit. He looked born to ride in limos. "I have to make a three-minute stop first," he said. "It's on the way to the Tunnel. I hope you don't mind."

Bonnie exhaled. "Not at all."

"Good." He stretched his legs, leaning into the soft leather seat. "So what's the big emergency anyway?"

"A missing button," she said, purposefully evasive. Mr. Kline and Mr. Charles were pals. If Mr. Kline told his school bud that he'd taken Bonnie to Mrs. Freed's bar mitzvah party to perform an emergency "zonkerectomy," Mr. Charles would be furious. Also, as titillating as it was to be alone in the backseat with a handsome man—this was how Bonnie lost her virginity—she found his interest in her suspicious.

"Serge needs to know where we're going," he prompted.

Bonnie recited the address and watched through the divider as Serge typed the info into the dashboard GPS. And then they headed downtown.

"Short Hills?" asked Steve. "Job interview at the Mall?" He was referring to the famous Mall at Short Hills, anchored by Bloomingdale's, Macy's, Neiman Marcus, and Nordstrom. Its hundreds of stores included upscale Chanel, Dolce and Gabbana, Louis Vuitton, Cartier, Gucci, Prada, and Hermés, trickling all the way down to low-scale (by comparison) Ann Taylor, Anthropologie, Juicy, and J. Crew.

"I'm very happy at Frankel's and have no intention of leaving," she said. "Are you spying on me for Mr. Charles?"

He laughed. "Hardly. If anything, it's the other way around."

And what did that mean? Bonnie didn't hazard a guess. Nervous now, unsure what to say, Bonnie looked out the window as the limo cruised downtown. Even if her eyes weren't on him, he engulfed her other senses. He smelled divine, as did the limo. His hand was within easy reach of hers. She could feel the magnetic pull of his body. She took a deep breath. Her hands felt sweaty, and her pulse raced. This was a powerful attraction. She hadn't felt like this since the early days with Mike, when she'd been in the throes of teenage hormones. Bonnie had no idea that someone in her thirties could feel like a teenager.

Mr. Kline asked, "Did you have a nice holiday?"

Christmas was weeks ago. "Yes, thank you. And you?"

"I went to Chicago and got to spend time with my sons."

Bonnie noticed that he didn't use the marital "we" pronoun. He hadn't mentioned his wife Joanne all day, in fact.

"Do any booking while you were gone?" she asked.

"Booking?" he asked, puzzled.

"Aren't you a bookie?"

He seemed confused, and then he remembered. "The proper term is 'book making.' And I'm not really a bookie."

"I know." Bonnie was as good a Googler as she was a stylist. One click of the mouse revealed that Mr. Kline owned nearly every strip mall in Illinois. He'd started out buying a single store on Lakeshore Drive in 1985, about five years before a huge real estate boom in Chicago. Mrs. Joanne Kline was equal partner in their corporation, which now did business in five states. The couple had two sons. Their younger son, Brian, a handsome kid and a senior at Northwestern, posted hundreds of photos of himself on Facebook partying at nightclubs, bars, and, recently, Caesar's Palace in Vegas. The older son, Jack, was a vice president at Kline and Co., although, according to an article she read in *Forbes*, Jack didn't have any real responsibilities. He was a VP by nepotism, not accomplishment.

As for the Kline marriage, it was a mystery. Whenever the couple was photographed together, they didn't touch. They seemed comfortable together, more like brother and sister than husband and wife. Or maybe that was Bonnie's wishful thinking.

"I got your note," he said.

Along with the text message, Bonnie sent a formal note to thank him for the silver platter. In fatter years, Bonnie received gifts from clients, such as bottles of champagne and beauty treatments at Elizabeth Arden (which she always found vaguely insulting). Mr. Kline's had been the most extravagant gift she'd received from anyone, ever, including her engagement ring.

"I can't thank you enough," she said.

"I hope you're getting some use out of it."

"I have put it to excellent use."

Immediately after unwrapping the platter, Bonnie kick-started her BlackBerry. She placed discreet calls to three of her favorite silver dealers. Within the hour, she'd sold the well-and-tree platter for enough to cover the tuition bill. The dealer was thrilled. Most likely he'd put the platter in storage for a few years until the design was unavailable. Then he'd show it as a Starck collectable and resell it for double the value. Although she'd recycled gifts before, Bonnie had never sold one off. In dire straits, she lost all sentimentality. The platter appeared on her desk. It might as well have been an envelope full of cash. Bonnie did what she had to do.

Now, weeks later, sitting next to Mr. Kline in close quarters, Bonnie felt a pang of regret and guilt. She would have loved to tell Mr. Kline the truth to alleviate her negative emotions. But she doubted he'd understand. Maybe Mr. Kline was the kind of self-made man who remembered what life was like before he could drop $15,000 without hyperventilating. Most of the wealthy—as opposed to the merely rich—blocked out the grubby reality of life beneath their class and hated to be reminded.

He'd probably dump her on the street if she told him about her reality. She'd *never* say, "The truth is, sir, my son is autistic with OCD and ADHD. I sold the platter to pay his tuition at a school where I know he'll be safe."

Instead, Bonnie said, "Are you meeting your wife downtown?"

Mr. Kline frowned. Before he could answer, the limo pulled to a stop outside an abandoned warehouse on Barrow Street in the West Village. "You like it?" he asked, pointing outside the limo window.

"What am I looking at?"

"The building."

It was a dilapidated graffiti-covered disaster. "It's a blight," she said. "I mean, a sight!"

He laughed. "Try to see the potential, the building as it might be."

Bonnie dutifully examined the structure, seeing only the rusted metal door, the crumbling façade, the windows x-ed with tape. She tried to dress it up and style it, like she would a woman who'd come into the Salon for a makeover. Bonnie started to see what this brick-and-mortar mess could be. She renovated in her mind, felt buoyed by the exercise. It reminded her of the satisfaction of making the perfect match between a client and a dress. She smiled and looked back at Mr. Kline.

He was staring *at her*. "I consider myself an expert on seeing potential where others don't—in buildings and people. I need two minutes," said Mr. Kline. "Be right back."

Serge opened the door for him. Bonnie watched out the window as Mr. Kline hailed and then shook hands with a man in a hat and overcoat, their breath visible in the cold.

He returned five minutes later, grinning. Serge pulled into traffic, and they were on their way to the Tunnel and New Jersey.

She had to ask. "Big plans for the warehouse?"

"I'm going to try something I've never done before. And that's why I wanted to take a ride with you."

Huh? Was that a proposition? "I'm sorry…"

"You probably know my company owns a lot of real estate," he said. "I rent to stores, but I've never opened my own store."

Oh. Not a proposition. Just shoptalk. Bonnie said, "Mr. Charles can tell you everything you need to know. You should pick his brain."

"I have. I picked his brain clean. And now I want to pick yours."

The limo reached the mouth of the Tunnel. Bonnie felt on the spot. "I have to defer to whatever Mr. Charles told you about Frankel's."

"He didn't tell me anything!" said Mr. Kline. "He might as well have been reading a press release about how wonderful the store is, how brilliant he is at running it, and how his employees revere and idolize him."

Bonnie stifled a snort. He looked so interested, so eager to talk, Bonnie felt herself wanting to open up. It'd been a long time since someone asked for her opinion—besides, "Does this make me look fat?"

"What do you want to know?"

"Tell me about customer loyalty. That's the holy grail of business."

"Like all relationships, you need trust," said Bonnie. "My clients have to trust me to make the right recommendations. I have to do the right thing for them, even if they don't agree." Bonnie told a few war stories. Like the time when she'd pushed a client to wear something and then they were rewarded with flattering press. Ego made her paint herself in a glowing light. Why not? She was good at her job and worked incredibly hard at it. She did have a sixth sense for fashion and many loyal customers. Some had followed her store to store over the years, like Gloria Rodkin.

Steve listened closely. He nodded and encouraged her, his body open toward her, an arm against the backseat, so close to her neck. His laser focus on her was seductive. She found herself espousing, liking the sound of her own voice. Bonnie had four years' worth of Frankel's stories she hadn't been able to tell Mike. They all came pouring out in the limo with Steve. The celebrity client who came in with a severe rash all over her body, maybe contagious, wanting to try on $10,000 gowns and bathing suits. The socialite who tried to sneak a huge bill past her stingy husband and, upon his discovering her charges, his divorcing her. The famous writer who bought designer outfits to wear to benefits and then returned them the next day with food and beverage stains on them, expecting a full refund. A starlet who shot up heroin in the fitting room. A local politician who bartered for free suits in exchange for voting to reduce sales tax in the city.

By the time they got to Short Hills, Bonnie and Steve were laughing like old friends. For a second, she was worried she'd said too much. But Bonnie had been careful. No names. No dates. Unlike name-dropper Chase Charles, Bonnie could keep a secret. She made that point to Steve, and he didn't once try to get real names out of her.

"I don't know what any of this has to do with opening your own store," she said.

He shrugged. "Helps to know what I can expect. What did you say to the actress with the rash? You didn't let her try on dresses, did you?"

"Of course not!" said Bonnie. "I called another client—a dermatologist—who agreed to see the actress right away. I took her to the appointment myself. I lost an hour of work, and Mr. Charles was…upset. But the actress came back a few weeks later, skin healed, and went on a wild spending spree. Plus, the dermatologist was so excited to have a celebrity client, she came into the store to thank me, and wound up buying a diamond necklace for herself."

"Well done!" he said, applauding.

"Thank you, thank you," said Bonnie, accepting the praise. "Selling jewels and saving lives, all in a day's work."

Serge said, "Sorry to interrupt. We'll be there in a few minutes."

Bonnie looked out the window as they drove through Short Hills, a tiny dot in the middle of northern New Jersey. Although Short Hills was small geographically, its twelve thousand residents had the eleventh largest per capita income in all of America.

Lee Freed grew up here. His parents lived at the top of Laurel Lane, a woodsy cul-de-sac with five-acre lots and turreted mansions. They reminded Bonnie of fairy tales and bucolic country scenes found on toilet wallpaper. Short Hills was only about twenty-five miles from midtown Manhattan, making it a Wall Streeter enclave.

"What's this?" asked Serge. He was confused by the fact that, halfway up the block, the pavement ended and red carpeting began.

The carpeting led to the Freed mansion, brilliantly illuminated by dozens of torches. Zachary had chosen a Hawaiian theme for his party. For his required charitable service, Vicki took Zach to Honolulu to feed the homeless. ("It would have been too easy to work at a soup kitchen in New York," Vicki explained. "But taking a ten-hour plane ride to help the poor? That was a legitimate sacrifice.")

"I'll run in," said Bonnie, grabbing her purse. "Back in ten minutes."

Steve said, "I'll escort you."

Serge had climbed out of the limo and opened the door for Bonnie. "No," she said. "It might embarrass my client to see me with someone. This is very hush-hush." The Freeds might recognize Mr. Kline. That would definitely start the gossip mill turning, which Bonnie didn't need.

After a moment's convincing, Steve agreed to stay with the limo. Bonnie hoofed toward the tiki-torch-lit house. It was a modern marvel with parallel flat roofs, stone masonry columns, glass walls, and deco window panes. The architect had tried to duplicate the drama of Frank Lloyd Wright's "Fallingwater" home in Pennsylvania. Like a knock-off designer handbag, the house was convincing at first glance. But as Bonnie looked closer, she saw it was a little shabby and outdated.

Vicki opened the front door, dressed in her Versace, hair and makeup perfect. Above their heads, the portrait of Zachary encased in glass.

"Thank God you're here. Hurry!" said Vicki, waving Bonnie inside.

The decor was minimalist to the point of Spartan. Through the interior glass walls, Bonnie saw several party tents in the backyard. A large rectangular swimming pool, uncovered, had rafts of tropical flowers floating on the water surface. From the rising steam, Bonnie guessed that the water was the temperature of a hot tub—in February. The pool's heating bill alone for the night would be astronomical.

Caterers, servers, suited planners, and florists were crawling all over the place like ants at a picnic. Vicki said, "This way. My in-laws are getting dressed down the hallway."

"The house is gigantic," said Bonnie.

"Notice how there's no furniture?" asked Vicki. "Bunny insisted on putting their possessions in storage so that the guests don't break or steal anything. Lee had to pay for the moving and storage, of course."

"How many guests?" Bonnie nearly collided with a florist carrying a towering birds of paradise hibiscus arrangement.

"Five hundred," said Vicki. "That is a lot of people. But they'll be outside in the tents, not trampling through the place. We offered to host a party at the country club. But *no*. Bunny and Benny insisted the bar mitzvah party be right *here*, where Lee and his two other sons had theirs."

"Bunny and Benny?"

"I know. This is it." Vicki stopped abruptly and knocked on a door. "Bunny? Are you decent?" Whispering to Bonnie, she said, "As if *that* were possible."

Bonnie was expecting a hatchet-faced battle-ax, so she was taken aback by the stooped, white-haired, little old lady who opened the door.

"This is Bonnie Madden," introduced Vicki. "She's here to remove the tag."

The elder Mrs. Freed smiled and then said, "Thank you for coming, dear. I hate to trouble you."

Her tone was pure sugar! This couldn't be the same harpy she'd heard on speakerphone last night. "No trouble at all," said Bonnie.

She entered the room, expecting Vicki to follow. But the old woman slammed the door in her daughter-in-law's face.

"Stupid slut!" hissed Bunny. Then, smiling sweetly at Bonnie, she said, "Tell me, dear, have you ever met a woman as shallow as my daughter-in-law?"

God, yes, she thought. Bonnie placed Vicki among the good ones, actually. Granted, the third Mrs. Lee Freed was not one of the great minds of her generation. But she meant well. She was generous and treated Bonnie with respect.

"I have the tag remover," said Bonnie neutrally. "If you show me the dress, I'll take care of it and get out of your way."

"Oh, so you're a bitch, too, huh?" snarled Bunny. "The dress is on the bed. If you damage it, I expect a full refund." She went into what Bonnie assumed was the master bathroom.

She was a bitch for *not* trashing her client? The elder Mrs. Freed had impossible standards for bitchery. After five minutes in the house, Bonnie's drama limit was maxed out. She found the dress on the bed. The zonker came off without a problem. Bonnie put the two plastic pieces in her bag along with the handheld device. What now? Sneak out, or announce her departure? It'd be rude just to leave, and Mrs. Freed probably wanted to inspect the dress.

She took a few steps toward the bathroom. Bunny and her husband, Benny, Lee's father and boss at Freed & Sons

Manufacturing, stood at their sinks. Bonnie overheard a snippet of conversation.

"Lee can't afford this party," said Mr. Freed in a gruff, quaking voice. "Carpeting the street? Heating the pool? Four-course meal for five hundred? I'm still angry about moving the furniture. And for what? To celebrate that brat of his? He'll go broke over this night. Mark my words."

"You don't have to tell me," said Mrs. Freed. "I begged him to keep costs under control. The carpeting is insane! But Lee insisted. It's Vicki's fault, of course. If Lee can't indulge that woman...with the way business has been lately...I'm afraid for his marriage. She's such a gold digger. If the business goes under, she'd leave him in a heartbeat."

"Better brace yourself for that possibility," said Mr. Freed. "We're looking at another very bad year. No one's buying."

Shocked for at least three reasons by this conversation, Bonnie backed away softly. Standing by the bed, she yelled, "The tag is off and the dress is fine. Okay, I'm leaving. Congratulations! Bye," and then dashed out of there.

Vicki intercepted Bonnie on the way out. "Everything okay?"

"She's all set. Just in time. Your guests have started to arrive." Through the glass walls, Bonnie counted a dozen cars lining up at the red carpet, attended to by a team of valets.

"Did she say anything about me?" asked Vicki, her eyes wide and hopeful. "She called me a stupid slut, right?"

"No!" said Bonnie.

Vicki arched one perfectly shaped eyebrow, leaned forward, and kissed Bonnie's cheek. "Thanks for coming. You're the first friendly face I've seen all day. I've been smiling for hours at people I barely know. And hardly any of them have seen me naked." Vicki smiled warmly.

"It was my pleasure," said Bonnie, almost meaning it. As superficial and narcissistic as Vicki seemed, she was a kind person. She didn't deserve the betrayal and plotting around her. Bunny was intentionally pushing Lee to bankrupt himself with the ulterior motive of breaking up his marriage. What did Bunny hope to gain? To drive her son back home, into her glass house? Was the old woman that selfish and spiteful?

Vicki's parents were both deceased. She was left with Lee's clan, and no one in that family—not her in-laws, her cheating husband, her greedy son—was on her side. Bonnie felt protective of her client suddenly, like an older sister.

"Well, you look breathtaking," said Bonnie. "Congrats to you and Zachary. This really is the beautiful setting for a party."

Vicki nodded and said, "The minute they're dead, I'm bulldozing this house to the ground."

On the drive back to the city, Bonnie was a lot quieter. As much as she loved talking with Steve Kline, she had to remember that her clients were people, not just stories to swap for fun and gossip.

"This isn't the best time to open a store," said Bonnie.

Steve nodded. "Not a luxury store, true. What do you think about disposable fashion, like H&M and Uniqlo?"

Disposable fashion was inexpensive trendy clothes, designed and intended to be worn for a season and then be thrown away. The philosophy was the opposite of what Bonnie sold at Frankel's: timeless investment pieces that transcended trends and were built to last. Of course, most people couldn't afford to pay as much for a coat as a used car.

"Cheap chic is doing well and will probably stay hot. A lot of my clients are going downtown with their kids to Top Shop and Uniqlo. The trends trickle up, too. The down market comes up with an idea, and then upscale designers adapt it for their lines a year later."

"Trends have always trickled up," he said.

"Not true," she said. "The mass versus class lines are blurrier than ever. The rich want to be cool, and the cool want to be rich. Designers who used to be huge snobs are now giving freebies to reality TV stars. It's a lowbrow and highbrow culture clash. Personally, I don't think that's going to change anytime soon."

"Fashion has gone socialist," said Steve. "I'd better alert my congressman."

Bonnie laughed. "I worry about high end, though. On a purely personal level. The idea of exclusivity drives my business. When that goes, what's left for Frankel's?"

"Maybe you'd be happier somewhere else."

The idea of switching jobs filled Bonnie with panic. She needed steady income, reliable benefits. Remembering suddenly that anything she said to Mr. Kline might be repeated to Mr. Charles, Bonnie said, "I'm very happy right where I am."

They'd already come through the Tunnel and were nearly back at the store. When Serge pulled up, Bonnie had only a few minutes to get the zonker key back to the Cage before closing.

"Thanks. I really appreciate this," said Bonnie, exiting the limo.

"I'd love to talk more," said Mr. Kline. "Get to know you better."

What did that mean? More brain-picking? Bonnie said, "We can talk shop anytime. Just call for an appointment." Her tone was clipped. Her mood had taken a hairpin turn from jovial to sober. She'd enjoyed his company tremendously. He was easy to talk to and look at. She could see herself giving in to temptation all too easily.

But not today. Not for as long as she could think straight in his presence. She closed the door, and Serge pulled away. She felt better, more in control of herself, now that he was gone.

God, she hoped he'd come back.

Chapter Nine

Sunday afternoon was the perfect time—and only time—Bonnie had for a mani-pedi with her sister. The salon trip was Anita's idea. Her way, as she said on the phone this morning, "to say 'sorry' for being a bitch at Christmas."

Anita was referring to that nasty "shopgirl" comment. Although Bonnie liked the idea that Anita had been stewing with regret for the last few weeks, Bonnie was already over it. Christmas was ancient history by now. Bonnie had moved on to bigger and thornier concerns, like her deepening feelings for Steve Kline and her warning at work. She couldn't possibly talk to Anita about either of those problems, though. Anita would be horrified about her flirtation with a married man, and she'd jump on any trouble at Frankel's as proof that Bonnie didn't fit in and didn't belong there anyway.

Anita, according to herself, had been true to her roots and true to herself. She'd barely moved a mile since high school. At twenty, she had married Frankie Alto, the boy down the block, and worked part time at his auto repair shop when she wasn't chasing her three kids. Anita's life looked nearly identical to their mother's—at least until Sylvia left Vinny and struck out on her own.

When Bonnie left home, she'd aimed upward. Anita, sideways. Today, they met on a level playing field: at Rita's, the Corona salon they'd been going to since high school. The space hadn't changed much since then, except for the pedicure chairs, which got higher-tech and cushier every year. Proprietress Rita looked exactly the same as when Bonnie was a teenager. She spoke salon English only. She could articulate "quick-dry topcoat, two dollar," and "back massage, ten minute, ten dollar," but she couldn't order an omelet at the diner across the street. That said, Rita's English was far superior to Bonnie's Korean. At this salon, Bonnie was the client. The manicurists were at her service. Only too sensitive to the dynamic, Bonnie was an extravagant tipper.

"I'm here," said Bonnie, breathless as she walked through the door. She was only five minutes late—good for her. Anita was perusing the polish selection.

"I just walked in," said Anita. They kissed hello. "You look good."

"You too." Anita, in jeans and a red fleece zip-up, looked a bit stressed and haggard. Or maybe it was just dry skin. As usual, upon her entrance, Bonnie was surrounded by manicurists who remembered her large tips from past visits.

"They love you here," observed Anita.

Bonnie shrugged. "How're the kids?"

"Pains in the ass. Spoiled brats. They don't know how good they have it," which was her sister's way of saying everyone was fine. "How's Peter?"

"He's doing really well." Although Bonnie hesitated to admit it, the blinking light glasses seemed to have a soothing effect on Peter. While wearing them, he was marginally less anxious. Mike was so encouraged that he'd started taking Peter to weekly therapy sessions with a shrink on Long Island who specialized in brain hemisphere balance. Bonnie had gone to the introductory assessment. Peter's autism was determined to be "mild" as opposed to his initial classification of "moderate." Mike was convinced the wacky glasses and brain balance exercises (stand on one leg while saying the alphabet backward, for example) were correcting Peter's neurological disorder. He believed that one day, he'd be able to take his son to a Giants game with fifty thousand screaming fans. The very idea of it filled Bonnie with anxiety on Peter's behalf, but she kept her fears to herself.

Anita said, "What do you think?" She held up a bottle of polish, the shade named "Siren Call," a garish red.

"I like it." Bonnie chose "Champagne Nights," a pink-gold neutral.

They were ushered to pedicure chairs. In hot, eucalyptus-scented water, they soaked their feet. Bonnie let herself relax—well, as much as she could.

"Have you spoken to Mom?" asked Anita.

"Not this week."

"She's serious with Carmine. They might get married."

"For Christ's sake, *why*? I thought she swore she'd never marry again."

Anita snickered. "Frankie's praying for it. Business would double overnight."

"Bullet holes and slashed tire repairs."

"Shush," said Anita, glancing around.

The pedicurist began the long-overdue process of shaping Bonnie's toenails.

"How's work?" asked Anita.

"Crazy," said Bonnie. "Yesterday, I had to make an emergency run to Jersey. A client had his chauffeur drive me out there in a limo. Last time I had an emergency, Mike took me to Midtown in the Crown Vic. I liked the limo better."

"Yeah. Don't get used to it."

"Ouch," said Bonnie, withdrawing her foot from a too-aggressive cuticle cutting. She felt her entire body tense, waiting for Anita's "apology" to feel like a fresh slap across the cheek. But the apology didn't come.

"Have you spoken to Mike lately?" asked Anita.

"I speak to Mike practically every day. I talked to Dad yesterday, too. Anyone else you want to grill me about?"

"Did Mike tell you he got engaged?"

Bonnie's eye widened. She couldn't speak. She tried, but only a squeak came out. Mike proposed to that Emily? How could he do that without asking Bonnie first? Bonnie had every right to weigh in on the woman who would become Peter's stepmother. This was wrong. She should at least get the chance to talk to this woman. A hot sting of tears hit Bonnie' cheeks. She wiped them away quickly. Anita studied her closely. Was her sister gloating?

"Yeah, Mike proposed to his girlfriend at Ragussa's,

probably around the same time you were cruising around Jersey in a limo. Mom saw the whole thing and she's freaking out."

Bonnie found it hard to breathe. "This was yesterday?"

"Last night. Valentine's Day."

Bonnie had forgotten. She'd remarked, months ago, that Zachary's bar mitzvah was on Valentine's Day, but that fact faded in significance as the event drew near. Valentine's Day had been an abstraction for years anyway. Bonnie realized she spent practically all of Valentine's Day with Steve Kline. Where was his wife? Why hadn't he been with her?

"Good for Mike," said Bonnie numbly. "I'm sure Emily is a very nice person."

"To be completely honest, I think it's weird you don't know her," said Anita. "She's been spending so much time with Peter. I thought you'd want to check her out."

Bonnie didn't like Anita's unspoken accusation. She was right, though. Bonnie should have demanded an introduction instead of passively waiting for Mike to initiate it. Would Emily, a police detective, be a devoted stepmom? Would she be patient? Loving? Emily probably wanted kids of her own. How would that affect Mike and Peter's relationship? No more Christmas mornings with just Mike, Bonnie, and Peter. No more Crown Vic high-speed rides to Manhattan. Mike belonged to another woman. Grim reality hit hard. *He's really gone now*, Bonnie thought. *No hope of his ever coming back.*

"I'm sorry to lay it on you like this," said Anita, looking genuinely pained. "But you needed to know, and no one else wanted to tell you."

"I guess I should thank you," said Bonnie sarcastically.

Anita frowned. "I know you don't want to hear the truth, Bonnie. But as your big sister, I have to say it. The emergency in your life? It's not some fashion fire to put out at Frankel's. Your problems are right here in Queens, with Mike and Peter, your family. *And you don't even know it.*"

The entire salon, customers and staff, had fallen silent. News of this scene would reach the farthest corners of Corona in approximately three minutes.

Bonnie tried to keep her expression blank. But then she lost it. She couldn't contain her anger any longer. "You don't know anything about what I need or what matters in my life. I want different things for myself, things you lack the creativity to even begin to imagine. You take a perverse pleasure in reminding me what's wrong with me. But not once have you ever tried to help me. You barely look at Peter. You don't talk to him. I've watched you turn your back on him when he asked you a question. You're afraid of him because he's different. You bristle around a harmless little boy who has never hurt anyone or ever will. He's got more compassion and love in his heart than you do, Anita. You don't know him or have the slightest understanding of our relationship. Don't you dare tell me I've failed my family again. You failed me, okay? You want to know what failure looks like, check in the mirror," said Bonnie.

She yanked her jeans down, putting her socks and shoes on wet feet. She made for the door, not looking back at Anita. Bonnie grabbed her coat and paused to rummage in her purse for a twenty. She was supposed to pick up Peter at Mike's house in a few hours. He'd tell her the news. Emily would be there (dear God). Bonnie would pretend to be happy for him. Did Peter know? He had to. He spent the weekend with Mike—and his fiancée. Bonnie felt sick.

Rita said, "No charge."

"I have to take care of the girl," said Bonnie, on the verge of tears.

In perfect English, Rita said, "Take care of yourself."

"Tell me another story," said Steve Kline on the phone.

"Have I mentioned the Wall Street baron who always bought four identical dresses for his wife, ex-wife, daughter, and mistress?" asked Bonnie.

"Oh, God," said Steve. "That's creepy."

"I've got to go," she said, although she didn't want to hang up. Steve had called or messaged Bonnie every day this week, and he never insulted, threatened, or complained to her. Ridiculous as it might seem, he was the bright light in her day. "Why don't you come in for some shirts? Then we can talk while I work," she suggested, surprising herself by how forward that sounded.

"I'm in Chicago, or I'd be sitting in your tiny office right now."

Amazing how chummy you could get on the phone and email. Texting was a shortcut to intimacy—the platonic kind. "In Chicago? Is Mrs. Kline with you?" she asked, none too subtly.

A few beats. "I know I've been asking all the questions, and you've been very open and generous with your answers. Maybe you have something you'd like to ask me?"

Sighing, not wanting to break the spell of their blossoming friendship, Bonnie said, "I'm not sure why you're paying so much attention to me. Mr. Charles knows more about Frankel's than I do."

"Chase might be an old friend, but he's also a competitive bastard going way back."

"I don't date married men," she blurted.

"We really do have so much in common. I don't date married men either."

She laughed. "I *was* wondering…"

"Joanne and I are partners in a large business. We have two children together. Our lives and finances are intertwined and would be the devil to separate. Socially, we have our own calendars and friends. It's unconventional, but it's worked well for us for years now."

An open marriage of convenience? That was a trend among the superrich. If it was just too expensive and complicated to divorce, couples stayed together legally, dividing time in their many houses, but never overlapping. Bonnie couldn't imagine staying married to someone you weren't passionately in love with. But the superrich were different than normal people. Although Bonnie couldn't relate, her heart leapt at the idea that Steve and Joanne Kline weren't together-together. He all but said he didn't love his wife anymore. And if that was true, his heart was available, even if he wasn't technically single. It wasn't so much a moral issue to fall for a man who had a clear understanding with his wife-in name-only.

"People! Gather 'round!" Mr. Charles's voice filtered in from Grand Central.

"I've got to go," said Bonnie.

"I'm back in New York in a few days. I'd love to continue this conversation at dinner."

Bonnie gulped. "I'm…goodbye." She hung up.

Stop talking yourself into it, Bonnie told herself. Married was married, regardless of their understanding. He was her client—and a big spender, which she needed. Those two major hurdles were dwarfed by what he didn't know about her. Would he still be hot for a dinner after he learned about her special needs son? That she was at war with her sister? That her mother was dating a wiseguy?

She could try to tell him the truth about her life, instead of keeping her two worlds separate. He was easy to talk to, and she wanted to be honest. She hadn't felt this kind of chemistry in years. When she wasn't working or with Peter, Bonnie thought about Steve. When she'd tried to get into an angry snit about Emily and Mike, her mind kept drifting back to Steve.

The idea of actually having an affair after years of celibacy was, frankly, terrifying.

"People!" called Mr. Charles again.

Bonnie joined the Salon staff and assorted others in Grand Central for the impromptu Friday morning meeting. "Gather 'round. I've got good news and better news," announced the boss.

Standing next to Bonnie, Roman said, "Oh, shit."

Megan, on Roman's other side, pressed her boobs into his arm coquettishly. They were officially a couple. Megan was unrelenting with her public display of affection. Roman, God bless him, seemed embarrassed by it.

Bonnie couldn't stand the sight of her. But since she was on probation and clinging to her own job, she was in no position to fire anyone. Until that changed, Bonnie kept a close eye on Megan—an unpleasant task because her every gesture, word, and action annoyed her.

"First, the good news," said Mr. Charles. "Overall sales have improved slightly. Our January friends-and-family sale brought in a lot of customers," he said. "Albert Frankel and the board of directors are pleased, and they want to reward the staff."

"Bonuses?" asked Tiffany, the store buyer.

"We can't give you money," said Mr. Charles. "But we're going to give promotions!"

Bonnie couldn't contain a scoff. As far as she was concerned, he could promote her to Exalted Ruler of the Universe and it wouldn't make a difference. A raise or a bonus—that would be greatly appreciated.

"Megan and Roman," said Mr. Charles. "I've seen how hard you've been working, and I believe you're ready to fly. I'm taking you out from under Bonnie's wing. You're both officially Salon stylists. Congratulations!"

There was a round of confused applause from Bonnie, Bella, Fran, buyers Tiffany and June, and the half dozen sales people in attendance.

Roman said, "Thank you."

"No raise, unfortunately. From now on, you'll answer to me."

Bonnie couldn't swallow her bitterness. Mr. Charles vaulted her assistants, who had three years of styling experience between them, to her level? This was a slap in the face. It was impossible not to take it personally.

"Will I get new assistants?" asked Bonnie, whose dozens of clients required more attention than one person could provide.

"I'm afraid not," said Mr. Charles. "Consider this an experiment. A test, if you will, of a new staff structure for the Salon. I realize I've been relying too heavily on just one person"—every eye in the room landed on Bonnie's blazing cheeks—"and that was, obviously, a mistake. I'm not installing a commission system for the Salon because of the full-service nature of the job. But I am going to offer a big carrot. The stylist with the largest sales for the quarter will be named the Salon's codirector, sharing the title with Bonnie. Bonnie will continue to work with celebrity clients, for continuity. But any new clients who come into the Salon arc up for grabs."

Bonnie said, "I'm competing with my assistants for my own job?"

Mr. Charles smiled. "Former assistants. The competition will be good for you. We all need a kick in the pants every now and again."

Bonnie would love to kick Mr. Charles in the front of his pants now and again in five minutes. And again five minutes after that. Probation was one thing. But having to share her title with people far below her experience level? Why would Mr. Charles do this, but to humiliate her? Was he trying to force her to resign?

"Excuse me," she said, ducking into her office and closing the door she'd paid out of her own pocket to have installed. It was an accordion door, the only type that worked for the tiny space. But it gave her the privacy she needed to muster a shred of dignity.

A rap on the door, which made it pop open. She cleared her throat and said, "Enter."

"A word," said Mr. Charles, stepping into her office. He sat on the edge of her desk. Bonnie just glared at him. She'd never hated anyone as much as she hated him at that moment.

"This isn't personal, Bonnie. Obviously it's never going to happen. Your sales will be five times theirs. But the idea that they could get bumped up will generate some enthusiasm quickly. Megan and Roman will be motivated."

"What's my incentive? Keep the job I already have? You know they'll go after my clients." Bonnie wondered if any of them would defect. Cody Deerlinger? She complained a lot. But she always bought something Bonnie chose for her.

Mr. Charles said, "Speaking of your clients, I got a phone call this morning from Lee Freed. He was very upset."

What fresh hell? It'd been a week since the bar mitzvah. She'd returned the handheld zonker key to the Cage by the end of business. Vicki's clothes were beautiful. "About what?"

"Vicki Freed's charges. He's reining in her spending. She's hereby cut off. He canceled her Frankel's account."

Cutting Vicki off from shopping? Lee Freed might as well chop off her hand.

"Mrs. Freed and I spoke a couple of days ago," said Bonnie. Vicki had gushed, actually, saying how grateful she was for all of Bonnie's hard work and advice over these many years, seasons, wardrobes…oh, boy. Bonnie suddenly realized the sad truth. What had sounded like a well-earned client appreciation call was actually Vicki's kiss-off.

Without Vicki Freed's sales, Bonnie couldn't guarantee a good quarter. The Peace on Earth annual event was several months away, but clients would start coming in for gowns soon. She'd have to hustle to keep Roman and Megan from getting to them first. Still scrambling, after all these years. Bonnie thought she'd be cruising by now.

There was a commotion in the main Salon room. Mr. Charles opened the door and stepped into the hallway. Bonnie followed. They saw three men in dark overcoats, fedoras over bushy eyebrows, and menacing frowns standing in triangle formation at Fran's reception desk. The biggest man stood at the point position.

To Fran, he said in a soft but authoritative voice, "I'm looking for Bonnie Salerno."

Mr. Charles blinked at Bonnie. "My maiden name," she explained.

"Do you know this person?"

"Friend of the family." Her mom's boyfriend, specifically.

"Is Bonnie Salerno here?" asked Carmine Ragussa, louder.

Megan, the clueless rube, cunningly approached Carmine and said, "I'd be happy to help you."

"Look at those rings," said Mr. Charles, gawking at the chunks of gold on each of Carmine's fingers. As if drawn to them by a magnetic force, Mr. Charles beelined to one of the most dangerous men in Queens.

"Hello," he said, hand out. "I'm Chase W. Charles, president of Frankel's. Allow me to introduce you to Megan Houlihan. She's got a wonderful eye for men's suits."

Carmine sized up Megan. Her Midwestern perk did not

move him. "I'll work with Bonnie Salerno, or nobody."

"I'm right here, Mr. Ragussa." Bonnie walked over to him. "It's a pleasure to finally meet you."

He took her hand and kissed it. "You're not blond like your mother, but I see the resemblance. You're both beautiful women."

Ha! Sylvia Salerno was a blond like the Pope was Buddhist. "Thanks," said Bonnie. "Now, what brings you to Frankel's?"

"Your mother sent me. She wants me to spruce up my look."

"He said 'spruce,'" one of his men snickered.

"Shaddup!" he barked.

Seeing a savior in a dark suit, Bonnie said, "You've come to the right place." *I owe you, Mom!* she thought.

PART FOUR

March:
Fashion Week

Chapter Ten

Carmine Ragussa waved a fan of one hundred dollar bills under Bonnie's nose. "What's that smell like to you?" he asked.

Like fresh-baked dough, right out of the oven, Bonnie thought while inhaling. *Like a bribe.* They sat in Bonnie's office at Frankel's. "Believe me, Mr. Ragussa, there is nothing I would like more than to take your money," she said. "But we have a certain way of doing business."

"Are you telling me I don't know how to do business?" His forehead wrinkled with consternation.

"If we don't charge sales tax, even for cash transactions, the IRS will know. Frankel's is audited quarterly."

"When you pay in cash," repeated Carmine, "you don't pay tax."

"Sales tax sucks. I hate paying it. I hate asking clients to pay it. But it is a rule. Some people call it 'the law.'"

Carmine closed his cash fan, put the stack in an envelope, and put it upon Bonnie's desk. "So we agree. I'll send over an envelope like this every week for five weeks."

She could bathe in all that green, but it wasn't going to happen. "I wish I could accept this." Bonnie handed the envelope back. "My boss is a stickler about cash transactions."

Carmine's bushy eyebrows knit. He seemed contemplative. This might be the expression he made right before he ordered a hit. Bonnie tried to remember from Catholic school if there was a patron saint for salespeople.

"Are we at an impasse?" asked Carmine.

Bonnie hated to think so. For the last week, she'd worked with Carmine every day. She'd canceled appointments with other clients to devote herself to her mom's boyfriend, winner of Bonnie's Most Impulsive Spender Award of the year. He was a point-and-shoot shopper. If they walked past a mannequin and he liked what he saw, he'd pull the trigger on it, buying one of everything. In five business days, he'd bought enough clothes to outfit Sylvia and himself for years. If Bonnie showed him a handbag or a sweater she admired, Carmine would say, "You like it? You got it!" Bonnie refused, of course. But then Carmine would grab the item anyway and try to stuff it into her desk drawer when she wasn't looking.

The week with Carmine had been pleasant. He was a sweet man, generous and polite, if quietly menacing. If Sylvia had sent him to Frankel's to soften Bonnie up before they announced their engagement, it worked. Bonnie could see what her mom saw in the gangster. But did Sylvia see his dark side at all? He was definitely crooked.

What kind of businessman didn't have a line of credit? Frankel's accepts cash, of course. It was legal tender. He could pay in pennies. But large cash purchases raised red flags. At the next audit, a dozen IRS agents would swoop in and take up residence in Mr. Charles's breast pocket. The store preferred clients to use charge cards, ideally a Frankel's Visa, for clean accounting.

Retail accounting had come under scrutiny in recent years. Two splashy cases had made the newspapers. The first involved a young salesman at another high-end department store who took cash payments into his pocket without ringing them up on the store registers. At another store, a jewelry saleswoman scammed her employers out of millions by inputting bogus returns into the system and letting the clients keep the goods. Lax security and inventory glitches kept her in the giveaway business *for years*. Speaking on her own defense at trial, the saleswoman called the not-returned jewelry "gifts" for deserving clients.

No. A jar of antiwrinkle crème with purchase was a "gift." A free diamond necklace? That was a steal.

When Bonnie heard what happened, she wondered, *What was in it for the saleswoman?* The clients got jewelry, and the saleswoman got fired, sued, and convicted. She made the fatal error of thinking her clients were "friends." Where were her "friends" now? They'd distanced themselves from the disgraced convict and refused to return the merchandise.

Now more than ever, it was essential to stick to Mr. Charles's neurotic *i*-dotting and *t*-crossing standards. If she lost her job, it would *not* be due to accounting or inventory mistakes.

Carmine Ragussa didn't do scrupulous. He was an off-the-grid kind of guy. He didn't have credit cards or a bank account. And he refused to open one now to make his purchase.

"You call this 'the most luxurious store in the world'?" he asked. "I call it 'the most ridiculous store in the world.'"

Bonnie laughed out loud. He was right. Frankel's was ridiculous, but not because it charged sales tax. "I'm sure we can work out a compromise," said Bonnie. If they didn't, and Carmine walked away, she'd wasted a week.

Roman and Megan hadn't wasted their first week as bona fide Salon stylists. They'd been frantically busy. Mr. Charles threw them every new customer who came through the doors. Bonnie banked on Carmine to put her over the top.

"Your mom will be very disappointed if we don't sort this out," he said. "She sends her love, by the way. She wants you to call her. I'm supposed to tell you that Anita is sorry, and she only means well."

Carmine, acting as Salerno family consigliere, had passed along Sylvia's "love" daily. Bonnie hadn't spoken to her mother all week. She was still angry about how the family decided to send Anita to do the dirty work and tell Bonnie about Mike's engagement. A lot of resentment toward Anita had finally come to the surface, and Bonnie couldn't let it go. Her big sister had been trampling her dreams since birth, and the way she'd treated Peter...Bonnie had turned a blind eye for too long.

"How about this," suggested Carmine. "You have a store account, right? In your name?"

"I do," she said warily.

"We put my stuff on your account. You get the sale. I don't have to open an account. And I get your employee discount."

"Except my employee discount is only for me."

"And family."

"But you're not family, unless you and Mom got hitched when I wasn't looking."

"You're a friend of mine." He winked.

Bonnie sighed. "Let me talk to my boss."

Carmine settled into the chair. "I'll wait here. Send in the girl with the coffee."

Bonnie left her office. The corridor was blocked by a full rack of clothing—all lacy, silky, and stretchy lingerie with ribbons and straps. She tried to move the rack to get by, but it was too heavy.

Roman appeared on the other side and lugged it out of the way. "Sorry about that," he said. Bonnie noticed he'd stopped calling her "Chief."

"Is this your rack?"

"Mine and Megan's. The clients are on the floor with her right now."

"She's on the floor, and you're organizing the rack? Megan will get credit for the sale," said Bonnie. She examined one of the items. Why anyone would want to wear a pearl G-string defied reason.

Roman shrugged. "Whatever. She asked for help, and I gave it."

"You're helping yourself out of a job, Roman. Megan will eat you alive. Trust me on that."

"Megan Houlihan is the sweetest woman I've ever met."

Poor smitten bastard, thought Bonnie. That she'd believed Megan's innocent act for a single day shamed her.

"Bonnie! There you are!" bellowed Mr. Charles, walking into the Salon, one arm around the slender shoulder of Mrs. Joanne Kline, Steve's in-name-only wife. Bonnie's heart iced over when she saw her rival. She had no business feeling competitive with her. Bonnie hadn't so much as winked at Steve. But if it wasn't for Joanne, Bonnie might have done a lot more than that.

"I called you two minutes ago," said Mr. Charles.

"I was in a meeting and turned my phone off. Hello, Mrs. Kline," she said. "It's lovely to see you. Mr. Charles, I need to speak with you privately for two minutes. It's about a friend of mine from Queens."

Mr. Charles had seen *Goodfellas*. He knew which client she meant. "Joanne, darling, do you mind?"

"I suppose not," she said matter-of-factly.

"Bonnie is all yours for the rest of the day," he said.

I am? "What are you shopping for today, Mrs. Kline?" she asked.

"A gown for the spring Peace on Earth event." Mrs. Kline fingered a negligee on Roman's rack. "Maybe some lingerie as well."

Lingerie? Bonnie's cheeks flamed with jealousy as she imagined Mrs. Kline strutting around in Steve's separate bedroom, trying to seduce him.

"Bonnie?"

"Yes?"

"Are you all right?" asked Mr. Charles.

"I'm fine."

Mr. Charles bowed slightly at the hip to Joanne, and then he and Bonnie ducked into an empty fitting room. "What?" he asked gruffly.

"Mr. Ragussa thinks sales tax is unAmerican," she said. "Same for opening a charge account."

Her boss nodded, took it in stride. Mr. Charles had been in the business for twice as long as she had. He'd seen it all, heard it all, and dealt with it all many times before. "What's his total?"

"Fifty thousand."

"Here's what we'll do," he said. "I'll have Cheryl in accounting arrange for weekly cash payments. That won't set off alarms."

"Okay," said Bonnie.

"You tell Mr. Ragussa that we'll forget the sales tax. Meanwhile, I'll sign off on an 8.75 percent discount for the entire order, and we'll use that to pay the tax."

Bonnie raised an eyebrow.

"Before the point of purchase," he said. "We'll have an accurate and legal receipt."

"You are a genius."

"You're noticing that *now*?"

They smiled at each other, like they used to during the golden years, circa 2009. Bonnie felt a wellspring of affection for him. Mr. Charles seemed on the verge of saying something sincere and apologetic to her about the way he'd been treating her lately. But then his expression hardened. The good feeling disappeared. Back to eggshells and tender hooks.

They exited the fitting room. Carmine had wandered out of Bonnie's office and was loitering by the lingerie rack. Bonnie thought, *Don't you dare suggest buying any of that for my mother.*

"Mr. Ragussa! Hello! We met before. Chase W. Charles, Frankel's president. I'm so glad to see you. Bonnie and I have just been talking. Perhaps you'd like to take a short walk with me to my office?"

Carmine nodded gruffly. "Bonnie, you coming?"

"Why don't we take care of business?" said Mr. Charles. "Let's leave the ladies to shop."

Yes, the men can go off and do important things, thought Bonnie. The entire building could be full of women and gay men, but the one straight white man would be in charge.

"Call your mother today. Swear it," said Carmine to Bonnie. Did he want blood? "I will."

That matter resolved, Bonnie turned her full attention to Mrs. Joanne Kline. She was dressed head to toe in Chanel, as usual. Although Bonnie would prefer her fat and ugly, Joanne looked good. Slim body, pearls, and flawless makeup. Overdressed for an afternoon of shopping, perhaps, but Bonnie had seen women wear diamonds and furs to try on jeans. The Klines had been New Yorkers for a few months by now. Joanne had changed her hairstyle from a matronly Midwestern helmet to an unstructured chic crop in an age-appropriate, natural-looking wheat hue. Bonnie had seen the same over-forty-with-an-edge look on half a dozen Salon clients in the last few weeks.

Bonnie wondered if Steve Kline liked his wife's new look. It'd been years since Bonnie updated her look. She'd worn the same style—long, thick, straight chestnut ponytail with just the right amount of backcomb—since design school. She'd thought of it as simple and classic. But seeing Joanne's new look, Bonnie thought she should update, too.

"My husband said you have wonderful taste in clothes." Joanne was frosty, matter-of-fact.

"We found him some beautiful suits." She felt butterflies in her belly, thinking of the day he'd come in, how he looked at her right in the eye instead of staring at his own reflection in the mirror.

"Let's see what you can do for me," said Joanne, getting right down to business.

And they were off. Bonnie decided to stay on the eighth floor with Joanne and browse the designer couture boutiques. The Peace on Earth event was a biggie. It takes place each year in the Waldorf-Astoria Hotel Ballroom, one of the only spaces in New York City that holds 1,200 people. The gala would be attended by New York's A-list celebrities, politicians, socialites, and the media elite. Attendees paid $50,000 for "a table." An individual seat went for $5,000. The Peace on Earth spring gala was among the priciest and hottest tickets on the charity calendar.

Bonnie had been once, in 2009. Cody Deerlinger wore a complicated Alexander McQueen gown that required the help of a dresser for bathroom use. Mrs. Deerlinger initially suggested Bonnie spend the evening in the ladies' lounge and wait there until needed. But Mr. Deerlinger vetoed that idea, saying it would come off badly for his wife's "help" to hide in the bathroom all night. In a rebellious snit, Cody did a full 180 and gave Bonnie a seat at their table. Mr. Charles approved lending Bonnie a gown—a sublime Oscar—for the night. Terrified about spilling or splashing, Bonnie barely touched the meal. She left the gala woozy from hunger and dazzled by the celebs. Even a jaded Frankel's stylist had to pinch herself when standing between Oprah Winfrey and Meryl Streep at the bar.

But that was then. Nowadays, clients who once purchased two tables to seat their teenage children and hairdressers were now buying two individual tickets instead.

"Will you and Mr. Kline be hosting a table at the event?" Bonnie asked.

"Of course," replied Joanne.

Steve Kline would wear his tux. She imagined them dancing in the ballroom. He'd look like Prince Charming—older version—waltzing her in the gorgeous flowing red Oscar, her hair up and shining, a devastating smile on his handsome face as they dipped behind one of the potted trees. He'd lower his lips to the white skin of her neck and take a little bite.

"Something sexy," said Joanne, puncturing Bonnie's daydream.

"Okay. I can do that." Naturally, Bonnie would rather Steve's wife looked dowdy. But that wasn't her job. It was her duty to turn a conservative Chicago businesswoman into a magical creature of the night.

"What about Chanel?" asked Joanne.

Enough already, thought Bonnie. Joanne was like a broken TV that ran on only one Chanel. "Do you have an open mind?" she asked, thinking that she would love to add, *Do you have an open marriage?*

Joanne nodded. "Wide open."

"Oh, my God!" screamed Gloria Rodkin from the Salon couch, phone to her ear, plate on her lap. Bonnie and Joanne were just returning with five gowns.

"Gloria! You look fantastic!" said Joanne. The two women hugged and air-kissed.

Into the phone, Gloria said, "Shelley, you will not believe it! Joanne Kline…yes, from Chicago…yes, on the committee… She just walked into the Salon with the same haircut I have!" To Joanne, she said, "You must have seen Sally Hershberger."

Joanne nodded. "She's incredible."

Gloria said, "I never thought I'd spend close to a thousand dollars on a cut and color until Sally. It's worth every penny, though."

"It looks much better on you," said Joanne, of Gloria's red version.

"It looks *so much better* on you! Hold still. We'll let Shelley decide." Gloria used her iPhone to snap Joanne's photo, then emailed it to her daughter. "Did you get it? Who looks better? Tell the truth, Shelley. I know when you're lying. You're lying!"

Bonnie pictured the entire planning committee for the Peace on Earth spring charity gala sitting in a well-appointed living room, sipping lattes, wearing Chanel suits, and sporting identical haircuts in different shades. It reminded Bonnie of high school, when every girl in her class showed up with "the Rachel." Bonnie's opinion on the matchy-matchy hairdos? On Gloria, the chop looked like a red Marianne Faithful wig. Joanne's ash blond suited her.

"I'll put your gowns in fitting room A, Mrs. Kline," said Bonnie. "Can I get you a cappuccino? Glass of Dom? Something to eat?" She gestured to the two trays of snacks, which Gloria was plowing her way through.

"I'll follow you." To Gloria, still arguing about trust and honesty with Shelley, Joanne mouthed, "See you later."

Client and stylist entered Fitting Room A, the second largest. The PS was occupied by Megan's client. As soon as the door closed behind them, Joanne removed her clothes. Off with the cardigan jacket and cashmere shell. Off with the tweedy skirt. Within a minute, the woman was down to her ivory slip.

Bonnie peeked at Joanne's figure. She was impressively fit for her age—a gym rat. Although Joanne didn't have the wiry Gollum arms of Madonna, her limbs were well-defined. Mike used to say too much sinew was unsexy. Bonnie tended to agree. A woman's body should be soft. That notion gave her some comfort when she got dressed each morning.

"Let's try the Herrera first," said Joanne.

Bonnie slipped the gold, sequined, strapless gown over Joanne's head and zipped it up. The fit was close. A roomy size six. The gown was old-fashioned glamour for the red carpet or a black-tie gala.

"I feel like a mermaid," said Joanne. "The sequins look like fish scales."

That was a "no" if Bonnie ever heard one. "Let's get it off you," said Bonnie, moving in to unzip.

But Joanne stopped her. "I think a man would like this dress, don't you?"

"Of course," said Bonnie. Did she mean Steve? She would have said, "I think Steve would like this." Bonnie knew him, after all, and would have an informed opinion. But Joanne said "a man," presumably another man. Or *the* other man. *Interesting,* thought Bonnie. She hadn't thought Steve had lied when he described the marriage as "open." But Bonnie was relieved to have some ambiguous confirmation.

"Let's try that one," said Joanne, pointing to a voluminous plum Marchesa silk organza gown, strapless, with ruffles and a plunging back. The dress was less expensive than the others on Joanne's rack—only $7,000—but the color would work well with her skin tone.

"Very dramatic," said Joanne once they got it on her. "It's beautiful. But is it sexy?"

"It's a fantasy gown," said Bonnie. "If it makes you feel sexy, the beholder will pick up your cues. The question is, do you feel sexy?"

"I'm in a fitting room in a department store," said Joanne. "Why on earth would I feel sexy?"

Not a sensual woman, thought Bonnie. She liked it that Joanne had a cold, practical demeanor. Steve was warm and welcoming. They were clearly mismatched. There was no way Steve and Joanne Kline had a passionate connection. If Bonnie had any doubt before, now she felt sure the marriage was a business partnership only. Had Joanne ever been warm and fun? She must have been for Steve to have fallen in love with her in the first place. But that was then. The past was history. The future? A mystery. Bonnie could see herself with Steve a little more clearly, though, having spent time with his wife.

"What's your opinion?" asked Joanne, turning side to side, watching herself.

Bonnie said, "Either gown would be appropriate for the event. The Herrera is sexier, but the Marchesa is more flattering."

"That's a mixed message," she said. "If you want to make a sale, you have to push me in the right direction. It's not up to the buyer. The seller controls the transaction."

What was she talking about? Schooling Bonnie on the art of the sale? "All due respect," said Bonnie. "I'm not selling a widget. This is a personal decision. Only you can make it. Both gowns look beautiful. The deciding factor has to be your emotional response. Which gown makes you feel special?"

"Interesting," she said. "I don't think clothes are emotional."

Hence all Chanel, all the time.

"I'll take the mermaid gown," said Joanne.

"It makes you feel the best?" asked Bonnie. Just double-checking. The gown cost $10,000.

"You should have stopped talking as soon as I said, 'I'll take it.'" Then Joanne lifted her arms to be helped out of the Marchesa.

"We have a few more to try on," said Bonnie.

"I've seen enough," said Joanne.

This had to be one of the weirdest gown styling episodes in memory for its bizarre lack of excitement. It was typical for a woman to cry, scream, moan, laugh, or cheer in the fitting room. Nine women out of ten, without any prompting from Bonnie, would reveal their hearts and souls when stripped to their underwear. The clothes came off, and the guard went down.

Apparently Joanne didn't have protective shields to lower, or she had absolutely nothing to hide. Either way, Bonnie couldn't relate to her at all. Steve deserved a woman who was as generous and giving as he was. Who'd laugh about tales from behind the fitting room door or share his excitement about a rundown abandoned warehouse. Did Steve and Joanne *talk*? Bonnie and Steve had spent hours on the phone in the last couple of months.

A knock on the fitting room door.

Joanne was nearly back in her suit. Bonnie said, "Excuse me," and opened the door a crack.

It was Megan. "There's a problem in the PS," she whispered. "Since you're Salon director, you have to deal with it."

Was this kid telling her what her job was? "Fix your own problem," Bonnie whispered.

Crash. It sounded like a wall had come down in the Salon. Joanne asked, "What was *that*?"

The three women rushed toward the noise. Gloria Rodkin, still on the couch, said, "Did you hear that crash, Shelley? I spilled my champagne!"

The sound had come from the PS. Bonnie asked, "Who's in there?"

Megan opened her mouth and then bit her lip. "No one."

Gloria said, "No one? Try Marco Standish and Gazelle!"

Anyone but them, thought Bonnie. The last time she'd seen the notoriously obnoxious actor and his chronically tipsy model girlfriend was about two years ago. The celebrity couple arrived at the Salon, and Bonnie showed them the store. In the bedding department, Gazelle playfully threw a decorative pillow at Marco. The zipper pull caught Marco in the cheek. He touched a tiny cut, not even bleeding, and screamed, "Not! The! Face!" He tackled his 110-pound girlfriend, and they landed on a display of overpriced down comforters. Their tussle ended in a sweaty dry hump that was filmed by dozens of shoppers and viewed ten million times on YouTube.

Mr. Charles banned Marco and Gazelle from Frankel's. Although celebrity customers were a reliable draw for tourists, they *always* demanded discounts, freebies, and special treatment—the standard "drop everything" entitlement Bonnie was used to. Celebs were important. But they didn't keep the store in the black. The Deerlingers, Freeds, and Mortimers of Manhattan paid full price as a point of pride. Well, they had until 2008, anyway, when everything changed. Now even Cody Deerlinger was looking for discounts.

Slam. Another jolt shook the PS wall.

"You know that Marco and Gazelle are banned from the store," said Bonnie.

Megan said, "You didn't tell me. This is your fault, Bonnie. They got by security, so it's also Mr. Greene's fault. They seemed okay. Not drunk or whatever, and they apologized for how they acted last time."

Smash. A mirror. *Scream*. Gazelle? She sounded hysterical.

Roman rattled the PS door. Locked and seemingly blocked, too.

To Fran at the reception desk, Bonnie said, "Call security." To Megan, she said, "Mr. Charles told you that I handle celebrity clients *for this reason*. You don't know what you're doing."

"Like you knew what you were doing with Archer Watson?"

A sore point. Bonnie still felt terrible about that.

"I can try to break in," said Roman.

Gloria Rodkin, meanwhile, delivered the blow-by-blow to Shelley. "It sounds like wild animals are attacking each other in there!"

"Security is on their way," said Fran.

Did they have time to wait, or would these two trash the room and each other first? "Fran, get the Key," said Bonnie.

"You sure?"

Bonnie nodded gravely. It was time.

Only two people in the Salon staff—Fran and Bonnie— were aware of the existence of the Key. Clients were guaranteed complete privacy in the PS. Unless they specifically requested the presence of a fitter or stylist, clients could expect to be left alone. No security cameras. The lock on the door was sacrosanct.

Except.

Bonnie, in her tenure, had never used the Key. She never talked about its existence. Mr. Charles made her sign a confidentiality agreement that it would not be used unless a client's life was at risk—if she were suffering a heart attack, for example. Or being attacked by her asshole boyfriend.

The Key was kept in a locked safe under Fran's reception desk. Only Bonnie, Fran, and Mr. Charles knew the combination. Fran ducked down to unlock the safe. She reappeared with the shining silver key in her hand. Bonnie strode over to the reception desk, took the silver object, and hurried over to the PS door.

A final crash and screech convinced Bonnie she was doing the right thing. She inserted the Key, turned it, and flung the Private Studio door open.

What Bonnie, Megan, Roman, Fran, Gloria, Shelley by proxy, Joanne, Mr. Charles (showing up with perfect timing, as usual), and the security guys who just ran in saw in there was...

Gazelle, in a La Perla fox fur bustier and thong set, along with a metal lattice garter belt, on her hands and knees on top of a pile of lingerie and hangers, facing the two remaining panels of the three-paneled mirror. Behind her, on his knees, *also* in a La Perla fox fur bustier and panties and a metal lattice garter belt, Marco Standish, with a large erection and a Stella McCartney lace bra hammocking his testicles.

In the mirror, Gazelle and Marco's faces, flushed, sweaty, completely shocked.

In the Salon, the Frankel's staffers and clients registered complete disgust.

Gloria Rodkin said, "Okay, now I've seen everything."

Marco slammed the door closed again. From behind it, he roared, "Guarantee of privacy!"

Gazelle sobbed, "I feel so violated!"

Mr. Charles glared at Bonnie. If looks could kill, her whole family would be dead.

"As it turns out, Shelley," said Gloria. "The Private Studio has a key!"

Mr. Charles groaned. That was that. The Key was "out."

"It sounded like he was killing her," Bonnie defended her decision.

"It's true, Chase," said Joanne. "Bonnie did the right thing."

Marco and Gazelle stumbled out of the PS. Their clothes were askew. Bonnie could plainly see they were still wearing the La Perla fox fur bustiers and, she assumed, the panties and garter belts. Marco dragged Gazelle by the wrist through the small crowd of spectators. The model hid her famous face with her hands.

"You'll be hearing from my lawyers!" bellowed Marco. And then the kinky couple was gone, stealing thousands of dollars in merchandise, causing thousands more in damage to the fitting room and the merchandise they'd used as a pallet.

"Who let those two in here?" roared Mr. Charles. He turned to the head of security, Mr. Greene. "You know they're banned!"

Mr. Greene was about to explain himself when Roman cut

him off. "It was me. I knew they slipped in, and I didn't throw them out."

"That *is* true," said Megan. "And you convinced me not to tell Bonnie. Plus, it was *your* idea to put the rack of lingerie in there with them instead of five items at a time, which is Salon policy."

That policy was largely ignored, as Mr. Charles knew full well. It hardly mattered. The expression on Roman's face almost made Bonnie weep. Naked heartbreak. He'd gallantly tried to play the hero and take the heat off his girlfriend. Part of him had to expect Megan to share the blame. But she only made it look worse for him.

Bonnie could not allow this betrayal to stand. "I'm still Salon director. I take full responsibility."

Mr. Charles opened his mouth to let a stream of invective flow forth, but then he stopped. Mrs. Rodkin and Joanne Kline were watching him. It'd be unseemly and against his elegant smoothie reputation to yell.

"Ladies, if you'll permit me, I'd like to treat you both to lunch at the Frankel's café," he said to Gloria and Joanne. "I think, after what we've just seen, we can all use a drink."

Gloria said to Shelley, "Oooh! Lunch with Mr. Charles!"

Joanne said, "Well done, Chase." She patted her old friend on the cheek and retreated to her fitting room to finish dressing. "Gloria, come with me, I want to show you the gown I'm not buying. It might be perfect for you."

The redhead followed the wheat blond into the fitting room. Mr. Greene's walkie-talkie squawked. He and his team exited in pursuit of a garden-variety shoplifter on six. That left only Salon staffers.

Fran said, "If Bonnie goes down for using the Key, I'll go down, too."

"No one's going down with anyone," said Mr. Charles.

Fran and Bonnie blinked and grinned.

Mr. Charles, realizing what he'd said, blushed furiously. "Grow up, women," he said. "Roman, you're fired. I want you out of the store within the hour."

Chapter Eleven

Bonnie waited outside Lincoln Center. It was cold for early March. Usually Fashion Week was in mid-February, when it was even colder, and the tents had to be heated with blazing furnaces that hissed "fire hazard" with every gust. Although Fashion Week was every bit as glamorous as civilians believed, for those who'd come to work, it was a grind. The excitement of seeing celebrities wore thinner every year. As the face of Frankel's and the store's president, Mr. Charles attended most of the major, and some of the minor, shows with Tiffany and June, the buyers. As Salon director, Bonnie escorted Cody Deerlinger, Vicki Freed, or a handful of A-list clients to top designer shows to entice them to buy, but also as a perk. This season, when Mr. Charles dispensed Frankel's allotment of tickets, he told Bonnie to take Joanne Kline as her guest.

"Not Mrs. Deerlinger?" asked Bonnie. Joanne was hardly a slave to fashion.

"I have my reasons," he said. "Just thinking a few squares ahead."

"The Klines own strip malls. Is Frankel's planning an outpost next to Jamba Juice?" she asked. It made no sense.

"Just do what I ask, Bonnie. Thank you."

Then he hung up. Since firing Roman—an unpopular decision staff-wide—Mr. Charles had been acting defensive and hostile. Spending time away from Frankel's would be a pleasure. Bonnie was disappointed not to take Cody Deerlinger to the shows. The woman was a demanding narcissist, but she was hilarious at Fashion Week. She trashed *everything*—the clothes, the models, her friends, the designers—with hateful glee. Plus, at the end of the show, Cody reliably placed a hefty order.

Joanne Kline, coldhearted and clueless about fashion, would be a colossal bore.

"I'm taking your wife to Fashion Week," Bonnie told Steve during his daily morning phone call.

"I know," he said.

"So you do talk."

"About you," he said teasingly. "She enjoyed shopping for gowns at Frankel's."

Bonnie might've gasped. "So she knows…that we're friends?"

"She knows I've got my eye on you," he said.

She almost dropped the phone. "This makes me uncomfortable. Is it unsophisticated to feel weird that my…"

"Friend," he inserted.

"That my friend talks about me with his wife?"

Steve paused and then whispered, "I have limits, Bonnie. For instance, I'd never kiss and tell."

Bonnie dropped the phone. She picked it up. "Gotta go. Bye!"

He shouldn't do that to her! His flirt style wasn't fair. She was teetering on the edge of taking the next step. He knew exactly how to knock her off-balance. *Would it happen?* Bonnie suspected that a better question would be *when?*

She couldn't not think about him, unless she forced her thoughts to other things. Such as why Mr. Charles was so hot for Joanne to go to Fashion Week? He had to be up to something.

She checked her BlackBerry. Joanne was cutting it close.

"Bonnie!" It was Lori, one of her ex-colleagues from Bloomingdale's, now a store buyer at a Frankel's competitor. She ran up the stairs at Lincoln Center to give Bonnie a kiss-kiss.

"Hey!" said Bonnie, hugging her friend, genuinely glad to see her.

"You never return my calls," said Lori, smiling when a photographer snapped her picture. "Come work for me. I hate my staff. Their taste level is atrocious."

"I'm happy at Frankel's."

"That's not what I hear," said Lori before sweeping toward

the tents.

A limo pulled up to the VIP entrance. Like the tourists behind the police blockades, Bonnie craned her neck to see who it was. A movie star? Famous designer? Society doyenne? Just standing here for five minutes, she'd seen Katy Perry, Heidi Klum, and Betsey Johnson.

The driver door opened, and Serge exited. For a delirious half second, Bonnie's heart leapt. Had Steve come to the shows? Serge opened the rear door, and Mrs. Kline stepped out. Alone.

Bonnie took a deep breath and walked down the steps to greet her guest. Joanne Kline looked lovely in, no surprise, a Chanel suit and Prada heels. Safe and predictable. She wouldn't be turning heads in the tents, but she wouldn't be mocked behind her back either.

Joanne said to Serge, "I'll text you when I'm ready to be picked up."

"Yes, Mrs. Kline." He ducked back into the driver's seat and pulled away.

Bonnie said, "You look wonderful, Mrs. Kline."

"Thank you."

Then testy silence. Okay. Not a single degree warmer today than last time. At least she was consistent.

"This way," said Bonnie, hoping Joanne would get into the spirit of Fashion Week. It'd be a long afternoon if she didn't. "We're seeing the Gideon Hauenstein show today." She hoped Mrs. Kline would get excited about *that*, or crack a smile at least.

"He designs for Target, right?"

Bonnie almost laughed. "Target, yes, but he also designs couture and ready-to-wear. He used to have a boutique off Madison, not too far from your apartment."

Mrs. Kline nodded. An upscale "whatever" gesture. If the woman wasn't impressed by Gideon Hauenstein, what would impress her? Maybe she was unwowable. No wonder Steve slept in a separate bedroom.

They queued up to get into the tent, preshow. While waiting, Bonnie smiled at and waved to a dozen people she knew. Other stylists. Former clients. Fashion directors and buyers. High-end retail in New York was a small world. Fashion Week was a biannual class reunion. Outside the tent, her colleagues, clients, and peers looked excited. Once they crossed through the canvas panel to get inside, the friendly faces were replaced by frozen stares. If you acknowledged someone inferior in title or status, that lowered you on his or her level, a major faux pas in Fashion Week etiquette. The person who could rebuff her colleagues with the sharpest disdain was the winner. The prize? To be ignored right back.

Bonnie sighed. Cynicism was oozing out of her in buckets.

She showed their tickets to the young woman in a Hauenstein creamsicle-colored, fifties-style dress at the entryway. At the top of each ticket, a number had been written in gold ink. The woman checked their numbers and names in her computer and confirmed Bonnie and Mrs. Kline's names. "First row, walk straight ahead to the runway, and go left."

"Thank you," said Bonnie.

The seats had their names on them. "Front row?" asked Mrs. Kline. "Even I know enough to be impressed."

Finally! A breakthrough. "Frankel's has a large Hauenstein boutique." Bonnie had personally sold hundreds of thousands of dollars in Hauenstein dresses and gowns to her clients over the last few years. "It's a courtesy."

"Will we sit next to Anna Wintour?" asked Joanne.

Groan. "She's in the front row, but in the center."

"Oh." Joanne's enthusiasm disappeared again.

It's going to be a long afternoon, thought Bonnie.

With the help of a model/usher, they found their seats. Front row, off to the right. They'd miss the turn, when the models stopped at the end of the runway to pose for the fashion press. No big deal, at least not to Bonnie. She glanced directly across the runway from her seat and noticed one of her former colleagues, now the associate fashion director at Barney's. This woman, around fifty, smartly dressed with a shock of black hair, was complaining loudly to her usher. She knocked a stack of programs out of the poor girl's hands and flapped her cape in protest like she might fly away.

Joanne followed her eye line. "What's that woman's problem?"

A bad case of myopia. The fashion director could only see to the end of her upturned nose. Granted, in her universe, she *was* all-powerful. It was her decision to order (or not) the collection for her store. A large purchase could make or break a season. God forbid she felt slighted by a designer. She'd be as spiteful as a jilted mistress. Didn't matter that hundreds of people logged months of hard work to get the collection to the runway. Didn't matter if her store's customers clamored for the styles seen here today.

Bonnie said, "She's the queen of her own fiefdom, and she expected to be seated at a throne."

"And her?" Joanne discreetly pointed toward a tantrum-throwing woman in a snakeskin trench coat, her pencil-thin legs stamping the ground.

Bonnie whispered, "That's the third in command at a second-rate magazine, who apparently feels she deserved a front-row seat."

"Second row isn't good enough?"

"Are you really interested in how it works?"

"That's why I'm here."

Huh? Not to see the clothes? Bonnie hoped Joanne would make a nice size purchase today. Maybe an insider take on the jostling would whet her appetite.

"Here's the breakdown," said Bonnie. "The prime front-row seats are for top-level editors, store presidents, and celebrities. The closer your seat is to the end of the runway, the more important you are, and the less likely it is that you'd actually pay for the clothes you've come to see. Editors and celebrities get it all for free."

Joanne said, "In exchange, the designers get bragging rights."

"If Lady Gaga wears Gaultier in a rock video, it's better than buying a dozen ad pages in *Elle*," said Bonnie.

"Lady *who*?" asked Joanne.

"That creature over there," said Bonnie, pointing to the blond pop star in kabuki makeup, a black leotard, red patent leather sky-high boots, a red bolero jacket, and red lacy hat.

Joanne said, "She's not wearing pants."

"I don't know about that."

Joanne raised her eyebrows and laughed. Bonnie was so surprised, she joined in. Finally, the glitter and oddness of Fashion Week was working on her. When she smiled, Joanne was quite pretty. Seeing that, Bonnie had to look away. She felt jealous, although she had no right to.

"Go on," said Joanne. "What about off-center seats?"

"They're for important buyers, clients, stylists, and fashion directors, people like the queen over there," said Bonnie. "And, ahem, us. The second row is for second-tier editors, the designer's personal friends, and clients—people who actually buy the clothes. Third row is for lesser buyers who order the clothes for stores all over the world. A buyer might want five dresses or five hundred, for a store in Boston or Berlin. Without them, the ordinary customer wouldn't have access to the clothes. The giveaway seats are up there, on the grandstand. Students at Parsons and FIT, fashionistas, and tourists. Even those spots are hard to come by."

"If and when I put on an event like this, the store buyers will be front row center," said Joanne.

"Spoken like a true businesswoman. But the photographers from *Women's Wear Daily* don't want a reaction shot of Shirley Peters from the Wichita Dress Barn. They want Nina Garcia and Kate Hudson."

"Understood," said Joanne. "Who are *those* people?" She gestured toward a long line of beautifully dressed spectators standing just outside the seated area.

It was the line of lost souls. All of them probably had an invite to the event, but that wasn't enough to score an actual seat. Preshow, you had to go through appropriate channels—usually the designer's "people"—to get a certified, *numbered* invitation for a chair. Otherwise, you were funneled into the line, where you had to stand in extreme footwear—since no one came to Fashion Week in less than a three-inch heel—until thirty seconds before the show began, at which point you could make a mad dash for any unclaimed gallery seat you could find.

Bonnie began to explain this to Joanne when her eyes lit on a pair of familiar faces in the line. "Oh, God," she said, looking away.

"What?" asked Joanne.

"I just saw someone I used to know."

Daring to take another look, Bonnie couldn't believe her eyes. Vicki Freed was cooling her Jimmy Choos in line next to Megan Houlihan. Judging by Vicki's ticked-off expression, Bonnie concluded that Megan landed a pair of tickets to this event and invited Vicki—but she didn't know to call ahead for a seat number. Vicki wasn't used to waiting—for anything, much less a chair. Meanwhile, why would Megan bring Mrs. Freed? Hadn't Lee, her husband, closed their account? With a cold rush, Bonnie wondered if Mr. Charles lied about that and secretly moved Vicki onto Megan's client list.

Joanne asked, "So what type of clothes are we seeing today?"

"Fall," said Bonnie.

"In March?"

"The collection is for next fall. Fashion operates six months ahead."

"I was hoping to see some flirty spring dresses." Joanne, a serious woman, just said "flirty." Was she being ironic?

Bonnie said, "I'd be happy to walk you through the spring collection at Frankel's next week."

"Next week is no good. I'm going back to Chicago in a couple of days, and I have tons to do."

Wasn't Steve coming to New York from Chicago in a couple of days? These two rarely spent time in the same city, a thought that made Bonnie smile. "Chicago in March. Must be cold."

Joanne shrugged. "It's warm indoors. When is this going to start? I have some meetings lined up for this afternoon."

A couple rushed by, the woman's Louis Vuitton tote bag hitting Joanne's face. If she'd been wearing glasses, they'd be on the floor. The rude woman didn't apologize or acknowledge Joanne. Incensed on her guest's behalf, Bonnie leaned over, tapped the woman on her shoulder, and said, "You should be more careful with your handbag."

The woman slowly turned around, saying, "And you should shut your bleeding pie ho...*you*!"

"Well, look who it is! Mrs. Kline, you remember these two," said Bonnie.

"I barely recognized them with their clothes on."

A classic Fashion Week moment. Marco Standish and Gazelle were seated to their right. Through their managers, the model and actor adamantly denied walking out of the store with thousands of dollars of merchandise. Bonnie was shocked to see that the gruesome twosome was, at that moment, wearing the La Perla garter belts and fur bustiers. Maybe the thongs, too, but Bonnie didn't want to confirm. The stolen items were designer exclusives and couldn't be purchased anywhere but Frankel's. Bonnie took out her pocket camera and started compiling evidence.

Marco yelled, "No flash photography. Security!" Gazelle covered her face as if she'd been attacked.

Alerted to the commotion, a security guard headed their way. Bonnie said, "Good, he can arrest you."

Marco said, "He'll arrest *you*! You're nothing. You're a loser!"

Joanne Kline put her fingers to her lips, silencing Marco and Gazelle. Weirdly, they responded to her. *She would have made an excellent Catholic school teacher,* thought Bonnie. Then Joanne wiggled one finger to draw Marco closer and whispered something in his ear.

Marco's wine ruddy cheeks paled. He nodded once and then unhooked the garter belt, which he handed to her. Then he untied the fur bustier and turned that over, too. Joanne said, "Thank you," and passed them over to Bonnie.

Gazelle, dumbfounded, said, "What'd you do that for?"

Marco whispered into her ear. Gazelle, already ghoulishly pale, turned downright transparent. She followed her boyfriend's lead and forked over the garments.

The security guard arrived. He said, "Do we have a problem?"

Marco said, "Only that you're blocking my friggin' view."

The security man looked at Bonnie and Joanne. They shrugged. He said, "No flash photography during the show," and left.

Near the front of the room, a trio of musicians started playing loud, chaotic jazz. The show was about to begin.

Bonnie folded the garments carefully and put them in her tote. She had to shout in Joanne Kline's ear. "What did you say to him?"

Joanne said, "Just a little something I'd heard on the South Side."

Bonnie grinned and then grimaced. It'd be a terrible mistake to get on this woman's bad side.

"I want that one, and that one. Definitely that one," said Joanne, pointing at models as they mingled with the crowd.

The show, only twenty minutes long, had worked its magic on Mrs. Kline. The music, the mood, the models, and, of course, Gideon Hauenstein's visions, activated the part of Joanne's brain that controlled reckless spending. Mrs. Kline was sold. She *loved* the collection. Hauenstein was the *greatest* designer *ever*. Excited, Mrs. Kline insisted they go to the VIP after party to buy dresses right off the models' backs.

For stylists and designers, postshow impulse shopping was the point of Fashion Week. At one Halston show a few years ago, Cody Deerlinger astonished Bonnie by buying one of each dress from the entire collection, dropping $100,000 in an hour. Bonnie was made a Friend to the House of Halston for life. They sent her a certificate.

"I want to meet Gideon," said Mrs. Kline.

She'd barely heard of him, but now they were on a first-name basis.

The designer was under siege, but Bonnie managed to elbow through the crowd and introduce her client. "Gideon, this is Joanne Kline, of Kline and Company," she shouted to be heard above the music. "She owns Chicago, and she loves your collection. She's buying five pieces today."

Hauenstein thanked Joanne. She tried to engage him in conversation about Target, of all things. One of his associates appeared at Bonnie's side to take Mrs. Kline's order and get her shipping and billing information. With the transaction completed and Joanne occupied for the moment, Bonnie drifted back to the periphery of the crowd for a breather.

A voice to her right: "Replaced me so soon?"

"Mrs. Freed," said Bonnie tepidly. "I'm so happy to see you."

"Surprised?" asked the blond. Vicki looked strained. Her boobs were vacuum-packed into a Prada sheath that Bonnie remembered selling to her a few years—and bra sizes—ago.

"I'm glad you and Megan Houlihan have…oh, forget it," said Bonnie. Why bother lying? "Why are you here with *her*?"

Vicki raised her arched brows. "Are you jealous?"

"I'm angry. We've worked together for years. I've done whatever you asked for, gone beyond the call of duty for you many times, as we both know. And then you dropped me for Megan? Did she call you? Or did you call *her*?"

"You've never spoken to me this way before. I like it!" Vicki sipped her champagne. "Really, I'm flattered. I didn't know you felt this way about me. I'm loyal to you, Bonnie. Do you honestly think I would work with that girl? She reminds me of me when I first got to New York—calculating, ambitious, desperate. I wouldn't trust her to pick out my panty hose. She called me out of the blue, said she had tickets to the show, and asked if I wanted to come. Who wouldn't? She pushed it hard. Every dress on the runway, she whispered, 'You'd look spectacular in that,' or 'It's so *you*.'" Vicki laughed. "When she wasn't selling dresses, she was selling herself. Did you know that Megan's father used to be the governor of Idaho?"

"Iowa," said Bonnie.

"I'd never work with anyone but you," said Vicki. "And when my husband's business picks up again, you're the first person I'll call. I have to say, anger is very cute on you. Your cheeks are a lovely shade of resentful."

"Thanks."

"Here comes your new client. Is she a shopaholic like me?"

"Getting there," said Bonnie.

"Who's her husband?"

Joanne joined them before Bonnie could answer. Bonnie made the introductions. Vicki said goodbye. Once she was gone, Joanne said, "Wife of Lee Freed, right? Her husband's company went bankrupt, and he's millions in debt. They're ruined. Vicki had to resign from Peace on Earth. Didn't you know?"

She didn't. Only weeks ago, the Freeds had paid to have the street carpeted. Bonnie felt terrible for Vicki. Women like her usually had a ten-year run. From marriage to divorce, or society debut to departure. They appeared on the scene in their twenties or thirties, and then, by their thirties or forties, they disappeared. Vicki had a longer run than average. She'd been the third Mrs. Freed for nearly fourteen years. Bonnie could imagine what would happen to her now. Her mother-in-law had plotted ruthlessly for this moment. Lee Freed would have to sell off his possessions, including their apartment. He'd be forced to move back to Short Hills with his son. Vicki might be frozen out.

Joanne said, "She'll be okay."

Bonnie remembered that the Freeds had a prenup. Vicki told her about it once when she was in her underwear. "I'll get nothing if we divorce before our fifteenth anniversary," she'd said.

Since Bonnie shopped for Mr. Freed's anniversary gifts for the last five years, Bonnie knew their fourteenth was coming up in a month or so. A year until their fifteenth. Plenty of time for him to pull the rug out from under her, as well as everything else, and leave her with nothing but memories.

For Vicki's sake, Bonnie hoped they were good ones. And even if they were, it didn't seem like a fair trade to Bonnie. She wasn't Vicki Freed, however—a woman who'd come to New York to find and marry a millionaire, who'd do anything to keep him happy or die trying. Bonnie would never put a man on top of her priority list. Being in a relationship was not the only way to be happy.

But it was a great way to be happy. She missed it badly. She could admit that now. That had to be the first step toward a relationship.

"What's next for us?" asked Joanne Kline.

Good question. Bonnie smiled and checked her BlackBerry for the next show on the schedule. She hadn't anticipated liking Joanne's company. It complicated things even more.

Chapter Twelve

The rules of the Italian game bocce are simple: One player throws a small ball called a "jack" to the opposite end of a sand alley. Then a player bowls a larger ball, a bocce, down the alley as close as possible to the jack. While similar to American lawn games like croquet or shuffle board, bocce is played with Italian style—passionately and slowly. Old men take forever to set up their bowls, then have gusty discussions about each toss. A round of eight tosses can take up to an hour, including espresso breaks.

Peter *loved* bocce. It was the only ball "sport" he played. He could, and often did, spend an entire afternoon at the Corona bocce court, a.k.a. "Spaghetti Park." Not much of a park. Just the center of an oversized traffic circle with some shrubs, trees, benches, concrete chess tables, and a few bocce alleys. The old men in hats and vests who seemed to live there adored Peter and fought to have him on their team. It was rare in a young person, they told Bonnie, to find Peter's patience and respect. Rare? It was *unique*, she thought proudly. Bonnie worried that her son should spend Saturday afternoons playing with kids his own age and not gray-haired septuagenarians. But friends were blessings, in whatever form they came.

Even if they were achingly handsome married men.

On that Saturday, Bonnie and Peter were meeting Mike and his fiancée Emily at the bocce court. Mike wanted to "talk." Bonnie waited on the park bench while Peter played. The couple arrived right on time, casually dressed. Mike wore his usual jeans and lightweight sweater that showed off his chest. He looked handsome and happy. Emily, who Bonnie had met now several times, looked good in slacks, a cropped jacket, and boots. She was dark, around thirty, petite, and intense, with a cop's alert eyes. A bundle of nervous energy, Emily preferred to stand and appeared ready to spring into action. It worked somehow with Mike's more relaxed demeanor. Yin and yang. They fit together.

Seeing them hold hands put a lump in Bonnie's throat, but she managed to say, "Hello."

Mike whistled and waved at Peter. The boy was focused on the game and barely noticed his dad's arrival. Mike understood Peter's laser concentration and took it in stride. He sat on the park bench next to his ex-wife and watched Peter for a moment. Then he said, "I've been thinking…"

"Not *again*," said Bonnie.

Emily laughed and said, "Right? I can smell wood burning."

Bonnie was beginning to like Emily. If she weren't engaged to Mike, she could imagine them being friends. Did she feel the same way about Joanne Kline? Too early to tell. She didn't want to like Joanne because of her attraction to Steve.

Mike nodded along as the women laughed at him. "Emily, can you give us…?"

Emily wisely took her cue. "I'm going to the deli for coffee. Anyone?"

What's happening now? Bonnie wondered. Mike had something to say to her in private? "Something on your mind?"

"I just wanted to say that Peter seems to be doing really well."

He was doing well. "True." She always suspected Mike thought Peter would one day be a normal kid, the kind he'd take to football games. She always heard herself hedging when they talked about Peter's progress. Just keeping the discussion in reality. But this time, she didn't disagree with Mike's assessment.

He blinked rapidly. "Emily thinks he's doing well, too."

Okay, this was about his fiancée. In the weeks since their official engagement, Bonnie had had a chance to spend time with Emily and to watch her interact with Peter. They were good together. Natural. Peter was comfortable with her, and he wouldn't take to anyone who gave off bad vibes. The only weird moment was when Emily tried to hug Peter goodbye once. After Bonnie explained his hypersensitivity, Emily seemed to understand. That awkward moment was, apparently, on Mike's mind. Why was it so hard for Mike to discuss his fears?

"Peter likes her, too."

"She wants kids," said Mike.

Bonnie figured as much. Why else get married at their age? Mike would have more children. Those kids would probably be neurologically "normal." He would get the son he'd always wanted, a companion at Giants Stadium. And, Bonnie saw plainly, he felt horrible guilt about how excited he was about it.

What surprised Bonnie was how unaffected she felt by the news. She'd guarded Peter and Mike's relationship closely. She'd been jealous of all of his previous girlfriends. But with Emily, she could imagine her and Peter's world expanding. Emily represented an emotional, social gain, not a loss.

"That's great!" said Bonnie. "No matter how many kids you and Emily have, I know you'll never stop loving Peter, or caring for him, or looking out for him."

"How do you know for sure?" he asked, looking at her strangely. *My God*, she thought. *He's absolutely terrified.*

"Poor Mike," she said, feeling the familiar protectiveness for this man, her childhood friend, her first and only love. "You aren't betraying Peter by falling in love with Emily and having kids. You're not betraying me. Peter will love having siblings. You have to have kids, for Peter's sake. Have five! The more, the merrier." Bonnie touched Mike on his cheek. He leaned into it, took her wrist, and kissed her palm.

He said, "Thank you. For everything."

She was just as grateful to him, for their child and their history. But he was moving on. Bonnie had resisted for so long, but she finally felt the romantic link between them, weak as it was, break.

Emily chose that moment to return. She asked, "We good?"

Mike said, "Perfect."

"Great," said Emily.

Peter came over and roped the couple into playing a round of bocce. Bonnie watched and reveled in how not jealous and bitter she was about Emily. She was more evolved than she thought. Logically, she should be ecstatic about Emily and their future children. More people in the world to love Peter.

She wondered briefly if her okayness was denial. It didn't feel that way. She was glad to cut the emotional tether to Mike. She gave her blessing to him. Was that the same thing as giving herself permission to move on? Of course, she wouldn't be nearly as magnanimous about Emily if she didn't have Steve Kline in her life.

Her phone vibrated. Steve? He always called when she was thinking about him. Then again, she was always thinking about him.

Bonnie answered, "Hello?"

"What are you doing?" asked Sylvia.

"Bocce," said Bonnie. "I might be stuck here for hours."

"Come by the restaurant for dinner."

"Peter doesn't like it."

Ragussa's was a loud, crowded place. Sylvia knew Peter reacted badly to noise. "You never come see me," she whined. "You can't still be mad at me about Anita. We screwed up, okay? I apologize for us both."

"Anita is going to have to apologize for herself." Bonnie wasn't quite ready to forgive.

"Be that as it may, things with Carmine worked out, right? You made some money there. But you're avoiding me."

She was, and Sylvia knew it. Why? Bonnie was afraid that, within five minutes of Mom's scrutiny, she'd crack. She'd admit to her fears for her job, how much it hurt when Anita accused her of letting her family down. Add to that her feelings for a married, older man and how close she was to taking it to the next level. Sylvia would never approve of Steve. Rich was good, but Steve was older, not in the market for more babies. He traveled way too often and would leave Bonnie behind. He wasn't close with his family, including his sons. He wasn't Italian or Catholic. Bonnie couldn't understand why Sylvia would care since she hadn't been to mass since the 1980s.

"I'm not avoiding you," said Bonnie lamely.

Sylvia asked, "Are you seeing someone?"

"No. Sort of."

"Why so secretive? Is he married?"

"Look, I've got to go. Peter needs me."

She hung up. Her phone vibrated immediately. Mom calling back?

No. A text message from Steve Kline. He wrote, "What are you wearing?"

His usual opener. Their little in-joke. She texted, "Should I send you a picture?"

He called and said, "Chicago sucks. I miss you. I can't wait to get back to New York."

"When?" she asked, her heart thundering. *I miss you*, he said.

"Tuesday. Let's have dinner. I'd like to see you when you're not working or thinking about work. Or running off to work. I want your undivided attention."

On a Tuesday night? How could she manage that? Lucee volunteered at her church on that evening. She'd worked late on Tuesdays for an hour or two, but Bonnie realized with a gulp she was planning for a really long date with Steve. He'd never said outright that he wanted her. Only that she was beautiful, funny, and that he missed her.

"Can we make it Wednesday?" Taking a deep breath, she said, "My ex has custody that night."

She thought she could hear him smile. "I see. Wednesday then."

A moment of silence. Bonnie's cheeks were so red, she thought she might pop a capillary. She said, "Well then. I'll let you…"

"Joanne told me she had a good time with you at Fashion Week. She likes you."

Talking about his wife? Now? After they'd just arranged an assignation? What was that about? Was this his way of letting her know Joanne had given their affair a stamp of approval? "I'm beginning to like her, too. If she weren't your wife, I'd love her."

"We'll go to the Four Seasons."

A hotel? she thought. No. That seemed sordid, even at one

of the best hotels in Manhattan. Suddenly she got nervous again and backpedaled. "You know, Wednesday might not work."

"Don't play hard to get," he said. "We'll meet there on Fifty-Second Street."

Oh, he means the restaurant, not the hotel, she thought, relief flooding over her chest.

"Uh-oh. Bonnie, Jack just came in. I've got to go. I'm going to be busy for the next couple of days, so forgive me if I can't call. Wednesday. I can't wait."

And then he hung up. Jack was Steve's son, the VP at Kline and Co. with the dubious credentials. So he was keeping his son in the dark about their relationship, such as it was, too. Bonnie hadn't breathed a word to Peter about Steve. She'd barely told Steve anything about Peter, for that matter. Obviously, if he were going to be a part of her life and not only her fantasies, he and Peter would have to meet. Bonnie frowned, worried how Peter would react to a man in her life or how Steve would handle Peter's unique perspective on the world.

Her fear about the two worlds colliding—Queens and Manhattan—had led her to keep them apart for her entire working life. The idea of crossover terrified her. She was afraid of being judged on all counts. To Anita and the Salernos, Steve would be a cheating stuffed shirt who thought he could buy anything or anyone. To Steve, the Salernos would seem crass and common. Peter would seem like an alien. Bonnie sat on the bench and tried to imagine seamlessly incorporating her family and the man she was growing closer to. When Peter said he was ready to go home, Bonnie realized an hour had gone by.

Joanne Kline's Hauenstein fittings took longer than expected. She had to leave New York without her new dresses. Bonnie swore she'd overnight them to the Kline residence in Chicago as soon as humanly possible.

"I'm never there. Send them to me at Sam's," Joanne instructed via email along with the home address of Mr. Samuel J. Kaufman. Bonnie Googled him. According to an article in the *Sun Times*, Mr. Kaufman owned every parking garage in Chicago. If parking there was anything like here, Kaufman had to be rolling with cash. Bonnie clicked through to his company website and found a photo. Physically, Kaufman was Steve Kline's opposite. Steve was sleek and athletic like a jungle creature. Mr. Kaufman was broad and rugged, like a fiftyish Clive Owen or Gerald Butler.

Joanne's flight was leaving LaGuardia right around now. Bonnie felt a huge weight lift off her shoulders. The week of tending to Steve's wife had been nerve-racking. Both Klines had the same caller ID, "Kline and Co." Bonnie didn't know what to expect when she answered her BlackBerry.

Her dinner with Steve was planned for this evening at 6:30 p.m. Bonnie wore a classic gray wool suit, patent leather pumps, and her favorite white silk bra and panty set. She wasn't sure if anyone but her would see it. She was of two minds about the scheduled seduction. Bonnie craved Steve physically. She'd worked hard to rationalize having sex with a dubiously married man. Whether she could go through with it remained to be seen. He'd be her first lover in years. That fact alone filled her with self-conscious anxiety. Wherever they wound up—his place, a hotel—she'd make sure to turn off the lights.

Fortunately, Bonnie's afternoon was packed. She didn't have a spare minute to obsess. Post-Fashion Week, a dozen socialites had made appointments to view the new collections. Also, the Peace on Earth spring gala was only two months away. It was the Super Bowl of society events. The ladies of New York needed a season of hard work and determination to get there in style.

The afternoon threatened to get away from her as clients flowed in and out of the Salon. Jesus texted that five new gowns from Zac Posen had just arrived. Bonnie knew a few of her clients would want first look and asked Jesus to hold them for her in the Cage. A Salon stylist could put a number of garments on hold in her own locked closet in the Cage to reserve for select clients. Bonnie's closet was bursting with looks for spring. Some of the designer gowns would never make it to the eighth floor boutiques if she could sell them to her clients at private showings at the Salon or in their homes. Bonnie's predecessor at Frankel's took advantage of the hold closet rule. *Every* incoming frock was delivered straight into his closet. Designers complained. Mr. Charles fired him.

Such tactics appalled Bonnie—back then. That was before she'd found herself in trench warfare at Frankel's, fighting a ruthless novice for her own job. For the month of March, Bonnie's sales were four times Megan's. But one big client could change that. Even though Mr. Charles thanked Bonnie profusely for bringing back the La Perla garments, he steered new clients toward Megan.

It was 5:30, a half hour from the Salon's closing time. A swarm of butterflies had taken residence in Bonnie's stomach as her date neared. She was checking her makeup when someone called, "I need some help out here!" Bonnie didn't recognize the voice, but she'd heard that tone before. The young, entitled, spoiled whine of a "special friend," a woman who'd just landed a sugar daddy. They wanted the world, and they wanted it *now*.

Bonnie peeked out of her office to get a look. A Naomi Campbell look-alike with a smirk, a bedazzled iPhone, and 3-D gel manicured nail tips. Her curvy body was packed into skinny jeans that made her bottom look enormous (the idea), topped with a red sequined top, and accessorized with the biggest gold hoop earrings Bonnie had ever seen.

Fran at reception made eye contact with Bonnie and mimed a finger down her throat. They'd both seen a hundred variations of this type in the Salon before, although less often since the recession.

"Bet you'd like some coffee," said Fran.

"Some service would be great. I don't have all freakin' day," she said. At moments like this, Bonnie wondered how she'd been doing this job for so long. Where was her millionaire savior? Was it really such a moral compromise to find a man to take care of her? This girl had done it. Her mother had done it. Half her clients were thrilled to tears not to have to worry about work or money. Bonnie exhaled and flashed to Steve and Joanne Kline, shopping together for their Manhattan home. Steve would never shop with her for sheets and towels. He had no intention of leaving Joanne. He'd told Bonnie as much.

I'm not interested in him for his money, she thought. Was that entirely true? Would Bonnie be as attracted to him if he were, say, a carpenter who built a mall rather than a financier who owned it?

"Coffee coming right up," said Fran, with feigned alacrity. Fran took every opportunity to get out from behind that desk and away from this type of client—the young and the breathless.

"How can I help you?" asked Bonnie.

The woman said, "I want to open a credit account. I've got a letter of introduction from the bank, instructing you to…"

"I love those jeans!" squealed Megan. She'd appeared in the room suddenly, as if lured by the scent of official letterhead.

Bonnie smiled—on the inside. She said to her former assistant, "This woman would like to open an account. Would you please take care of her? I've got a previous appointment."

Megan grinned. "Of course. How can I help you?"

The Naomi clone sized up Megan. She seemed mildly happier at the prospect of working with her. They were the same age, spoke the same language. "I was just telling this woman that I've got a letter from the bank. I need to set this up NOW, before my friend gets here."

"I can help with that. I'm Megan, by the way."

"Shawnee."

"Right this way, Shawnee," Megan said, steering her new client into Fitting Room C, which Mr. Charles had converted into a makeshift office for her.

Bonnie grabbed her phone and purse and ran out of the Salon. Shawnee's sugar daddy probably told her to set up an account before his arrival just moments before closing time. That way, they'd be able to shop for shoes and clothes with some privacy. Last time Bonnie worked with a flavor-of-the-month, the married boyfriend threw the girl out of her kept apartment the day her Frankel's order was ready to ship. The girl wanted her packages delivered to her ex-doorman. In a fit of operatic paranoia, she wouldn't give her name, the doorman's name, or his cell phone number. She'd only supply the address and an AmEx number, which had been invalidated the day before. The ordeal had been a huge waste of time for Bonnie. Another secret mistress tried to exit the store in a new outfit of designer clothes, tags still on. When she was stopped by security, she screamed, "Don't you know who I am?" She called her boyfriend, a foreign diplomat who was also a "close and personal" friend of Mr. Charles. From that day forward, photos of the diplomat's girlfriends were posted in the security office, and the girls were allowed to walk out in whatever they could pile on their backs—all charged to the man's account.

By passing Shawnee to Megan, Bonnie felt like she'd dodged a bullet. She laughed to herself, imagining the paces Megan would be put through. The happy feeling didn't last long. Out on Madison, Bonnie remembered her nerves.

Irma, the blind, homeless woman in dark sunglasses was on her milk crate out front as always. She sniffed in Bonnie's direction and said, "Hey, White Linen."

"Mind the store," said Bonnie, giving her a dollar. At that moment, a limo pulled up on the curb. Limos pulled up to Frankel's many times per day. No big deal. The back door opened, and a glamorous long-legged woman stepped out.

Okay, not your ordinary, run-of-the-mill limo arrival, thought Bonnie, her jaw unhinged like every other person on the street.

"Latisha!" screamed Irma. "Oh, my sweet Jesus! It's Latisha!" The blind cripple jumped to her feet with catlike fluidity and proceeded to mimic the dance steps from Latisha's latest music video—which Irma had apparently seen. With her eyes that seemed to work just fine.

As the world-famous singer and her entourage approached the entrance, Irma shouted, "Check me out! I got moves!"

Latisha smiled at her. A man walking next to her in a porkpie hat said into his phone, "Shawnee? We're coming up. Did you set up the account? We're good? Nice. Two minutes." To Bonnie, he said, "Excuse me."

This would be the moment. She could introduce herself, welcome Latisha to the store, escort the hip-hop icon to the

Salon, and cut Megan out of what was sure to be a massive sales day.

Seanceé or Steve?

Bonnie hesitated. Work or romance? Profession or personal? It boiled down to that. Then the moment was over. The singer was inside, surrounded by her people as well as Frankel's security. She was already on her way up to the Salon, where Shawnee—not a girl-of-the-month, but a member of the singer's entourage—and Megan waited.

She'd missed her chance or had willfully let it go. Bonnie frowned, not sure if she'd made a huge mistake.

Irma sat back down on her milk crate, blackout glasses back on, weaving à la Stevie Wonder.

"You can see," said Bonnie flatly. "And walk. And *dance*."

"I have no idea what you're talking about," said Irma.

Bonnie rolled her eyes and headed down Madison toward the Four Seasons. She'd been faced with a choice, and her subconscious had made it. She'd gone with romance. Happy and feeling settled about the date for the first time all day, Bonnie headed toward the restaurant and maybe her future.

Bonnie's eye went right to Steve when she entered the room. He looked fantastic in the charcoal Zenga suit she'd picked out for him. It fit his slim body perfectly. She flashed to what his body looked like underneath. Breathtaking.

He had already been seated at a table for two in a discreet corner of the Pool Room at the Four Seasons. Bonnie had been to the famous restaurant once before, when Mr. Charles was courting her for her current job. She remembered the ambiance to be dazzling, with impeccable waiters and classically simple decor. She'd felt wooed back then, seduced into moving to Frankel's from Bloomingdale's. Around that time, the extent of Peter's problems had come to light. Her marriage was unraveling. The new job had been a blessing, an exciting distraction from her personal problems. Striving to prove her worth and title gave her a daytime focus. Without it, she might have slipped down the rabbit hole. Now she was back in the Pool Room to meet another man for another seduction. The promise of an exciting distraction quickened her pulse and her steps.

"You look lovely," he said, gesturing for her to sit.

"Good to see you, too," she said, accepting his compliment and believing it. She knew she looked good in the Theory suit. The soft wool jacket hit right at the hip with a pretty rounded hem, making her look feminine and young. The cropped trousers helped take a few years off and made her legs look skinny and long. Heather gray made her hazel eyes pop and her skin glow. She wore patent high-heeled pumps, stepping out of her usual boots. Bonnie felt tall and as beautiful as she had in years. Steve's attention did this to her. He'd inspired the fluttering in her core. As uncomfortable as it was, Bonnie didn't want it to stop.

He helped her into her chair. A waiter appeared to take her drink order. "Chardonnay," she said, needing something to calm her nerves.

Steve said, "Vodka, rocks."

Once alone again, Bonnie glanced around the room. A lot of the women had matching "Sally" haircuts.

"Does every woman in New York go to the same hairdresser?" he asked.

Hairdresser. She smiled at the old-fashioned word. "Hair stylist," she corrected.

"I thought you were a stylist."

"I am," she said. "For clothes and shoes. I cover everything below the neck."

"Not hats?" he asked, grinning.

"I'm not a big hat person."

Her clients were dotted around the room. Bonnie was careful not to acknowledge any of them, although she did admire her work out of the corner of her eye. Smart-dressed women made her swell with pride.

Steve asked, "Hungry?"

"Yes!"

"Is it my imagination, or are we being watched?"

"Unfortunately. But no one will try to talk to us. Most of

my clients shun me in public. It shatters the illusion that they shop for themselves."

"I'm proud to be seen with you," he said.

She blushed. It couldn't be helped. She was ridiculously flattered and grateful. "Thank you," she said softly.

The waiter brought their drinks. He said, "Tell me a story about someone here. But don't tell me who. I'll have to guess."

She took a sip of her wine. "Okay. A woman in this room once plotted to land her financier husband the old-fashioned way—by cyberstalking him. She hired a hacker to get access to his travel agent and found out he was flying to China on business. With her last dollar, she booked a first-class seat on the same flight right next to him. She had twenty hours in the air to work her charm. By the time they landed in Hong Kong, he was ready to leave his wife and children and marry her."

"My God," he said, glancing around the room. "What'd she do to him?"

"It's a mystery, wrapped in an enigma. She is an extremely resourceful woman."

Steve smiled. "You are, too."

What did he mean by that? She must have looked confused. He said, "You are, aren't you? I knew that about you the moment I first saw you. Remember? Back in September. You were going up the escalator, and I was walking around Frankel's with Chase. We made eye contact for just a few seconds, but I thought, *Who's that?* And then we saw each other again in the lobby at the St. Regis."

Of course, Bonnie remembered each moment as if it were set in amber. Steve had seen her. He'd noticed her, picked her out of the crowd, just like she'd zeroed in on him. It was wonderful, but confounding.

"You do realize I'm not young. I'm divorced. I've got a kid, and I live in Queens. I sell dresses for a living."

He said, "All I know is that you're beautiful, talented, funny, and honest."

Honest? Well, that wasn't exactly true. She'd already lied to him about the well-and-tree platter she'd sold.

"I know you'll be perfect," he said. "Joanne is coming around to it, too."

"Your wife?" Okay, this was too weird, even for Bonnie. "What, what are you talking about?"

"My new store," he said. "At the site of that warehouse I showed you on Barrow Street. A mix of high- and lowbrow fashion culture. Cheap chic, to compete with Target and H&M."

"What does that have to do with me?" Bonnie got a sick feeling in her belly. Was all this about a store? The phone calls and texts? The limo ride to Short Hills, the long looks, and big dinner date? Was he courting her like Chase Charles had done, for a *job*? Bonnie's mind replayed their relationship thus far. Now that she thought about it, they talked about clients and her work half of the time. He talked about his big New York City store plans the other half. They'd barely spoken about their personal lives. With a cold chill, Bonnie realized she'd misinterpreted his attentions. It all made sense now. The drive to see his warehouse. Having Joanne, his business partner, come to the Salon and Fashion Week as her client. All this time, he'd been conducting a protracted job interview.

"Wait, did you think I was…" he asked, and his cheeks turned red.

She'd spent the better part of six months fantasizing about this man. She'd realigned her morals to convince herself to sleep with him. Totally embarrassed, Bonnie gulped down her wine and fought back mystified tears.

She was mortified. But Bonnie had years of practice pretending to be placid on the outside while she crumbled inside. Her voice tart, she said, "Not interested in a move. I'm vested at Frankel's. I love my clients. As long as they'll have me, I'm staying."

"You hate your clients!" he said. "You've been trashing them to me for weeks."

"I'm devoted to them. They make me crazy, but they need me." *And I need them*, she thought.

"With respect, I think you're capable of more. Maybe you're afraid to make a change."

"I'm afraid of being unemployed," she corrected. The humiliation was turning into anger. Good. She could handle that more easily. "This would never work." How could she spend all day with this man? It'd be a nightmare of suppressed desire on top of embarrassment.

"I know you'd be perfect."

"You don't know that. You don't really know anything about me."

"I have good instincts about people."

"Your instincts are off. I've already lied to you. You know the well-and-tree platter you gave me for Christmas? I sold it within an hour of receiving it."

He looked hurt. "Why?"

"To pay for private school for my son. His name is Peter. He's six," she said, smiling, thinking of his face. "He has special needs."

Bonnie stared at Steve, gauging his reaction. He said, "I'm sorry to hear that, Bonnie."

Oh, God. He seemed to mean it. She felt a sudden need to explain herself. "He's okay. But I do have to make smart decisions about where I work." She had to protect her income, and thereby her son. She was intensely protective about everything that affected Peter. For a long time, that feeling was the only powerful emotion in her life. *And then I met you*, she thought, *and my world cracked open a little bit*. But now, she saw her wishful thinking for what it was. He did like her, but not in the way she hoped he did. He was her friend, if nothing more, and Bonnie could use one. She smiled, trying to lighten the moment.

"I have sons, too. Jack and Brian," said Steve. "They're older, as you know. My relationships with them are...complicated. They work for me. There are issues about money and advancement, resentments real and imagined. I remember six, though. It's a good age. I missed a lot."

Bonnie could easily guess what he meant by "issues" and things being "complicated." She'd spent enough time with the Deerlinger twins and the Zachary Freeds of the world. It was strange how Bonnie and Steve had spent so many hours talking, but only in the last five minutes had they actual revealed some real truths to each other. She told him about Peter to explain about keeping her job at Frankel's. Why had he told her about the touchy subject of his fatherhood? He might think opening up about his doubts would earn her trust. Smart men knew that by giving a little, they'd get a lot back.

"I really do appreciate you thinking of me for the new store," she said. "Making a change isn't a possibility for me. I need old, reliable Frankel's. I can't take the risk of jumping ship."

"I'm disappointed," he said.

He didn't know the half of it.

With the job off the table, the frankness they'd shared moments ago disappeared as quickly as it'd come. They sat in silence. Bonnie felt deflated. The day's emotional ride had come to an abrupt halt. She said, "So. I should probably go."

"No, stay," he said, putting his hand over hers. "We're just getting started. We won't talk about the store. Tell me more about Peter."

She shrugged, not in the mood. She felt her heart close up again.

He frowned. "We're friends, aren't we?"

She'd hoped they'd be more. And if they couldn't be, well, she'd settle for less, eventually. But right now, she was just wrung out. "Thank you for the drink."

"Bonnie, something went wrong here, obviously. I don't care that you sold the platter. If anything, I'm impressed you were able to put it to good use. I didn't mean to imply that you aren't reaching your potential at Frankel's. Stay, please. You seem upset. I've insulted you somehow."

Her phone vibrated. Saved by the BlackBerry again. She checked caller ID. Gloria Rodkin? It wasn't like her to call after hours.

"Excuse me," she said to Steve, removing his hand from hers. "Hello?"

"Something terrible has happened!" said Gloria.

This was not Gloria's usual hysterical tone when she broke a heel or couldn't get a table at Le Bernardin. "What's wrong?"

"I knew this was coming! You heard me predict this! I'm suing the doctors. All ten of them!"

"I still don't know what..."

"Elliot Snyder, my son-in-law! He's dead! Shelley is a thirty-year-old widow! We have to plan the funeral. By Jewish law, it has to be tomorrow. I need you, Bonnie! I can't do this by myself."

Bonnie's blood froze. Elliot was dead? She'd styled their wedding not two years before. "Okay, I can be at your apartment in fifteen minutes." She hung up. To Steve, she said, "It's a client. Someone died. No one you know."

"I'm so sorry. Can I call you?"

Flustered, Bonnie nodded vaguely and left. She was three blocks away before she realized she never said goodbye.

PART FIVE

April:
The Funeral

Chapter Thirteen

"Did I not see this coming?" asked Gloria Rodkin, her daughter Shelley next to her on the couch in their living room. "I knew that man was going to drop dead."

Bonnie had never been inside the Rodkins home before. Since she knew her client's taste in clothes—conservative—Bonnie hadn't expected an über-modern, Frank Stella-inspired loft space with white walls, bare wood floors, and huge sculptures. It was like walking into the art deco floor at the Museum of Modern Art. Mother and daughter were perched on the pea green, molded hard plastic couch. Bonnie was directed to a tiny stool on a thin pedestal she was sure she'd break.

No wonder Gloria spent so much time at Frankel's, thought Bonnie. *The Salon had comfortable furniture.*

"I'm so sorry for your loss," said Bonnie. "What happened? Was it his…ulcer?" She remembered hearing something about an ulcer listening to Gloria's phone conversations.

Shelley was in shock, staring spookily at the wall. Last time Bonnie saw her, she was twenty pounds thinner, standing on a dress platform in her wedding gown. Bonnie got to know Shelley while working on the gown and styling the bridal party. She liked her. They were close to the same age. She was, like a lot of upper-class Manhattan daughters, a bit dependent on her wealthy parents. Shelley was particularly attached to her mom and came off as wishy-washy. Mike, a *Star Wars* fan, would say, "The force is weak in this one."

Gloria answered for her distraught daughter. "That's the bitter irony, Bonnie. His ulcer was *cured.* He'd just received a clean bill of health from his doctor, and then he had a brain embolism and died on Park and Eighty-Sixth Street."

Shelley sobbed. Her hands covered her face.

"Oh my God," said Bonnie, horrified.

Gloria said, "They'd only been married two years. They were trying, but now…it's a blessing Shelley and Elliot had no children."

Was it ever a blessing *not* to have children? A baby would have been Elliot Snyder's legacy and given Shelley a reason to carry on. A baby would be a source of joy for the grieving family.

"I understand," said Bonnie.

"I can't make any more phone calls," said Shelley, barely able to speak.

"She called her in-laws in Orange County. They're distraught," Gloria said. To her daughter, "I'll do the rest." Back to Bonnie: "Our doctor should be arriving any second to give Shelley a shot. I already called Rabbi Menchen at the Lexington Avenue Synagogue. The funeral is supposed to be the day after the death, according to our faith. But I explained to the rabbi that we simply can't plan a proper funeral in just one day. I made a large donation to the temple, and he gave me three days."

Bonnie nodded. "You want my help?"

"I need more than *help*, Bonnie. I want you to handle the whole thing."

"Me? What about your usual planner?" Her name escaped Bonnie. She was the same woman who did the wedding.

"You mean Savoy San Sullivan? That woman is *useless*. If you recall, Bonnie, she screwed up one thing after another, and you know that better than anyone since you fixed all her mistakes. This has to be done right this time. Announcements in the papers, burial arrangements. Limos to take us from the temple to the cemetery—thank God Elliot had a plot already at Shady Hills in Queens. Very respectable cemetery. Very clean. We need caterers for the shivah at Shelley's apartment. Shelley and I need new suits and dresses for the funeral and seven days' worth of sitting. I told Rabbi Menchen that I want a reception— tasteful, a buffet and bar—after the service, but before we take the body, before the burial, so the mourners can express their condolences to Shelley in the holy setting… Listen closely, Bonnie." Gloria continued, "Shelley needs to look beautiful. This whole thing is tragic enough. It'd be adding insult to injury if the mourners thought Shelley looked bloated."

"I look bloated?" asked the widow, as horrified by that as anything else that'd been said.

"Bite your tongue," said Gloria, aggressively stroking Shelley's hair. "You're beautiful, and now you're tragic, too. There's nothing as romantic as a tragic young widow. And you look gorgeous in black."

Shelley nodded, sniffled. Despite her grief, she was glad to hear she'd look pretty at the funeral. If it seemed pathologically shallow, Bonnie wouldn't hold it against her. Any comfort in the face of sudden death was welcome.

"Why don't you go lie down, Shelley?" said Gloria. "I need to talk to Bonnie about funeral logistics."

The widow nodded, trancelike, got up on shaky legs, and dragged herself out of the room.

Gloria waited until Shelley was gone. "That one phone call to California was all she could stand to do. The mother fainted, and Shelley promised the father she'd take care of everything, that all they had to do was get to New York. And then Shelley swallowed three Lorazepams and has been barely functional since. It's for the best, though. I'm going to make the doctor give me enough to keep her doped until June. Can you *believe* this, Bonnie? It's a nightmare! How dare Elliot let his brain explode! If he weren't dead, I'd kill him!"

Shelley had confided to Bonnie during one of their fittings that Elliot was the first man who'd told her she was beautiful and the first lover to fully satisfy her. Bonnie vaguely remembered their backstory. College friends who rediscovered each other at a party. Mutual parental approval. A good match. A love match. Shelley had been looking—as had Gloria on her behalf—for quite some time when she hooked up with Elliot. God, this was awful.

"Does Shelley have anything to fall back on?" asked Bonnie, tears forming. "A career, friends?" No siblings.

"Nothing!" whispered Gloria. "Elliot was her whole life. I guess she has her apartment, which is breathtaking. But she can't buy art all day. I could send her on a European tour. I'll call my travel agent. She can pull an itinerary together quickly."

Her son-in-law dropped dead, making her daughter a widow, and Gloria was talking about sending Shelley on a trip? "Maybe it's a bit soon. Shelley needs to stay close for now."

"She's been close her whole life! She only left home two years ago. She's never had a job. Never taken care of herself. This death is like God is forcing her back home."

Gloria's losing it, thought Bonnie. The weight of responsibility for Shelley had fallen, apparently, on her head. Bonnie would gladly support Peter for the rest of his life. But Peter's dependence was neurologically based. Shelley could, theoretically, create her own life apart from Gloria. Was it too late? Healthy separation was supposed to occur when a kid was around thirteen years old. Shelley was in her thirties. It might be too late for her to become her own woman. Bonnie had no choice in the matter. Her father refused to pay for college or for one dime of rent money when she could just live in his house. She understood—before thirteen—that her life was what she made of it.

"I don't mean that," said Gloria, backpedaling. "This is just a horrible situation in a million ways. I really need your help."

"It's absolutely no problem—wardrobe, the funeral, and shivah—but I'm just not qualified to plan an event." Not to mention, Bonnie would be off-site for three days. Mr. Charles would never allow it. The Salon was full-service, which meant running the occasional errand or shopping in other stores for clients. But organizing an event? That would be a first. "I can put you in touch with an event specialist, someone better than Savoy. We can call a few of them right now," Bonnie said, holding up her BlackBerry.

"No!" shouted Gloria. Then softer, "I can't trust any planner, Bonnie. This is extremely delicate. I don't want some stranger with a walkie-talkie in a suit clicking around my apartment, seeing us like this. Seeing Shelley like this. Our private lives exposed. I can't trust anyone else, Bonnie." She drew a deep breath. "Shelley's birth father, he's a deadbeat. He left Shelley and me with nothing, but she worships him anyway, the prick. You know my husband, Stan. He and Shelley...their relationship isn't great. We had some lean years, but Stan supported Shelley all the way through. Brearley, Wesleyan, he paid for everything. Shelley never thanked Stan for any of it. She never gave him a chance, despite everything he did for us. He really tried to win her over, Bonnie—a lot harder than I would have. I promised him that when Shelley was finally settled with Elliot—Stan paid for the wedding, too—that we'd travel, have adventures, do whatever his heart desired. That's over. And now Stan will have to pay for the funeral."

Gloria started to cry. Bonnie jumped off her stool, making it fall over. The clunk echoed in the sparse room. She sat next to her client and put an arm around her. "I understand," she said.

She did feel for Gloria. Stan was her white knight, and Gloria was terrified of losing him. If Bonnie found a similarly supportive man, she'd feel beholden to him, too. Stan Rodkin had taken in Gloria and Shelley. The guy was a sweetheart. Shelley repaid him with aloofness. He'd endured a lot. So had Gloria, torn between her child and husband.

No wonder Gloria had been obsessed with Elliot's health.

"You're the only person in the world I've ever told about Stan and Shelley," said Gloria, wiping under her eyes so as not to smear her mascara. "I've built up a façade of our happy little family. I've tried to hold it all together, to be strong. Elliot was a very kind man, Bonnie. Their marriage was a blessing. I have no idea how she'll get over this. It's shameful, how helpless she is, isn't it? Is it my fault? Did I do that?"

"Let's just get through the next few days. The soul-searching can wait until later. Pencil it in for April or May," said Bonnie. Planning a funeral would be a new challenge. She should push herself. She'd speak to Mr. Charles about this. He'd figure out some way to bill the planning through the store. Peter was with Mike this weekend, which made things easier.

"Or next year. Or never," said Gloria. She paused and composed herself. "You're right. We should focus on the task at hand and make this funeral the talk of the town. Elliot would have wanted it that way."

"The mayor?" asked Bonnie at her BlackBerry. In the twelve hours between the time Bonnie had left Gloria's last night and Thursday morning, Gloria had sent dozens of texts about the funeral. This last one instructed Bonnie to "book" the mayor to speak at the service. If that wasn't possible, Gloria would settle for Bill Clinton or Oprah Winfrey.

Her head pounding, Bonnie rushed up the subway stairs. She scrolled through texts while hoofing over to Frankel's and asked herself, "What have I gotten myself into?"

Bonnie blew right by Irma today as she entered the store. She went for the elevator and got off on the fifth floor, Shoes. She walked through the vast maze of sandals, boots, pumps, and flats to the back of the floor, where Mr. Charles's private office was located.

"I need to see him now," she said to Craig, Mr. Charles's assistant. He'd been there a week. Mr. Charles went through assistants like socks.

"He's in a meeting," said Craig.

"I'm not asking your permission," said Bonnie. She ignored the protests, opened Mr. Charles's door, and entered the two-hundred-square-foot office. The decor was as luxurious and claustrophobic as an Arabian harem chamber. Mr. Charles was an avid Orientalist. After the minimalism of Gloria's apartment, the opulence of Mr. Charles's overlapping rugs, silk pillows, damask curtains, and inlaid wood Chinese desk and chairs made Bonnie's eyes hurt.

She was also assaulted by the sight of Megan Hooligan—ahem, *Houlihan*—sitting on the corner of Mr. Charles's desk. One leg was dangling, the other on the floor. Her skirt rode enticingly high. Mr. Charles sat behind the desk. From Bonnie's perspective, Megan was aiming her crotch right at his face. Talk about moral equivalency. Bonnie had never, would never use sexual appeal for career advancement. She'd use her good taste, wit, attractiveness, such as it was, to win people's confidence and trust. If exposing her thighs was a job requirement, Bonnie didn't want the position. She felt a wellspring of disgust rise in her throat. She had to compete with Megan this way, too?

He said, "Bonnie! Megan and I were just kicking around ideas about the future of the Salon. We need to appeal to younger women. We can't just go for the older crowd. We'll die out as they do. We need young energy around here. A new focus."

"Mr. Charles really understands what's going on out there with the youth market," said Megan. "I'm blown away by how in touch he is. I mean, it's like he's got his finger on the pulse of my generation."

He'd love to get his finger on the... "I need to speak to you privately," said Bonnie to Mr. Charles.

Megan said, "Nothing's wrong with Peter, I hope."

Bonnie almost snarled protectively. She didn't want Megan to say his name. She'd rather Megan didn't know his name. "He's great."

"You're amazing, Bonnie," said Megan. "I don't know how you do it. Most working moms wouldn't do half the job you do."

What she really meant was that a woman without a child would do twice the job Bonnie did. Mr. Charles wasn't falling for this, was he? "Thank you," said Bonnie. "Cool celebrity shopper sighting. I think I just saw Angelina Jolie browsing in pumps."

"Angelina??" Megan flew off Mr. Charles's desk, checking her phone for a text alert to the star's arrival. "Gotta go," she said. She couldn't leave fast enough.

Mr. Charles smiled. "And she's off."

"Good riddance."

He said, "I read in the *Post* this morning that Ms. Jolie is in Burma. I also heard you had dinner with Steve Kline last night."

"Excuse me?"

"I got five texts from clients at the Four Seasons. Was he recruiting you for that monstrosity they're building downtown? Good luck competing with Target and H&M. I've known him for twenty-five years. He's never been short on ego. Only he could waltz into New York and expect the city to bow at his feet."

"I wouldn't characterize it like that," said Bonnie, torn between wanting to defend Steve and not revealing any information to Mr. Charles.

"He's fooling himself. And I assume he's tried to fool you, too. Don't take this the wrong way, but the only reason he wants you is to screw with me. We've always been a bit competitive."

If that were true, Bonnie wondered if Mr. Charles had ever won, in any fashion, against Steve Kline. She knew he was inflating his involvement in Steve's decision making. But his words stung nonetheless. She'd felt hurt that Steve's proposal hadn't been romantic. Mr. Charles now forced her to wonder if his professional proposal hadn't been valid. No, he had to be wrong. Steve valued her. He liked her. Their relationship had nothing to do with this jealous jackass. Or did it?

Change the subject. "Gloria Rodkin's son-in-law died yesterday," said Bonnie. "She wants me to plan the funeral. She'll pay for all of it—cars, catering, clothes, flowers—on her Frankel's card, but only a fraction of the expense will be purchased in store."

He was already shaking his head. "No."

"She'll also pay a flat fee for my services."

"How much?"

"Fifteen thousand."

"That's *it?*" He was not impressed. "You can earn that much for the store selling one Valentino."

"Mrs. Rodkin is my oldest client," said Bonnie. "We've worked together for ten years, since before I came to Frankel's."

"Megan had a *very* successful afternoon yesterday. Latisha might be the only woman left in the city with money to burn. Those are the clients we need more of, and Megan knows exactly how to appeal to them. Your clients are literally dying off, Bonnie. Or going broke."

"Mrs. Rodkin isn't exactly broke. It'll take three days to earn her eternal loyalty to Frankel's."

"Her loyalty will be to you, Bonnie, not Frankel's," he said. "I've noticed this about you. You care more about your own ambitions than the health of the store. You're not thinking of the big picture, only of your own self interests."

It was so off base, Bonnie couldn't fathom a response. As far as Bonnie was concerned, she'd been the epitome of the hardworking employee.

"You also let the clients control you. You want them to like you and respect you so badly, you do anything they want. When Gloria Rodkin asked for this huge favor, did she cry?"

Oh, God, thought Bonnie. She had cried. Was he right to say she was easily manipulated? Bonnie flashed to two recent memories: the Cody Deerlinger shoe crisis at the St. Regis and the emergency trip to Short Hills for Vicki Freed. What both crises had in common? Steve Kline had been present both times. Bonnie couldn't help seeing his eyes connect with hers through that glass elevator in the hotel lobby. Or how close they sat in the backseat of his limo while driving to New Jersey.

"Any of the stylists would go out of their way to help the clients," said Bonnie. "That is my job."

"No. Your job, which I shouldn't need to tell you, is to sell frocks. It's a matter of perspective. I can't believe I'm telling you this. You've been here for five years already. You don't get it. Maybe you never did."

"And Megan does?" Was he firing her?

"The retail business gets more ruthless every day. You, Bonnie, are getting softer by the hour. Where's your killer instinct? Megan will do anything to make a sale. She would have demanded $30,000 for Gloria Rodkin. When you started at Frankel's, it was impossible *not* to put up huge numbers. Those days are gone. We have to adapt to a new economic environment or die. "

Bonnie felt stung, condescended to. He would have wanted her to jack up the price on a grieving mother-in law? The deal with Gloria Rodkin was fair. She'd thought Mr. Charles would praise her for being at the service of a loyal client. But he didn't care about Gloria, or Bonnie's initiative, or the strength of the relationship. It was a sucker bet to think of clients as friends. But Bonnie had to think of them, at the very least, as human beings with feelings. Otherwise, she might as well be playing dress-up with paper dolls.

Helping Gloria Rodkin, a decent person in need, was the right thing to do, period. If Bonnie's job didn't include compassion and caring, then she'd find one that did. Other people—her former colleagues and Steve Kline—had made offers. Why had she felt so trapped? It was the psychology of the oppressed to believe you didn't have anywhere else to go. She realized with a jolt that her job had been like an abusive spouse. She'd cowered and clung like a battered wife.

Her mother had been begging her to take more risks in life. Sylvia meant romantically, but Bonnie had been playing it safe across the board. Look where it'd gotten her: alone in life and afraid of losing.

A new reality struck her. She could see herself escaping this office, the store, her own self-imposed loneliness. But first, she had work to do.

"I already promised Gloria I'd do it," she said to Mr. Charles.

"Go ahead," he said, shrugging. "It's your funeral."

"I'll need an assistant."

"Take it out of the $15,000."

"Fine," she said and walked out. By the time she hit the elevator, she'd reached candidate number one.

"Chief!" said Roman Jones. "How's it going?"

It had been a month or so since he'd been fired. "You tell me."

"Busy, in debt, but happy."

"I want to apologize, Roman. I should have been able to protect you." She was on the eighth floor now, heading for the main entrance of the Salon.

"No worries, really. Look, I'm walking into a class…"

"I'll get to the point. I'm working on a special project. Speed is a major factor, and I could use a hand. Good money."

He was silent for a second. "Hello?" she asked.

"Sorry, Bonnie, you can't pay me enough to walk into Frankel's."

"Because of Megan?"

He laughed. "No. I'm over her by a mile. It's the store, the atmosphere. I can't kiss one more rich bitch ass. And the merch stresses me out. Remember the red Valentino gown that never turned up? I still have nightmares."

Phone pressed to her ear, Bonnie entered the Salon, nodded at Fran, squeezed between a few racks of clothing, nearly collided with a delivery guy, and almost tripped over a shoe on the floor. Five people called her name as she walked to her office. Roman was right. The Salon was stressful.

"It's only a few days."

"Sorry. You take care, Bonnie."

"You too." She hung up.

Fran appeared in her office door. "A bunch of messages," she said. "You've got dresses on hold for the spring gala, and Jesus wants to know when to send them up. You missed two appointments with clients this morning, too."

"How long have you been sitting at the reception desk?" asked Bonnie.

Fran said, "An hour?"

"I mean, how long have you had this job?"

"Fifteen years. I've seen a lot of shit."

"Want to see *more*? Do more? Make more money?"

"What'd you have in mind?"

"Three days, $5,000," said Bonnie.

"I'll take it."

"Don't you want to know what it is?"

"As long as it's mostly legal."

"It involves a dead body," said Bonnie, smiling.

"What do I have to do to it?" asked Fran.

The expression on her face! Steely, yet disgusted. Bonnie laughed. "We're going to bury it," she said. "With style."

Chapter Fourteen

"Great turnout," said Fran. "The lilies are giving me a headache, though. We cornered the market on 'the flower of death.' Hope no one else dies this week."

Bonnie and Fran stood just inside the Lexington Avenue Synagogue's ornate doorway. Fran's beehive was exceptionally high today, with large bobby pins holding it up and a black scarf keeping it neat. Bonnie tried to keep track of the people coming in. They'd planned on five hundred for the brunch in the temple reception room. Elliot Snyder's favorite food had been caviar blinis, little pancakes topped with crème fraiche and sturgeon eggs from the Caspian Sea. Bonnie hired four sous chefs from Petrossian to make them to order. If more than five hundred people showed up, she'd have to get behind the griddle and compile them herself.

"Three twenty," said Bonnie, counting heads. "Twenty-one, twenty-two…"

"I'm going to check the valet situation," said Fran. Her son and nephews worked for a valet service and were available at a moment's notice. Even though most people arrived via taxi, they'd petitioned the city to cordon off Lexington Avenue between Eighty-Sixth and Eighty-Ninth Streets for private parking. It cost a fortune, but Stan Rodkin said price was no concern. If Bonnie thought he was a mensch *before*, she didn't know the half of it.

Fran's son, Paul, was quite possibly the sweetest, dumbest, twenty-five-year-old, drop-dead gorgeous, Italian hunk alive. He helped the mourners out of their Mercedes and Lexuses, making eighty-year-old society dowagers gawk. After Gloria Rodkin got a load of him, she practically ran over to Bonnie. "Is he single?" she asked. "Does he like Jewish girls?"

If Paul was handsome, his cousins were fallen Gods. Bonnie asked Fran, "What do you *eat* in Bensonhurst?"

"Lotsa pasta."

"I grew up eating spaghetti. But none of the guys in Corona look that good."

"Was it cooked with love?"

Fran Giagoni, apparently, could make water boil with her heart. It was but one of her hidden talents, which Bonnie became aware of over the last few days. Not only could Fran find every last white lily in New York City, she had a flare for obituary writing, and could start any car without a key. "What? You can't? You're kidding!" she said when she hotwired their rental at the cemetery.

Bonnie could not have pulled off the funeral without Fran. This genius of organization had been sitting, literally, right under Bonnie's nose for five years. As soon as they returned to Frankel's, Bonnie was going to petition Mr. Charles to give her a raise and a job in the marketing department to work on Frankel's special events and promotions.

The bereavement business itself was a well-greased machine. The cemetery people knew the headstone people, who knew the limo services. The temple people knew the body prep people, the contacts for placing announcements, and worthy charitable organizations for donations in the name of the deceased. Gloria and the Snyders, Elliot's family, fielded and placed calls to his friends and colleagues. Stan dealt with the estate lawyers and death certificates, the cumbersome paperwork of dying. Bonnie ran down her checklist. With so much reliable support, the funeral was a pleasure to plan. She felt competent and accomplished, or the opposite of how she'd been feeling lately at Frankel's.

Everyone else had done his and her jobs so well, Shelley had precious little to do herself. The function of funerals was to distract the bereft. On the Upper East Side, emotionally healthy duties were consigned to others. Shelley was left with her sadness, a daily appointment with her doctor for "shots," and morning fittings for mourning clothes.

Ironically, styling Shelley, which should have been the easiest part of the planning, was the most challenging. Shelley hated *everything*. Contrary to what Gloria predicted, Shelley thought she looked ugly in black. "Don't you have something in black that isn't so dark?" she asked at one point.

Bonnie gently explained the tradition of the widow wearing somber shades to reflect their grief. Shelley broke down in the Private Studio and called Rabbi Menchen for spiritual guidance. After she regained control of herself, she handed the phone to Bonnie.

He said, "Is this Ms. Madden?"

"Yes, sir."

"Don't let her call me again."

Eventually Shelley settled on a dignified Jil Sander dress and a Fendi jacket with a ruffled sweetheart neckline. Gloria would be the image of maternal support in a lightweight black cashmere Donna Karan wrap dress and jacket. The jacket, an investment piece, was as soft as butter and woven with the faintest silver threads. The Rodkins and Shelley were already seated in the front row. Being so close to the casket—closed—was rough on Shelley. She kept trying to flee. Gloria had her hands full keeping the widow in her seat.

Bonnie wore a new dress for the occasion. It'd been two years since she spent any money on herself. All her funds were usually funneled into Peter's tuition, the car, and the house. That was fine. She didn't need to buy each season. Her collection of classic pieces held up year to year. It inspired her to stay at the same weight, too. But Gloria's new Donna Karan jacket reactivated Bonnie's long-dormant lust for something brand-new. She took an hour at Frankel's to shop for herself (what a concept), choosing a black-belted Dior cap-sleeved dress that fit like a second skin, right off the rack. She also bought Fran a classic Calvin Klein suit, her way of saying thanks. Considering what Fran was making, the gift might've been unnecessary. But Bonnie wanted to make sure Fran dressed appropriately for the funeral. And she did look perfect, except for the hair.

Bonnie felt the profound joy of knowing she looked fabulous in her Dior—even if it was for a funeral. It wasn't a conceit, but a calm confidence. She'd taken special care with her hair and makeup, too. Paying close attention to detail was usually something she did only for her clients. That hour of browsing for clothes in her size, to suit her body and coloring, made her realize how badly she'd neglected herself for years. How long had it been since she'd looked in a three-way mirror and thought, "I look good. I feel pretty." The simple moment was profoundly gratifying. She'd let thousands of those moments go by. No longer.

If only Steve Kline could see me in this dress, she thought when she'd tried it on, and a hundred times since then. She hadn't heard from him since she'd left him at the Four Seasons. She thought about him whenever she had two seconds to spare. And sometimes when she didn't. As mourners filed in, Bonnie's gut was fluttering, imagining every tall, slim man with graying hair might be Steve. He might come. Joanne was friendly with Gloria.

"Looking for me?" asked a woman's voice from behind. It was Cody Deerlinger, sneaking up behind Bonnie. "You look… there's no reason that boring dress should be so sexy," she said.

"Er, thank you?" said Bonnie. "And thanks for coming to pay your respects. Is Mr. Deerlinger with you?" Bonnie cringed inside at the thought of Cody's Heathcliff of a husband.

"He's in Japan closing a billion-dollar deal," she said, loud enough for Moses and King David to hear. "I heard that you pulled this little shindig together for Gloria. True?"

Shindig? More like grave-dig. "Things were slow at Frankel's. Haven't seen you there in a while."

Cody shrugged. "How'd you get the mayor to show up?"

"He and Stan Rodkin used to sit on some of the same boards. Years ago, before he was elected."

"Look at all those bodyguards. I want a bodyguard." She said it like a child would say, "I want an ice cream cone."

"Shall I look into that for you?" asked Bonnie, deadpan.

"Since you're freelancing," said Cody, "I have a job for you. Top secret. If you tell anyone, I'll run you out of town on a rail."

"Sounds reasonable."

"You know Lee Freed is bankrupt."

Bonnie nodded. The news was bad for the Freeds. The company was in deep trouble, and Lee personally was underwater.

"Vicki Freed is holding a private sale of all her jewelry and handbags out of their apartment tomorrow at noon," said Cody.

Bonnie hadn't heard about that. Granted, she'd been out of the loop for a few days. "And you want her Kelly bags," she said. Vicki Freed had collected a few of the rare Hermés purses over the years. Cody was famously obsessed with them.

Cody shushed toxically. "Keep your voice down, for Christ's sake." The nearest person was twenty feet away. "I *must have* her green crocodile mini Kelly. It's one of a kind. But I want to be able to tell people that it was custom made for *me*."

"Got it. You need a bag woman."

"Exactly. Go there and get it for me. Pay any price," said Cody. "I'll give you 10 percent."

Bonnie remembered a piece of diamond jewelry of Vicki's that Cody had once lusted after. "What about that chandelier necklace?" asked Bonnie. "Vicki wore it to the spring gala a few years back? Looked like diamond drops trickling down her chest? You admired it quite a bit." Cody's exact words were, "I could kill her for that necklace."

Cody's eyes popped. "Oh. My. God. I *want* it." She grabbed Bonnie's cap sleeves. "You have to get it. Show up at Vicki's at six in the morning. Be first in line!"

Get up that early and miss another half day at work on Monday? For 10 percent, it'd be worth it. Interesting that as soon as Bonnie could see herself leaving Frankel's, opportunities presented themselves.

She felt bad for Vicki, though. Bonnie hated to pick the bones.

The sound of piano music filled the room suddenly. The two women turned toward the lectern. The rows of pews were tightly filled. A cantor began singing in Hebrew.

. . .

The reception room at the synagogue reminded Bonnie of the Metropolitan Opera House, with giant stained-glass windows by Marc Chagall, the favorite artist of American Jewry. The chefs from Petrossian were hard at work, filling platter after platter of blinis and other caviar-based hors d'oeuvres that were passed by handsome Russian servers.

Bonnie scuttled around the vast room, clearing tables of used plates and champagne glasses, keeping the food and beverages moving, helping mourners into chairs, and making sure the Rodkins and Snyders were comfortable. Scores of her regular clients were there. The ladies of the Peace on Earth charity committee kept Shelley surrounded, which unfortunately was not what Gloria had in mind.

She found Bonnie and whispered in her ear, "Shelley has to circulate. I want people to see she's holding up well and looks beautiful."

"What do you want me to do?" asked Bonnie.

"We need to find a man to escort her around the room."

Why on Earth was that a good idea? wondered Bonnie. "I think Shelley would prefer to keep a low profile."

"I didn't throw the funeral of the century so she could hide. Now, who should we choose? Over there. Jack Kline. The man by the bar."

"Jack…Kline?" Bonnie's heart had leapt into her throat. Steve's son from Chicago was here? Was Steve also here? How had he gotten by Bonnie? She'd watched the door like a hawk.

"You see him? He's cute, right? He's Joanne and Steve Kline's son. I love Joanne to death—shouldn't use that expression today—but she's as cold as glacial rock. Weird couple. Well, not really a couple at all. I heard from a friend in Chicago that Joanne practically lives with another man and that Steve doesn't care. The three of them have dinners together. They only stay married for the sake of their company and their children—not that the kids care."

While Gloria gossiped, Bonnie's stomach did somersaults.

Her eyes tracked Jack Kline's move from the bar to the blinis station. "He looks like Joanne," she said.

"Rich, single, and handsome," said Gloria. "Please, please, please, take him to Shelley. If I do it, it'll seem obvious."

Bonnie swallowed her nerves and did as Gloria asked. As odd as it was to approach the son of the married man she was secretly, wildly attracted to, Bonnie found his smile open and kind. He shook her hand.

"Hello," she said. "I'm Bonnie Madden, a friend of the family. The widow would like to thank you for coming." His hand was soft and dry. Jack, in his midtwenties, was an interesting mix of Joanne and Steve's genes. He had Joanne's bone structure and fair coloring. But he had Steve's height and expressive eyes as well as his father's languid body. He was sexy, but he lacked Steve's gravitas. He was more like Kline *lite*.

Jack nodded and said, "Lead the way."

They crossed the room together, and Bonnie introduced him to Shelley. She was seated on a cushioned bench between two friends. After Jack finished speaking, Shelley turned to Gloria and asked, "Who the hell is he?" She was woozy, on the edge of consciousness. Jack smiled in just the right way and proceeded to introduce himself to Shelley's friends. The blond brigade, the Ashleys and Cordelias of the Peace on Earth committee, fluttered around the new man in town.

Shelley seemed relieved to get some breathing room. Without friends holding her up, she listed to one side and closed her eyes. "Shelley!" said Gloria, shaking her. "You should mingle."

"Leave me alone," slurred the widow. "My husband's dead. I don't care about mingling!"

"She needs to lie down," said Bonnie.

"She needs to circulate," said Gloria.

Frowning, Bonnie leaned in to whisper in Gloria's ear. "I know you're nervous about Shelley's future. But you have to deal with the daughter you've got right now, not the daughter you want someday. Look at her! She's miserable!" Bonnie had never been quite so direct with Gloria before. But what was the point of thinking of her clients as human beings if she couldn't speak honestly to them? It was another breakthrough for Bonnie. Maybe her new dress gave her courage. She was outfitted as Gloria's equal. She'd speak to her like one mother to another.

Gloria blinked, realization setting in. "Jesus, Bonnie, you're right."

"She needs a time-out, just for a few minutes."

"Okay. I'll take her to the rabbi's office to rest until we head to the cemetery. Will you tell Stan what's going on?"

Gloria and one of her friends were able to get Shelley on her feet and walk her out of the reception area. Bonnie scanned the room for Stan. She found him twenty feet away, deep in conversation with a tall man. His back was to Bonnie, the perfect angle to judge the tailoring of his suit. Bonnie admired the expert cut of his Zenga, how snugly it fit across his broad shoulders... *Oh, good Christ.* Instant belly butterflies. She knew that suit and those shoulders.

Steve Kline seemed to sense her eyes on his back. He turned in her direction. When their eyes connected, he smiled. A current passed between them. It was undeniable. They *were* powerfully attracted to each other. Her instincts hadn't been completely off. Their break from emailing and texting might've made him miss her and understand the true nature of his attraction. It wasn't only about work. Whether or not he wanted her for his store, he also wanted her.

The dress helps, she thought, and smiled pleasantly, politely, as she joined the two men.

Stan asked, "Is everything okay?"

"Mrs. Rodkin and Mrs. Snyder are in the rabbi's office," she said to Stan. "They needed some space for a few minutes."

"Understood," said Stan. "Do you two know each other? Ms. Bonnie Madden, this is Stephen Kline."

Steve said, "We're already good friends. If it weren't for Bonnie, I wouldn't be wearing this suit."

She smiled as blandly as possible. "Very nice to see you."

"And you," he said. Jack just joined them. "And this is my older son, Jack Kline, whom I've mentioned to you."

They smiled at each other and both said, "Hello again."

Something caught her eye across the room. Fran was signaling to her by the door. Bonnie said, "Excuse me," but Steve put his hand on her elbow.

The smallest, lightest touch, a glancing contact, lit her skin on fire. She might've gasped.

Steve said, "Don't leave. Stay and talk to us."

Stan said, "Bonnie, I can't thank you enough for what you've done for us this week. If they didn't have all this to think about, I can't imagine what the last few days might've been like."

"Funerals are for the living. I wish I could do more for your family." Out of the corner of her eyes, Fran had given up discreet hand signals and was now waving with both arms. "I'm getting the signal. Excuse me."

"Excuse me, too. I'll be right back," said Steve. Lightly holding Bonnie's elbow, he walked with her toward Fran. "We need to finish our conversation. I've been thinking about it a lot. I took the wrong tack at dinner the other night. I do want you for the store. But we have other things to talk about."

He *had* missed her. *Thank God.* She hadn't made up the attraction. As to whether he expressed his intention explicitly, or she'd acted on it, she wasn't sure. But just knowing it was real was a huge relief.

"Let me apologize," he said. "I tend to get one-track minded when I'm starting a new venture. I should have talked about our friendship first." He put his hand on her bare upper arm—in front of all these people. Her skin heated on contact.

She said, "Your son is watching us."

Steve said, "Do I have to make an appointment to talk to you?"

A few of her clients loomed ahead. They, too, were watching. She said, "I'll call you." Her heart pounded at the exposure and his touch.

He let her go. Bonnie could barely breathe. She kept her eyes facing front and went over to Fran. "The cars and limos are lined up on Lex behind the loaded hearse," said Fran. "Mr. Bernard at Shady Hills called. They want to know when we're coming."

Bonnie looked around the room at the five hundred people drinking, eating, and mingling. "We'll have to make an announcement."

"Just close the bar. Works like a charm."

Nodding, Bonnie was still reeling from the conversation with Steve. *He wants me*, she thought. She wished she could sing it.

"Wait," said Fran. "I got these."

She opened her clutch and pulled out a stack of business cards.

"What?"

"Women have been slipping me their cards," said Fran. "Bonnie, seriously, have you ever thought about starting your own business? I'd go with you. We could get out of Frankel's. You have to know your days there are numbered."

Chapter Fifteen

"I'm so excited!" piped Sylvia Salerno, standing with Bonnie in Vicki Freed's lobby.

"Mom, shhhh," pleaded Bonnie, eyeing the two dozen other proxies who'd been sent to scope out rare and precious treasures among the ruins of Vicki Freed's former fabulous life. She recognized a few personal assistants, young women in headbands who trailed their bosses around Frankel's. Bonnie also spotted a few of the diamond district dealers she'd worked with to find vintage Harry Winston pieces, for example. Bonnie wondered why Vicki hadn't used Christie's or Sotheby's auction houses. But that would be too humiliating, too public a defeat.

"Carmine said I could buy whatever I wanted," said Sylvia. She giddily opened her Vuitton bag and showed Bonnie the stacks of cash inside.

The sight of all that money made Bonnie nervous. "Close that. Can't you…just be cool, okay, Mom?"

"Forgive *me* for enjoying myself. If you're embarrassed by me, just *say* so. I'll go stand by myself in the *corner*. Sorry I'm not *discreet* enough for your society friends."

Great, now Sylvia was in a snit, and Bonnie would have to deal with that on top of taking care of Cody Deerlinger's business. She had no one to blame but herself. She was supposed to have brunch with her mom today. Instead of rescheduling, Bonnie invited Sylvia to come along to the Freed sale on Monday.

"I'm not embarrassed," said Bonnie, averting her eyes from her mom's leopard print silk blouse—not from Frankel's—heavy black eyeliner, and too-tight black pencil skirt. "These private sales are very fussy. The objective is to show as little excitement as possible. If you act too excited, it'll draw attention and you might wind up in a bidding war with another buyer. We have to downplay. Show as little emotion as possible."

Sylvia nodded, happy to play the game now that she knew the rules. "Got it," she said.

A woman in a gray suit announced to the women waiting in the lobby, "The Freed sale is now open. I'll take the first group to the penthouse now."

It was like waving red at a bull. Sylvia's elbows came out and she pulled Bonnie along, plowing through the crowd of ladies. They didn't see her coming.

"See? I can be useful," said Sylvia, at the head of the line to get in the elevator.

Bonnie laughed, despite her better judgment. "We're in a good position. Remember what we're looking for?"

Sylvia whispered, "Green crocodile purse, diamond necklace."

They rode up to the triplex. As soon as the doors opened right into the Freed living room, Sylvia was off, running into the vast space, not knowing where to look first.

Bonnie would have used her Queens instincts and followed, but she stood in shock at the sight. The room she'd once found visually chaotic with chintz and floral wallpaper had been stripped bare. Even the wallpaper had been steamed off. How long had it been since Zachary's bar mitzvah? February to April. To go from carpeting the street to selling the wallpaper in a matter of months? Bonnie felt terrible for Vicki.

Buyers scurried around the long tables set up with hundreds of items on display. Among them were half a dozen security guards and as many official sellers behind the tables, poised to answer questions and take the money.

Bonnie did a quick scan. No sign of the items Cody Deerlinger wanted. She did notice a leather duffle bag by Louis Vuitton. Retail, new with tags, it would be in the $15,000 range. It was appraised as "mint condition," used once or twice. Vicki probably bought it and then forgot about it. The private sale price tag: $3,000.

Private sale? More like a fire sale, she thought. Vicki could do better on eBay. The bank probably forced the Freeds to do this sale. Bonnie shook her head and glanced toward the balcony landing two flights up, where Vicki had been standing the last time Bonnie had come over. And there she was now, in dark wash jeans and a silk top, her hair in an uncharacteristic ponytail, watching the opportunists paw through her things.

Taking out her BlackBerry, Bonnie called Vicki's cell. She watched as Vicki reached into her jeans pocket and answered her phone.

"Bonnie?" asked Vicki.

From two stories below, Bonnie said, "I'm down here."

Vicki scanned the room, found Bonnie, and waved. She said brightly, "I've got Fresca. Want to come up?"

"I've got…I'd love to, in a few minutes."

"You're shopping for someone, aren't you? That bitch Cody Deerlinger? She wants my green Kelly mini, doesn't she? And my diamond teardrop necklace."

"Are they here?"

"Nope, and you can text Cody and tell her she's out of luck."

"Still want me to come up?" asked Bonnie, feeling dirty all of the sudden.

"Of course! I need company. One thing no one warns you about bankruptcy: It's so boring! *Always* a dull moment."

Bonnie laughed and saw Vicki's superwhite smile spread across her face from flights below.

"I'll be right there," said Bonnie. She found Sylvia trying on an emerald bracelet. A bank seller watched carefully.

"You think it's a good price?" asked Sylvia, draping it across her wrist.

The tag on the bracelet was $4,000. Since Bonnie had personally picked it out—for Vicki to give to Lee to give back to his wife for their eleventh anniversary—Bonnie knew that the bracelet was worth about three times as much.

"A steal. Look, Mom, I've got to say hello to someone."

"Now?"

"She's the owner," said Bonnie, pointing at Vicki leaning on the balcony landing.

"Can I meet her?" asked Sylvia, waving.

Really? Her mother and the socialite? Bonnie got a strange, uneasy feeling about introducing them. Queens, meet Manhattan. Upper East Side, allow me to present Corona. Bonnie had been straddling her two universes—work and home—for her entire professional life. She wasn't sure how the idea got in her head, but she'd been superstitious about keeping them apart, believing that if the two worlds collided, the impact would destroy both. But then again, she'd been questioning a lot of her assumptions lately. She thought, *Why not? Let's see how this goes.*

"Right this way," said Bonnie to Sylvia. They walked toward the stairs.

Vicki had to come down to convince the security guard stationed at the spiral stair to let them through. She said, "You look so pretty today, Bonnie. I've never seen you in pink before. You're always in black and gray."

Sylvia said, "I noticed that, too. And her skin looks brighter. Healthier."

"And your eyes are smiling, even with that anxious frown on your face. If I didn't know better, I'd guess…"

Sylvia and Vicki finished the thought together, speaking in giddy unison, "Bonnie's got a boyfriend!"

"I do not!"

"But you're thinking about it," said Sylvia.

Okay, yes, Bonnie couldn't stop thinking about Steve since he touched her upper arm at the funeral.

"You must be Bonnie's mama," said Vicki, holding out her hand. "I can see the resemblance."

They introduced themselves. Sylvia said, "I'm sorry you have to go through this. Everything you've accumulated over the years, gone? How can you stand to watch?"

"You're right. This is borderline masochism. Let's go to my office upstairs."

Mother and daughter followed Vicki up to the top floor of her soon-to-be-former apartment, to a wing that Bonnie hadn't seen before. "In here," Vicki said, opening a door to a stunning room with wraparound windows set in dark, wood-paneled walls and three-quarter views of Central Park in spring. A door was open to a terrace with lilac trees in marble pots, ivy covering the demi-wall outside.

Sylvia gaped at the terrace view. "I'd never leave. I'd camp out in the winter."

Right. Sylvia wasn't what anyone would call an "outdoor" person. But the terrace was otherworldly beautiful. The three women plopped their elbows on the demi-wall, gazing from on high at the people milling in the Park.

"Fourteen years," said Vicki. "It's a lot more than most people get of such a spectacular view or of this kind of life. I came to New York with nothing, and that's how I'll leave it. No, that's wrong. I've got my son, and a few good friends. My green Kelly bag and my diamond necklace."

She'd forgotten to mention her husband. Had they separated? Bonnie flashed back to the scene in the home gym, of Mr. Freed doing push-ups on top of his very personal trainer.

Sylvia said, "I bet you've seen some crazy stuff from up here."

Vicki shrugged. "Actually, I hardly ever looked. I'd come out with a big hat and a book and pretend I was floating on a cloud. But now that I'm leaving, I can't stop looking down at the little people." Overly dramatic, she said, "I'll soon be walking among them."

Bonnie, who had always walked among them, said, "It's not so bad."

Vicki rolled her eyes. "Please."

She went back inside. Sylvia and Bonnie followed. This room hadn't been cleared out yet. A black leather sectional couch hugged the corners, lined bookshelves behind it. On the glass table, Vicki had been looking at family scrapbooks.

Sylvia pointed at the open page. "Your son?" she asked.

"Zachary," said Vicki. "He's in Short Hills, living with his grandparents. We didn't want him to see his things being sold off piece by piece. Lee and I will be joining him soon, to live with my in-laws who call me a stupid slut to my face. So. Who wants a Fresca?"

"Me," said Sylvia. "With a splash of vodka, if you've got it."

"Have I *got* it?" laughed Vicki. "It's *all* I've got." She went to the bookshelf, pushed a shelf, and the door of a hidden-in-plain-sight mini fridge opened. Inside it was a six-pack of Fresca and bottle of Grey Goose. To Bonnie, Vicki said, "Bella turned me on to this, remember?"

She did. If Bonnie were in Vicki's pumps, she'd be hitting the Fresca pretty hard herself. After pouring the drinks, Vicki said, "Now. Bonnie. Tell us all about your new boyfriend."

Bonnie's face turned fire engine red. Sylvia said, "Look at her cheeks! Out with it. I've been waiting for you to find a man for years. I hope he's rich!"

"To rich men!" said Vicki.

Should she tell them? Bonnie wondered. She'd kept her thoughts about Steve Kline to herself for months now. If she didn't say his name, it was safe to talk, right? "Okay, yes, I do like someone, and he's given me just enough of a hint to believe he likes me, too. But there are a couple major problems. For one, he hasn't made a move on me. Romantically. For another, he's married, which I'm not sure I'll be able to get over."

"Oh, big deal," asked Vicki.

"Excuse me?"

"They've been married for a while?" asked Vicki.

"Twenty-five years."

"Then don't worry about it. And don't look so shocked. Every long-term marriage has its own set of rules, whether they're about time away from each other or with other people. You can't judge from the outside what's right for them."

"That's very tolerant."

"Oh, come on, Bonnie. You were married once. You know how hard it is to keep it going. People disappoint each other. There's no unblemished long marriage. But husbands and wives who stay together figured out how to forgive each other for their sins."

"How do you know about my marriage?" asked Bonnie.

"You mentioned it once," said Vicki. "What? It only looks

like I've got a head stuffed with cotton. I do have a brain, and I listen."

Sylvia asked, "What's the story with the wife?"

"She's kind of cold. I heard she had a boyfriend out of town. He told me their marriage is in name only for the sake of their business," said Bonnie. "The gossip mill confirmed it. I have it on good authority."

"Who?"

"Gloria Rodkin."

Vicki nodded. "She does know everything."

"Carmine was married when I started up with him," said Sylvia. Catching Bonnie's reaction, she said, "Don't you look at me like that. His wife had been sick for a long time. He needed comfort, and she was okay with it."

"Lee was in a dead marriage when we started up. His wife was thrilled by our affair," said Vicki. "She got millions more in the settlement. So, happy parties, all around. To married men!"

They toasted and drank. Two big sips were enough to relax Bonnie on the conversation. She'd been guarding her attraction to Steve Kline for so long. The secret was increasingly painful to keep in. It was tugging at her soul to burst into the light. She should have told her mom sooner. Sylvia was the one person in her life that really cared—in her nagging, meddling way—about Bonnie's romantic happiness. That both her mom and Vicki brushed off the immorality of cheating made Bonnie feel better about doing it. "If we did start something, it'd be a short-term fling. Why would he commit to me? I'm a middle-aged single mother."

"Is that how you see yourself?" asked Vicki, horrified. "I never want you to say 'middle-aged' again. You're not even forty, and you're drop-dead gorgeous! Whoever this guy is, he'd be lucky to have you."

"She's right, Bonnie," said Sylvia. "This is what I've been telling you for years. After you and Mike broke up, you put yourself on a shelf. But you've got to dust yourself off and get involved in life. You have no idea what's in store for you."

What's in store…interesting word choice, thought Bonnie. She knew, to the last inventory list, what was in store at Frankel's. But she spent zero time mulling what was in store for the rest of her life, except caring for Peter. She'd been so focused on protecting her son that she'd shelved more than her love life. When Bonnie was young and idealistic, she had dreamed of one day running a boutique or a store of her own. Steve was offering her a chance at romance and her dreams. By all logic, she should grab it with both hands. She should be running toward it, not squirming away from it. She had no idea how things would play out. She could regret either decision.

As if reading her mind, Vicki said, "Four months ago, I never would have guessed I'd be broke, moving in with my in-laws, and probably getting divorced. I know about my husband's affairs. He hadn't been faithful to his first and second wives—I was one of his girlfriends. But I thought back then, by the time he's bored with me, he'll be too old to cheat. Well, I was wrong about that. He'll probably cheat when he's ninety. The necklace Cody Deerlinger would love to get her claws on was a gift from Lee. He gave it to me when Zachary was born, a year after we got married. I always thought of it as my personal insurance. The necklace is in my name, so the bank can't take it to pay off Lee's debts. I've got it in the safe. Want to see it?"

Sylvia said, "God, yes!"

Vicki popped open another faux bookshelf panel to reveal a hidden safe. She spun the dial and opened the gray metal door. Carefully, she extracted two boxes. One was orange—Hermés. The other was robin's egg blue—Tiffany's. She put both boxes on the table in front of the women delicately, almost religiously.

"My two prized possessions," said Vicki. First she opened the Hermés box. Inside, wrapped in tissue, lay a triangular-shaped purse about the size of a paperback novel—the mini green Kelly. The shiny crocodile caught the light, as did the platinum clasps. Bonnie had never actually seen it before, although she'd heard the legend. Women stewed for ten years on a wait list for the standard red leather Kelly bag. A rare material, like croc, in a special color, like hunter green, in an irregular size, like the mini, was an endangered species. A truly unique creature—none existed in the wild, and only one remained in captivity.

"Cody will go as high as $50,000," Bonnie had to say.

"For a purse?" said Sylvia. "That's insane."

Vicki next turned to the blue box, which was flat and as long, wide, and thick as an issue of *Vogue*. She gingerly pulled off the lid to reveal a thick blue leather envelope with a silver snap. She undid the snap and unfolded the envelope. Inside, atop a cushion of midnight blue velvet, lay dozens of tear-shaped diamonds artfully placed along several platinum chains. The sun hit the necklace, and rainbow prisms appeared on the walls, the couch, and their faces.

"Thirty flawless carats," said Vicki, staring hypnotized at the sparkler.

Sylvia was speechless. Bonnie was awed, humbled, by the sight of such artistry and beauty. "I can offer you $500,000," she said solemnly. "If Mr. Freed does…if things don't work out, you'll have something to fall back on."

Vicki held up the necklace, making the prisms dance. She said, "My plan was to wait until he leaves me before I sold it. I won't last long in New Jersey. Lee is a good man, but he's a mama's boy. Either Bunny will get to him, or his girlfriend Chris will. He'll keep me around for emotional support while we liquidate. And then, when he finds his confidence again, he'll get rid of me."

She'd be far better off, thought Bonnie. *Lee Freed doesn't deserve her.* "Whenever you're ready to sell," said Bonnie. "Mrs. Deerlinger will be ready to buy."

"She'll *hate* waiting," said Vicki, her eyes shining like the diamonds at the thought of making Cody twist in the wind.

"Sell now," said Sylvia. "Take the money and run. You don't owe your cheating husband another day, let alone three months."

Vicki said, "You know what? I think I will sell now. And I'm going to give the money to Lee."

"*What??*" said Bonnie and Sylvia together.

"When I married him, I was only twenty and looking for a rich husband. I was a total gold digger, I admit it. I don't blame myself for the bankruptcy—not completely—but I certainly put my credit cards to good use."

That is true, thought Bonnie.

"He gave me a great life. If it weren't for Lee, I wouldn't have these objects—and they are just things. If it weren't for him, I wouldn't have Zachary, or have seen the world, or lived in luxury. He gave me everything I wanted. Now I'm in the position to give back. These objects aren't much. A drop in the ocean of his debt. But I wouldn't feel right keeping the money or abandoning him. Despite the lies and the cheating, he's my husband, and I love him."

Bonnie was shocked and impressed. The woman had courage and a heart, if not a pot to pee in.

"Call Cody," said Vicki with cold certainty.

Taking out her BlackBerry, Bonnie started dialing.

"Hang up," said a voice in the doorway.

"Lee!" said Vicki. "What are you doing here? I thought you were in court."

He was dressed like a lawyer in a gray pin-striped suit and brown shoes. "A little privacy, please," he said to Bonnie.

To Sylvia, Bonnie said, "We should go."

When they left, Vicki was still on the couch. Lee stared at her from the doorway. Bonnie had no idea how much he'd heard. If he heard any of it, he should be thanking his lucky stars to have found one of the few honest trophy wives in New York.

In the taxi downtown, Sylvia admired her emerald bracelet and said, "What's Vicki's phone number? I want to thank her."

"For what?" asked Bonnie, scrolling through her messages and emails. Her eyes and smile grew big to see that three were from Steve Kline.

"For the Fresca," said Sylvia.

In five years of Frankel's Monday morning meetings, Bonnie never once received flowers from Mr. Charles. She'd had weeks with sales tallies in the hundreds of thousands of dollars. A few times, he'd said, "Well done," or "Keep up the good work." But usually, he congratulated her by saying, "Don't think this means you can slack off, Bonnie."

Today, the first Monday in May, Mr. Charles presented a gigantic bouquet of peonies in a crystal vase to Megan for being the top seller in the month of April.

Megan blushed as pink as the peonies. "Gosh, this is unexpected! I'm just so embarrassed!" she said, taking the flowers like Miss America making her acceptance speech. "Mr. Charles, you are too, too good to me. I can't take credit for this—although my one-week sales volume was the best of any Salon stylist all year. The biggest thanks goes to Mr. Charles, of course, for being such a cutting-edge visionary and so in touch with what my generation wants. Also, thank you, Bonnie, for letting me ride your coattails all the way to the top. If you hadn't left the Salon on non-Frankel's business all week and generously let me keep all of your appointments, I wouldn't be where I am today. I guess you know what you're doing, since you've been at it for so, so, so, so very long."

Bonnie just sat there, shaking her head. Megan was the definition of shameless. Mr. Charles beamed at her, obviously smitten. Bonnie had never seen him like this. Leave it to conniving Megan—a girl cut from the same cloth—to bring him to his knees.

Although Bonnie had been wording her resignation speech for weeks, she worried now that Megan and Mr. Charles had been writing their own version for her. Bonnie had a reputation to uphold in the industry. It was one thing to leave one job for a better opportunity. It was quite another to be forced out, without another position lined up. As of this morning, a pip-squeak had been elevated to her level. That wouldn't look good. Megan was probably gloating and trashing Bonnie's name all over town. If Bonnie left now, would it seem like sour grapes, or righteous indignation? Ideally, Bonnie could reclaim sole possession of her title and *then* quit. Because of her obligations, she wasn't going to up and leave without something lined up first.

Mr. Charles said, "A round of applause for Megan, our new Salon codirector!"

Perfunctory clapping from Bonnie, Bella, salespeople, and

buyers. Fran snapped her gum a few times. Megan bowed and preened. The news might've come as a surprise to some of the staffers. But Bonnie had been forewarned in an email from the Frankel's accounting department that outlined the Salon sales figures for the week. Although the Rodkin funeral resulted in charges of $90,000 on Gloria's store card, she'd only purchased $25,000 worth of store merchandise, including Bonnie's fee. Bonnie had worked herself ragged, but she'd had the lowest weekly sales total in her Frankel's history.

She fired an email to Mr. Charles, asking, "Am I 'on probation' or 'on warning'?"

The reply came from Ms. Schnew in Personnel. "Being 'on probation' is the step before being 'on warning,'" she wrote. "When an employee transitions from 'on probation' to 'on warning,' she has two weeks to turn the situation around. Otherwise, she will be officially terminated."

Or officially "on unemployment."

Although Bonnie promised Fran to put in a word for her about moving to the marketing department, a recommendation from her to the personnel department at this point in time would not help. Now that the path toward her destruction was so clearly lit, Bonnie should have felt panicked. But, weirdly, she felt an eerie calm. The kind that comes before the storm.

She could try event planning with Fran. She would call her old friend Lori, who'd made overtures. She could ask Steve Kline if he was still interested in hiring her and about the particulars. Most importantly, when would the checks start to arrive, how much, and would health insurance kick in immediately? She hesitated to ask. The ground of their friendship was forever shifting beneath her feet. She had a sense that it was an either/or proposition. A job or a relationship. That might be a paranoid projection, though. Either/or was how she'd organized her own life. More likely, with all-business Steve, the proposition was everything or nothing. The job *and* the relationship, or nothing. She craved job security. If the relationship didn't work out or even get off the ground, what would happen? Likewise, if she wasn't a good fit at his store, would he dump her and move on personally as well? She hated the idea of failing on one level. But letting Steve down in two distinct arenas? The anticipatory pressure was paralyzing.

What would wind up happening if she got forced out of Frankel's? A retreat to Queens. She'd return to the borough of her birth, humbled, and take her place among her siblings and siblings-in-law at the car repair shop. Anita was right about Carmine's interest in the family business. He was now a major investor in Salerno Auto. Bonnie's brother (and brothers-in-law) were opening a new garage in Bayside. Mike would love it if Bonnie were closer to home during the day, for Peter's sake. His wedding was in two weeks. Would it be so terrible to take a low-pressure job that let her talent go to waste and sucked her soul dry of inspiration and beauty?

No. I will NOT let that happen, she thought.

Bonnie loved what she did. Not only making the big sale, but the beauty and glamour, the passion for fashion. Her identity was wrapped up in her career as an arbiter of style. Okay, yes, she was a bit of a snob about her talent. Why should she apologize for that? Men didn't say "sorry about being talented." Why should Bonnie? She had experience, education, skills, and an amazing sense of style. Surely she could continue to earn a decent living at it, supporting herself and her son, which was her duty and privilege. She shouldn't have to resort to being an auto repair shop bookkeeper in Bayside. No way.

At the meeting, Mr. Charles had another announcement to make. "I am also proud to welcome Hortense Clout to the Salon staff. Hortense has been a salesperson in Designer Ready-to-Wear for many years and has shown initiative and creativity during that time. She will be reporting to Megan. Welcome, Hortense!"

Another tepid round of applause as the anorexic accepted her welcome. Hortense smiled smugly. As far as she was concerned, this promotion was a long time coming.

Her moment was cut short. Tiffany and June, the erratic store buyers, ran into the Salon, teetering in their heels. "Emergency!" yelled Tiffany. "Mr. Charles, come quick!"

The boss followed them out of the Salon. He wouldn't run

if the building were on fire, but he did walk briskly. Bonnie and other staffers went along, too. Tiffany and June rushed over to an eighth floor boutique—a ten by ten, three-walled section nestled between two dozen others. It was the space for Chang Feng, a Chinese designer who rocketed to stardom off the back of the First Lady. She wore his dress at a state dinner in France.

And there he stood, in his trademark outfit, covered head to toe in black, including a veil over his lower face, like a ninja. The visit was ninja-like, too. Feng hadn't let them know he was coming. Ordinarily designers liked a little fanfare from the staff. Next to Mr. Feng stood a young, pretty Chinese woman.

Mr. Charles, in kiss-ass mode, held out his hand to Feng and said, "Welcome to Frankel's. I'm Chase W. Charles, president, and a great admirer of your work."

The designer didn't shake. The young woman whispered into his ear. Then he whispered something back. She said, "Chang wants to know where his gowns are." She gestured toward the racks of his boutique, empty except for a few items on hangers.

Tiffany and June jabbered apologies to the designer and then huddled with Mr. Charles and Bonnie. Softly, Tiffany said, "We ordered a dozen gowns from his collection. We know they arrived because Jesus called me when they got here. I assumed they'd be on display by now. Jesus tracked them to the Salon over a week ago."

June added, "We've been looking for them, but they've disappeared."

Bonnie was reminded of the white mink stole and the red Valentino dress that had also gone missing. Occasionally an item did get misplaced. But never an entire collection. A dozen one-of-a-kind gowns by an important designer, lost? This was bad.

Mr. Charles turned back to Mr. Feng and said, "I'm very sorry about the delay. Your gowns will be on display by this afternoon. In fact, we'll put some in the windows and in what we call the 'hot spot,' a display that's the first thing clients see when they walk in."

Usually designers pay a premium to get promotional

exposure on store displays or in the legendary street-view windows. The hot-spot mannequin was worth tens of thousands of dollars. Mr. Charles was giving Mr. Feng the moon and the stars.

The designer lent his ear to the Chinese woman and then muttered a reply in her ear in return. She said, "Mr. Feng should have taken his collection to Bergdorf Goodman."

Oof. A direct hit to Mr. Charles's solar plexus. He turned to Tiffany, June, and Bonnie and mouthed, "Find the collection NOW." Then he said a few words in Chinese.

The young woman stared at him. "I don't understand."

Mr. Charles repeated his Chinese. For all Bonnie knew, he'd just told the designer to run naked down Fifth Avenue.

The translator was baffled. She said to Mr. Feng, "I think he's speaking Chinese. I guess he assumes that you don't speak English."

The designer's eyes, the only visible feature, narrowed with rage. He whispered frantically into the woman's ear. She said, "Mr. Feng was born and raised in San Mateo, California. He thinks you might be racist."

"Forgive me," blathered Mr. Charles. "I assumed this woman was your translator."

"Mr. Feng does not like to speak directly to strangers."

Not foreign, thought Bonnie. *Just crazy.*

In exasperated English, Mr. Feng raised his ninja veil and said, "Read my lips, Mr. Charles. If the gowns aren't on display in an hour, I'm suing the store for replacement costs and damages."

And so began a frantic search. The Salon carpet was practically torn up to find the gowns, as if they could've crawled there on their own. Bonnie called Jesus and went over the chain of acceptance and delivery.

Jesus said, "According to the form, you signed for them, Bonnie."

Her blood ran cold. "I never saw them."

About forty-five minutes into the search, Hortense Clout asked, "Has anyone checked Bonnie's hold closet in the Cage?"

Mr. Charles called Jesus and instructed him to search Bonnie's hold closet in the Cage. Bonnie knew full well that she hadn't put a hold on any of Mr. Feng's designs. His aesthetic was too modern for her traditional clients. She grumbled, "Search all you want. It's a waste of time."

Mr. Charles's cell phone vibrated a minute later. Bonnie watched her boss's face while he listened to the person on the other end. Snapping the phone closed, he said, "Jesus found the entire collection—still covered in plastic inside garment bags—in Bonnie's hold closet. The collection is on the way up via the service elevator now. I want everyone here to get those dresses unwrapped and in the Feng boutique in the next fifteen minutes."

And then Mr. Charles exited the Salon, probably to go find Mr. Feng and tell him the good news. He glared at Bonnie on the way out. She swallowed a lump and went to greet the gowns at the elevator.

She'd been set up, of course. Someone had managed to unlock her closet door and forge her signature. But no one got by Jesus in the Cage, and she tracked carefully every single designer delivery that came and went from the Salon, regardless of who signed the receipt. Was the Feng collection connected to the Lanvin mink and the Valentino gown? The number one suspect, Megan, couldn't have been responsible. She simply didn't have the necessary access or, as a relatively new employee, an understanding of the way things worked logistically.

Bonnie was under attack from at least two enemies on multiple fronts. Now she had to defend herself. She'd been raised never to back down from a fight. She might go down. But she'd do so swinging.

PART SIX

May:
The Gala

Chapter Sixteen

Not again, thought Bonnie, reading the *New York Post*'s "Page Six" gossip column later that week. The headline: "Frankel's Puts First Lady Favorite Chang Feng in the Closet."

> Celebrated Chinese-American designer Chang Feng got the shock of his life last week while visiting Frankel's to show his ailing mother his new collection of twelve couture gowns at the luxury Mecca. When they arrived at his in-store boutique, the racks were bare. According to a source at Frankel's, the priceless collection had gone missing. Mr. Feng's mother—a five-foot-tall, ninety-pound Chinese national who'd flown from Shanghai just to see the boutique—was so upset, she had to be sedated. The gowns were eventually found in a salesperson's "holding closet," a dank, moldy room in the store's subbasement. "The saleswoman is a hoarder, like those women on television who live among piles of garbage. She has a psychological problem," said the source. "I felt *so bad* for Mr. Feng and for his poor, frail mother! Broke my heart, seeing her cry." Mr. Feng threatened to sue the store. Frankel's spokesperson did not return calls.

Fran poked her head into Bonnie's office. "Did you see it?"

"If that woman was his mother," said Bonnie, "she gave birth to Mr. Feng before she was even born."

"Mr. Charles is on the warpath. Check your email."

Bonnie checked her BlackBerry and saw a message from her boss, with an all-caps subject line: "MANDATORY STAFF MEETING TODAY AT 10:30 A.M." It was a little after ten, so

Bonnie had time to sip her coffee and check her schedule. The Peace on Earth gala was only weeks away, and she was booked solid. She felt anxious about the gossip item, even though it was 99 percent lies. The true part—the misplaced collection—had been grossly exaggerated by the anonymous source. Probably the same person who leaked the Archer Watson story months ago. That time, Bonnie swallowed the half truths and rightfully took the blame. Not this time. The Feng incident wasn't her fault. Someone framed her and lied to the press.

Bonnie laughed bitterly. The person who was campaigning secretly to get rid of her must not have thought this through. The Page Six item made it almost impossible for her to quit. It'd be like she was leaving in disgrace. Her reputation would never recover, and potential employers would believe the lies they read in the paper. She was more stuck now than ever. She felt completely alone and on her own.

A fantasy popped into her head of Steve Kline riding in on a white horse, plucking her up, riding her and Peter to a mansion in Chicago with a cook, a tutor, and a child psychiatrist on twenty-four-hour call. It was a ridiculous little mental movie. She thought about calling him and complaining about the item. She knew he read three papers every morning. Surely he'd seen it. Usually he called her by this time each morning. No calls or texts from him yet. Was he embarrassed for her? Bonnie mustered her courage. She had no reason to be ashamed. She hadn't done anything wrong, except feel sorry for herself.

She had to think and fight back.

"Has Hortense come in yet?" she asked Fran. A Salon stylist now, Hortense moved her base of operations to Fitting Room B.

"Putting on her war paint," said Fran, thumbing toward the restroom down the narrow hallway.

Bonnie grabbed the *Post* and stormed into the ladies room. The potpourri-scented, mint green powder room—three times larger than her office—was a convenient retreat. A little slice of calm amid the chaos. It was Bonnie's idea to install a trickling fountain against the wall and a Zen sand garden box with a tiny rake on the vanity.

Hortense sat on a cushioned stool, an eyeliner poised to draw life into her face. Bonnie slapped the paper on the counter in front of her. "You are the source," she accused. "You'd throw the entire store under the bus to get me fired."

"That'd be an awfully big bus," said Hortense, placidly applying her makeup.

"You admit it?"

"Sure. I have an old friend at the *Post*. We talk occasionally."

Bonnie hadn't expected her nemesis to crack so easily. Now that she had a confession, she didn't know what to do with it.

Hortense said, "You can tell Mr. Charles, but I'll deny it. Not that he'd believe you anyway—or defend you. The fact is, if you hadn't hoarded the Feng collection, none of this would have happened."

I didn't hoard the collection! Bonnie wanted to shout. But then she realized there was no point. For all she knew, Hortense herself bribed one of Jesus's staff to stuff them into Bonnie's closet.

"Just tell me why," said Bonnie. "You've hated me from day one. What have I ever done to you?"

Hortense stopped primping and glared at Bonnie. "Why do I hate you? Are you fucking kidding me? Look in the mirror, Bonnie. You're young, beautiful, and talented. You have exquisite taste, and it comes naturally. You have a family and a son. Your clients adore you. Designers respect you. You had Mr. Charles in your back pocket *for years*. But now I do." Hortense flashed her evil version of a grin. "I've been waiting a long time for my moment. It's here, and you're not getting in my way."

Bonnie stood there, frozen and confounded. Hortense thought she was *young*? Didn't she know? Bonnie was within sight of forty! How old *was* Hortense? A hundred? As for *beautiful*, well, that was in the eye of the beholder. Bonnie would describe herself as attractive, but not beautiful. Talented? Bonnie agreed with that. A natural? Maybe. She did have a way with clients and designers. Bonnie was blessed with a big family that, at times, drove her nuts and might actually be crazy. And thank God for Peter. He was her life's guiding light.

Except for her career and financial problems—Bonnie

noticed that Hortense didn't say, "young, beautiful, talented, *and rich*"—she had a good life. From her rival's point of view, Bonnie had a great life. She'd spent too much time thinking about what she didn't have and not nearly enough time giving thanks for her many blessings. Bonnie smiled, relieved and grateful for the perspective shift.

And she had her sworn enemy to thank for the insight.

Hortense waited for Bonnie to respond bitterly in kind. But how could she? The woman's jealousy made Bonnie feel better about herself. She was her own savior on a white horse. Why did she forget that?

She said, "Thanks, Hortense. From now on, whenever I look at you, I'll remember how lucky I am to be me." Bonnie walked over and wrapped her arms around her, which felt like embracing an iceberg. The hug didn't cost a thing. But the shocked expression on Hortense's face? Worth her weight in gold.

"Gather 'round, people! This is Mr. Curtis Rial," said Mr. Charles at the mandatory meeting soon after. The entire staff of Frankel's, minus the wrapping and shipping crew, security, administration, and about half the sales people, who stayed at their counters lest the customers run amuck, crowded into the Salon's main space, making it feel very much like Grand Central at rush hour.

Looking perturbed and nervous, Mr. Charles ceded the floor to Mr. Rial, a forensic accountant and short man with thick spectacles, an oversized brown suit, and tasseled loafers. "Good morning," he said in a soft tone. Bonnie leaned forward from her spot on the couch between Fran and Bella. "As a representative of the Frankel family and the board of trustees, I have been asked to read a statement from Mr. Albert Frankel himself, which he sent me from his home in Tuscany this morning. These are *his* words, which I will now recite to you." He coughed, clearing his throat.

Channeling Mr. Frankel, Mr. Rial bellowed, "'What *the*

fuck is going on over there? Every time I pick up the fucking phone, there's a problem. Some bimbo's brat gets lost? Some Chinese woman has a fucking heart attack? Not in my store! Chase Charles: What kind of monkey house are you running? I didn't give you a $60,000 bonus to get the store trashed in the New York fucking *Post*! Get your shit together, man! As of this morning, the store's accounts are going under a microscope. You will all do whatever Mr. Rial asks. I want every holding closet emptied *immediately*. Every item, down to the last tube of lipstick, must be moved to the floor and priced to sell."

Mr. Rial lowered the sheet. In his own voice, he said, "Ordinarily, I would never use such language. I apologize to the women in the room."

Bella whispered, "Apology fucking accepted."

"No Christmas bonuses for us, but Mr. Charles got $60,000?" said Fran. "That is just wrong."

Like the rest of the staff, Mr. Charles was hearing Mr. Frankel's email for the first time. Red-faced and ruffled, Mr. Charles looked rightfully chagrined. To be upbraided by Mr. Frankel, via Mr. Rial, in front of his staff? That had to hurt. The fact that Mr. Charles got a bonus and the staff went without? In an instant, any last drops of sympathy she felt for her boss dried up. She suddenly stopped caring about him, the store, her own security. It was like a light flickering on, a real a-ha moment. The whole store was going down. She no longer cared about clinging to the railing of the Titanic.

"I'd like to meet with Mr. Charles and the two Salon codirectors privately," said Mr. Rial. For lack of a better place, the four of them went into the PS. "There's another matter. An ongoing forensic accounting investigation of the store's bookkeeping," he said, his eyes shifting from Chase, to Megan, to Bonnie. "My team has been on-site since seven this morning, and we've already discovered a dummy account. It was set up like a staff account." All staffers had a number account they entered into the computer to make a sale, log a return, or make a personal purchase. "The dummy account is registered under the name Harold Hill. Mr. Hill has logged $500,000 in returns.

None of those items have been sent back to our warehouse, restocked to the sales floors, or returned to their place of origin. Half a million dollars of merchandise is missing. Do you know anything about this, Mr. Charles?"

Dumbfounded, he said, "No one by that name is employed by the store."

Mr. Rial sighed. "We know *that*. As I said, it's a *dummy* account, with a *fake* name. Harold Hill? Doesn't ring a bell? He's the main character from *The Music Man*, a con artist who swindles money from gullible rubes by promising them glory and happiness."

That's where I've heard the name, thought Bonnie. She'd been scrambling in her mind to place it.

Megan raised her hand. "Excuse me, Mr. Rial, sir? I just want to say that Mr. Charles is an excellent boss. The stress of running the store gets to him, but he does a fantastic job. Think about what he has to deal with. The staff is out of control. The designers and buyers are disrespectful. If it weren't his daily therapy sessions and the morning visits with Olga, his masseuse, I don't know how Mr. Charles would get through the workday. He's incredibly dedicated! He has weekly colonics for weight maintenance, facials, and laser hair removal on his back and chest. He has every right to bill the store for all of his beauty treatments!"

Bonnie laughed. Mr. Rial turned toward her, and she tried to squelch it. He asked, "You are?"

"Bonnie Madden."

"Do you find it amusing, Ms. Madden, that Mr. Charles is having laser hair removal treatments and facials at the expense of your employer?"

"Not nearly as amusing as the colonics."

Dead silence. Megan's jaw dropped, and Mr. Charles almost died, right there, of embarrassment.

"And you are?" asked Mr. Rial, pointing.

"Megan Houlihan."

"You seem to know what's really going on here. I believe Mr. Frankel might wish to speak with you via Skype about Mr. Charles's colonics and whatnot." The accountant turned toward

Mr. Charles. "To your office, now."

The three of them left. Bonnie returned to find the rest of the staff milling around the Salon, begrudging Mr. Charles's bonus, plotting a rebellion that would never happen before wandering back to their departments and desks.

"*The Music Man*," said Bonnie to Fran and Bella. "It's been a while since I saw it. Where was it set?"

"River City," said Bella instantly. She sang a few bars of a song with the town's name. Seeing Fran and Bonnie's reaction, she said, "I like musicals. In Russia, people don't sing. If you hum on the street in Moscow, you are dragged to mental hospital for electric shock. I come to New York, I see movie with Robert Preston and decide Americans are very stupid—but not so bad if they like to sing."

"Remind me," said Bonnie. "River City is in what state?"

"Iowa," said Bella.

The three women took turns giving each other meaningful looks. "Who else do we know from Iowa?" asked Bonnie.

"I smell a ginger rat," said Fran.

An hour later, after tracking the rat's movements to the basement, Bonnie, Fran, and Bella walked down the dark corridor of the subbasement to the Cage's main gate. Jesus wasn't guarding the entrance as usual. Bonnie tried to flag down one of the other shipping guys, but they were either too busy or too far away.

"I could yell," said Bella.

"But then she'll hear us," said Bonnie.

Fran said, "Stand aside."

She removed a bobby pin from her beehive and made quick work of the lock.

Bonnie asked, "How'd you do that?"

"Just a little something I picked up in Bensonhurst," she said of picking the steel-reinforced, five-gauge, two-pound Master Lock.

They pushed the Cage door open and headed straight for the row of hold closets about fifty feet inside, on the right.

Bonnie's closet had already been emptied, probably within minutes of Mr. Rial's proclamation. The doors of a few other hold closets were wide open, the spaces empty and cleaned up, save for some bubble wrap and empty garment bags.

"They're like ghost closets," said Bonnie.

The chain link door of the last hold closet was closed, and it was covered by a black nylon tarp. Bella said, "This is it."

The three women leaned against the tarp and listened. Bonnie thought she heard some rustling, but no voices.

She whispered, "Now what?"

They heard a squawk. "Jesus, come in," said the voice over the walkie-talkie.

"I'm busy," said Jesus from inside the closet.

Squawk. "Cage door lock's open," said the voice.

"Goddamn it," said Jesus, and then the closet door flew open.

Fran, Bella, and Bonnie, who'd been leaning against it, tumbled into the hold closet, falling on top of Jesus, who fell against Megan Houlihan.

As they clamored to their feet, Bonnie was the first to notice that the closet was packed with garments, shoes, and coats, all with the tags on. Bonnie recognized dresses from seasons past, things she'd tried to pull for a few of her clients, but had gone missing—including the white mink Lanvin stole.

"Here you are," said Bonnie, reaching for the one-of-a-kind red Valentino gown, the one that Roman was apoplectic about losing. "I've been looking all over for you. But you were tucked away in the hold closet of Harold Hill." Megan and Jesus had been pulling this scam for nine months. It was dumbfounding that no one noticed for all that time. "You logged the returns, the money went into Harold Hill's dummy account, and then you resold the garments off the books? Not the special pieces, though. They were too dangerous to move. Someone might notice."

"Jesus made me do it!" said Megan.

Fran asked, "But you're no computer genius. How'd you access the Frankel's…whatever—main frame, server?"

Bella said, "She probably paid off or slept with one of the tech guys."

"That's the lowest...I can't believe you'd...I would never..."

Fran, Bella, and Bonnie nodded at each other. "Guilty," they agreed.

"Even if I did—and I didn't—it's only because Jesus threatened me! He said he'd hurt me if I didn't do what he wanted. He brainwashed me with intimidation. The truth is... *Jesus raped me.*" Megan started blubbering, real theater, looking through her fingers once to see if they were buying it.

Jesus blinked at his coconspirator and said, "Woman, you're crazy."

Squawk. "Dude, where you be?" said the voice.

"I'm coming."

"Hold on, Jesus," said Bonnie. "You stashed the Chang Feng collection in my hold closet. You put the extra zonker on that dress for Vicki Freed's bar mitzvah. No one else could have gotten the garment bag through the sensors."

"But I made it okay," said Jesus. "I got you the key."

She couldn't believe he'd purposefully try to ruin her. "You sabotaged me."

"Megan offered me real money, Bonnie. A lot more than free Starbucks," he said. "Times are tough. My whole family is out of work. It's hard to work here and not let your mind imagine ways to cash in. Staffers had always offered me little bribes. Giants tickets. Yankees tickets. Sometimes envelopes with cash. But nothing life-changing. Just a drop in the bucket. I just couldn't pass up what Megan offered. She had it all figured out. It started small, reselling fake returns. But the market just blew up. We came up with creative ways to get more merchandise."

"He's lying! How can you believe him? He's Mexican!"

"My mother is Puerto Rican, and my father is Dominican," he said. "On what planet does that make me Mexican?"

Bonnie said, "Creative ways to get merch. You mean hijacking the delivery truck at Christmas time? That was you."

Jesus shrugged. "It wasn't only me."

"I had nothing to do with it!" said Megan. "I'll swear it

in court."

"Megan, for once, just tell the truth, no matter how much it hurts. Archer Watson. Did he really run away from you, or did you abandon him on purpose?"

Of all Bonnie's alleged mess-ups, the Archer Watson incident continued to bother her. The thought of that boy afraid and alone made her sick. She couldn't help imagining Peter in that position. It was unfathomable that anyone could be ruthless enough to use a child to harm a rival. But Megan could. She was amoral. She didn't care about anyone. Not Bonnie, Roman, or Mr. Charles. Accusing Jesus of rape was another new low.

Megan's face turned crimson. Her freckles nearly popped off her cheeks. She said, "What happened with Archer was your fault! How dare you suggest that I…Mr. Charles is going to hear about this!"

Bonnie nodded. Megan would never tell the truth. She was a pathological liar, user, and manipulator. Bonnie had known she was a dangerous woman. But who could have imagined she was also a devious criminal?

The ultimate assistant from hell stormed out of the hold closet, swearing revenge on Jesus, Bonnie, and everyone else. The air lost its chill, but Bonnie felt cold inside.

Jesus said, "I didn't mean to get you in trouble, Bonnie."

"That's not an apology." She was hurt. He was supposed to be her friend.

"I'm sorry." Sounded like he meant it.

Bonnie now had the proof needed to exonerate herself, get Megan fired, and reclaim her title. One phone call to Mr. Charles and Mr. Rial would do it. Bella and Fran were witnesses. Jesus would admit the truth. Wrongs would be righted. Order would be restored.

Squawk. "Dude, hot brunette just kicked over a pile of boxes on her way out."

"What're you going to do?" Jesus asked Bonnie.

Bonnie took a deep breath. "I have no choice."

Jesus sighed heavily, seemingly accepting of his fate. "It's okay. I deserve what's coming. I knew the risks."

She shook her head. "I'm not going to rat you out, Jesus. If I were you, I'd empty this closet ASAP." She wasn't going to destroy his career. Bonnie wouldn't destroy anyone's career, even those who had it coming. That was the difference between her and Megan and Hortense. Mr. Charles was right. Bonnie didn't have the killer instinct. She could defend herself, but not if it meant ruining another person.

That said, Bonnie wasn't going to kiss and make up either. Oh, she'd get over Jesus's sabotage in time. She could see herself forgiving Hortense and Mr. Charles eventually—never Megan. She'd try to forgive, but she wouldn't forget. Although fashion was a brutal industry, the toxic environment of greed and consumption at Frankel's had led decent people to do terrible things. She had to get away from here.

Funny how the obvious became glaring only when a light shined upon it. Despite what quitting now with the store under investigation might look like and the harm it could do to her reputation, she was out of there. Bonnie couldn't control the gossip and rumors in the best of circumstances. Bonnie had to do what she knew in her heart was best.

She turned on her heel and walked toward the Cage exit.

Bella called after her, "Where are you going?"

"To tell Mr. Charles I quit."

"I quit," said Bonnie, on the couch at home and on the phone with Mike. "No going back, no collecting a parting gift, no severance. Just free."

"Holy shit," he said.

"Exactly," she said, taking a long sip of wine. She opened the chardonnay as soon as she put Peter to bed.

"Are you drinking?"

Bonnie hardly ever drank. "I'm celebrating."

"Are you? Most people wouldn't celebrate losing their income with tuition due next month."

"Hey, you're the one who never understood why I put up with my job. 'Can't those rich bitches shop for themselves?'"

"Yeah, but it paid the bills," he said.

That had been her trade-off forever. "At what cost, though? My job was basically to make other people look and feel good. But it was impossible to succeed. My boss was rooting against me. My clients were never satisfied. When I was an FIT student, I fantasized about a career in fashion, like we all did. I swore I'd do anything, sell my soul, whatever, to be part of the business. And I was. I made it. But my career wasn't about fashion. It became nothing more than kissing ass. My boss's. My clients'. Designers'. I had to stop before my soul was completely gone. No career is a fair trade for your soul. I'm out. I feel great."

"What about Peter?"

"Peter will be happier and more relaxed to have a happy, relaxed mother."

"All this time, you said you had to slave away at Frankel's for Peter's sake, and now you're saying you quit for his sake."

"I quit for me," she said. "But he'll reap the benefits. I'll mortgage my house for the Mason tuition, or I'll sell some jewelry."

Mike sighed. "I don't see that as a long-term solution."

Bonnie laughed. She'd been giggling randomly all evening. "I'll get another job," she said. "I have a few ideas. Fran, a colleague, wants to start an event-planning business. Or I'll go back to Bloomingdale's or go to another store. I can always get a job at Salerno Auto. I'll find the money. Can't you be happy for me? We used to laugh about how horrible these people were."

"We were laughing all the way to the bank!"

"It got a lot less funny when my clients went bankrupt and my colleagues stabbed me in the back."

How had she gotten through it? Now that it was over, she felt an avalanche of relief. It felt great to talk to Mike, to speak the truth about work and other things.

"I liked myself when we were together," she said. "I haven't liked myself so much since we broke up."

"Bonnie…"

"I'm not hitting on you, Christ. What I was about to say before you interrupted was that quitting, in a weird way, was like coming back to myself. I'm here. I can open up to someone else now."

"Anyone in particular?" he asked. Did she hear a hint of jealousy?

Saved by the doorbell.

"I've got to go. My pizza is here."

"Wait a minute…" he said, but she hung up.

She finished her glass of wine and went to get her dinner. She meant it that she was open to letting someone else into her life. She was open to a different kind of work, too. Both avenues—love and career—seemed to point in the same direction.

"Anita?" Bonnie was shocked to find her sister standing outside her front door holding a box of pizza.

"I got here at the same time the delivery did," said her sister. "I paid for it. So…"

So…Bonnie had no choice but to let Anita inside. She held the door wide open for her. "Thanks. I'll pay you back."

"Forget it."

"I wasn't expecting to see you," said Bonnie. Tonight or anytime soon. It'd been a while since their fight at Rita's. Avoiding each other hadn't been so easy. Bonnie always called her dad first to make sure Anita wasn't over. She never did get to Frankie's shop to drop off her car.

"I heard about Frankel's," said Anita.

"I'm sure you're thrilled. Now you get to say 'I knew you didn't belong there,' or 'they used you up and kicked you out.'"

Anita dropped the box on the Formica table and went to get plates. "I'd never say that to you, Bonnie. I never thought you couldn't make it there."

Bonnie put a slice on each plate. They sat down and ate for a minute. "That explains why you've been obnoxious about my career since Bloomingdale's."

"Okay, I'll own up to that," said Anita. "And that I've been jealous and mystified by what you do. You don't understand how I feel about Peter. I am nervous to say something wrong when I'm with him. I admit it. I'm not afraid of him. I love him. I just don't want to upset him."

She could've made more of an effort, but whatever. Bonnie wouldn't harp on it. Anita had three kids of her own and a business and a husband. She was just as stressed out and busy as Bonnie was. "Why are you here? To apologize?"

"I'm here to welcome you home," said Anita. "And to say I'm sorry. It's not that I didn't want you to succeed in Manhattan. I felt like you'd turned your back on us and looked down on us. The way you talked about your job, you were queen of Manhattan. Maybe I did try to take you down a peg."

"Well, now I'm down a few."

"You'll get back up there," said Anita.

Bonnie nodded. There was some truth to that. She might've misrepresented herself a bit to her family. She wanted them to be proud of her and envious. But she'd alienated them in the process.

Anita finished her slice. "I'm also here to offer you a job if you want it, doing the books at Frankie's. We're expanding, and you're better at the business stuff than I am."

"That's...I don't know what I'm going to do next. But I really appreciate the offer."

"Your family is always there for you, Bonnie," said Anita. "I've always got your back, no matter what."

Bonnie felt choked up. In the craziness of the last few months, she'd forgotten her roots—and just how deep they were. "Thanks, Anita."

Her big sister dusted flour off her hands and stood up to go. "I've got to get Frankie Jr. Think about coming to work with us. We'd love to have you."

They hugged at the door. Bonnie sank into it. Anita smiled when they parted and gave her sister a kiss. "Call me."

Bonnie closed the door behind her and her phone rang.

"Bonnie?" asked Steve Kline. "What the hell is going on? Chase Charles just called me to say he wanted to talk to me about the top job at Barrow Street."

Now that was interesting. "He had a rough day at Frankel's."

"He told me you quit."

"I did."

"So you're available for the Barrow Street job?" asked Steve. "Can you meet me tonight to talk? Come to my apartment. Joanne is in Chicago. We'll have the whole place to ourselves."

"Can't," she said, her heart thumping. "My son."

"I'll come to you. Where are you?"

"I'm in Queens. And you're not invited here." She hadn't brought a man home since the divorce. Peter would freak out if he saw one here. She'd have to introduce them. What was Steve to her? It'd be confusing and uncomfortable. Not going to happen.

"I want to thank you for how much you've helped me," she said. "You got me to open up, to think about the dreams I used to have. Frankel's was like a destructive lover I couldn't tear myself away from. You showed me a way out. I appreciate it."

He said, "Why does this sound like a kiss-off?"

"You've been a good friend," she said. How could she work at Barrow Street and not die a little every day, looking at what she wanted and couldn't have? It would be worse than at Frankel's.

"What will you do?" he asked, seeming to understand.

"I'm not sure."

"What about your son?" he asked. "Do you have a secret stash of well-and-tree platters to sell off?"

"I'll work it out."

"How?"

"I've got a few ideas." She didn't want to get into specifics—there were none yet. "I'll be in touch." Before he could reply, she hung up.

Bonnie polished off the bottle. She felt that she'd done the right thing all around today by quitting her job and letting Steve Kline off the hook. Now she had to move on and start over.

Chapter Seventeen

Leonard's La Dolce Vita in Great Neck, Long Island, was a catering hall, but it could be considered a museum of the world's gaudiest, cheesiest decor. From the wallpaper to the ceiling murals of cherubs, nymphs, and satyrs, the faux palace was dripping with crystal, gold paint, and damask. It was like crawling into the fever dreams of Federico Fellini and Donatella Versace's bastard child. As soon as guests pulled up the half-moon driveway, saw the Trevi fountain water feature, the white columns, and the ten-foot-tall "Leonard's" chiseled into the side of the building, they knew they'd left New York and entered a world of pure kitsch.

Bonnie *loved* Leonard's. Its tackiness overload was the antithesis of Frankel's snooty austerity. The staff of Leonard's was totally in on the joke. The decor was *supposed* to make your eyes triple in size and to inspire laughter and bafflement.

"How many weddings have you been to at Leonard's?" Bonnie asked Sylvia, who was seated to her right at Mike and Emily's reception.

"Ten, including Anita's and Connie's."

"How about you, Mr. Ragussa?" asked Bonnie.

"Carmine, for the last time," he said. Bonnie had a block about calling her clients by their first names. "I've been to weddings here, family reunions, business parties, bar mitzvahs…"

"Bar mitzvahs?"

"Yeah, my lawyer's son, my accountant's son, my doctor's son…"

One of Mike's nephews, Jimmy, ran by their table. Carmine grabbed his Sunday suit lapel. "Hey, kid. Go to the bar and get me a scotch, no ice. Tell them Carmine sent you." He reached in his pocket, pulled out a roll of money and peeled off a hundred dollar bill. Tucking it into ten-year-old Jimmy's palm, he added, "Come back every half hour in case I need something else, okay, kid?"

Jimmy stared open-mouthed at the money. He glanced at Bonnie, his former aunt. "It's okay, Jimmy," she told him.

The boy said, "Scotch, no ice, coming right up," and ran at top speed toward the bar.

Sylvia said, "Carmine, you realize there are about fifty cops in this room and that it's illegal to serve alcohol to a minor."

Carmine said, "They don't care."

Sylvia agreed. "They're off duty anyway. I've been meaning to ask, Bonnie. What's with the black dress? Is it a tradition? The first wife wears black to her ex's wedding?"

Bonnie was wearing the Dior she bought for Elliot Snyder's funeral. With some statement jewelry, the dress was appropriate for a wedding. She accessorized it with long strands of oversize pearls and a big starburst brooch.

Jimmy was back with the drink and five cherries on a napkin. "Here you go, sir."

"Thanks, kid," said Carmine. "Remember, come back in a half hour."

"You got it!"

Bonnie shook her head. "Corrupting minors."

"He's having the time of his life," said Carmine. "*Salute!*"

They drank. Bonnie watched Jimmy join his cousins on the dance floor. He showed them the hundred and pointed at Carmine. Every kid's eyes lit up, and Bonnie laughed. Pretty soon, they'd be swarmed with boys asking to get them food, drinks, anything.

Peter was not among the circle of his cousins. Bonnie leaned down to look under their table. There, in the relative calm, somewhat protected from the flashing lights and loud music by the heavy tablecloth, sat her son.

"How's it going?" she asked.

Peter looked up from his DS. "I beat level twelve," he said.

"We'll stay another hour, tops," said Bonnie.

"I'm okay, Mom," said Peter, going back to his game.

Two years ago, Peter wouldn't have lasted five minutes at this reception. The visual and aural stimulation would have triggered a retreat into himself that he wouldn't come out of for hours. But today, thanks to his behavioral therapy and his meds, Peter was able to stand at the altar as Mike's best man for the length of the service. He didn't fidget too much, either.

The reception took place on the other side of a movable wall. Their table included Bonnie, Peter, Sylvia (invited by Mike as a gesture of respect and as Peter's grandmother), Carmine, and two couples who were friends of Emily (complete strangers). Vinny Salerno was invited, too, but he declined.

Peter was able to sit still for dinner, to participate in the group conversation, to order chicken for himself, and eat well.

He danced three times. A slow dance with Mike and Emily, which made Bonnie cry a little; a fast dance with Bonnie; and a fast dance with Sylvia. Afterward Bonnie said, "Mom. You can move."

"You didn't know?" asked Sylvia.

"I have never seen you dance before," said Bonnie. Not at her own wedding, nor any of her siblings'.

Sylvia said, "What can I say? I'm in love. We dance all the time." She put her arm around Carmine. They kissed disgustingly.

Peter said, "I'm going under the table now."

"Can I join you?" Bonnie asked.

That was an hour ago. Bonnie watched Jimmy and the cousins tearing up and down the dance floor. Peter would probably never join them. He'd never be that free of his anxieties. He'd always have to retreat to a safe place to hide. No question, Peter had come a long way and would continue to improve. Bonnie felt that in her heart. But she also knew Peter would have a harder time getting through life than other kids.

"I worry," said Bonnie to Sylvia. "When I really let myself think about it, I feel genuine terror." She meant Peter primarily, but also her uncertain future.

Sylvia said, "Who can say, of all these kids, whose life will be hard, or easy, or exciting, or dull. You can't. No one can. Peter has problems. We all have problems. But Peter has you, and that makes up for a lot."

"Stop." Bonnie waved off the compliment.

"I mean it," said Sylvia. "You're a great mother, Bonnie. Peter trusts you. He knows you love him unconditionally. You're ten times the mother I was. I was distant when you were growing up. I was just so unhappy in my own life. You did the right thing, quitting a job that made you miserable."

It had been a week. She did feel better about Frankel's. Even better still because of a certain phone call she received yesterday.

"It was you and Carmine, right?" asked Bonnie.

"What was us?"

"The Mason School? Come on, Mom."

"What about it?"

The finance office secretary at the school left a couple of messages on Bonnie's home voicemail. Naturally, she assumed it was about the upcoming tuition bill. Gritting her teeth, Bonnie answered the third call. "Good news, Mrs. Madden. We received an anonymous donation to the school to cover Peter's tuition for the remainder of this year and next."

"*What?*" asked Bonnie. That was $45,000.

"I was as shocked as you sound," said the secretary. "The donation was made in cash. You can imagine how it felt to open the envelope."

Confused, Bonnie asked, "In the mail?"

"No, it was hand delivered, and the man waited until I counted it and logged in a receipt."

"What did he look like?"

"Young, white, didn't say his name," she replied. "I was so stunned by the donation, I forgot what he looked like."

The cash donation tipped Bonnie off. It had to have been Carmine. Bonnie had told Sylvia about the tuition shortfall a few days before, and her mom vowed to help cover it.

"Deny all you want," said Bonnie. "I know what you did, and I'm beyond grateful. I swear, I'll pay you back, every penny."

Sylvia blinked. "I honestly have no idea what you're

talking about."

"You and Carmine didn't send an envelope full of cash to Peter's school?"

Sylvia's jaw dropped. "How much cash?" She seemed as shocked as Bonnie had been. It wasn't like Sylvia not to take credit where it was due.

"A year and a half tuition's worth."

"Sweet Jesus! Wow! Maybe it was Mike?"

"Mike doesn't have money like that."

"A bribe from a drug dealer or something."

Funny how Mike, the cop, was sketchy in Sylvia's mind, but Carmine, the gangster, was a saint. "Mike swore he didn't know anything about it."

"I wish I could say I did it. Who else could have? Do you know anyone rich?"

Bonnie laughed. "I know loads of rich people. But none of them would do that for me. Hardly any even know I have a son, let alone where he goes to school."

Except Steve Kline.

"How's your mystery man?" asked Sylvia. "Was it him? Maybe he gave the money."

"We…we ended the relationship." If she could call it that. They'd never even kissed.

"Call him. Right now. Ask him," said Sylvia.

If the anonymous donor wasn't Steve, it'd be awkward to call. And if it was him? What did she owe him for his generosity? Joanne Kline was currently in Chicago, essentially living with Sam Kaufman, the parking lot baron. Gloria Rodkin still called her to talk about Shelley's state of mind and to gossip. (Another tidbit: After Bonnie resigned, Megan Houlihan blamed everything on Jesus, who was fired. Megan was given a battlefield promotion to Salon director.)

So Steve was alone in New York. He might've made a grand gesture to get Bonnie's attention. But she just couldn't reach out. She felt a wall of…what was it, exactly? No point in denying her feelings. She was afraid.

Sylvia watched Bonnie struggle with the idea of placing a

phone call. She put her hand on her daughter's shoulder. "Don't get mad," she said. "I want to say something to you I've held back on saying for a long time."

"Oh, God," said Bonnie. "Where's Jimmy? I need a drink."

"You know how Peter gets overwhelmed and he hides in the closet or under the table, like right now? That's you, sweetheart. You've been hiding in the closet, too. It happened to be the most luxurious closet in the world. But you're still hiding. Unlike Peter, you don't have the excuse of being autistic, either."

"Mom!"

"Well, it's true! This man overwhelms you, and instead of facing your feelings, you've done the emotional equivalent of crawling under the table. I see good changes, though. You're dressing nicer and calling attention to yourself in that way. You quit Frankel's and got out of that closet. But you need to take one more step. It's a biggie."

"He's married, Mom. I have to be an example to Peter."

"So be an example! Show Peter that you know how to be brave and take a chance in life!"

A nice argument, thought Bonnie. She felt the stirrings of courage and the desire to show herself that she could face her fears. But practically, she couldn't pursue it. "I can't just leave. What about Peter?" asked Bonnie.

"I'll take him home with us."

And then the sun crashed into the Earth. The oceans bled into the sky. Those scenarios were more probable than Sylvia Salerno *volunteering* to babysit *any* of her grandchildren, especially Peter.

Seeing her daughter's reaction, Sylvia said, "Now I'm starting to feel insulted."

"No," said Bonnie. "I mean, thanks. You think you can handle it?"

"If I can't, I'll call you," she said. "Or I'll call Mike and ruin his wedding night."

Bonnie laughed, her excitement growing. Could she really call Steve Kline and pursue him? To throw her fears and morals aside and reach out for selfish, foolish pleasure? *Yes*, Bonnie thought. *I can do it. I want to do it.*

"Call him," urged Sylvia.

"Let me clear it with the boss first." Leaning under the table, Bonnie said, "You okay going home with grandma and Carmine?"

"Sure," said Peter.

"Really?"

"I can bring the DS?"

"Yes."

"And they have TV."

"True."

"It's just like being at home," he said. "With better food."

Also true. Bonnie righted herself and smiled at Sylvia. "Last chance to back out."

"Not on your life," said Sylvia.

"All right." Bonnie took her phone out of her purse and called Steve's cell.

"Can I come over?" she asked when he picked up.

"I had the phone in my hand to call you," he said. "I've been thinking about you. I would have called sooner, but Jack's been here all week. He went to Philadelphia today to look at some property and won't be back until tomorrow. Yes, come over! Where are you? I'll send Serge."

This is really happening, thought Bonnie, her pulse rocketing. She was going to be alone with Steve. Suddenly, she couldn't move fast enough to get out of Great Neck and into Manhattan.

"I've got a car," she said. "I'll be there in an hour."

Ninety breakneck minutes later...

After making a quick stop at her place in Corona to pack an overnight bag, Bonnie sped to the Kline residence on Park Avenue. The doorman announced her, and she took the elevator up to the fourteenth floor. Steve opened the door—natty yet casual in a white shirt, chinos, and, beguilingly, bare feet—and immediately took her in his arms.

Incredibly, they hadn't hugged until that moment. Bonnie

remembered the electric charge when he touched her hand and her arm before, at lunch, at the funeral. But this full envelopment in his arms was bliss. She sank into his chest and melted into his body.

Wisely, Steve stayed silent. His hands spoke for him, stroking her shoulders and back. He smiled at her face, his eyes warm and welcoming, sending the message that he wanted her and cared about her. The physical contact and warm looks were overwhelming. Bonnie resisted the impulse to worry about what she was getting into.

"I know what you did," she said, a bit breathless.

"What are you talking about?"

"The donation?"

"What donation?"

"Liar."

He smiled, and said, "Is that why you're here?"

"No," said Bonnie. "Well, yes. I want to thank you properly. A note doesn't seem to be enough."

"A note would have been fine," he said, smiling.

"Why'd you do it? I have to know."

Steve paused. "If I feel guilty about anything in my life, it's my relationship with my sons. I gave them too much stuff, and too little attention. If I could rewind, I would have been supportive in a different way. I'd have put my sons first, like you do with Peter. I know how hard you've worked to protect him. I haven't met him yet, but I have an image in my head of this sweet, little kid who asks for nothing. I just couldn't stomach the idea of his education and comfort being disrupted. The money is... You know I can afford it."

"Would you like to meet him?" asked Bonnie.

"Is that a good idea? He won't be upset?"

"He'll like you. He'll like us." *Peter will be happy for me*, thought Bonnie, with a flash of insight. He won't care about Steve's marital status. He won't judge the way an adult would. Peter will see through all the layers and just absorb Bonnie's happiness, just like he was happy for Mike and lovingly accepting of Emily. Bonnie realized she had used Peter's confusion as an excuse.

She'd had a lot of layers of fear to peel back.

She felt nakedly free of fear now. Bonnie smiled and kissed Steve. The kiss was light and lingering. It was empty of doubt and full of promise. The contact with his lips sent her heart thumping in her chest. His, too. She could feel it through their clothing.

Steve said, "I want to show you something."

"Here?"

He laughed. "Not in the living room. In the *dining* room."

She followed him into the apartment toward a large parlor. The room was painted a soft gray, with elaborate teardrop ceiling molding and a crystal chandelier hanging from a center medallion. An oak sideboard loomed along one wall, dark and massive. But otherwise, the space was empty, save for a fifteen-by-fifteen, one-of-a-kind antique Persian rug.

"Oh my God!" gushed Bonnie.

Last time she'd seen it, the rug had been hanging on a wall at Frankel's. The colors were muted. But now, they were vivid.

"I had it restored and cleaned. Amazing difference, isn't it?"

"It's incredible."

"The furniture looked shabby in comparison, so I sent it out to be restored, too."

"This rug would make anything look shabby in comparison."

"Not you. You look beautiful," he said, coming up behind her and wrapping his arms around her waist. "Whenever I come in here, I think about you and what I'd do if I ever got you alone."

"What would you do?" she asked, pulse thundering.

He turned her around to face him, lifted her chin, and kissed her gently. At first. But then the kiss deepened. His lips were hard against her soft ones. She stood on her toes to snake her arms around his neck. Bonnie could feel his heart beating against her chest and his excitement rising. Her temperature was going up, and she had to get out of her clothes or they'd burn off her body.

"Why hasn't this happened before?" he asked.

"You move faster with your other girlfriends?" The words

slipped out. Bonnie might have a layer of fear left to shed after all.

"I don't have girlfriends," he said, "not for a long time."

They kissed again. He sealed his lips on hers, one arm around her neck, the other at her waist. Bonnie turned to liquid. Good thing he was holding her so tightly, or she would have spilled onto the carpet. His lips were soft on hers, but they got harder with each sigh, taking more of her breath without asking.

Bonnie felt her own long-dormant desire come back to life. It was wide awake and rampaging across her chest, her cheeks, and lower as the kiss intensified. It was almost too intense. "I think I need to lie down," she gasped.

"Good," he said as he lowered her carefully to the magic carpet. He arranged her hair, his fingers stroking her face and neck. "You okay?"

"Yes," she sighed, his hands on her collarbone now, the length of his body pressed against hers.

"Because you look kind of startled," he said.

"Are we talking now?" she asked impatiently.

Another kiss. This time, she held him as tightly as he did. Steve pried her arms loose and held them over her head, pinning her wrists on the carpet with one hand. With his other hand, he touched her cheek, her chin, and her cashmere sweater. What lay underneath the layer of softness, Bonnie's even softer skin, heated.

He said, "We'd better get you out of these clothes." Peeling off her top, Steve gaped at the sight of her torso. She'd always been proud of her breasts and trim upper body, probably one of the reasons for her bra fetish. Steve approved of her choice today, a black silk demi, and bent his head to kiss her above the front clasp. Then he unhooked it and grazed her sensitive olive skin with his lips. Looking down, Bonnie marveled at his face, his smooth tongue, her own pink and taut nipples. She'd imagined this happening so many times. For once, reality was as delicious as fantasy.

Rising up, Steve shrugged off his shirt and pulled off the T-shirt underneath. Bonnie stared openly at his chest, the hair in a heart shape across well-defined muscles. Her fingers itching to run through it, she reached for him. They clung to each other, skin to skin, kissing, on the carpet, grasping and clutching. Bonnie broke the kiss to look at him. He wasn't just some masculine body of fantasy. It was beautiful, generous Steve Kline, who saw her the way she wanted to see herself, who'd singled her out and made her feel special. The way he looked at her right now—adoring and a little bit pained—sent a shock wave down her belly, all the way down to her most sensitive spot.

She had to have him inside her *now*. Would pay any price to feel him *now*. She sat upright and unzipped her boots, kicked off her pants and the black panties. He'd undone his belt, slipped off his shoes, and was pulling down his jeans. Only his boxers remained between her and his high and hard erection.

Bonnie slipped her hands inside the waistband, and yanked it down, his penis exposed to her eyes. Before Bonnie could properly admire it, Steve positioned himself between her legs.

"We'll have to do it once quickly," he said. "And then, I swear, I'll make love to you for the next ten hours, slowly."

Bonnie was in just as big a hurry. She reached for him and guided him in. Slick and ready, Bonnie gasped when he entered her, her eyes wide open. One stroke and her body melted. He moved inside her. It was like she'd been reborn. She saw no reason to control her response, not that she could have, and wrapped her arms and legs around him to draw him in deeper.

Steve moaned. "I'll come if you do that," he warned.

Just hearing him say the word made Bonnie coil and release. Four and a half years of celibacy ended in a wild implosion that made her cry and gasp and hold on or else break apart into a million pieces. She was aware that Steve was watching her face, and that just made the orgasm last longer. When he sensed she was nearly at the end, he sped up his pace and looked into her eyes when he came, too.

Five panting minutes later...
"It *is* a magic carpet," said Steve, floating back to Earth.

Bonnie, incapable of speech, just smiled and sighed.

He helped her up. "Come on. I don't know about you, but I need a bed."

Naked, they padded down another hallway to a blue bedroom, masculine and comfortable, with a king-size bed and sailcloth curtains. He pulled back the covers that Bonnie had helped select way back in the fall, and she climbed into the bed between clean Egyptian cotton sheets.

Steve stood next to the bed, naked. "Round two?" he asked.

"Already?" she asked. "How old are you, really? Twenty?"

Steve laughed. "It's all you. I have no control over it. If you can stand to be away from me for two minutes, I'll get us something to drink."

"Just hurry back," she said. "You promised me ten hours of slow lovemaking, and I mean to get it."

He laughed. "Oh, you will, Bonnie. I'm a man who keeps my promises."

Twelve hours later...

Bonnie stretched, felt the deep comfort of a warm bed and soft sheets beneath her. The pillow was super soft, too. Different. And the light was coming from the wrong side of the room. Weird.

"Oh, shit," she said, lurching upright, remembering that, for the first time in *years*, she'd woken up in a strange bed.

Looking around for a clock or anything that told the time, Bonnie noticed her purse and overnight bag on a chair next to the bed. She rummaged for her BlackBerry and found three text messages from Sylvia, sent over the course of the last night and this morning. "P is fine, asleep." "R U having fun?" and "P awake, eating pank8s." Bonnie was glad all was well in Queens. But her seventy-year-old mother texting "U" for "you" and "R" for "are"? Using abbreviations? It was just wrong.

She checked the time. She'd been up half the night, entwined and active. When had they finally drifted off? Despite having had only four or five hours sleep, Bonnie hadn't felt so blissfully well-rested since before Peter was born. She could get used to this lazy-cat-in-the-sun feeling.

Steve was not in bed next to her. She had fuzzy memories of half waking up and feeling his chest at her back, her butt nestled against his belly and thighs. Bonnie must have crashed hard, tumbling into unconsciousness after the long day, long year, long decade. Every satisfied fiber in her body rejoiced and called out, "Thank you!" and "About time!" She'd never felt more grateful for the relief and the soul-purging release of passionate sex, deep orgasms, and uninterrupted sleep. Surely this simple recipe was what human beings were born to follow.

I'm madly in love with Steve, she realized.

She loved him and had felt what it meant to have him. Maybe she'd never experience having him completely, not 100 percent. That wasn't possible as long as he was legally bound to Joanne. But, for good or ill, she was in it now, and she was glad.

But she had to get home and relieve her mom. Bonnie grabbed her overnight bag and went into the bathroom. She washed, dressed, and put on a little makeup. "Home in 1 hr," she texted to Sylvia.

Following the smell of fresh coffee, Bonnie found Steve in the kitchen. The room was surprisingly small, but cozy and inviting. Steve wore jeans and a white shirt, buttoned askew. Bonnie flashed back to peeling that shirt off his shoulders, her palms sliding over his taut muscles. He stood at the Viking stove, cutting a thick dollop of butter into a hot pan. It sizzled temptingly. Sensing her behind him, Steve turned to greet her and smiled, his graying hair a charming mess. Bonnie's heart might as well have been the butter, melting instantly.

"Good morning," she said.

"Coffee?" he asked. "Pancakes almost ready."

Same breakfast as Peter, she thought. "I hate to go, but my son is alone with my crazy mother and her gangster boyfriend."

"Sounds fun," he said, pouring batter into the pan. Then he came toward Bonnie, giving her one of his enveloping, protective hugs. Her nose found its place in the delicious hollow at the base of his throat. He smelled deliciously like butter and sleep.

"Okay, one pancake," she said.

He beamed and jogged the two steps back to the griddle. "In college, I was a short order cook at a disgusting diner on the South Side," he said happily. "Grease literally dripped down the walls. Every surface in the place was sticky. The gum under the table was older than I was. One time, this couple came in and ordered double-fried chicken-fried steak, with a side of double-fried chicken-fried fries. I am dead serious."

Bonnie laughed at his story. She loved his voice and his high spirits. She felt lighter suddenly, her misgivings forgotten.

He served her a plate. His batter was as irresistible as his patter. "This is good," she said.

"Real buttermilk," he said, serving himself and sitting across from her.

"I mean, this is really good," she said. Did pancakes always taste so good, or was this an aftereffect of sex and sleep?

"We are really good. Last night was truly incredible, Bonnie. It has to happen again. When? Tonight? No, Jack will be here. Tomorrow?"

"When is he going back to Chicago?"

Steve frowned. "I don't know. I can come to Queens. I'd like to see your house and meet Peter."

She wasn't ready for that. It was one thing to imagine their meeting someday, but not tonight. "What about Joanne?"

"She's in Chicago until the Peace on Earth gala next week." Looking into her eyes, he said, "It doesn't matter where she is. She has nothing to do with my personal life."

A strange thing to say about your wife, she thought. Bonnie exhaled. She was involved now. There was no going back. She had to accept his bizarre marriage arrangement and take joy in whatever imperfect form it came in. "We'll figure something out."

"Okay. I'll call you this afternoon."

They cleaned up the breakfast plates together. After a goodbye kiss that put wings on Bonnie's feet, she left the building and walked down Park Avenue in the bright sunlight toward her car—which, thank God, hadn't been ticketed or towed.

Her BlackBerry vibrated. She checked caller ID. Kline and

Company. Smiling, she answered. "Couldn't wait a few hours to talk to me?" she asked.

"Joanne Kline for Bonnie Madden."

Oh, God. "This is Bonnie." She froze, midstep.

"I'll be back in New York this evening. Are you available for lunch tomorrow? There's something I'd like to discuss with you." Joanne's tone was crisp, no nonsense, businesslike.

Did Joanne have spies in the woodwork? Bonnie wondered. How on earth had she found out about them so quickly? Video surveillance? Phone taps? Did Steve call his wife the minute Bonnie walked out the door to tell her what he'd done? *No, not possible.*

Maybe this wasn't about Steve at all. "Will Mr. Kline be joining us?" Bonnie asked neutrally, trying to get a feel for Joanne's sudden interest in lunch.

"No," said Joanne, terse and crisp as ever. "Four Seasons Grill, noon."

Joanne hung up. She might as well have said, "High noon."

Freaking out, Bonnie dialed Steve. "Your wife just set up a lunch with me. I hate to ask, but were we on candid camera last night?"

He said, "Joanne called you? It's not about us. No security cameras that I know about. She probably heard about Frankel's and wants to get you on board at Barrow Street. I do, too, for the record."

That remained to be seen. Just because Steve thought they'd had privacy didn't necessarily make it so. Bonnie didn't push it with Steve, but her anxiety increased bit by bit as she imagined being alone with her lover's wife.

Chapter Eighteen

The next day, Bonnie's first Monday as an unemployed person since the age of fifteen, she walked into the Four Seasons Grill Room dressed in a suit that might as well have been made of armor. It was a black Jil Sander power suit she bought years ago, and she felt like she could take on Godzilla in it. She assumed Joanne had called the lunch to draw territorial lines around Steve. It was a turf war. Bonnie was braced for battle.

So it was a bit of a surprise when, after she sat down at the table, Joanne leaned forward in her seat, looked into her eyes, and said, "I like you, Bonnie."

Bonnie said, "Thank you?"

"I'm impressed that you quit Frankel's. Chase Charles bragged at dinner a few months ago that he had every member of his staff under his thumb. Well, you managed to wiggle free. You may or may not be aware, Bonnie, that your quitting caused a firestorm at Frankel's. Twenty of your clients—including Cody Deerlinger—are demanding explanations from Mr. Frankel."

Fran had told her about the tension in the Salon since she left, and Gloria had been filling Bonnie's ear, too.

"That's very flattering," she said.

"When Steve brought you to my attention, I had doubts, certainly. You're a woman. The women I've hired for Kline and Co. turned out to be disappointments. But I've seen you in action. I think you can handle difficult people."

"I do my best," said Bonnie, even more confused. "Forgive me, Mrs. Kline, but what exactly are we talking about?"

"Don't be coy. Steve and I want you."

Bonnie nearly spilled her water. "Excuse me?"

"For Barrow Street. Our primary investor, Stan Rodkin, likes you. Lee Freed likes you. I had the brilliant idea of hiring Freed and Sons at rock bottom prices to manufacture the clothes we intend to sell."

Joanne bragged about taking advantage of the Freeds when they were desperate? Then again, by doing so, she probably pulled them out of total ruin. Bonnie said, "Congratulations."

"The Klines, Freeds, and Rodkins are in agreement about the most important next step. The job of store president. The president will oversee the staff, obviously, work with designers to create a store aesthetic, and work with the marketers and the customers. Are you up for it?"

Of course, it'd been her dream to be the boss of her own store. That she was in the position to discuss it was beyond the realm of what she thought would be possible. Steve liked her for the job. Bonnie had assumed Joanne would keep her from it. Now she was offering? It didn't smell right.

"Why you? Why isn't Steve making the offer?"

"This is a business proposition," she said. "Your personal relationship with Steve might confuse the matter. Don't give me that face. I know all about it. The doorman in my building texts me the name and time of anyone who enters and leaves the apartment."

So Bonnie *had* been spied on. How could Joanne, or any woman, regardless of the understanding, be so bloodless about her husband's affair? "Does Steve know?" she asked.

"I assume he was there."

"About the doorman."

Joanne shrugged. "Probably not. He's not nearly as careful as I am."

"Do Gloria and Vicki know about this?"

"Know about what? The job offer, or that you spent the night with my husband?"

Bonnie felt her skin crawl. Hearing Joanne talk about Bonnie and Steve's relationship made her extremely uncomfortable. "I meant your offering me the position at Barrow Street."

"Gloria and Vicki are just wives. They don't know about

Barrow Street from me. Maybe their husbands talk business in bed. Steve and I certainly talk business, but we don't share a bed. Maybe that's the secret to our success."

This made no sense. Their marriage was a success because they didn't share a bed? Or their business was a success because of separate rooms? Joanne clearly prized her career over her marriage and believed that business and love didn't, couldn't, mix.

That didn't bode well for Bonnie's working at Barrow Street. Which was more important to Bonnie? Finding love after years of loneliness, or being the boss after years of subservience at Frankel's?

"You do have to choose," said Joanne, as if reading her mind. "Not today or right away. But one day you'll have to decide. I know you, Bonnie. I know which way you'll eventually go. That's the reason I'm making the offer. To keep the water clear in the meantime, you'll report to me. I'm hiring you. Should we decide to make a change, I'll fire you."

"You really don't care about Steve?"

"I'm happy for Steve. He's been alone for a long time."

"But you're married."

"You did fill out the delivery slip to me at Sam Kaufman's house, correct? Gloria Rodkin must have told you the gossip. Why look so surprised? It's all above board. Except for my spying—and I consider that a security measure, not a personal one—Steve and I don't have secrets. We're best friends. Our relationship isn't about staying together as much as it's about not dissolving our family and business."

That was even worse! Bonnie hated the idea that Steve and Joanne confided in each other about their affairs. "Call me old-fashioned, but I believe in divorce."

"Steve and I are both comfortable with how we live. A divorce would be an incredible legal nightmare. A lot of couples stay married in name only for legal reasons. Steve and I have children. We started Kline and Co. when we were just out of college. Our company is intertwined with our marriage and our sons. Divorce is just a piece of paper, Bonnie. In our case, it'd be a very expensive piece of paper. A settlement would cause rifts, cost millions, and last for years. I say, why rock the boat?"

"Marriage is just a piece of paper. Divorce is just a piece of paper. But to me, they matter."

"Then get married," said Joanne. "I don't care what you do. But I'm never divorcing Steve. That is nonnegotiable. The Barrow Street presidency, on the other hand...we'd have a lot to discuss."

Bonnie looked at the older woman, her hand hovering between them, over the bud vase. If she took that hand, she'd be in business and in bed with both Klines. Her instinctual first reaction was elation. She was being offered everything she'd ever wanted. Her second reaction? Wariness. What would she be trading off by accepting? Her sense of right and wrong challenged her, or was it fear of moving forward that was paralyzing her again?

"How much would the job pay?" she asked. "In salary, bonuses, and shares? Roughly?"

Joanne lowered her arm and wrote a number on the tablecloth with her nail. "For starters," she said.

The number, already starting to fade, was five times her salary at Frankel's. If Barrow Street became a success and she could keep it in business for a few years at least, she'd be safe. Her son would be secure. She'd get a new car and renovate her bathroom. Even if Barrow Street crashed and burned after a year, she'd still be in better shape than she was now.

It started to sink in. Bonnie was being offered a golden ticket. Mr. Charles would choke if he knew—and she hoped she'd get the chance to tell him. Her own store! Creating a design aesthetic! Making all the decisions, from the hem of a skirt to the free gifts with purchase to employee promotions.

"Yes," said Bonnie, holding out her hand.

Joanne shook. "Good. We'll start working with the lawyers after the Peace on Earth gala. You do have a lawyer?"

"Not yet," she said. Her head was spinning.

The waiter came over, and the ladies ordered lunch.

"I would like to hire my own people," said Bonnie.

"Upon approval." Joanne found an envelope in her purse.

"Here's a ticket to the gala. We need to start appearing in public as a team. You'll sit at our table with the Freeds and the Rodkins. My son will also be there. And Sam Kaufman. He'll be your dinner partner. This is how we've done it in the past, so Steve and I can invite our special friends to events."

Their respective beards escorted each other. Bonnie was entering a whole new world here. It made sense, logically. Bonnie pushed aside any misgivings whenever she thought about that number Joanne wrote on the tablecloth.

They ate crab cakes and discussed Barrow Street. After Joanne left, Bonnie called Steve. She got his voicemail. "Your wife and I had a lovely lunch and a frank discussion about marriage. If you want to know the details, call me back."

She hung up and speed-dialed the Salon at Frankel's.

"You?" asked Bella, apparently not at liberty to mention her name in close quarters.

"Yes, me."

"I can't talk now. Mr. Charles is having a hissy fit and I have to watch. I can video and send later."

"I need you to make me a gown."

"Fit a gown?"

"No, design it for me to wear to the Peace on Earth gala," said Bonnie. "I'll pay you, of course."

"You're going to gala?"

"I'm going with the Klines, if you can believe that. Can you make me an incredible gown for $300 or less? I want to knock them dead. Are you in?"

"You will tell people who made the gown?" asked Bella.

"Oh, I'm going to sell it hard," said Bonnie. "I want you think of it as your own personal *Project Runway* challenge, with the possible reward of making your own label and selling it in the retail store of your dreams."

"I have no idea what you are talking about," said Bella. "But, for you, I make gown."

Next, Bonnie called Fran. "You should be so glad you're out of here," she said. "Mr. Charles just blew through here screaming like a banshee about putting a hat boutique on the seventh floor."

"I heard he was having a tantrum from Bella."

"Did you hear he's been put on probation for not being innovative enough or 'in touch with the younger generation'? Hence, hat boutique. Don't ask me to explain that."

"On probation? Well, I know how that feels."

"What's up?"

"Have you ever written a marketing plan?"

"Nope," said Fran.

"Go to Frankel's marketing department and look at theirs. Think about how you'd improve on it or any ideas that come to mind."

"Why?"

"Just familiarize yourself with the lingo," said Bonnie. "Study up. And trust me."

"What's going on, Bonnie?"

"Can't say. But I'll be in touch."

Chapter Nineteen

The plan was for Bonnie to meet Sam Kaufman outside the Waldorf-Astoria. He'd been a gentleman and offered to pick up Bonnie at her house. But that would be confusing to Peter, and she wouldn't allow it. She spent an hour getting ready (other women would have spent days preparing for the event by having every beauty treatment on the menu at Elizabeth Arden), and then she left her bedroom and walked across the hall to Peter's.

His room was simply decorated. Too much stimulation would be upsetting to him. There were a few under-the-sea posters of fish and ocean plants on the walls. His bed was dressed in plain white, supersoft fabrics, and his pillow was hypoallergenic foam with an all-cotton cover. Peter loved his room. It was his safe haven. Bonnie and Lucee were the only ones allowed to enter. Even Mike had to wait in the hall outside before Peter could let him in.

Her son was at his computer, wearing his blinking light therapy glasses. On screen, Bonnie saw weird alien-like creatures.

"What's this game?" she asked.

"It's called Spore," he said. "Carmine bought it for me."

Carmine. His new favorite "grandfather." From a kid's perspective, Carmine was a lot more fun than his real grandfather Vinny, who barely left his armchair. Or Mike's sports maniac father, who acted as if his own happiness depended on the Mets winning the pennant.

"I'm going out now," she said. "Lucee is in the kitchen making spaghetti and meatballs." His favorite.

"When will you be back?" asked Peter.

"By the last stroke of midnight," she couldn't resist staying.

Peter nodded, taking it literally. "Like Cinderella. How old was she?" he asked.

"A lot younger than me," she said. "It'll be around midnight. Don't worry if it's a little bit later. I'll bring back cake."

He surprised her by grabbing her around the neck and pulling her toward him. Bonnie had learned to wait patiently for his special tight hugs, which were bestowed less often as he got older. Whenever Peter was demonstrably affectionate, Bonnie choked up. "I love you," she said, hugging back. "So much."

"Don't cry, Mom," he said flatly, emotionless.

She dabbed under her eyes, kissed the top of his head, and left. With a final word to Lucee, Bonnie got in her car and drove herself to the ball.

Sam Kaufman was waiting for Bonnie on the carpet outside the Waldorf-Astoria Hotel. She recognized him immediately. He smiled as she approached and held out a plastic box. "For you," he said.

Bonnie said, "Thank you. It's lovely." She hadn't been given a corsage since Mike took her to the senior prom. The purple orchid was a bad match for her black-and-white gown. Should she wear it? How insulted would he be if she didn't? Oh, what the hell. She slid it on her handbag. No one else was giving her flowers. With luck, the corsage would read as ironic. Besides, it was sweet.

Mr. Kaufman smiled, a bit forced. "You're the prettiest beard yet."

"Thanks again," she replied, not knowing what else to say. He'd made his peace with having to pretend about his romantic life. Bonnie was uneasy to say the least. She shouldn't feel insulted about arriving by herself and entering an event on the arm of her boyfriend's wife's boyfriend, right? She was a New Yorker and had seen a lot of unconventional relationships. But she'd never been in one before. She'd have to get used to the fast lane, such as it was. For Steve and Barrow Street, the unsettled feeling was a fair trade.

Sam's hand on her arm, they walked into the hotel, through the vast lobby, and up to the Grand Ballroom. Several tables were set up outside with a sign over each designating a portion of the alphabet. Mr. Kaufman approached the G–K table, spoke to an immaculate young lady in a black satin gown, and collected their table assignment. He gestured for Bonnie, and they entered the ballroom.

Despite the airplane hangar size of the room, it was buzzing loudly with guests and service staff. On the stage, an orchestra played a classical piece probably called, "Music to Be Fabulous By." At each of the one hundred tables for ten or twelve sat a centerpiece of fresh roses, peonies, and irises that filled the air with fragrance. In the middle of the flowers, a long white stick with hooks had been stuck into each bouquet. At some of the tables, pink, orange, and gold balloons on strings were tied to the hooks. The balloons represented donations to the charity. A pink balloon meant someone at the table donated $5,000. Orange was $10,000. Gold was $20,000. At the end of the night, the table with the largest donation total got the door prize. A few years ago, it had been a week's luxury vacation to a private Bahamian island. The balloons, as well as the gold lamé tablecloths, silver, crystal glasses, and candles, made the room sparkle. The men in their tuxes and the bejeweled women added to the glamour. Bonnie was dazzled.

"We're number twenty-four," said Mr. Kaufman over the din.

As she followed him toward their table, Bonnie's eyes popped at the spectacular gowns—as well as a few fashion train wrecks. Bonnie spotted several of her clients. She smiled and waved at them and watched their shocked reaction.

It *was* shocking! Not only was Bonnie walking among them like an equal, she was better dressed, too. The stress of quitting and the excitement about Steve and her new job had been good for a five-pound weight loss. The black belt of her gown cinched her narrow waist. Her bosom was lifted by Bella's invisible inside corset. The white silk skirt shimmered across her long legs, tickling her ankles, which were tucked into black, barely-there high-heeled sandals. She'd done her own hair and makeup simply, deciding to let her dress be the star of her look.

Bella had worked a miracle, creating a sublime gown for only $300 of fabric and a day of her life. Bonnie felt like a million dollars in it. It was another feeling she wasn't used to. This one, she liked. A lot.

Bonnie's eye fell on a painfully thin woman in a Marchesa embroidered gown, a couture piece with literally a thousand hours of hand-stitching. So distracted was she by the dress, Bonnie didn't notice the gentleman standing directly in front of her. Not until he was impossible to avoid.

"Mr. Charles," she gasped.

"Bonnie," he nearly choked. "You look...you look incredible, as I'm sure you know." He leaned in to kiss her cheek.

She instinctively recoiled, but then politely accepted the contact. The last time she saw him, Mr. Charles was at his desk, his jacket off and sleeves rolled up, poring over his computer ledgers, a man possessed by the flaw in his system. As far as Bonnie was concerned, the flaw in his system was the bottom-line mentality that inhibited creativity and compassion. But he was the boss. Not hers anymore, thank God.

In a pressed and perfect tuxedo, Mr. Charles looked haggard. She said, "I didn't know you'd be here."

"Mr. Frankel kindly invited me."

The store owner rarely left his mansion in Italy. "That's quite an honor."

"I'm very flattered. He wanted to meet some of our regular clients face-to-face. In fact, he's thinking about moving back to New York."

"How fun for you," said Bonnie, deadpan. "Let me introduce you to Sam Kaufman of Chicago. Mr. Kaufman, this is Chase Charles."

When he heard "Chicago," Mr. Charles perked up. "Do you know the Klines? They're old dear friends of mine."

Sam said, "Never heard of you."

Mr. Charles scowled. "What brings *you* to the event, Bonnie? Last time you were here, weren't you Cody Deerlinger's bathroom attendant?"

God, she hated him.

"Is Mrs. Deerlinger here? I'll have to give her my love," she said, and took Sam's arm to walk on.

"Elevator to the balconies is that way," said Mr. Charles, assuming she was in the section of second floor tables—the cheaper seats for plebs and media freebies.

"We're looking for table twenty-four," she said. When she said the number, Mr. Charles went a little grayer.

The lower the number, the higher the prestige. Their table was right in the middle of the action on the main floor, among the billionaires and celebrities. Bonnie spotted it easily enough. She noticed Joanne first, in her gold, sequined gown, the one she helped her pick out. Steve was seated next to her.

When Bonnie and Sam worked their way over, Steve rose to his feet, took her hand, kissed it, and said, "Ms. Madden, you are breathtaking."

"Agreed," said Stan Rodkin.

Gloria, in a tasteful, vintage Bill Blass, asked, "That dress is divine! Who are you wearing?"

"It's a Bella Orloff original."

"If I knew Bella could design," said Vicki Freed, "I would have hired her to do all my dresses."

"But what is that horror on your bag?" asked Gloria. "Dear God, is that a corsage? My eyes are burning! Get rid of it, Bonnie!"

Mr. Kaufman said, "What's wrong with it?"

Joanne said, "Everyone, this is my dear friend, Sam Kaufman. Vicki and Lee Freed. Gloria and Stan Rodkin. They're the parents of Jack's date, Shelley. Jack, you know Sam."

Jack Kline, next to Shelley Snyder, said, "Hey" to Sam. And then went back to buttering a roll.

Bonnie smiled at the young couple. Shelley, the widow, wore a Versace that was as conservative as the designer went, which was to say, not very. By her taste, it was too sexy for a widow in mourning. Steve hadn't told Bonnie Jack was dating Shelley. Were they, or was it a last-minute fix-up? Neither one of them seemed happy to be there. Jack was the only man at the table who didn't stand up when Bonnie arrived. Shelley gave Bonnie a feeble wave. Gloria probably pushed her to "get out there." Bonnie's heart broke a little at how hard Shelley was trying.

Lee Freed greeted Bonnie warmly, which he hadn't done before. "Good evening. It's wonderful to see you again." Something different about him. No hair! He was bald! Oddly, he looked ten years younger without the toupee.

Vicki said, "He looks better, right?" Bonnie nodded and gave her attention to Vicki. Her dress was a modest sheath in crepe de chine...wait, modest? Bonnie took a closer look and blinked at Vicki's new figure.

"Mrs. Freed? You've...er...changed."

Vicki laughed heartily. "You mean these?" She cupped the space on her chest where her enormous breasts used to be. "Lee and I have been scaling back all over the place." Rubbing his bald head, she said, "Bankruptcy made us take a cold, hard look at our lives, and we've been rethinking our unnecessary expenses. Club memberships—canceled. Salon treatments—over. Lee got rid of his personal trainer, too. You met her once, Bonnie, remember?"

"Of course," she said.

"Chris is no longer part of our lives."

Bonnie understood her meaning: Lee's affair was over. Whether Lee dumped the trainer or the trainer dumped him—because he was broke, probably—was irrelevant.

"Your necklace," said Bonnie, clasping her heart. "Gorgeous." Mrs. Freed wore her diamond showstopper, the one her husband wouldn't let her sell to Cody Deerlinger. It was a flashing thirty-carat sign to their friends and enemies that they weren't dead yet.

Joanne said, "Everyone, sit." The tablemates complied. Joanne had assigned the seating with engraved place cards—clockwise: Joanne, Steve, Bonnie, Sam, Shelley, Jack, Gloria, Stan, Vicki, and Lee. "I paid for a half dozen balloons. The committee should have brought them to our table by now. I don't want to look cheap." It was all about how things looked to Joanne. Including Bonnie's place at the table and the faux date with Sam.

"What's the door prize this year?" Shelley asked.

Gloria put her finger to her lips. "It's a surprise."

"Oh, come on. Just tell," whined Shelley.

Jack winced when she spoke. Her voice was a bit nasal, but it wasn't that bad. Was the Kline/Rodkin match supposed to unite two strong families, like the Bourbons and the Habsburgs? They both seemed miserable, as a couple and individually. Shelley shouldn't be here at all, let alone in that sexy dress. Jack? He clearly wished he were anywhere but here.

Steve used his fork to tap his glass. "A toast," he said. "To the reason we're all here tonight—apart from the worthwhile charity, of course. What brought our group together…to Barrow Street!"

Stan Rodkin seconded it, "To Barrow Street."

Everyone drank. Lee Freed flagged down a waiter, pressing a five dollar bill into the young man's hand. "More wine," he said. Bonnie smiled to herself, thinking of Carmine's hundred.

Joanne said, "To a happy partnership."

Vicki said, "To Freed factories clogging the skies over Elizabeth, New Jersey again!"

They all raised their glasses again, draining them.

The waiter arrived with a single bottle of red wine. He began pouring it and ran out after four glasses. Lee Freed gave the waiter another fiver, and said, "Bring us a few bottles, okay?"

Looking at the pathetic bribe, the waiter—an obvious model/actor/server—almost laughed. Steve waved him over, gave him a twenty, and said, "We'd appreciate it." The twenty was better than the five, but not by much. Maybe Bonnie should introduce Steve to Carmine.

Flash. A camera went off, and Bonnie was temporarily blinded.

"Can I get a group shot?" asked the photographer.

"David!" called Gloria Rodkin. "Joanne, have you met David Patrick Columbia? He's the genius behind the New York Social Diary website."

Introductions were made. Some repositioning went on before the group photo. The ladies were asked to remain seated, and the men stood behind their chairs. Sam Kaufman stood behind Bonnie. She posed. Fake smile.

When Sam sat back down, he took Steve's seat next to Joanne. Steve silently took Sam's chair next to Bonnie. Sam leaned over to say something private to Joanne. She nodded, leaned on him a little. Seated close to Joanne, the burly man seemed softer, even cuddly. Bonnie sensed true affection, a real love.

Bonnie was now seated next to Steve. Under the table, he squeezed her thigh, which almost made her spill her water. She glanced around the table to see if anyone noticed and found all eyes on her. Gloria and Stan were smiling at her. Vicki, too. Did they know Steve had touched her? She felt totally exposed.

How was Sam Kaufman so comfortable with this awkward setup? Maybe being from the upper class equipped someone with a high tolerance for pretense. Bonnie felt chafed by it.

Joanne said, "Another toast. To Bonnie Madden. We've all been impressed by your taste, work ethic, and devotion to your clients. I know firsthand that you expertly handle difficult people. We couldn't have asked for a more qualified and inspiring store president."

She blushed. The rest of the table raised their glasses to drink. Everyone except Jack Kline. Bonnie already knew he wasn't thrilled to be passed over for the job. But he'd grudgingly accepted it for a position in the company to be named later. Still, he wasn't about to celebrate Bonnie's rise either.

He said, "Excuse me," and headed for the bar.

Shelley said, "Alone again. Naturally."

Gloria sighed heavily. "It's not you, sweetheart."

Joanne said, "I'll go get him. Sam, come with me. Jack will talk to you."

Sam said to Steve, "Maybe I can offer him something for now. I've got a few big projects going on."

Steve said, "I'd appreciate it, Sam."

Joanne and Sam walked off together, in search of Jack. How weird was it that Sam was so friendly with Jack? He was best buddies with his mom's lover? This whole family dynamic made zero sense to Bonnie, and yet, by getting involved with Steve, being hired by Joanne, and being Sam's beard, she was now part of it. Bonnie didn't feel all warm and happy, like she'd been enveloped by a large, loving new set of in-laws. Also, it suddenly occurred to her, would she and Sam be expected to conduct an entire fake relationship, just to be seen in public with their real partners? Sam was very nice and well-dressed. But pretending to be his girlfriend night after night would get old fast.

"Can we move on to far more important matters, like how much each woman's gown cost and how much Juvaderm they've injected?" asked Gloria.

"Yes, let's," said Vicki. "Starting with you, Gloria."

"There's Martha Stewart. Bonnie?"

Bonnie said, "Brocade gold and silk coat. Looks like vintage Comme des Garçons. She might have had it in her closet for years."

"How about Barbara Walters?" asked Vicki, pointing.

"Black Oscar. Very chic. At her right, Anna Wintour…"

"That's easy," said Gloria. "Prada, obviously."

The ladies smirked. Bonnie discreetly avoided saying any prices.

Steve and Stan started talking about the store again. Lee Freed leaned over Vicki to join their conversation. Bonnie and Lee would be working closely together on manufacturing, but that would be later on, after she'd hired her design and production team.

Days later, it still seemed that this fantasy job wasn't actually hers. Reality had become a hazy fantasy. It didn't seem real.

"Three o'clock, Julianne Moore giving Kate Winslet an air-kiss," whispered Vicki. Even Bonnie gawked.

I'm a garbage collector's daughter from Queens, she thought. Then again, how many native Manhattan socialites were at this table? Vicki grew up poor in Spokane. Gloria was a suburban Long Island girl before she came to the city to work in magazines in her twenties. Stan was self-made. Steve was self-made. Only Lee Freed had been born rich, and he'd learned the hard way how to pull himself back up from failure. *This is New York City,* she thought. *Anyone can make it here.* The question wasn't whether making it could be done. The question was, "How?" On whose terms? By what set of principles? Bonnie had worked hard. She deserved her place at the table. Her son deserved the relief of financial security the Barrow Street job could provide.

And I deserve a real relationship that could be exposed to the open air, she thought.

"I'd love to kiss you right now," whispered Steve in her ear.

Bonnie frowned. She'd love to kiss him, too, but just smiled, nodded, and squeezed his knee under the table.

After the appetizers, Bonnie excused herself to the ladies room. Stepping out of her stall, she went to the communal mirror to check her makeup.

"Bonnie! What the *hell* are you doing here?"

Flinching at the language, like every other woman in the women's lounge, Bonnie turned toward the speaker.

"Mrs. Deerlinger," said Bonnie. *She's drunk.*

"I'm furious with you," said Cody. "I told Mr. Charles he'd better offer you a big pile of money to come back to Frankel's. The new director, that idiot from Nebraska or wherever? She tried to sell me a space suit by Christian Siriano for tonight. I had to drag out this old thing." She twirled in a navy strapless gown by Armani.

"You're exquisite," stated Bonnie. "Mr. Deerlinger must be proud to show you off tonight."

"Bastard!" shouted Cody. "He *left* me, if you can believe that. He's here with his twenty-year-old dental hygienist with boobs the size of watermelons. Come meet Daddy. He's my date. He flew in from Fort Worth to chop off Dan's balls. But he's decided to go for the jugular instead. I'd make a better widow than divorcée, don't you think?" That comment made every woman glance at Cody.

Bonnie tried to quiet her down, but Cody's speech got longer and louder. "Seriously, if I could kill Dan, I would. But I'll settle for destroying everything he holds dear. Like his precious hedge fund!"

"We should have this conversation in private," whispered Bonnie, noticing that some women in the lounge weren't even bothering to eavesdrop subtly.

"We'll see how long his new girlfriend hangs around when the truth about his bogus derivative trading is exposed! It's criminal. He should be thrown in jail!" she hollered. "But you're right, Bonnie. I should be discreet." Then Cody winked slyly at her.

Not drunk. But she was pretending to be. Bonnie glanced around, to see if she recognized any of the other women in the lounge. Maria Bartiromo, CNBC's financial reporter, just emerged from a stall. Cody had made this spectacle for her benefit.

Cody said, "Now, we leave."

The two exited the rest room. Waiting outside was a tall man in a ten-gallon hat, cowboy boots, a huge silver belt buckle, and a bolo tie. Mr. Lloyd Proctor from Fort Worth made John Wayne look like a sniveling coward. Bonnie felt sorry for Dan Deerlinger.

Cody kissed her dad and said, "Done."

"That's my girl," he said.

"My accomplice. Daddy, this is Bonnie Madden."

"Pleasure, ma'am."

"Nice to meet you, sir."

"I have to insist that we continue to work together on a freelance basis. I saw Vicki Freed. I want that necklace!"

"I'll send her your love."

Cody laughed, clearly in a great mood. Separating from Dan Deerlinger would make any woman feel giddy.

"You ever been to Fort Worth, Ms. Madden?" asked Mr. Proctor.

He bragged to Bonnie about his hometown—daily cattle drives down Main Street and the world's largest Honky Tonk. Bonnie listened politely. Her eye wandered and landed on a couple partially obscured by a potted tree.

The woman—white shoulders in a red dress—was definitely Megan Houlihan. The man was older, in a distinctive charcoal gray tux, short, slim, with boot-black dyed hair (or a toupee), and too-taut skin with telltale horizontal lines across his cheekbones.

He had an ageless, waxy look, like Dorian Gray with a tan.

Mr. Albert Frankel. The boss of bosses, the chairman of the board was kissing Megan Houlihan, who was at least fifty years his junior. Yet another man who'd fallen under her spell, be it about sex (Roman), money (Jesus), or ego (Chase Charles). This ghastly sight was just further proof that Bonnie couldn't compete with her former assistant. She simply could not sink that low. Nor was she willing to trade sex with a man three times her age for a job.

Spooked, Bonnie rushed back to her table. Waiters started to maneuver through the tables, serving the entree. Someone was sitting in her seat next to Steve Kline.

Chase W. Charles was leaning in, talking eagerly to his old chum. Bonnie knew only too well that Mr. Charles looked into people's eyes and saw dollar signs. Steve seemed to tolerate his old chum's conversation, barely.

It occurred to Bonnie just then how much they looked alike. Steve was far more handsome. But they had a similar affect. Funny how she'd never seen it before.

Over Mr. Charles's shoulder, Steve beamed at Bonnie. "Here she is," he said, standing.

Mr. Charles stood, too. He wasn't pleased to see her. "You're in my seat," she said.

"You're sitting...here?"

"Is Megan Houlihan here tonight?" she asked.

"She's with me," he said, and the fool couldn't stop himself from pumping out his chest.

Not anymore. Megan had moved on, yet again. But Bonnie would let Chase Charles figure that out for himself. "Yes, well, she's looking for you," Bonnie said. "I saw her by the ladies room."

Mr. Charles nodded and left to find his date. Good riddance. She hoped she'd never see him or Megan again.

"Chase asked me for a job," said Steve as he helped Bonnie into her seat. "The guy practically begged."

"What'd you say?"

Steve said, "I told him we'd found someone perfect."

"But you didn't tell him who. You didn't mention my name."

"What's wrong?" he asked.

"You should have told him about me." Steve should tell the whole world about her, not only as store president, but also as his girlfriend.

When you were really in love, you put the other person first. Steve was a businessman at heart. As romantic as it seemed, he wasn't willing to make Bonnie his number one or put her before Joanne.

Bonnie realized with a thud in her stomach that if she worked for Steve and Joanne, she'd always be the number three (or lower) on their books. She'd have even less job security than at Frankel's. Joanne wouldn't hesitate to cut her out if things didn't go according to her schedule. The invitation to work in the store—and to sleep in Steve's bed—was a devil's bargain. She could see it playing out plainly now. They knew she worked like a dog. They knew she had professional standards and would devote herself to the store's success. But she would never be their equal. Steve would never leave Joanne.

Bonnie deserved better. For her sake, and her son's.

"You look like you're upset," said Steve. "I'll call Chase back here and tell him about you if it's so important."

They were alone at the table. All of the other couples were milling or dancing, including Shelley and Jack. Bonnie took advantage of their momentary privacy (in a room full of people) to speak her mind.

"That's not the point," she said.

"So why are you upset?"

"I thought I'd made a good trade. But now I realize I shortchanged myself."

"About the job? Your salary is…"

"About us. I believe you and Joanne have an understanding. But I don't understand how you can live with it. Well, I can't. It's not enough to have you if I can't have you all the way. I'm not saying we have to get married. But you do have to get divorced."

Steve was speechless. She'd made a real demand on him. He appeared to be shocked. Thus far, Bonnie had been Ms.

Compliance. The longer his silence stretched, the less patience Bonnie had with it.

She stood up. "I've got to go."

"What? The night just got started," said Steve.

She apologized and started walking toward the ballroom exit.

"Bonnie!" Steve caught up with her in the hotel lobby. "Stop. This is ridiculous."

"This isn't going to work out," she said. "The store, the relationship, none of it," she said. "I can't believe I'm walking away. The job is wonderful, but at the end of the day, it's serving other people again, being at their beck and call, including yours. I have to start taking care of myself and asking what I really want to do for the next ten years. I convinced myself it was a good idea to be absorbed by you, but I can't do it. I'll lose myself again, right when I was just starting to come out of the shadows."

"Okay, so the job is out. But you sound like you're leaving me," he said.

Relief flooded her senses. It was the right thing to do. "You're offering me the crumbs, Steve. Incredible, delicious crumbs. I was tempted, believe me. You are a wonderful man, and I'm grateful for what you've shown me and what you've given me. I'll never be able to thank you enough for the Mason School donation. But I can't shake the feeling that I'm being bought or paid off. I can't compromise on what's most important for me and Peter. I want a love I don't have to pretend doesn't exist. I'd like to get married again, give Peter a stepfather he won't have to lie about. Neither is possible with you."

He shook his head. "I'm not giving up on you."

Bonnie said, "I'll send you some names tomorrow to replace me at the store."

As she turned away, her dress twirled around her hips and legs. Bonnie strode away and felt stronger than she had in years. She'd been tested and she passed. From this point on, she was sure only good things would flow her way.

EPILOGUE

One Year Later

"Sorry I'm late," said Bonnie, rushing in as always, even if it was a Saturday morning. Peter held on to her hand. Now that she was her own boss, she could bring him to work with her on weekends.

"Hello, Peter!" said Vicki Freed from atop the dress platform in the middle of the room. Bella was at her feet, making last-minute alterations in her dress. Vicki was having her final fitting for this year's Peace on Earth gala, scheduled for the upcoming weekend.

Peter sort of smiled, and then he said, "Can I go?"

Bonnie said, "I'll check on you in a few minutes."

The boy ran over to the skirted table by her desk that Bonnie set up for him. He crawled underneath it like he had at Mike's wedding. The place was his special spot, where he felt safe and secure. He could play peacefully with his DS in there for hours. Bonnie was happy to be near him, even if he was in his own world. If she'd known being her own boss would allow her to spend more time with Peter, she would have figured out a way to do this years ago.

"You outgrow the dress every few hours," complained Bella, who'd designed Vicki's gown and had to re-fit it several times already.

Vicki laughed and put her hand protectively on her ever-expanding belly. "For once in my life, I'm going to eat whatever

I want. And you can't stop me."

Vicki continued to shop and buy new dresses at every stage of her pregnancy. Bonnie smiled and walked into her office. It was really just a desk in the back of the showroom in their Garment District space. They'd expand someday, Bonnie hoped, but at this point, the business she started with Bella a year ago—Bella Orloff Designs—was just keeping its head above water. They had only a handful of clients. Thanks to Cody Deerlinger, Vicki Freed, and Gloria Rodkin, they were paying their bills. Their aesthetic, the new modern classic, was tailor-made for Cody and her generation of socialites. Bella designed whatever the clients needed—a gown, a suit, anything. After years at Frankel's, Bella was lightning fast. She could turn around a cocktail dress in twenty-four hours.

Fran Giagoni, office manager, was on her Bluetooth headset at her desk. She put her hand over the mouthpiece and said, "Stew wants you to call him." Stew was their accountant and business guy. He'd been highly recommended to Bonnie by her silent financial backer, back when this little company was just a vague idea. Now Bonnie couldn't imagine getting through a day without talking to Stew. "Also, check out Page Six." She pointed at the open newspaper on Bonnie's desk.

What now? Bonnie gasped at the lead item headline: "Frankel Heirs Fight Over Iowa Governor's Daughter."

Bonnie read the item, titled "Trouble in Tuscany."

> The sons of Albert Frankel, chairman and majority shareholder of Frankel's LLC, the company that owns the luxury department store, are duking it out over a pretty Midwestern politico scion. Alex and Yuri Frankel, ages 47 and 50, brothers and heirs to the Frankel fortune, both claim to be engaged to Megan Houlihan, 25, the director of the Salon at Frankel's and daughter of Henry "Slappy" Houlihan, former governor of Iowa.
>
> Our sources tell us that Ms. Houlihan was staying at the Tuscan villa as the senior Mr. Frankel's personal

guest. The two have grown close in the months since the departure of ex-store president Chase W. Charles. When Alex and Yuri visited their father's estate last week, they both became smitten with Ms. Houlihan. Our source tells us the Frankel sons routinely try to steal their father's girlfriends, and each other's. But, by all accounts, this is the first time all three have fought over the same woman. Repeated attempts to contact the Frankel family have been ignored. Ms. Houlihan's spokesperson, Harriet Gorson, public relations maven to the stars, issued this statement: "Ms. Houlihan is honored to be associated with the Frankel family, personally and professionally. If anything were to happen to her standing at the store, she'd be terribly upset and wouldn't know what to do about it." When Page Six asked if her statement was a thinly veiled threat, Ms. Gorson refused to comment.

Slappy? Bonnie laughed.

Fran said, "I won't be surprised to pick up the paper one day and read that Megan is the Queen of England."

Bonnie checked her iPhone. She had upgraded. The Blackberry was so 2010. "Oh, God, not again," she said when she saw the caller was Mr. Charles. He'd been after her to hire him as their retail guru. He had a new company, too, called Chase Consultants. Bonnie'd put him off several times, telling him that since he taught her everything she knew (as he'd told her), she didn't see why she needed to pay him to do it all over again. If he was still after her, business must be slow. Oh, well. He'd made his bed. He could flounder in it.

Vicki Freed, radiant and eight months pregnant, burst into the office. "What do you think?" she asked, spinning. Her empire waist gown was a marvel of engineering. Bella had outdone herself.

"You're magnificent," said Bonnie.

"Stunning," agreed Fran, already printing out the final bill for the dress, sealing it in an envelope, and handing it to Vicki.

"How's your table shaping up for the gala this year?" Bonnie asked.

"It's in flux, actually," said Vicki. "Gloria and Stan aren't attending the gala because of Shelley's wedding." The event was one week after the gala, and the consuming fire of Gloria's life. The gown and all the bridesmaid dresses were Bella Orloff originals, of course. Shelley was marrying a man she met online, a young architect. The Rodkins were thrilled for her. Vicki continued, "Out of politeness, I invited Joanne and Sam. Of course, they refused. They hardly ever leave Chicago anymore. I never liked her, to be honest. And Lee still blames her for the Barrow Street mess."

As plugged into the gossip grapevine as Vicki was, she'd never known the full story.

After Bonnie walked out of the Waldorf Hotel lobby in her glorious Bella Orloff gown, she'd knocked down the first domino in what would become a mile-long chain in the Kline universe. Her declaration that she needed more from Steve inspired him to say what he'd wanted to say to Joanne for over ten years:

"I want a divorce," he told Joanne later that night.

For months she refused, making her usual points about the business and their sons.

But once Steve's resolve to stay married fell, Sam Kaufman was the next domino to fall. He said the one thing he'd wanted to say to Joanne for years:

"I want to get married." He declared himself to her when she finished ranting about Steve going off the deep end.

When Joanne turned to her sons for support, Jack and Brian confided to her that they'd been uncomfortable with their parents' masquerade as a happily married couple for years and would rather they split up than keep up the façade.

Suddenly the construct of Joanne's life came crashing down all around her, and she started to question why exactly she'd held on so tightly to Steve as her husband. They called in a team of lawyers and accountants, including Stew Grossman, to dissolve their marriage, but keep Kline and Co. intact. Unfortunately, the

Barrow Street warehouse became mixed up in that negotiation, and the store never happened. Joanne saw no reason to stay and left New York. She told Bonnie that she never felt like she fit into Manhattan society anyway. Steve kept his apartment on Park Avenue, where Bonnie spent many nights when Peter was at Mike and Emily's house.

Vicki said, "You and Steve are still coming, right? If you cancel, I'll kill you."

Bonnie opened her mouth to reply, but a voice answered for her. "We'll be there," said Steve, striding into the room. "But Bonnie is going to wear the same dress as last year. We never got to dance together with you wearing it."

"Romantic," said Bella, scoffing. "But Bonnie cannot be seen wearing same dress two years in a row. That's bad for business."

"You don't need to worry about business ever again," said Steve. "I come with news."

That got all of their attention. Bonnie leaned forward in her chair and stared at her silent backer and fiancé (although it'd probably be a while until they could marry, with the divorce still in progress). Bonnie couldn't help but think how sexy he looked in his new suit. It'd been designed by Bella, who had used him as her muse for the new menswear concepts. He'd been happy to spend days working with Bella. The fact was, Steve didn't have a whole lot to do now that he'd decided to take a backseat to Joanne and Jack at Kline and Co. for the time being. He was now helping his fledgling company get off the ground. He'd also been spending a lot of time with Bonnie and getting to know Peter. They were going slow, but Peter seemed to like Steve, and Bonnie had high hopes.

"Joanne called me an hour ago. She has a certain political somebody who she ran into at a gala the other night in Chicago."

"Michelle Obama?" asked Bonnie.

"Close! So she saw this woman again at a fundraiser last night, and this certain somebody was impressed with Joanne's gown."

"The black silk?" asked Bella.

"The very same," said Steve happily. "Joanne told her all about you. And this woman told her that she intended to come here the next time she's in New York, which will be very soon. There's something major going on at the UN, and apparently this woman needs a gown."

At that moment, the business phone rang. Fran picked up. "Orloff Designs. Yes. Yes. Okay." Then she put the phone down. "I think we just got a prank call. It was someone saying they were from the Secret Service and that the Secretary of State wants to stop by tomorrow for a walk-through."

Steve hooted. "That was fast!"

"Oh my GOD!" screamed Bonnie. Everyone in the room started screaming and jumping up and down.

Peter peeked out from under the table. "Can you keep quiet?" he asked and then went back under.

Bonnie stopped yelling and turned to Bella. "Can you do it?"

"Oh, I will make 'Madame' look so good, no one will ever make a nasty comment about her taste again."

"We have to start planning, now!" said Bonnie. This is huge, an opportunity to put her little company on the world stage. The team got busy, Bella and Fran kicking into action, Vicki making calls to spread the word. Bonnie would call all her buyer friends to drop hints that they potentially had a major new client. She glanced up and noticed the one calm presence in the room.

Amid the craziness, Steve Kline stood solidly and still, smiling at her. It was all for her. She was his focus. And now, her company was poised for a breakthrough, thanks, indirectly, to him. She went over, hugged the love of her life, and said, "It's going to be kind of hectic around here for a while."

"If I want to see you," he said, "I'm probably going to have to make an appointment."

"No need. I'll squeeze you in," she said.

Acknowledgments

It is with deep appreciation we would like to thank our agent, Yfat Reiss Gendell, Foundry Literary+Media, for guiding us, encouraging us and believing in *The Trade Off* these past 7 years. Along with her team, Kirsten Neuhaus, Director of Foreign Rights; Jessica Regel, Foreign Rights Associate; Michon Vanderpoel, Rights and Finance Team; Sara DeNobrega, Controller; and Deidre Smerillo, Contracts Director; Yfat has enabled us to share with the world the inside scoop of life in a New York luxury department store, the people who work there, and the high end clientele they help.

To all the wonderful people at Diversion Books, Senior Acquisitions Editor, Laura Duane; Sarah Masterson Hally, Production Manager; and Brielle Benton, Marketing and Publicity Associate; we give our heart felt thanks for their professional advice and making our dream come true by getting *The Trade Off* to the marketplace.

We would like to give a big "thank you" to our dear and talented friend Jared R. Pike for his technical advice and never-ending patience without which this manuscript would never have come together; to Claire Hentschker, whose creative cover captures the essence of *The Trade Off*; to Frank Hentschker for his never-ending support and facilitating multiple reader copies; to Eve Schaenen, Inda Schaenen, and Michael Dee for their editing talents along the way and the enormous amount of time and energy they spent on this project; to Brian Hauenstein, Alexandra Maniscalco, Thomas Maniscalco, Rose and Anthony Simone, Gail Hauenstein, and Jack Rudin for putting up with our stress levels during this project; and to Joe Cullen for reading so many drafts and always saying each was perfect.

Because of the medical challenges in both our families, we give our deepest gratitude to our nursing staff, especially Mary Timoney and Bridget Kirby. Without their support on the home front, we never would have been able to carve out the time in our lives to complete *The Trade Off*.

Of course, we cannot thank Josh Seftel enough. He was our first fan. From an accidental meeting on a Jersey beach, Josh spent hours with us discussing story line and teaching us about the construction of a novel. Without Josh's encouragement, advice and patience, *The Trade Off* would never have seen the light of day.

And to our friends, you have been remarkable and have listened to our chatter about this book for the past 7 years. You never gave up encouraging us to carry on. THANK YOU!

SUSAN RUDIN is a retired retail executive who loves to shop. After moving to New York, she worked as a personal shopper in a major Manhattan department store. While raising her two daughters as a single mother, she became the director of all the shopping services in the store and its branches. Traveling to Paris with the buyers, Susan suggested purchases for her clients. Today, Susan involves herself in community and charitable causes that interest her and understands life on both sides of the register.

While raising a special needs child, **LOUISE MANISCALCO** worked for some of the luxury retail giants in New York, including Bloomingdales, Neiman Marcus, and Saks Fifth Avenue. At Barney's New York, she created and directed their Personal Shopping and Studio Services for motion pictures, television and advertising. Today, Louise has her own studio in Manhattan, as well as being a co-founder of Luxe Axcess, an exclusive five-star network of luxury fashion stylists gathered from the upper echelon of the luxury fashion community.

CPSIA information can be obtained
at www.ICGtesting.com
Printed in the USA
BVHW030443220219
540919BV00001B/38/P